PENGUIN BOOKS

# *Three Novels*

Arthur Annesley Ronald Firbank was born in 1886, a grandson of Joseph Firbank, a Durham miner who later amassed a fortune as a railway contractor. His mother, to whom he was greatly attached, was an Irishwoman of considerable beauty and cultivated tastes. Owing to a weak constitution, Firbank was educated mainly at home; in 1906 he went up to Trinity Hall, Cambridge, where he was received into the Roman Catholic Church. Until 1914 Firbank travelled a good deal but lived mainly in London, habitué of the Café Royal, well-known for his extreme and deliberate aestheticism, his sinuous, loosely-jointed figure, and his morbid nervousness, which issued in hysterical laughter in an elaborately capricious manner. The First World War was spent in retreat in Oxford; then again until his death in Rome in 1926 he travelled widely.

Firbank's first work was published in 1905, a volume of two short stories, *Odette d'Antrevernes* and *A Study in Temperament*. Ten years later Grant Richards brought out his first novel, *Vainglory*. The following were published later: *Inclinations* (1916); *Caprice* (1917); *Valmouth* (1919); *The Princess Zoubaroff*, a play (1920); *Santal* (1921); *The Flower Beneath the Foot* (1923); *Prancing Nigger* (1924 – published in England in 1925 under Firbank's original title, *Sorrow in Sunlight*); *Concerning the Eccentricities of Cardinal Pirelli* (1926). All save *Prancing Nigger* were published at the author's own expense. An early, but fully 'Firbankian', novel, *The Artificial Princess*, had been put away unpublished, though in the last year of his life Firbank revised it with a view to possible publication. It appeared posthumously in 1934.

His writing was admired by a number of significant writers. John Betjeman considered his work 'polished . . . like a jewelled and clockwork nightingale among London sparrows', and Anthony Powell described his creation of 'a world, in the last resort, absolutely original; one that causes a cavalcade of wish-fulfilment myths to sweep gaily past the reader's vision'. In a critical essay on Firbank, Evelyn Waugh described his 'radiant lucidity', and wrote: 'When everything has been said which can intelligently be brought against him there remains a figure of essential artistic integrity and importance . . . From the fashionable chatter of his period, vapid and interminable, he has plucked, like tiny brilliant feathers from the breast of a bird, the particles of his design'.

Alan Hollinghurst was born in 1954. He is the author of three novels, *The Swimming-Pool Library* (1988), *The Folding Star* (1994) and *The Spell* (1998).

# RONALD FIRBANK

# *Three Novels*

*The Flower Beneath the Foot*

*Sorrow in Sunlight*

*Concerning the Eccentricities of Cardinal Pirelli*

*With an introduction by Alan Hollinghurst*

PENGUIN BOOKS

PENGUIN BOOKS

Published by the Penguin Group
Penguin Books Ltd, 27 Wrights Lane, London W8 5TZ, England
Penguin Putnam Inc., 375 Hudson Street, New York, New York 10014, USA
Penguin Books Australia Ltd, Ringwood, Victoria, Australia
Penguin Books Canada Ltd, 10 Alcorn Avenue, Toronto, Ontario, Canada M4V 3B2
Penguin Books (NZ) Ltd, Private Bag 102902, NSMC, Auckland, New Zealand

Penguin Books Ltd, Registered Offices: Harmondsworth, Middlesex, England

*The Flower Beneath the Foot* first published 1923
*Sorrow in Sunlight* first published 1924
*Concerning the Eccentricities of Cardinal Pirelli* first published 1926
This edition published in Penguin Classics 2000

10 9 8 7 6 5 4 3 2 1



Set in 11/12.5 pt Monotype Fournier
Typeset by Rowland Phototypesetting Ltd, Bury St Edmunds, Suffolk
Printed in England by Clays Ltd, St Ives plc

# *Contents*

[illegible]

[illegible]

[illegible] Pr[illegible] [illegible] [illegible] [illegible]

[illegible]

[illegible] there was [illegible] of the [illegible] and [illegible]
had plunged [illegible]
The flag [illegible]

# *Introduction*

This book contains the last three novels of Ronald Firbank – three works of remarkable economy, brilliant humour and disconcerting pathos. Each of Firbank's novels is a daring experiment in style and form. He threw away almost everything he inherited from the Victorian novel, and what he retained he treated in bizarre and unpredictable ways. He owed something to earlier comic writers – Restoration comedy, Pope's satires, *Tristram Shandy* – and a great deal to writers of the 1890s. His first book, published in 1905, pays homage in two short tales to two sides of Oscar Wilde: 'Odette d'Antrevernes' is a religiose fairy story, 'A Study in Temperament' an unresolved fragment of social comedy. Wilde was to remain a presence in all his work, and Firbank was to become best known for a kind of social camp, in which the certainties of Wildean epigram are suggestively unpinned and unpicked; but the element of fairy story also survives until the end in a vein of fable and fantasy. By the time Firbank published his first novel *Vainglory* in 1915, however, he had achieved a revolution in technique; over the next four years he went on to refine it in three more startlingly original novels, *Inclinations*, *Caprice* and *Valmouth*: books which constitute an aesthete's witty defiance of the war and of the depression into which it had plunged him.

The main features of Firbank's stylistic revolution were the suppression, or at least concealment, of plot; a texture made up of elliptical-seeming fragments; and an extraordinary brevity. After *Vainglory*, his longest novel, he settled on what was to be his natural length for a book, about 20,000 words. Unlike his great contemporary Proust, who expanded the novel to unprecedented length to do justice to the complexity of his narrator's consciousness and world, Firbank, who shared many of Proust's preoccupations, arrived early on at an aesthetic which required almost everything to be left out. 'I am all design – once I get going,' he wrote. 'I think nothing of filing fifty pages down to make a brief, crisp paragraph, or even a row of dots.'

Firbank is described by several contemporaries as writing his novels on post-cards; none of these manuscripts survives, but the notebooks for each novel, in which he amassed descriptive phrases, lines of dialogue, sketches of dresses and hats, can still be read, and suggest something of his mosaic-like practice. One of the most commented-on procedures in the earlier novels is a kind of verbal collage, by which he conveys the atmosphere of a party as if with a roving microphone, picking up and juxtaposing random snippets of talk:

> 'Heroin.'
>
> 'Adorable simplicity.'
>
> 'What could anyone find to admire in such a shelving profile?'
>
> 'We reckon a duck here of two or three and twenty not so old. And a spring chicken *anything to fourteen*.'
>
> 'My husband had no amorous energy whatsoever; which just suited me, of course.'
>
> 'I suppose when there's no more room for another crow's-foot, one attains a sort of peace?'
>
> 'Cruelly lonely.'
>
> 'Leery . . .'
>
> 'Vulpine.'
>
> 'Calumny.' [. . .]
>
> 'If she pays her creditors *sixpence* in the *pound* it's the utmost they can expect.' [. . .]
>
> 'It's a little pain-racked face – not that she really suffers.'

At its best the result is convincingly nonsensical: as V. S. Pritchett said, 'Firbank must have been the first disinterested, clinical listener to the lunacy of conversation.' But the effect is also an analogue of his wider technique, which brings things into unexpected proximity by simply leaving out the narrative padding which would normally keep them apart. Firbank combines rich, sharp observation with the dictates of a genuinely modernist sensibility. His urge to refine a modern aesthetic out of the murky legacy of the 1890s, his cutting-out of superfluities, his amassing of fragments, are processes we see at the same time in the work of Eliot, Pound and Yeats; and there are ways in which Firbank seems as close to the most innovative poets of his time as he does to the novelists, such as James Joyce and Virginia Woolf, who always crowd him out of histories of modernism in English.

Certainly Firbank's early books challenged the priorities of the novel and the assumptions which traditionally underpinned it. His narratives, if you try to sum them up, are slight: *Vainglory* is 'about' the determination of Mrs Shamefoot, the neglected wife of a clever husband, to have a window to herself installed in an English cathedral, whilst she is still alive; in *Inclinations* a lesbian biographer travels to Greece with a fifteen-year-old girl and loses her to an Italian count, to whom she becomes happily married; in *Caprice* a stage-struck country girl escapes to London to follow an acting career and is killed by falling into a well beneath the stage of the theatre where she is playing Juliet; in the benign climate of *Valmouth*, the characters survive to an immense age, and are helped in the pursuit of their amorous inclinations by Mrs Yajñavalkya, a mysterious black masseuse. As plots these may sound whimsical or merely anecdotal; but as with Henry James, who often turned small 'shocking' plots into complex extended fictions, the treatment is all. Firbank must have learnt much from James's mastery of obliquity, before passing on to his own more extreme and absurdist position; *Inclinations*, in particular, which is written almost entirely in dialogue, shows a Jamesian preference for presenting events not as they happen but as they are refracted and analysed in conversation which touches on them. Thus, much of the book is a kind of conversational fantasia, counterpointing the tomboyish bluntness of young Mabel Collins with the disillusion of her refined but vampiric admirer Geraldine O'Brookomore. (Miss O'Brookomore's heartbreak, when it comes, is conveyed in a chapter which consists simply of the word 'Mabel!' repeated eight times.) From the start Firbank's novels, so witty in tone and confidently languid in tempo, none the less required total concentration from their readers; in the earlier novels in particular there are passages of heady difficulty, and unannounced transitions which require a kind of intuitive alertness to be properly followed. Ordinary fictional expectations are largely disregarded. Rather, as we tease out the aspirations of the characters from their talk – by turns extravagant and commonplace, obscurely meaningful and boldly irrelevant – it is as if we were witnessing some strange hybrid of a Symbolist drama and a play by Congreve: both highly artificial forms, but each contributing its peculiar kind of truth.

*Vainglory* is an astonishingly achieved first novel, and part of its audacity lies in Firbank's unfaltering adherence to his entirely new way of doing things. The story of Mrs Shamefoot and her window is a strand in the whole, but much of the novel's activity happens quite independently of it. Mrs Henedge, widow of the Bishop of Ashringford, is going over to Rome. The early chapters take place in London, and the longest episode is a party at Mrs Henedge's house for the recitation (significantly enough) of a newly discovered fragment by Sappho. Then the scene moves to Ashringford, the small cathedral town on which Mrs Shamefoot has fixed her hopes. Figures from London move in and out of a quaintly old-fashioned provincial milieu which is treated with mischievous fondness by Firbank. An adulterous affair takes place; an actress recovers from a role and prepares for another; the bishop's wife and sister-in-law discuss the new curate; but the various elements are prevented from coalescing into a Trollopean whole. Design, juxtaposition, omission and selection of detail assert their priority over plot. And the effect is both liberating and disquieting. The massive prosecution of a system of cause and effect, so characteristic of the Victorian novel, is overturned by Firbank in favour of a different model, where characters move in response to whim, desire, ambition, under the fluctuating magnetism of class and religion, but without the security of any clear social or moral system. As Mrs Shamefoot remarks, 'The world is disgracefully managed, one hardly knows to whom to complain.' And the novel in which she finds herself has a superficial air of mismanagement too. The subsidiary elements, ostensibly sub-plots, are never resolvingly tied in. Indeed, there is no certainty as to what is plot and what sub-plot, what matters and how much. In *Inclinations*

Miss O'Brookomore will disappear entirely in the second part of the novel. There is often a sense that the major characters in Firbank's novels are perhaps only minor characters in them: an adjustment which discomfortingly illuminates a bleak truth about life as well as a time-honoured presupposition of fiction.

Firbank the man has tended to be known through a distorting haze of miscellaneous anecdote. He appears as a somehow fabulous figure, dandyish, exquisite, made up, an habitué of the opera and ballet and later of black jazz-bands; pathologically shy, but with the boldness and determination which sometimes accompany shyness; a drinker rather than an eater; an admirer but not a lover of young men; an incessant traveller; a giggler and writher and towards the end of his life a cougher; a man who often laughed when he was alone. But even the kindest and most marvelling stories, by those who counted themselves his friends, convey a sense of distance from their exotic and unknowable subject. In the years before the war, whenever Firbank was in London, he was a figure in the bohemian world of the Café Royal and the Eiffel Tower restaurant. But during the war, when he lived for four years in isolation in Oxford, he recedes further from view, and in effect disappears into his work. There is something movingly exemplary about his dedication to his writing during this period of deep depression and separation from the reality that culture and travel represented for him – the more so since the often wildly funny books he wrote then were greeted with incomprehension and distaste, and he was obliged to pay for their publication himself. When the war was over, he resumed his travelling, and apart from brief summer visits to London he was abroad for the rest of his life, in hotels and rented apartments, and in climates better suited to his tastes and appetites and his always frail health. His intense solitariness and nervous restlessness were embraced and transcended in the lonely experiment of his art. He never settled down, never bought a place of his own. The date-lines of his later novels – 'Versailles, Montreux, Florence', 'Havana, Bordighera' – emphasize the fact that he shaped his own life into an itinerary of occasions and opportunities to write books. If he ever receives the biography he deserves it will be one especially sensitive to the fact that his art was what mattered most to him.

Of course there is much in the life to suggest why Firbank took the view he did of the instability of society and the likelihood of disappointment. To take just a few possible topics. He was himself the exotic third-generation bloom of a typically Victorian social success story. His paternal grandfather was a Durham miner who had made a fortune as a railway contractor; his father, who served as Unionist MP for East Hull from 1895 to 1906, was knighted in Edward VII's Coronation honours. But when Sir Thomas died in 1910 and Ronald assumed control of the family's finances he discovered that the fortune had largely gone; property had to be sold, his mother and sister accommodated, and the wherewithal for his single but not exactly austere way of life to be secured. The desire for quasi-aristocratic independence was shadowed by the fear of penury, just as his whole life was shadowed by his own weak health, and the fear of the early death which had been the fate of his two brothers, Joey (1884–1904) and Bertie (1887–1913).

Ronald spent his childhood, up to the age of eleven, in Chislehurst, a small town to the south of London, which had also been the adopted home of the Empress Eugénie, widow of Napoleon III, whose tomb was for some years in a chapel of the Catholic church near the Firbanks' house. Later the little court in exile moved to Farnborough, but it seems unquestionable that its presence in Chislehurst coloured Firbank's imagination, and fed his fascination with royalty (and especially royalty seen in its homely and off-guard moments) and with Catholicism.

The very feminine world in which Ronald spent his childhood must account in some way for the feminine nature of his fictional world. With his father often away in London or in his constituency Firbank grew up in a mutually adoring relationship with his mother, for whom he wrote poems and stories, and to whom he would later dedicate ('In all the world to the dearest of mothers') the 1916 reissue of his mawkish early tale *Odette*: a gesture of reassurance perhaps as his considerably more outré mature work began to appear. (Lady Firbank, however, remained an ardent admirer of her son's books until her death in 1924; one can only speculate as to how much she understood or screened out their provocativeness and sexual unorthodoxy.) Firbank's fictional world seems to replicate the female world of his childhood home, of his mother and her friends. It was not until his final and very personal masterpiece *Cardinal Pirelli* that he wrote a book 'about' a man. The mood of passivity and frustration in his work stems in part from the fact that he chose to write about a female world, shut off, like that of Jane Austen's women, from power and action. His dramatis personae are spinsters, widows, or grass widows, who refer with pity or disdain or horror, but very rarely with regret, to the absence of men: the counterpart to their powerlessness is a paradoxical sense of freedom, and relief from the stuffiness, difficulty and physical exactions of the opposite sex. The model of society divided into separate male and female realms had become deeply institutionalized in Victorian upper-class life, and it is one which continued to fascinate Firbank in more personal ways. His play *The Princess Zoubaroff* is an unconventional marriage comedy in which, under the aegis of an idealized Oscar Wilde, the men very happily go off with the men and the women with the women. And in his later books the female viewpoint becomes more obviously a sly means of expressing his own homosexuality. The spinsters and widows of the English colony in *The Flower Beneath the Foot* debate the merits of being alone, and take out from the circulating library's high-camp catalogue such volumes as *Man, and All About Him*, *Men – my Delight* by Cora Velasquez, *The Beard throughout the Ages*, and *Men Are Animals* by the Hon Mrs Victor Smythe. Along with this goes a sort of emotional transvestism. No male novelist and few female ones have shown such an absorbed delight in women's clothing as Firbank does, and it is surely no coincidence, in terms of family psychology, that his sister Heather collected a remarkable wardrobe of contemporary fashion (it is now in the Victoria and Albert Museum). Firbank's collection, equally fashion-conscious, is in the pages of his novels.

In the three novels in this book, the experiments of the earlier work are absorbed and refined, but in general there is a greater directness of treatment. Chapters of *The Flower Beneath the Foot* open with clear expositions of plot, and *Sorrow in Sunlight* has a classic transparency of design. All three of them, though written in Firbank's thirties, seem retrospectively to show the fused complexity and trenchancy of the best 'late' work.

*The Flower Beneath the Foot* is the book in which Firbank turned his back on England, and the tone of parts of it has a satirical asperity not heard before in his writing. In earlier books he'd sometimes sought to settle a private score, though sometimes he also changed his mind at proof-stage. But in *The Flower* the invigorating vein of malice noted by some of his acquaintances gives a complex personal shading to the story of youthful heartbreak and retreat from the world. 'Vulgar cynical & "horrid"', Firbank described the book, 'but of course beautiful here & there for those that can see.' For the first time he introduced thinly disguised real people, and always with the purpose of mockery. In a letter to his mother saying how 'dangerous' the book was he offered a key:

> 'Princess Elsie' = Princess Mary. 'Mrs Chilleywater' = Mrs Harold Nicolson. 'Eddy' = Evan Morgan – and of course 'King Geo' & 'Queen Glory' are the king & queen. The English Ambassadress is founded on Mrs Roscoe & Lady Nicolson . . . The lady journalist must be 'Eve' of the Tatler or any other of the prattling busy-bodies that write for the magazines.

Mrs Harold Nicolson was of course better known as V. Sackville-West, here rather wildly satirized as a representative of all that Firbank had set himself against in the English novel. 'Who among us today', she asks rhetorically, 'is carrying on the tradition of Fielding? Who really cares? I know *I* do what I can . . . and there's Madam Adrian Bloater, of course. But I can think of no one else; – we two.' (It's interesting that Firbank gives only the vaguest hint of Sackville-West's lesbianism, and indeed makes Lady Something, also modelled on her, so prudish and confused in the face of the advances of the Queen of Dateland.) Evan Morgan (1893–1949) was more central to the novel, a fact attested to by his more ruthless marginalization. Morgan was the only son of the third Viscount Tredegar. Firbank had first seen him in 1914 in the British Museum, where he was struck by his resemblance to the mummy of Ramses II and dragged him off to show him the 'original'. They became friends of a sort, Morgan enjoyed Firbank's 'dubious and speculative' conversation, while it seems clear that Firbank fell somewhat in love with Morgan. In 1920 he offered him the dedication of *The Princess Zoubaroff*; but machinations by Morgan's family, who objected to the association in general and to moral and religious aspects of the play in particular, and who felt the dedication would compromise his chances of an expected diplomatic posting, led to its rejection at a late stage in the book's production. The Hon 'Eddy' Monteith is Firbank's revenge for this rejection, and, like the best satirical portraits, a wonderful comic creation in its own right. Like Firbank, Morgan was a Catholic convert, and Firbank's own camp ambivalence about Rome is here focused on his victim. Morgan was also a prolific and extremely bad poet, and the glimpse we get of 'Eddy''s poems perfectly captures their derivativeness and infantilism. 'Eddy''s death, in a footnote, is a master-stroke of controlled malice: 'the shock received by meeting a jackal while composing a sonnet had been too much for him. His tomb is in the Vale of Akko, beside the river Dis. Alas, for the *triste* obscurity of his end!'

Alongside the satirical rejection of English culture ('the very apotheosis of worn-out *cliché*'), the disdain for British royalty ('more at home in the stables than in a drawing-room'), and the wilful disregard for English grammar (exemplified by the novel's very first sentence), runs a new boldness about homosexuality, itself so fiercely repudiated in Firbank's homeland. It is clearly a subject which becomes more approachable in the Ruritanian ambience of Kairoulla, an 'imaginary Vienna' as Firbank describes it in the short preface, as arch as it is startlingly candid, that he wrote for the American edition of the novel after his mother's death. (It is reprinted here with the novel for the first time.) Of course there is much about Kairoulla that is not Viennese; it is a typical Firbankian hybrid, a traveller's montage of longed-for and remembered places, and with its palm-trees and Arab flower-sellers 'half-way to the East already'. (Firbank uses the term 'the East' in the old Orientalist sense to mean North Africa and the Middle East, not the Orient itself.) A significant part of its charm, evidently, and of the novel's genesis, is the '*wonderful boys*' that are to be found there.

*The Flower* comes at a suggestive juncture in the literature of homosexuality; and again there are connexions with Proust which might bear further investigation. The first volume of Proust's *Sodome et Gomorrhe*, with its account of the overheard sexual encounter between the Baron de Charlus and the tailor Jupien, and its extended metaphor of floral pollination for human sexual activity, was published on 2 May 1921. Firbank arrived in Paris on 22 May, left after a week for a short visit to London, and returned on 3 July, when he moved into an apartment at Versailles and began writing *The Flower Beneath the Foot*. There are no direct references to Proust in his books, but it seems at least likely that Firbank, who read widely in French fiction and poetry, would have looked at this much-discussed and arrestingly named new instalment of Proust's novel. When he reveals in the first chapter of *The Flower* that it is a pet project of the Queen of Pisuerga to 'form a party to excavate (for objects of art) among the ruins of Chedorlahomor, a *faubourg* of Sodom', the use of the biblical motif is as striking as his choice of the word *faubourg*, which means a suburb, but in society parlance meant particularly the *faubourg* Saint-Germain, the Parisian milieu of Proust's upper-class characters. As for the floral conceit, it is a preoccupation of both writers, and one which Firbank takes to a daring extreme in this book by realizing the metaphor of the 'language of flowers' and actually having a shopful of flowers speak. ('Life's bound to be uncertain when you haven't got your roots!') When the Queen of Dateland wants to convey the sexual freedom of her 'Eastern' homeland, it is with the metaphor of 'the little amorous jessamine-flower . . . that twines itself sometimes to the right hand, at others to the left, just according to its caprices!'

Coincidence or not, it is fascinating that the two novelists should be propounding visions of counterbalanced male and female homosexualities at the same time. Usually Firbank's homosexuals are lesbian, but in the lulled 'soul-trip' chapter of *The Flower* he suspends both males and females for a moment in their private spheres outside the world of the court, Count Cabinet and Peter Passer on their island in the lake, Olga Blumenghast and the Countess of Tolga, on their way to visit them with a volume of Uranian verse, becalmed in their boat into a rapturous discovery of each other. In his last two novels, and particularly in *Cardinal Pirelli*, Firbank would boldly obtrude his own unignorably gay presence as observer and commentator. Proust disguised his own sexuality in his largely autobiographical novel, converting his male lovers into female ones, and treating the subject with an affected objectivity which André Gide, amongst others, found timid and hypocritical. Firbank, in his oblique and fantasticated way, is characteristically more reckless. And the shocking last page of *The Flower*, in which the story of trampled and disregarded Laura reaches a temporary close, throws a painfully personal shadow back across the whole novel.

It seems probable that despite his famous postcard to Osbert Sitwell, 'Tomorrow I go to Haiti. They say the President is a *Perfect Dear*', Firbank did not in fact visit that country (which was then under US military occupation). He did, however, go to Cuba and Jamaica in the summer of 1922, and it was in Cuba that he 'found' his new book; as he travelled between Santiago de Cuba in the east and Havana in the west he would have experienced the contrast between the simplicity and remoteness of the sugar-growing countryside and the intense excitement and glamour of the capital – a contrast and a journey which form the template of *Sorrow in Sunlight*. Of course he reinvented the place, turning Havana into Cuna-Cuna, 'Little city of cocktails', and borrowing features from elsewhere (the May Day Mountains, for instance, from southern Jamaica); the name of the island itself, Tacarigua, he took from a lagoon on the Caribbean coast of Venezuela. As in the cosmopolitan fantasy of *The Flower*, the sources are less important than the habit of mind which absorbs and synthesizes them, and which reacts so keenly to the euphony and suggestiveness of proper names. Both things had been demonstrated by Mrs Yajñavalkya in *Valmouth*, who claims abstrusely to come from 'Taihaiti'. That exotic compound says a lot about Firbank's love of what we would call the multi-cultural, his attraction to the racially hybrid culture of Egypt or Cuba, and his fascination with figures (maids, flower-sellers, jazz musicians, kings and queens) adrift from their ethnic moorings. His reactions are partly aesthetic and voyeuristic, no doubt, but they are also underpinned by a poignant sense of identification. The nomad in him is full of sympathetic intuitions about the nomads he describes, and in a way Firbank's blacks carry the burden of expressing his own sense of difference, of having come, emotionally, from somewhere distant and misunderstood. (They carry also, therefore, a sense of mystery, glamour and secret supremacy.)

It is this that makes the Mouth family so touching as well as so funny. They are his most objectively seen characters, the most solid, and in a sense the most conventional. Like everything in the novel they are presented with miraculous economy, yet they have an almost Dickensian presence, achieved largely through their speech and the way Firbank notates it. There is, untypically for Firbank, nothing oblique about the Mouths, who all say exactly what they mean and what they want; like characters in a play they seem to be fully present in their speech, and we grasp their hopes, fears and misunderstandings without the author's further intervention. Unlike some phonetic procedures Firbank's is always audible and persuasive, though of course in a British West Indian idiom cheerfully at odds with the Hispanic setting. The acuteness with which it is heard accommodates effects not far from Sam Weller or Mrs Gamp – 's'poge', 'kimpoged', 'ticklers' (for particulars) – alongside the long Jamaican *a*s of 'Ah cyan pramas'; and it is subtly adjusted to the speakers. Little Edna comes out with 'gemplum' for gentleman and childish 'bokkles' and 'buckler' for bottles and butler, while her mother veers closer to Mrs Malaprop ('bombax' for bombast) and favours elaborate locutions and French phrases: 'We go to Cuna-Cuna for de finishing ob *mes filles*!' Sometimes the registers overlap significantly: 'Dis an event to take exvantage ob', declares the socially aspiring Mrs Mouth, whilst Edna blithely recalls the necklace she was given 'de time he take exvantage ob my innocence' – one phrase whose two contradictory meanings sum up the tragic misapprehensions of the novel. For the Mouths, like many of Firbank's creations, are comic characters with tragic destinies.

As always Firbank had a very clear sense of the book's aesthetic, and its expressive significance. On the day he finished it he wrote to his mother: 'As a bit of colour & atmosphere it is the best of all my others & some of the figures negroes and Spanish South American are as wonderful as their setting! It is an amazing affair altogether & some no doubt will be horrified by it while others will be carried away by its vivid unusualness & the crude touches left purposely unshaded.' Later he described it as 'purposely a little "primitive", rather like a Gauguin in painting – extremely gay'. The novel's destiny, however, lay in a slightly different cultural perspective.

In March 1922 the American novelist and critic Carl Van Vechten had written to Firbank: 'I am very sorry to be obliged to inform you that I think there is some danger of your becoming the rage in America.' Van Vechten had already published a magazine article on Firbank, and his letter was effectively the next step in creating the 'rage' he was predicting. He clearly responded to the scandalous 'subterranean' element in Firbank: thirty years later he wrote that 'Almost all of Firbank is quaint reading and enough to make your hair, even pubic hair, stand on end when you understand it'; he also had an eye to publicity which was far from unwelcome to a writer starved of recognition, who had literally never earned a penny from his work. Van Vechten took up the Firbank case, and when he received the manuscript of *Sorrow in Sunlight* convinced Brentano's to publish it in the States; he also flung together an introduction to the novel, emphasizing its lightness and fashionableness ('The whole book hovers delightfully between a Freudian dream and a drawing by Alastair, set to music by George Gershwin'), and proposed a change of title, to *Prancing Nigger*. Firbank professed himself to be delighted with this, moved too perhaps by Van Vechten's assurance that 'beyond a doubt the new title would sell at least a thousand more copies'; he had never visited the United States, but he learned that Van Vechten was an active promoter of black writers, and relied on his sense of the apt and the topical. *Prancing Nigger* was published in New York in March 1924.

As a title it has the benefit of gaiety and animation, as against the melancholy abstraction of *Sorrow in Sunlight*, and doubtless it helped

Firbank's case by appearing to align him with the emerging spirit of the Harlem Renaissance. But it is also, strictly speaking, misleading, in a way that none of Firbank's other titles is: Prancing Nigger is Mrs Mouth's affectionately ironic nickname for her morose hymn-droning husband, a memorable character, but not the protagonist of the book. To call the novel *Prancing Nigger* is a bit as if *Pride and Prejudice* were to be called *Mr Bennet*. Still, whatever its emblematic value, when Brentano's brought out an English edition ten months later Firbank insisted on reverting to his earlier title. Presumably it reflected more clearly his own sense of the book's emotional chiaroscuro, as well as being more appropriate to a readership remote from black culture, to whom *Prancing Nigger* might have seemed inexcusably (or rather, perhaps, excusably) offensive. When Duckworth and Brentano's together brought out a five-volume *Works* of Firbank three years after his death, they stuck with *Prancing Nigger*, which evidently had the wider currency; and it has always been published under that title since. But in reverting here to *Sorrow in Sunlight* we have the authority of Firbank's first and last thoughts; and the book, in which the word 'nigger' is never used pejoratively, is saved from seeming, to a casual modern eye, to misadvertise itself. Whilst even readers who see the use of the word 'nigger' in its particular historical context (Van Vechten's novel *Nigger Heaven*, for instance, was published two years later) are saved from an apologetic reflex which necessarily focuses attention on a period aspect of the book's publishing history.

'Ah, the East . . .', Firbank wrote in the preface to the American *Flower*, 'I propose to return there, some day, when I write about New York.' It was a little joke that summed up his sense of elsewhere, his belief that absence from a place was an essential condition of writing about it; and it was also a promise that he would reciprocate the attention that New York had accorded him. Duly, in Cairo, in October 1925, he started work on his New York novel, *The New Rythum*. He had finished six chapters of it when he died the following spring.

So *Concerning the Eccentricities of Cardinal Pirelli* turned out to be his last book, and if it seems in retrospect to have been designed as a farewell then that is in part because Firbank himself, clear-sighted as well as morbidly superstitious, anticipated the end. In each of his previous two books, death capriciously seizes a minor character: the Archduchess Elizabeth dies of a chill caught while paddling, Bamboo is eaten by a shark; but in *Cardinal Pirelli* death comes for the archbishop himself.

Of all Firbank's novels, with their various cryptic personal elements, it is in this one that a portrait seems most clearly to have been painted over a self-portrait; and it is surely significant that he chose a prominent churchman as its subject. Like many aspects of his inner life, Firbank's religious feelings and beliefs are always hard to assess. He had been received into the Catholic church in 1907, whilst he was at Cambridge; and two years later he tried but failed to enter the Guardia Nobile at the Vatican. He later told Lord Berners that 'The Church of Rome wouldn't have me and so I laugh at her.' But spiteful though Firbank could be, the laughter he directs at the Catholic church seems of a kind with his general amused observation of human attitudes and institutions; and he often takes a mischievous pleasure in the 'otherness' of Catholic ritual in an English context. (In *Cardinal Pirelli* the old Pope recalls his dealings with Queen Victoria, 'who for so many years had corresponded with the Holy See under the signature of *the Countess of Lostwaters*'.) Firbank also claimed to be very moved by the mystical element in religion, and in the lonely months between his mother's death and his own often went to pray in the crypt of St Peter's, with Evan Morgan, to whom he had become reconciled. Spanish Catholicism, of course, had a further dimension of syncretic ritual and display which clearly fascinated Firbank. He had spent six months in Madrid in 1905, and visited Seville, where he 'found' his city of Clemenza and his Cardinal-Archbishop, in the summer of 1923. The scandalous baptism of a police-dog which opens the novel may well have been suggested by the feast of San Antón on 17 January (also Firbank's birthday), when animals are blessed in Madrid. The six dancing choirboys of Clemenza Cathedral are clearly a version of the Sevillian *seises*, choristers who dance a slow minuet before the high altar of the cathedral on certain festivals. Firbank's typical sensitivity to this supposedly Mozarabic survival is reflected too in his vignette of the 'Moorish' maid who cannot forget that 'the great basilica of Clemenza was a Mosque profaned', and in the legend of the ghostly black dervish who still 'walks' the *coro*. Before *The Flower* he had written a short novel *Santal*, which he saw as recasting *Odette* in an Arab setting, the story not of a girl seeking the Virgin but of a boy seeking Allah. To Pirelli himself the Bible and the Koran are old Eastern cousins, 'hardy old perennials, no less equivocal and extravagant, often, than the ever-adorable *Arabian Nights*!'

The beautiful sequence set in the decaying monastery of the Desierto (chapter 8) epitomizes the particular sweetness and humour of this novel, and reveals much about Firbank's method and voice. The Cardinal is in retreat, preparing his defence, looking out from the remoteness of the monastery at the appealing lights of Clemenza on the plain below: 'Dear beckoning lamps, dear calling lamps; lamps of theatres, cinemas, cabarets, bars and dancings; lamps of railway-termini, and excessively lit hotels, *olé* to you, enchantress lights!' It is a classic Firbankian motif, the longing for tranquillity and contemplation weighed against the allure of the world of pleasure; it is the underlying tension of *The Flower*, where in a similar passage Laura and Prince Yousef identify the lights of Kairoulla from the Palace gardens, and where, in the culminating scene, Laura gazes out from the convent walls at Yousef's wedding procession in the streets below. *Sorrow in Sunlight* contains Firbank's most insistent celebration of the world of bars and streetlife in the 'feverish sadness' of the tropical evening, and the end of the novel reverses the emotional perspective of its predecessor, with Edna and Vittorio looking down from their balcony at the procession of penitents and planning an evening of pleasure: 'Dair's a new dancer at de Apollo tonight. Suppose we go?' Pirelli is himself a sensualist and adventurer, prone to nostalgic enumeration of his old conquests, and we have already learnt of his habit of going into 'the dear street . . . The adorable Avenidas' in disguise, sometimes as a woman. The little apostrophe to the city's lights carries a melancholy sexual charge (it seems indeed, for all Pirelli's heterosexual leanings, like a catalogue of gay cruising spots).

For now, however, he has fled from the world, and from the 'malice and vindictiveness of men', and in the ambience of the old monastery, where St Theresa of Ávila is said to have written a part of *The Way of Perfection*, he gives himself up to the semi-random reflections that Firbank so excels at. Firbank never laboured in any systematic way at the evocation of a stream of consciousness, but a significant part of all his books is made up of the tracing of his characters' thoughts as they uncurl in droll or wistful arabesques. The musings of the Hon 'Eddy' Monteith on the language of bees (pp. 50–51) are a wonderfully funny nonsense of false consequences: Firbank seems always to have had a sense of the shape of thoughts, the frail chains of ideas, the easy distractions of the suggestible mind. He is a poet of solitariness who understands how huge a part of our conscious lives is given over to idle speculation, reminiscence, and the purely fragmentary associations evoked by what we see and hear. His own habit as a writer is often to chase a thought into a surprising decorative epiphany, or to slide, like the half-focused mind, between different tones, humming a line of a hymn or a popular song or echoing the quaintly poetic formulae of fairy-tales and works of piety. So the Cardinal wanders in the garden and in the 'forsaken splendour of the vast closed cloisters', talks with the old priest from the village church nearby and with the young acolyte who waits on him; and his memories, plans and reflections, ranging from former mistresses to points of theology, are woven into Firbank's rich but sparing evocations of place, colour and light. We see the things Pirelli shares with his creator: personal vanity (should he have a henna shampoo?) and feminized dandyism (in 'a creation of dull scarlet crêpe, a cobweb dubbed "summer-exile"'); a relish for the taboo, and a not-unrelated sense of persecution. And at this point too Pirelli's sensual yearnings seem to merge with Firbank's to envelop young Chicklet, the boy who will lead him, in the book's last pages, to the literal defrocking of his naked death. The mood of mortality ('Ahi; this death . . .') intensifies the isolation; and after dusk, as Pirelli gets progressively drunker, Firbank seems to be drawing on a deeply personal register of experience: 'It's queer, dears, how I'm lonely', the Cardinal exclaims to the old Zurbarans on the wall. 'The evenings are suicide.' And then comes the drunken delusion, absurd but touching in the longing for consolation it reveals, that St Theresa herself, 'sublime in laughter, exquisite in tenderness', has visited him.

The relative success of *Prancing Nigger* in the States had encouraged Firbank in the candour with which he depicted Pirelli's unorthodoxy and the relish with which he evoked the choirboys of the Cathedral. In the spring of 1924 he told his sister that the book in progress was under offer in the States, 'where people seem less hypocritical and narrow than in England'. Sadly this proved an illusion. A year later he learnt that 'Brentano is shocked with The Cardinal', and the novel was indeed rejected on 'moral and religious grounds'. So Firbank returned for his last book to Grant Richards, and to paying for its publication out of his own pocket. However, the General Strike, and Richards's bankruptcy proceedings, repeatedly delayed the novel's appearance. It was finally published on 29 June 1926, five weeks after Firbank's death.

## TEXTUAL NOTE

When Duckworth reissued Firbank's works after his death they regularized his punctuation, corrected his grammar, made numerous small verbal changes, and greatly reduced the frequency of hyphenations and of the expressive capitals he favoured, especially for the names of flowers. Firbank punctuated for emphasis and rhythm rather than in accordance with any strict modern system, and his capitals and italics lend his texts a more personal, and on occasion a more eighteenth-century, character. This volume reverts to the last texts revised by Firbank himself (*The Flower Beneath the Foot*, New York: Brentano's, 1924; *Sorrow in Sunlight*, London: Brentano's, 1924; *Concerning the Eccentricities of Cardinal Pirelli*, London: Grant Richards, 1926), with very occasional corrections of spelling (particularly of foreign words) and of obvious typographical errors.

# *The Flower Beneath the Foot*

*Being a record of the early life of St Laura de Nazianzi and the times in which she lived*

# *Draft preface to the first American Edition* (1924)

I suppose the Flower beneath the Foot is really Oriental in origin, although the scene is some imaginary Vienna. The idea came in Algeria while writing Santal. One evening (or it may have been early morning) just as the lights were being extinguished of a supper-restaurant in Algiers, a woman, almost assuredly an American, sailed unconcernedly in, & sank down with charming composure at a table not far from mine, & to myself I murmured: 'her Dreaminess, the Queen!' Later, in the radiant dawn, just outside, I beheld an Arab boy asleep beside the summer-sea, & to myself I murmured: 'his Weariness, the Prince!' And from these two names the Flower just came about. It did not occur to me, at the time, I believe, to fabric a story from so singularly little; but a short while afterwards, in another town, his Weariness I saw again. Everywhere in fact his Weariness, or his simulacrum, appeared; all Princes, all weary – *wonderful boys* – wearier, even, than me! And his Weariness recalled her Dreaminess, & then, quite naturally, & quite cosily, figures & objects composed themselves about them. The Queen's Ladies – her hectic Maids, the Palace, the Furniture, the Gardens &, above all, the ambitions of her Dreaminess the Queen for his Weariness the Prince – an alliance with England, poor woman, was the nadir of her dreams! Thus, gradually, characters & dialogue came together in my mind, & my tale of Islam began to bore me unutterably, & I longed to begin the Flower. A kind of nostalgia (which *may* only have been waywardness,) turned all my thoughts towards Vienna. And it was a veritable craving for Vienna, too. I remember it was at Touggourt in mid-Sahara while assisting at a sunset from the minarette of a Mosque, that I found the Duchess of Varna's court-dress

– the green of Nile water. 'Vi' & Olga's little soul-trip on the Lake, chapter, (I think,) *eleven*, suggested itself while watching two shed rose-leaves in a Moorish fountain. Such clinging, tender, courageous little rose-leaves they were – curious ones as well. Other elements, of course, went towards the shading & formation of my Flower, which really is as much a country-buttercup as a cattleya-orchid!

Ah, the East . . . I propose to return there, some day, when I write about New York.

Ronald Firbank

*To* MADAME MATHIEU
*and* MADEMOISELLE DORA GARNIER-PAGÈS

Some girls are born organically good: I wasn't.

St Laura de Nazianzi

It was about my eighteenth year that I conquered my *Ego*.

Ibid

# I

Neither her Gaudiness the Mistress of the Robes, or her Dreaminess the Queen were feeling quite themselves. In the Palace all was speculation. Would they be able to attend the *Fêtes* in honour of King Jotifa, and Queen Thleeanouhee of the Land of Dates? – Court opinion seemed largely divided. Countess Medusa Rappa, a woman easily disturbable, was prepared to wager what the Countess of Tolga 'liked' (she knew), that another week would find the Court shivering beneath the vaulted domes of the Summer-Palace.

'I fear I've no time (or desire) now, Medusa,' the Countess answered, moving towards the Royal apartments, 'for making bets,' though turning before the anteroom door she nodded: 'Done!'

She found her sovereign supine on a couch piled with long Tunisian cushions, while a maid of honour sat reading to her aloud:

'*Live with an aim, and let that aim be high!*' the girl was saying as the Countess approached.

'Is that you, Violet?' her Dreaminess enquired without looking round.

'How is your condition, Madam?' the Countess anxiously murmured.

'Tell me, do, of a place that soothes and lulls one —?'

The Countess of Tolga considered.

'Paris,' she hazarded.

'Ah! Impossible.'

'The Summer-Palace, then,' the Countess ejaculated, examining her long slender fingers that were like the tendrils of a plant.

'Dr Cuncliffe Babcock flatly forbids it,' the Royal woman declared, starting slightly at the sound of a gun: 'That must be *the Dates!*' she said. And in effect, a vague reverberation, as of individuals cheering, resounded fitfully from afar. 'Give me my diamond anemones,' the Queen commanded, and motioning to her maid: 'Pray conclude, mademoiselle, those lofty lines.'

With a slight sigh, the lectress took up the posture of a Dying Intellectual.

'*Live with an aim, and let that aim be high!*' she reiterated in tones tinged perceptibly with emotion.

'But not *too* high, remember, Mademoiselle de Nazianzi . . .'

There was a short pause. And then –

'Ah Madam! What a dearest he is!'

'I think you forget yourself,' the Queen murmured with a quelling glance. 'You had better withdraw.'

'He has such strength! One could niche an idol in his dear, dinted chin.'

'Enough!'

And a moment later, the enflamed girl left the room warbling softly: *Depuis le Jour*.

'Holy Virgin,' the Countess said, addressing herself to the ceiling. 'Should his Weariness, the Prince, yield himself to this caprice . . .'

The Queen shifted a diamond bangle from one of her arms to the other.

'She reads at such a pace,' she complained, 'and when I asked her *where* she had learnt to read so quickly, she replied "On the screens at Cinemas".'

'I do not consider her at all distinguished,' the Countess commented, turning her eyes away towards the room.

It was a carved-ceiled, and rather lofty room, connected by tall glass doors with other rooms beyond. Peering into one of these the Countess could see reflected the 'throne', and a little piece of broken Chippendale brought from England, that served as a stand for a telephone, wrought in ormolu and rock-crystal, which the sun's rays at present were causing to emit a thousand playful sparks. Tapestry panels depicting the Loves of *Mejnoun and Leileh* half concealed the silver *boiseries* of the walls, while far down the room, across old rugs from Chirvan that were a marvellous wonder, showed fortuitous jardinières, filled with every flowering-kind of plant. Between the windows were canopied recesses, denuded of their statues by the Queen's desire, 'in order that they might appear suggestive', while through the windows themselves, the Countess could catch across the fore-court of the castle, a panorama of the town below, with the State Theatre and the Garrisons and the Houses of Parliament, and the Hospital, and the low white dome, crowned by turquoise-tinted tiles of the Cathedral, which was known to all churchgoers as *the Blue Jesus*.

'It would be a fatal connexion,' the Queen continued, 'and it must never, never be!'

By way of response the Countess exchanged with her sovereign a glance that was known in Court circles as her *tortured-animal* look: 'Their Oriental majesties,' she observed, 'to judge from the din, appear to have already endeared themselves with the mob!'

The Queen stirred slightly amid her cushions.

'For the aggrandisement of the country's trade, an alliance with Dateland is by no means to be depreciated,' she replied, closing her eyes as though in some way or other this bullion to the State would allow her to gratify her own wildest whims, the dearest, perhaps, of which was to form a party to excavate (for objects of art) among the ruins of Chedorlahomor, a *faubourg* of Sodom.

'Am I right, Madam, in assuming it's Bananas? . . .' the Countess queried.

But at that moment the door opened, and his Weariness the Prince entered the room in all his tinted Orders.

Handsome to tears, his face, even as a child had lacked innocence. His was of that *magnolia* order of colouring, set off by pleasantly untamed eyes, and teeth like flawless pearls.

'You've seen them? What are they like . . . Tell Mother, darling?' the Queen exclaimed.

'They're merely dreadful,' his Weariness, who had been to the railway-station to welcome the Royal travellers, murmured in a voice extinct with boredom.

'They're in European dress, dear?' his mother questioned.

'The King had on a frock coat and a cap . . .'

'And she?'

'A tartan-skirt, and checked wool-stockings.'

'She has great individuality, so I hear, marm,' the Countess ventured.

'Individuality be —! No one can doubt she's a terrible woman.'

The Queen gently groaned.

'I see life today,' she declared, 'in the colour of mould.'

The Prince protruded a shade the purple violet of his tongue.

'Well, it's depressing,' he said, 'for us all, with the Castle full of blacks.'

'That is the least of my worries,' the Queen observed. 'Oh, Yousef, Yousef,' she added, 'do you wish to break my heart?'

The young man protruded some few degrees further his tongue.

'I gather you're alluding to Laura!' he remarked.

'But what can you *see* in her?' his mother mourned.

'She suits my feelings,' the Prince simply said.

'Peuh!'

'She meets my needs.'

'She's so housemaid . . . I hardly know . . . !' the Queen raised beautiful hands bewildered.

'Très gutter, ma'am,' the Countess murmured dropping her voice to a half-whisper.

'She saves us from *cliché*,' the Prince indignantly said.

'She saves us from nothing,' his mother returned. 'Oh, Yousef, Yousef. And what *cerné* eyes, my son. I suppose you were gambling all night at the Château des Fleurs?'

'Just hark to the crowds!' the Prince evasively said. And never too weary to receive an ovation, he skipped across the room towards the nearest window, where he began blowing kisses to the throng.

'Give them the Smile Extending, darling,' his mother beseeched.

'Won't you rise and place your arm about him, Madam,' the Countess suggested.

'I'm not feeling at all up to the mark,' her Dreaminess demurred, passing her fingers over her hair.

'There is sunshine, ma'am . . . and you have your *anemones* on . . .' the Countess cajoled, 'and to please the people, you ought indeed to squeeze him.' And she was begging and persuading the Queen to rise, as the King entered the room preceded by a shapely page (of sixteen) with cheeks fresher than milk.

'Go to the window, Willie,' the Queen exhorted her Consort fixing an eye on the last trouser button that adorned his long, straggling legs.

The King, who had the air of a tired pastry-cook, sat down.

'We feel,' he said, 'today, we've had our fill of stares!'

'One little bow, Willie,' the Queen entreated, 'that wouldn't kill you.'

'We'd give perfect worlds,' the King went on, 'to go, by Ourselves, to bed.'

'Get rid of the noise for me. *Quiet them.* Or I'll be too ill,' the Queen declared, 'to leave my room tonight!'

'Should I summon Whisky, Marm?' the Countess asked, but before there was time to reply the Court physician, Dr Cuncliffe Babcock, was announced.

'I feel I've had a relapse, Doctor,' her Dreaminess declared.

Dr Babcock beamed: he had one blind eye – though this did not prevent him at all from seeing all that was going on with the other.

'Leave it to me, Madam,' he assured, 'and I shall pick you up in *no* time!'

'Not Johnnie, doctor?' the Queen murmured with a grimace. For a glass of *Johnnie Walker* at bed-time was the great doctor's favourite receipt.

'No; something a little stronger, I think.'

'We need expert attention, too,' the King intervened.

'You certainly are somewhat pale, sir.'

'Whenever I go out,' the King complained, 'I get an impression of raised hats.'

It was seldom King William of Pisuerga spoke in the singular tense, and Doctor Babcock looked perturbed.

'Raised hats, sir?' he murmured in impressive tones.

'Nude heads, doctor.'

The Queen commenced to fidget. She disliked that the King should appear more interesting than herself.

'These earrings tire me,' she said, 'take them out.'

But the Prince, who seemed to be thoroughly enjoying the success of his appearance with the crowd, had already begun tossing the contents of the flower vases into the street.

'Willie . . . prevent him! Yousef . . . I forbid you!' her Dreaminess faintly shrieked. And to stay her son's despoiling hand she skimmed towards him, when the populace catching sight of her, redoubled their cheers.

Meanwhile Mademoiselle de Nazianzi had regained again her composure. A niece of her Gaudiness the Mistress of the Robes (the Duchess of Cavaljos), her recent début at Court, had been made under the brightest conceivable of conditions.

Laura Lita Carmen Etoile de Nazianzi was more piquant perhaps than pretty. A dozen tiny moles were scattered about her face, while on either side of her delicate nose, a large grey eye surveyed the world with a pensive critical glance.

'Scenes like that make one sob with laughter,' she reflected, turning into the corridor where two of the Maids of Honour, like strutting idols, were passing up and down.

'Is she really very ill? Is she *really* dying?' they breathlessly enquired.

Mademoiselle de Nazianzi disengaged herself from their solicitously entwining arms.

'She is not!' she answered, in a voice full of eloquent inflections.

But beguiled by the sound of marching feet, one of the girls had darted forward towards a window.

'Oh Blanche, Blanche, Blanchie love!' she exclaimed, 'I could dance to the click of your brother's spurs.'

'You'd not be the first to, dear darling!' Mademoiselle de Lambèse replied, adjusting her short shock of hair before a glass.

Mademoiselle de Lambèse believed herself to be a very valuable piece of goods, and seemed to think she had only to smile to stir up an Ocean of passion.

'Poor Ann-Jules,' she said: 'I fear he's in the clutches of that awful woman.'

'Kalpurnia?'

'Every night he's at the Opera.'

'I hear she wears the costume of a shoe-black in the new ballet,' Mademoiselle de Nazianzi said, 'and is too strangely extraordinary!'

'Have you decided, Rara,[1] yet, what you'll wear for the ball?'

'A black gown and three blue flowers on my tummy.'

'After a shrimp-tea with the Archduchess I feel I *want* no dinner,' Mademoiselle Olga Blumenghast, a girl with slightly hunched shoulders said, returning from the window.

'Oh! Had she a party?'

'A curé or two, and the Countess Yvorra.'

'Her black bordered envelopes make one shiver!'

'I thought I should have died, it was so dull,' Mademoiselle Olga Blumenghast averred, standing aside to allow his Naughtyness Prince Olaf (a little boy wracked by all the troubles of Spring), and Mrs Montgomery, the Royal Governess, to pass. They had been out evidently among the crowd, and both were laughing heartily at the asides they had overheard.

''Ow can you be so frivolous, your Royal 'ighness?' Mrs Montgomery was expostulating: 'for shame, wicked boy! For shame!' And her cheery British laugh echoed gaily down the corridors.

'Well *I* took tea at the Ritz,' Mademoiselle de Lambèse related.

'Anybody?'

'Quite a few!'

'There's a rumour that Prince Yousef is entertaining there tonight.'

Mademoiselle Blumenghast tittered.

'Did you hear what he called the lanterns for the *Fête*?' she asked.

'No.'

'A lot of "bloody bladders"!'

'What, what a dearest,' Mademoiselle de Nazianzi sighed beneath her breath. And all along the almost countless corridors as far as her bedroom door, she repeated again and again: 'What, *what* a dearest!'

1 The name by which the future saint was sometimes called among her friends.

## II

Beneath a wide golden ceiling people were dancing. A capricious concert waltz, drowsy, intricate, caressing, reached fitfully the supper-room; where a few privileged guests were already assembled to meet King Jotifa and Queen Thleeanouhee of the Land of Dates.

It was one of the regulations of the Court, that those commanded to the King's board, should assemble some few minutes earlier than the Sovereigns themselves, and the guests at present were mostly leaning stiffly upon their chair-backs, staring vacuously at the olives and salted almonds upon the table-cloth before them. Several of the ladies indeed had taken the liberty to seat themselves, and were beguiling the time by studying the menu or disarranging the smilax, while one dame went as far as to take, and even to nibble, a salted almond. A conversation of a non-private kind (carried on between the thin, authoritative legs of a Court Chamberlain) by Countess Medusa Rappa and the English Ambassadress, was being listened to by some with mingled signs of interest.

'Ah! How clever Shakespere!' the Countess was saying: 'How gorgeous! How glowing! I once knew a speech from "Julia Sees Her! . . ." perhaps his greatest *oeuvre* of all. Yes! "Julia *Sees* Her" is what I like best of that great, great master.'

The English Ambassadress plied her fan.

'Friends, Comrades, Countrymen,' she murmured, 'I used to know it myself!'

But the lady nibbling almonds was exciting a certain amount of comment. This was the Duchess of Varna, voted by many to be one of the handsomest women of the Court. Living in economical obscurity nearly half the year round, her appearances at the palace were becoming more and more infrequent.

'I knew the Varnas were hard up, but I did not know they were *starving*,' the Countess Yvorra, a woman with a would-be indulgent face, that was something less hard than rock, remarked to her neighbour the Count of Tolga, and dropping her glance from the Count's weak chin she threw a fleeting smile towards his wife, who was looking 'Eastern' swathed in the skin of a blue panther.

'Yes, their affairs it seems are almost desperate,' the Count returned, directing his gaze towards the Duchess.

Well-favoured beyond measure she certainly was, with her immense placid eyes, and bundles of loose, blonde hair. She had a gown the green of Nile water, that enhanced to perfection the swan-like fairness of her throat and arms.

'I'm thinking of building myself a Villa in the Land of Dates!' she was confiding to the British Ambassador, who was standing beside her on her right: 'Ah, yes! I shall end my days in a country strewn with flowers.'

'You would find it I should say too hot, Duchess.'

'My soul has need of the sun, Sir Somebody!' the Duchess replied, opening with equanimity a great black ostrich fan, and smiling up at him through the sticks.

Sir Somebody Something was a person whose nationality was written all over him. Nevertheless, he had despite a bluff, and somewhat rugged manner, a certain degree of feminine sensitiveness, and any reference to the *soul* at all (outside the Embassy Chapel), invariably made him fidget.

'In moderation, Duchess,' he murmured, fixing his eyes upon the golden head of a champagne bottle.

'They say it is a land of love!' the Duchess related, raising indolently an almond to her sinuously-chiselled lips.

'And even, so it's said, too,' his Excellency returned: 'Of licence!' when just at this turn of things the Royal cortège entered the supper-room, to the exhilarating strains of King Goahead's War-March.

Those who had witnessed the arrival of King Jotifa and his Queen earlier in the afternoon, were amazed at the alteration of their aspect now. Both had discarded their European attire for the loosely-flowing vestments of their native land, and for a brief while there was some slight confusion among those present as to which was the gentleman, or which the lady of the two. The king's beard long and blonde, should have determined the matter outright, but on the other hand the Queen's necklet of reeds and plumes was so very misleading . . . Nobody in Pisuerga, had seen anything to compare to it before. 'Marvellous, though terrifying,' the Court passed verdict.

Attended by their various suites, the royal party gained their places amid the usual manifestation of loyal respect.

But one of the Royal ladies as it soon became evident was not yet come.

'Where's Lizzie, Lois?' King William asked, riveting the Archduchess' empty chair.

'We'd better begin without her, Willie,' the Queen exclaimed, 'you know she never minds.'

And hardly had the company seated themselves when, dogged by a lady-in-waiting and a maid-of-honour, the Archduchess Elizabeth of Pisuerga rustled in.

Very old and very bent, and (even) very beautiful, she was looking as the Grammar-books say, 'meet' to be robbed, beneath a formidable tiara, and a dozen long strands of pearls.

'Forgive me, Willie,' she murmured, with a little high shrill tinkling laugh: 'but it was so fine, that after tea, I and a Lady went paddling in the Basin of the Nymphs.'

'How was the water?' the King enquired.

The Archduchess repressed a sneeze: 'Fresh,' she replied, 'but not too . . .'

'After sunset, beware dear Aunt, of chills.'

'But for a frog, I believe nothing would have got me out!' the august lady confessed as she fluttered bird-like to her chair.

Forbidden in youth by parents and tutors alike the joys of paddling under pain of chastisement, the Archduchess Elizabeth appeared to find a zest in doing so now. Attended by a chosen lady-in-waiting (as a rule the dowager Marchioness of Lallah Miranda) she liked to slip off to one of the numerous basins or natural grottos in the castle gardens, where she would pass whole hours in wading blissfully about. Whilst paddling, it was her wont to run over those refrains from the vaudevilles and operas (with their many shakes and rippling *cadenze*), in favour in her day, interspersed at intervals by such cries as: 'Pull up your skirt, Marquise, it's dragging a little my friend below the knees . . .' or, 'A shark, a shark!' which was her way of designating anything that had fins, from a carp to a minnow.

'I fear our Archduchess has contracted a slight catarrh,' the Mistress of the Robes, a woman like a sleepy cow, observed, addressing herself to the Duke of Varna upon her left.

'Unless she is more careful, she'll go paddling once too often,' the Duke replied, contemplating with interest, above the moonlight-coloured daffodils upon the table board, one of the button-nosed belles of Queen Thleeanouhee's suite. The young creature, referred to cryptically among the subordinates of the Castle, as 'Tropical Molly', was finding fault already it seemed with the food.

'Take it away,' she was protesting in animated tones: 'I'd as soon touch a foot-squashed mango!'

'No *mayonnaise*, miss?' a court-official asked, dropping his face prevailingly to within an inch of her own.

'Take it right away . . . And if you should *dare* sir! to come any closer . . . !'

The Mistress of the Robes fingered nervously the variously Orders of Merit on her sumptuous bosom.

'I trust there will be no contretemps,' she murmured, glancing uneasily towards the Queen of the Land of Dates, who seemed to be lost in admiration of the Royal dinner-service of scarlet plates, that looked like pools of blood upon the cloth.

'What pleases me in your land,' she was expansively telling her host, 'is less your food, than the china you serve it on; for with us you know there's none. And now,' she added, marvellously wafting a fork, 'I'm for ever spoilt for shells.'

King William was incredulous.

'With you no china?' he gasped.

'None, Sir, none!'

'I could not be more astonished,' the king declared, 'if you told me there were fleas at the Ritz,' a part of which assertion Lady Something, who was blandly listening, imperfectly chanced to hear.

'Who would credit it!' she breathed, turning to an attaché, a young man all white and pensieroso, at her elbow.

'Credit what?'

'Did you not hear what the dear king said!'

'No.'

'It's almost *too* appalling . . .' Lady Something replied, passing a small, nerveless hand across her brow.

'Won't you tell me though,' the young man murmured gently, with his nose in his plate.

Lady Something raised a glass of frozen lemonade to her lips.

'Fleas,' she murmured, 'have been found at the Ritz.'

'. . . . . . . . . . . . ! . . . . . . . . . . . . . . ? . . . . . . . ! . . . . . !!!'

'Oh and *poor* Lady Bertha! And poor good old Mrs Hunter!' And Lady Something looked away in the direction of Sir Somebody, as though anxious to catch his eye.

But the British Ambassador and the Duchess of Varna were weighing the chances of a Grant being allowed by Parliament for the excavation of Chedorlahomor.

'Dear little Chedor,' the Duchess kept on saying, 'I'm sure one would find the most enthralling things there. Aren't *you*, Sir Somebody?'

And they were still absorbed in their colloquy when the King gave the signal to rise.

Although King William had bidden several distinguished Divas from the Opera House to give an account of themselves for the entertainment of his guests, both King Jotifa and Queen Thleeanouhee with disarming candour declared that, to their ears, the music of the West was hardly to be borne.

'Well, I'm not very fond of it either,' her Dreaminess admitted, surrendering her skirts to a couple of rosy boys, and leading the way with airy grace towards an adjacent salon, 'although,' she wistfully added across her shoulder, to a high dignitary of the Church, 'I'm trying, it's true, to coax the dear Archbishop to give the first act of *La Tosca* in the Blue Jesus . . . Such a perfect setting, and with Desiré Erlinger and Maggie Mellon . . . !'

And as the Court now pressed after her the rules of etiquette became considerably relaxed. Mingling freely with his guests, King William had a hand-squeeze and a fleeting word for each.

'In England,' he paused to enquire of Lady Something, who was warning a dowager, with impressive earnestness, against the Ritz, 'have you ever seen two cooks in a kitchen-garden?'

'No, never, sir!' Lady Something simpered.

'Neither,' the King replied moving on, 'have *we*.'

The Ambassadress beamed.

'My dear,' she told Sir Somebody, a moment afterwards, 'my dear, the King was simply charming. Really I may say he was more than gracious! He asked me if I had ever seen two cooks in a kitchen-garden, and I said no, never! And he said that neither, either, had he! And oh isn't it so strange how few of us ever have?'

But in the salon, one of Queen Thleeanouhee's ladies had been desired by her Dreaminess to sing.

'It seems so long,' she declared, 'since I heard an Eastern voice, it would be such a relief.'

'By all means,' Queen Thleeanouhee said, 'and let a *darbouka* or two be brought! For what charms the heart more, what touches it more,' she asked, considering meditatively her babouched feet, 'than a *darbouka*?'

It was told that, in the past, her life had been a gallant one, although her adventures, it was believed, had been mostly with men. Those, however, who had observed her conduct closely, had not failed to remark how often her eyes had been attracted in the course of the evening towards the dimpled cheeks of the British Ambassadress.

Perceiving her ample form not far away, Queen Thleeanouhee signalled to her amiably to approach.

*Née* Rosa Bark (and a daughter of the Poet) Lady Something was perhaps not sufficiently tactful to meet all the difficulties of the rôle in which it had pleased life to call her. But still, she tried, and did do her best, which often went far to retrieve her lack of *savoir faire*. 'Life is like that, dear,' she would sometimes say to Sir Somebody, but she would never say what it was that life was like, '*That*,' it seemed . . .

'I was just looking for my daughter,' she declared.

'And is she as sympathetic,' Queen Thleeanouhee softly asked, 'as her mamma?'

'She's shy – of the Violet persuasion, but that's not a bad thing in a young girl.'

'Where *I* reign, shyness is a quality which is entirely unknown . . . !'

'It must be astonishing, ma'am,' Lady Something replied, caressing a parure of false jewels, intended, indeed, to deceive no one, 'to be a Queen of a sun-steeped country like yours.'

Queen Thleeanouheee fetched a sigh.

'Dateland – my dear, it's a scorch!' she averred.

'I conclude, ma'am, it's what *we* should call "conservatory" scenery?' Lady Something murmured.

'It is the land of the jessamine-flower, the little amorous jessamine-flower,' the Queen gently cooed with a sidelong smiling glance, 'that twines itself sometimes to the right-hand, at others to the left, just according to its caprices!'

'It sounds I fear to be unhealthy, ma'am.'

'And it is the land also, of romance, my dear, where *shyness* is a quality which is entirely unknown,' the Queen broke off, as one of her ladies, bearing a *darbouka*, advanced with an air of purposefulness towards her.

The hum of voices which filled the room might well have tended to dismay a vocalist of modest powers, but the young matron known to the Court as 'Tropical Molly', and whom her mistress addressed as Timzra, soon shewed herself to be equal to the occasion.

> 'Under the blue gum-tree
> I am sitting waiting,
> Under the blue gum-tree
> I am waiting all alone!'

Her voice reached the ears of the fresh-faced ensigns and the beardless subalterns in the Guard Room far beyond, and startled the pages in the distant dormitories, as they lay smoking on their beds.

And then, the theme changing, and with an ever-increasing passion, fervour and force:

'I heard a Watch-dog in the night . . .
Wailing, wailing . . .
Why is the Watch-dog wailing?
He is wailing for the Moon!'

'That is one of the very saddest songs,' the King remarked, 'that I have ever heard. "Why is the watchdog wailing? He is wailing for the Moon!"' And the ambitions and mortifications of kingship, for a moment weighed visibly upon him.

'Something merrier, Timzra!' Queen Thleeanouhee said.

And throwing back her long love-lilac sleeves, Timzra sang:

'A negress with a margaret once lolled frousting in the sun
Thinking of all the little things that she had left undone . . .
With a hey, hey, hey, hey, hi, hey ho!'

'She has the air of a cannibal!' the Archduchess murmured behind her fan to his Weariness, who had scarcely opened his lips except to yawn throughout the whole of the evening.

'She has the air of a —' he replied, laconically, turning away.

Since the conversation with his mother earlier in the day, his thoughts had revolved incessantly around Laura. What had they been saying to the poor wee witch, and whereabouts was she to be found?

Leaving the salon, in the wake of a pair of venerable politicians, who were helping each other along with little touches and pats, he made his way towards the ballroom, where a new dance known as the Pisgah Pas was causing some excitement, and gaining a post of vantage, it was not long before he caught a glimpse of the agile, boyish figure of his betrothed. She passed him, without apparently noticing he was there, in a whirlwind of black tulle, her little hand pressed to the breast of a man like a sulky eagle; and he could not help rejoicing inwardly, that, *once* his wife, it would no longer be possible for her to enjoy herself exactly with whom she pleased. As she swept by again he succeeded in capturing her attention, and nodding meaningly towards a deserted picture-gallery, wandered away towards it. It was but seldom he set foot there, and he amused himself by examining some of the pictures to be seen upon the walls. An old shrew with a rose . . . a drawing of a man alone in the last extremes . . . a pink-robed Christ . . . a seascape, painted probably in winter, with cold, hard colouring . . .

'Yousef?'

'Rara!'

'Let us go outside, dear.'

A night so absolutely soft and calm, was delicious after the glare and noise within.

'With whom,' he asked, 'sweetheart, were you last dancing?'

'Only the brother of one of the Queen's Maids, dear,' Mademoiselle de Nazianzi replied. 'After dinner, though,' she tittered, 'when he gets Arabian-Nighty, it's apt to annoy one a scrap!'

'*Arabian-Nighty*?'

'Oh, never mind!'

'But (pardon me dear) I do.'

'Don't be tiresome, Yousef! The night is too fine,' she murmured glancing absently away towards the hardly moving trees, from whose branches a thousand drooping necklets of silver lamps palely burned.

Were *those* the 'bladders' then?

Strolling on down hoops of white wisteria in the moon they came to the pillared circle of a rustic-temple, commanding a prospect on the town.

'There,' she murmured smiling elfishly, and designating something, far below them, through the moonmist, with her fan: 'is the column of Justice and,' she laughed a little, 'of *Liberty*!'

'And there,' he pointed inconsequently, 'is *the Automobile Club*!'

'And beyond it . . . The Convent of the Flaming-Hood . . .'

'And those blue revolving lights; can you see them, Rara?'

'Yes, dear . . . what are *they*, Yousef?'

'Those,' he told her, contemplating her beautiful white face against the dusky bloom, 'are the lights of the Café Cleopatra!'

'And what,' she questioned, as they sauntered on, pursued by all the sweet perfumes of the night, 'are those berried-shrubs, that smell so passionately?'

'I don't know,' he said: 'Kiss me, Rara!'

'No, no.'

'Why not?'

'Not now!'

'Put your arm about me, dear.'

'What a boy he is!' she murmured, gazing up into the starry clearness.

Overhead a full moon, a moon of circumstance, rode high in the sky, defining phantasmally far off, the violet-farded hills beyond the town.

'To be out there among the silver beanfields!' he said.

'Yes, Yousef,' she sighed, starting at a Triton's face among the trailing ivy on the castle wall. Beneath it, half concealed by water-flags, lay a miniature lake: as a rule now, nobody went near the lake at all, since the Queen had called it '*appallingly smelly*', so that, for rendezvous, it was quite ideal.

'Tell me, Yousef,' she presently said, pausing to admire the beautiful shadow of an orange-tree on the path before them: 'tell me, dear, when Life goes like that to one – what does one do!!'

He shrugged. 'Usually nothing,' he replied, the tip of his tongue (like the point of a blade) peeping out between his teeth.

'Ah, but isn't that being strong?' she said half-audibly, fixing her eyes as though fascinated upon his lips.

'Why,' he demanded with an engaging smile that brought half-moons to his hollow cheeks: 'What has the world been doing to Rara?'

'At this instant, Yousef,' she declared, 'it brings her nothing but Joy!'

'You're happy, my sweet, with me?'

'No one knows, dearest, how much I love you.'

'Kiss me, Rara,' he said again.

'Bend, then,' she answered, as the four quarters of the twelve strokes of midnight rang out leisurely from the castle clock.

'I've to go to the Ritz!' he announced.

'And *I* should be going in.'

Retracing reluctantly their steps they were soon in earshot of the ball, and their close farewells were made accompanied by selections from *The Blue Banana*.

She remained a few moments gazing as though entranced at his retreating figure, and would have, perhaps, run after him with some little capricious message, when she became aware of someone watching her from beneath the shadow of a garden vase.

Advancing steadily and with an air of nonchalance, she recognised the delicate, sexless silhouette and slightly hunched shoulders of Olga Blumenghast, whose exotic attraction had aroused not a few heartburnings (and even feuds) among several of the grandes dames about the court.

Poised flatly against the vase's sculptured plinth, she would scarcely have been discernible, but for the silver glitter of her gown.

'Olga? Are you faint?'

'No; only my slippers are *torture*.'

'I'd advise you to change them, then!'

'It's not altogether my feet, dear, that ache . . .'

'Ah, I see,' Mademoiselle de Nazianzi said, stooping enough to scan the stormy, soul-tossed eyes of her friend: 'you're suffering, I suppose on account of Ann-Jules?'

'He's such a gold-fish, Rara . . . any fingers that will throw him bread . . .'

'And there's no doubt, I'm afraid, that lots do!' Mademoiselle de Nazianzi answered lucidly, sinking down by her side.

'I would give all my soul to him, Rara . . . my chances of heaven!'

'Your chances, Olga —' Mademoiselle de Nazianzi murmured, avoiding some bird-droppings with her skirt.

'How I envy *the men*, Rara, in his platoon!'

'Take away his uniform, Olga, and what does he become?'

'Ah *what* —!'

'No . . . Believe me, my dear, he's not worth the trouble!'

Mademoiselle Blumenghast clasped her hands brilliantly across the nape of her neck.

'I want to possess him at dawn, at dawn,' she broke out: 'Beneath a sky striped with green . . .'

'Oh, Olga!'

'And I never shall rest,' she declared, turning away on a languid heel, 'until I *do*.'

Meditating upon the fever of Love, Mademoiselle de Nazianzi directed her course slowly towards her room. She lodged in that part of the palace known as 'The Bachelors' Wing', where she had a delicious little suite just below the roof.

'If she loved him absolutely,' she told herself, as she turned the handle of her door, 'she would not care about the colour of the sky –; even if it snowed, or hailed!'

Depositing her fan upon the lid of an old wedding-chest that formed a couch, she smiled contentedly about her. It would be a wrench abandoning this little apartment that she had identified already with herself, when the day should come to leave it for others more spacious in the Keep. Although scarcely the size of a ship's cabin, it was amazing how many people one could receive together at a time merely by pushing the piano back against the wall, and wheeling the wedding-chest on to the stairs, and once no fewer than seventeen persons had sat down to a birthday *fête*, without being made too much to feel like herrings. In the so-called salon, divided from her bedroom by a folding lacquer screen, hung a few studies in oils executed by herself, and which, except to the initiated, or the naturally instinctive, looked sufficiently enigmatic against a wall-paper with a stealthy design.

Yes it would be a wrench to quit the little place, she reflected, as she began setting about her toilet for the night. It was agreeable going to bed late without anybody's aid, when one could pirouette interestingly before the mirror in the last stages of déshabille, and do a thousand (and one) things besides[1] that one might otherwise lack the courage for. But this evening being in no frivolous mood she changed her ball-dress swiftly for a robe-de-chambre bordered deeply with ermine, that made her feel nearer somehow to Yousef, and helped her to realise, in its various facets, her position as future Queen.

'Queen!' she breathed, trailing her fur flounces towards the window.

1 Always a humiliating recollection with her in after years. *Vide*: 'Confessions'.

Already the blue revolving lights of the Café Cleopatra were growing paler with the dawn, and the moon had veered a little towards the Convent of the Flaming-Hood. Ah . . . how often as a lay boarder there had she gazed up towards the palace wondering half-shrinkingly what life 'in the world' was like; for there had been a period indeed, when the impulse to take the veil had been strong with her – more, perhaps, to be near one of the nuns whom she had *idolised* than from any more immediate vocation.

She remained immersed in thoughts, her introspectiveness fanned insensibly by the floating zephyrs that spring with morning. The slight sway-sway of the trees, the awakening birds in the castle eaves, the green-veined bougainvilleas that fringed her sill – these thrilled her heart with joy. All virginal in the early dawn what magic the world possessed! Slow speeding clouds like knots of pink roses came blowing across the sky, sailing away in titanic bouquets above the town.

Just such a morning should be their wedding-day! she mused, beginning lightly to apply the contents of a jar of Milk of Almonds to her breast and arms. Ah, before that Spina Christi lost its leaves, or that swallow should migrate . . . that historic day would come!

Troops . . . hysteria . . . throngs . . . The Blue Jesus packed to suffocation . . . She could envisage it all.

And there would be a whole holiday in the Convent, she reflected falling drowsily at her bedside to her knees.

'Oh! help me heaven,' she prayed, 'to be decorative and to do right! Let me always look young, never more than sixteen or seventeen – at the *very* outside, and let Yousef love me – as much as I do him. And I thank you for creating such a darling, God (for he's such a perfect dear), and I can't tell you how much I love him; especially when he wags it! I mean his tongue . . . Bless all the sisters at the Flaming-Hood – above all Sister Ursula . . . And be sweet, besides, to old Jane . . . Shew me the straight path! And keep me ever free from the malicious scandal of the Court: Amen.'

And her orisons (ending in a brief self-examination) over, Mademoiselle de Nazianzi climbed into bed.

## *III*

In the Salle de Prince or Cabinet d'Antoine, above the Café Cleopatra, Madame Wetme the wife of the proprietor, sat perusing the Court gazettes.

It was not often that a *cabinet particulier* like Antoine was disengaged at luncheon time, being as a rule reserved many days in advance, but it had been a 'funny' season, as the saying went, and there was the possibility that a party of late-risers might look in yet (officers, or artistes from the Halls), who had been passing a night on the 'tiles'. But Madame Wetme trusted not. It was pleasant to escape every now and again from her lugubrious back-drawing-room that only faced a wall, or to peruse the early newspapers without having first to wait for them. And today precisely was the day for the hebdomadal *causerie* in the *Jaw-waws' Journal* on matters appertaining to society, signed by that ever popular diarist 'Eva Schnerb'.

'Never,' Madame Wetme read, 'was a gathering more brilliant than that which I witnessed last night! I stood in a corner of the Great ball room and literally *gasped* at the wealth of jewels . . . Beauty and bravery abounded but no one, *I* thought, looked better than our most-gracious Queen, etc. . . . Among the supper-guests I saw their Excellencies Prince and Princess Paul de Pismiche, – the Princess impressed me as being *just* a trifle pale: she is by no means strong, and unhappily our nefarious climate does not agree with everybody! Their Excellencies, Sir Somebody and Lady Something (Miss Ivy Something charming in cornflower *charmeuse* danced indefatigably all the evening, as did also one of the Lambèse girls). The Count and Countess of Tolga – she all in blue furs and literally *ablaze* with gorgeous gems (I hear on excellent authority she is shortly relinquishing her post of Woman of the Bedchamber which she finds is really too arduous for her). The Duchess of Varna, looking veritably radiant (by the way where has she been?) in the palest of pistachio-green mashlaks, which are all the rage at present.

'*Have you a Mashlak?*

'Owing to the visit of King Jotifa and Queen Thleeanouhee, the Eastern mashlak is being worn by many of the smart women about the Court. I saw an example at the Opera the other night in silver and gold *lamé* that I thought too —'

Madame Wetme broke off to look up, as a waiter entered the room.

'Did Madame ring?'

'No! . . .'

'Then it must have been "Ptolemy"!' the young man murmured, bustling out.

'I daresay. When will you know your bells?' Madame Wetme retorted, returning with a headshake to the gazette: Her beloved Eva was full of information this week and breathlessly she read on:

'I saw Minnie, Lady Violetrock (whose daughter Sonia is being educated here) at the garden *fête* the other day, at the Château des Fleurs, looking chic as she *always* does, in a combination of petunia and purple ninon, raffling a donkey.

'I hear on the best authority that before the Court goes to the Summer-Palace later on, there will be at least *one* more Drawing-room. Applications, for those entitled to attend, should be made to the Lord Chamberlain as *soon* as possible.'

One more Drawing-room –! the journal fell from Madame Wetme's hand.

'I'm getting on now,' she reflected, 'and if I'm not presented soon, I never will be . . .'

She raised imploring eyes to the mural imagery – to the 'Cleopatra couchant', to the 'Arrival of Anthony', to the 'Sphinx', to the 'Temple of Ra', as though seeking inspiration: 'Ah my God!' she groaned.

But Madame Wetme's religion, her cruel God, was the *Chic*: The God Chic.

The sound of the music below reached her faintly. There was not a better orchestra (even at the Palace) than that which discoursed at the Café Cleopatra – and they played, the thought had sometimes pleased her, the same identical tunes!

'Does it say when?' she murmured, reopening the gazette. No: But it would be 'before' the Court left . . . And when would that be?

'I have good grounds for believing,' she continued to read: 'that in order to meet his creditors, the Duke of Varna is selling a large portion of his country estate.'

If it were true . . . Madame Wetme's eyes rested in speculation on the Oleanders in the great flower-tubs before the Café, if it were true, why the Varnas must be desperate, and the Duchess ready to do anything. 'Anything – for remuneration,' she murmured, rising and going towards a table usually used for correspondence. And seating herself with a look of decision, she opened a leather writing-pad, full of crab-coloured ink-marked blotting paper.

In the fan-shaped mirror above the writing-table she could see herself in fancy, all veils and aigrettes, as she would be on 'the day' when coiffed by Ernst.

'Among a bevy of charming débutantes, no one looked more striking than Madame Wetme, who was presented by the Duchess of Varna.' Being a client of the house (with an unpaid bill) she could *dictate* to Eva . . . But first, of course, she must secure the Duchess. And taking up her pen she wrote: 'Madame Wetme would give the Duchess of Varna fifty thousand crowns to introduce her at Court.' A trifle terse perhaps?? Madame Wetme considered. How if the Duchess should take offence . . . It was just conceivable! And besides, by specifying no fixed sum, she might be got for less.

'Something more mysterious, more delicate in style . . .' Madame Wetme murmured with a sigh, beginning the letter anew.

'If the Duchess of Varna will call on Madame Wetme this afternoon, about five, and partake of a cup of tea, she will hear of something *to her advantage*.'

Madame Wetme smiled: 'That should get her!' she reflected, and selecting an envelope, she directed it boldly to the Ritz. 'Being hard up, she is sure to be there!' she reasoned, as she left the room in quest of a page.

The French maid of the Duchess of Varna was just putting on her mistress's shoes, in a private sitting-room at the Ritz, when Madame Wetme's letter arrived.

The pleasure of being in the capital once more, after a long spell of the country, had given her an appetite for her lunch and she was feeling braced after an excellent meal.

'I shall not be back, I expect, till late, Louison,' she said to her maid, 'and should anyone enquire where I am, I shall either be at the Palace, or at the Skating-Rink.'

'Madame la Duchesse will not be going to her corsetier's?'

'It depends if there's time. What did I do with my shopping-list?' the Duchess replied, gathering up abstractedly a large, becoroneted vanity-case and a parasol. She had a gown of khaki and daffodil and a black tricorne hat trimmed with green. 'Give me my other sunshade, the jade – and don't forget –: On me trouvera, Soit au Palais Royal, soit, au Palais de Glace!' she enjoined sailing quickly out.

Leaving the Ritz by a side door, she found herself in a quiet, shady street, bordering the Regina Gardens. Above a sky so blue, so clear, so luminous seemed to cry out: 'Nothing matters! Why worry? Be sanguine! Amuse yourself! Nothing matters!'

Traversing the gardens, her mind preoccupied by Madame Wetme's note, the Duchess branched off into a busy thoroughfare, leading towards the Opera, in whose vicinity lay the city's principal shops. To learn of anything to one's advantage was, of course, always welcome, but there were various other claims upon her besides that afternoon, which she was unable, or loath to ignore – the palace, a *thé dansant* or two, and then her favourite rink . . . although the unfortunate part was, most of the rink instructors were still unpaid, and, on the last occasion she had hired a man to waltz with her, he had taken advantage of the fact by pressing her waist with greater freedom than she felt he need have done.

Turning into the Opera Square with its fine arcades, she paused, half furtively, before a Florist's shop. Only her solicitors and a few in the secret were aware that the premises known as *Haboubet of Egypt* were her own; for fearful lest they might be occupied one day by sheriffs' officers, the little business venture had been kept the closest mystery. Lilies 'from Karnak', Roses 'from the Land of Punt' (all grown in the gardens of her country house, in the purlieus of the capital) found immediate and daily favour among amateurs of the choice. Indeed as her gardener frequently said, the demand for Roses from the Land of Punt, was more than he could possibly cope with without an extra man.

'I may as well run in and take whatever there's in the till,' she reflected – 'not that, I fear, there's much . . .'

The superintendent, a slim Tunisian boy, was crouching pitcher-posture upon the floor, chanting languidly to himself, his head supported by an osier pannier lately arrived from 'Punt'.

'Up, Bachir!' the Duchess upbraided. 'Remember the fresh consignments perish, while you dream there and sing.'

The young Tunisian smiled.

He worshipped the Duchess, and the song he was improvising as she entered, had been inspired by her. In it (had she known) he had led her by devious tender stages to his Father's fondouk at Tifilalet 'on the blue Lake of Fetzara', where he was about to present her to the Cheikh, and the whole assembled village, as his chosen bride.

The Duchess considered him. He had a beautiful face spoiled by a bad complexion, which doubtless (the period of puberty passed) he would outgrow.

'Consignment him come not two minute,' the youth replied.

'Ah Bachir? Bachir!'

'By the glorious Koran, I will swear it.'

'Be careful not to shake those *Alexandrian Balls*,' the Duchess peremptorily enjoined pointing towards some Guelder-roses – 'or they'll fall before they're sold!'

'No matter at all. They sold already! An American lady this morning, she purchase all my Alexandrian-Balls; two heavy bunch.'

'Let me see your takings.' . . .

With a smile of triumph, Bachir turned towards the till. He had the welfare of the establishment at heart as well as his own, and of an evening often he would flit, garbed in his long gandourah, through the chief Cafés and Dancings of the city, a vast pannier heaped high with flowers upon his head, which he would dispose of to dazzled clients for an often exorbitant sum. But for these excursions of his (which ended on occasion in adventure) he had received no authority at all.

'Not so bad,' the Duchess commented: 'And, as there's to be a Court again soon, many orders for bouquets are sure to come in!'

'I call in outside hands to assist me: I summon Ouardi! He an Armenian boy. Sympathetic. My friend. More attached to him am I than a branch of Jessamine is about a Vine.'

'I suppose he's capable?' the Duchess murmured, pinning a green-ribbed orchid to her dress.

'The garlands of Ouardi would make even a jackal look bewitching!'

'Ah: he has taste?'

'I engage my friend. Much work always in the month of Redjeb!'

'Engage nobody,' the Duchess answered as she left the shop, 'until I come again.'

Hailing one of the little shuttered cabs of the city in the square she directed the driver to drop her at the palace gates, and pursued by an obstreperous newsboy with an evening paper, yelling: 'Chedorlahomor! Sodom! Extra Special!' the cab clattered off at a languid trot. Under the plane-trees, near the Houses of Parliament, she was overtaken by the large easy-stepping horses of the Ambassadress of England, and acknowledged with a winning movement of the wrist, Lady Something's passing accueil. It was yet not quite the correct hour for the Promenade, where beneath the great acacias Society liked best to ride or drive, but, notwithstanding, that zealous reporter of social deeds, the irrepressible Eva Schnerb, was already on the prowl and able with satisfaction to note: 'I saw the Duchess of Varna early driving in the Park, all alone in a little one-horse shay, that really looked more elegant than any Delaunay-Belleville!'

Arriving before the palace gates, the Duchess perceived an array of empty carriages waiting in the drive, which made her apprehensive of a function. She had anticipated an intimate chat with the Queen alone, but this it seemed was not to be.

Following a youthful page with a *resigned* face, down a long black rug woven with green and violet flowers, who left her with a sigh (as if disappointed of a tip) in charge of a couple of giggling colleagues, and who, in turn, propelled her towards a band of sophisticated-looking footmen and grim officials, she was shewn at last into a vast white drawing-room whose ceiling formed a dome.

Knowing the Queen's interest in the Chedorlahomor Excavation Bill, a number of representative folk, such as the wives of certain Politicians or Diplomats, as well as a few of her own more immediate circle, had called to felicitate her upon its success. Parliament had declared itself willing to do the unlimited graceful by all those concerned, and this in a great measure was due to the brilliant wire pulling of the Queen.

She was looking singularly French in a gold helmet and a violet Vortniansky gown, and wore a rope of faultless pearls, clasped very high beneath the chin.

'I hope the Archbishop will bless the Excavators' tools!' she was saying to the wife of the Premier, as the Duchess entered. 'The *picks* at any rate . . .'

That lady made no reply: In presence of royalty she would usually sit and smile at her knees, raising her eyes from time to time to throw, beneath her lashes, an ineffable expiring glance.

'God speed them safe home again!' the Archduchess Elizabeth who was busy knitting said. An ardent philanthropist she had begun already making 'comforts' for the men, as the nights in the East are cold. The most philanthropic perhaps of all the Royal Family, her hobby was designing, for the use of the public, sanitary, but artistic, places of Necessity on a novel system of ventilation. The King had consented to open (and it was expected appropriately) one of these in course of construction in the Opera Square.

'Amen,' the Queen answered, signalling amiably to the Duchess of Varna, whose infrequent visits to court disposed her always to make a fuss of her.

But no fuss the Queen could make of the Duchess of Varna, could exceed that being made by Queen Thleeanouhee, in a far-off corner, of her Excellency, Lady Something. The sympathy, the *entente* indeed that had arisen between these two ladies was exercising considerably the minds of certain members of the diplomatic corps, although had anyone wished to eavesdrop, their conversation upon the whole must have been found to be anything but esoteric.

'What I want,' Queen Thleeanouhee was saying, resting her hand confidentially on her Excellency's knee: 'what I want is an English maid with Frenchified fingers — Is there such a thing to be had?'

'But surely —' Lady Something smiled: for the servant-topic was one she felt at home on.

'In Dateland, my dear, servant girls are nothing but sluts.'

'Life is like *that*, ma'am, I regret indeed, to have to say: I once had a housemaid who had lived with Sarah Bernhardt, and oh, wasn't she a terror!' Lady Something declared, warding off a little black bat-eared dog who was endeavouring to scramble on to her lap.

'Teddywegs, Teddywegs!' the Archduchess exclaimed jumping up and advancing to capture her pet: 'He arrived from London not later than this morning,' she said: 'from the Princess Elsie of England.'

'He looks like some special litter,' Lady Something remarked.

'How the dear girl loves animals!'

'The rumour of her betrothal it seems is quite without foundation?'

'To my nephew: ah alas . . .'

'Prince Yousef and she are of an equal age!'

'She is interested in Yousef I'm inclined to believe; but the worst of life is, nearly everyone marches to a different tune,' the Archduchess replied.

'One hears of her nothing that isn't agreeable.'

'Like her good mother, Queen Glory,' the Archduchess said, 'one feels, of course, she's all she should be.'

Lady Something sighed.

'Yes . . . and even *more*!' she murmured, letting fall a curtsy to King William who had entered. He had been lunching at the Headquarters of the Girl Guides, and wore the uniform of a general.

'What is the acme of nastiness?' he paused of the English Ambassadress to enquire.

Lady Something turned paler than the white candytuft that is found on ruins. 'Oh *la*, sir,' she stammered, 'how should I know!'

The King looked the shrinking matron slowly up and down: 'The supreme disgust —'

'Oh *la*, sir!' Lady Something stammered again.

But the King took pity on her evident confusion: 'Tepid potatoes,' he answered, 'on a stone-cold plate.'

The Ambassadress beamed.

'I trust the warmth of the girls, sir, compensated you for the coldness of the plates?' she ventured.

'The inspection, in the main, was satisfactory! Although I noticed that one or two of the guides, seemed inclined to lead astray,' the King replied, regarding Teddywegs, who was inquisitely sniffing his spurs.

'He's strange yet to everything,' the Archduchess commented.

'What's this – a new dog?'

'From Princess Elsie . . .'

'They say she's stupid, but I do not know that intellect is always a blessing!' the King declared, drooping his eyes to his abdomen, with an air of pensive modesty.

'Poor child, she writes she is tied to the shore, so that I suppose she is unable to leave dear England.'

'Tied to it?'

'And bound till goodness knows.'

'As was Andromeda!' the King sententiously exclaimed . . . 'She would have little, or maybe nothing, to wear,' he clairvoyantly went on: 'I see her standing shivering, waiting for Yousef . . . Chained by the leg, perhaps, exposed to the howling winds.'[1]

'Nonsense. She means to say she can't get away yet on account of her engagements: that's all.'

'After Cowes-week,' Lady Something put in, 'she is due to pay a round of visits before joining her parents in the North.'

'How I envy her,' the Archduchess sighed, 'amid that entrancing scene . . .'

Lady Something looked *attendrie*.

'Your Royal Highness is attached to England?' she asked.

'I fear I was never there . . . But I shall always remember I put my hair up when I was twelve years old because of the Prince of Wales.'

1 *Winds*, pronounced as we're told, 'in poetry'.

'Oh? And . . . which of the Georges?' Lady Something gasped.

'It's so long ago now that I really forget.'

'And pray, ma'am, what was the point of it?'

The Archduchess chuckled:

'Why, so as to look eligible of course!' she replied, returning to her knitting.

Amid the general flutter following the King's appearance, it was easy enough for the Duchess of Varna to slip away. Knowing the palace inside out it was unnecessary to make any fuss. Passing through a long room, where a hundred holland-covered chairs stood grouped, Congresswise, around a vast table, she attained the Orangery, that gave access to the drive. The mellay of vehicles had considerably increased, and the Duchess paused a moment to consider which she should borrow, when recollecting she wished to question one of the royal gardeners on a little matter of mixing manure, she decided to return through the castle grounds instead. Taking a path that descended between rhododendrons and grim old cannons towards the town, she was comparing the capriciousness of certain bulbs to that of certain people, when she heard her name called from behind, and glancing round perceived the charming silhouette of the Countess of Tolga.

'I couldn't stand it inside: Could you?'

'My *dear*, what a honeymoon hat!'

'It was made by me!'

'Oh, Violet . . .' the Duchess murmured, her face taking on a look of wonder.

'Don't forget, dear, Sunday.'

'Is it a party?'

'I've asked Grim-lips and Ladybird, Hairy and Fluffy, Hardylegs and Bluewings, Spindleshanks, and Our Lady of Furs.'

'Not Nanny-goat?'

'Luckily . . .' the Countess replied, raising to her nose the heliotropes in her hand.

'Is he no better?'

'You little know, dear, what it is to be all alone with him chez soi when he thinks and sneers into the woodwork.'

'*Into the woodwork?*'

'He addresses the ceiling, the walls, the floor – me never!'

'Dear dove.'

'All I can I'm plastic.'

'Can one be plastic ever enough, dear?'

'Often but for Olga . . .' the Countess murmured considering a little rosy ladybird on her arm.

'I consider her ever so compelling, ever so wistful – ' the Duchess of Varna averred.

'Sweet girl –! She's just my consolation.'

'She reminds me, does she you, of that *Miss Hobart* in de Grammont's *Memoirs*.'

'C'est une âme exquise!'

'Well, au revoir, dear: We shall meet again at the Princess Leucippe's later on,' the duchess said, detecting her gardener in the offing.

By the time she had obtained her recipe and cajoled a few special shoots from various exotic plants, the sun had begun to decline. Emerging from the palace by a postern-gate, where lounged a sentry, she found herself almost directly beneath the great acacias on the Promenade. Under the lofty leafage of the trees, as usual towards this hour, society, in its varying grades had congregated to be gazed upon. Mounted on an eager-headed little horse his Weariness (who loved being seen) was plying up and down, while in his wake a '*screen artiste*', on an Arabian mare with powdered withers and eyes made up with kohl, was creating a sensation. Every time she used her whip the powder rose in clouds. Wending her way through the throng the duchess recognised the rose-harnessed horses of Countess Medusa Rappa – the Countess bolt upright, her head carried stiffly staring with a pathetic expression of dead *joie-de-vivre* between her coachman's and footman's waists. But the intention of calling at the Café Cleopatra caused the duchess to hasten. The possibility of learning something beneficial to herself was a lure not to be resisted. Pausing to allow the marvellous blue automobile of Count Ann-Jules to pass (with the dancer Kalpurnia inside), she crossed the Avenue, where there seemed, on the whole, to be fewer people. Here she remarked a little ahead of her the masculine form of the Countess

Yvorra, taking a quiet stroll before *Salut* in the company of her Confessor. In the street she usually walked with her hands clasped behind her back, huddled up like a statesman: '*Des choses abominables! . . . Des choses hors nature!*' she was saying, in tones of evident relish, as the duchess passed.

Meanwhile Madame Wetme was seated anxiously by the samovar in her drawing-room. To receive the duchess, she had assumed a mashlak à la mode, whitened her face and rouged her ears, and set a small, but costly aigrette at an insinuating angle in the edifice of her hair. As the hour of Angelus approached, the tension of waiting grew more and more acute, and beneath the strain of expectation even the little iced-sugar cakes upon the tea-table looked green with worry.

Suppose, after all, she shouldn't come? Suppose she had already left? Suppose she were in prison? Only the other day a woman of the highest fashion, a leader of 'society' with an *A*, had served six months as a consequence of her extravagance . . .

In agitation Madame Wetme helped herself to a small glassful of *Cointreau* (her favourite liqueur), when, feeling calmer for the *consommation*, she was moved to take a peep out of Antoine.

But nobody chic at all met her eye.

Between the oleanders upon the curb, that rose up darkly against a flame-pink sky, two young men dressed 'as Poets' were arguing and gesticulating freely over a bottle of beer. Near them, a sailor with a blue drooping collar and dusty boots (had he walked poor wretch to see his mother?) was gazing stupidly at the large evening gnats that revolved like things bewitched about the café lamps. While below the window a lean soul in glasses, evidently an impresario, was loudly exclaiming: 'London has robbed me of my throat, sir!! It has deprived me of my voice.'

No, an 'off' night certainly!

Through a slow, sun-flower of a door (that kept on revolving long after it had been pushed) a few military men bent on a game of billiards, or an early *fille de joie* (only the discreetest *des filles 'sérieuses'* were supposed to be admitted) – came and went.

'Tonight they're fit for church,' Madame Wetme complacently

smiled as the door swung round again: 'Navy-blue and silver-fox looks the goods,' she reflected, 'upon any occasion! It suggests something sly – like a Nurse's uniform.'

'A lady in the drawing-room, Madame, desires to speak to you,' a chasseur tunefully announced, and fingering nervously her aigrette Madame Wetme followed.

The Duchess of Varna was inspecting a portrait with her back to the door as her hostess entered.

'I see you're looking at my Murillo!' Madame Wetme began.

'Oh . . . Is it o-ri-gi-nal?' the duchess drawled.

'No.'

'I *thought* not.'

'To judge by the Bankruptcy-sales of late (and it's curious how many they've been . . .) it would seem from the indifferent figure he makes, that he is no longer accounted chic,' Madame Wetme observed as she drew towards the duchess a chair.

'I consider the chic to be such a very false religion! . . .' the duchess said, accepting the seat which was offered her.

'Well, I come of an old Huguenot family myself!'

'— . . . ?'

'Ah my early home . . . Now, I hear, it's nothing but a weed-crowned ruin.'

The duchess considered the ivory cat handle of her parasol: 'You wrote to me?' she asked.

'Yes: about the coming court.'

'About it?'

'Every woman has her dream, duchess! And mine's to be presented.'

'The odd ambition!' the duchess crooned.

'I admit we live in the valley. Although I have a great sense of the hills!' Madame Wetme declared demurely.

'Indeed?'

'My husband you see . . .'

'. . . . . . . . . . . . . . .'

'Ah! well!'

'Of course.'

'If I'm not asked this time, I shall die of grief.'

'Have you made the request before?'

'I have attempted!'

'Well?'

'When the Lord Chamberlain refused me, I shed tears of blood,' Madame Wetme wanly retailed.

'It would have been easier, no doubt, in the late king's time!'

Madame Wetme took a long sighing breath.

'I only once saw him in my life,' she said, 'and then he was standing against a tree, in an attitude offensive to modesty.'

'Tell me . . . as a public man, what has your husband done —'

'His money helped to avert, I always contend, the noisy misery of a War!'

'He's open-handed?'

'Ah . . . as you would find . . .'

The duchess considered: 'I *might*,' she said, 'get you cards for a State concert . . .'

'A State concert, duchess? That's no good to me!'

'A drawing-room you know is a very dull affair.'

'I will liven it!'

'Or an invitation perhaps to begin with to one of the Embassies – the English for instance might lead . . .'

'Nowhere . . . ! You can't depend on that: people have asked me to lunch, and left me to pay for them . . . ! There is so much trickery in Society . . .' Madame Wetme laughed.

The duchess smiled quizzically: 'I forget if you know the Tolgas,' she said.

'By "name"!'

'The Countess is more about the throne at present than I.'

'Possibly – but oh *you* who do *everything*, duchess?' Madame Wetme entreated.

'I suppose there are things still one wouldn't do however —!' the duchess took offence.

'The Tolgas are so hard.'

'You want a misfortune and they're sweet to you. Successful persons they're positively hateful to!'

'These women of the Bedchamber are all alike so glorified. You would never credit they were Chambermaids at all! I often smile to myself when I see one of them at a *première* at the Opera, gorged with pickings, and think that, most likely, but an hour before she was stumbling along a corridor with a pailful of slops!'

'You're fond of music, Madame?' the duchess asked.

'It's my joy: I could go again and again to *The Blue Banana*!'

'I've not been.'

'Pom-pom, pompity-pom! We might go one night, perhaps, together.'

'. . .'

'Doudja Degdeg is always a draw, although naturally now she is getting on!'

'And I fear so must I' – the duchess rose remarking.

'So soon?'

'I'm only so sorry I can't stay longer —!'

'Then it's all decided,' Madame Wetme murmured archly as she pressed the bell.

'Oh I'd not say that.'

'If I'm not asked remember this time, I shall die with grief.'

'Tonight the duke and I are dining with the Leucippes, and possibly . . .' the duchess broke off to listen to the orchestra in the café below, which was playing the waltz-air from *Der Rosenkavalier*.

'They play well!' she commented.

'People often tell me so.'

'It must make one restless, dissatisfied, that yearning, yearning music continually at the door?'

Madame Wetme sighed.

'It makes you often long,' she said, 'to begin your life again!'

'Again?'

'Really it's queer I came to yoke myself with a man so little fine . . .'

'Still —! If he's open-handed,' the duchess murmured as she left the room.

## *IV*

One grey, unsettled morning (it was the first of June) the English Colony of Kairoulla[1] awoke in arms. It usually did when the Embassy entertained. But the omissions of the Ambassador, were, as old Mr Ladboyson the longest-established member of the colony declared, 'not to be fathomed', and many of those overlooked declared they should go all the same. Why should Mrs Montgomery (who, when all was said and done, was nothing but a governess) be invited and not Mrs Barleymoon who was 'nothing' (in the most distinguished sense of the word) at all? Mrs Barleymoon's position as a captain's widow with means, unquestionably came before Mrs Montgomery's, who drew a salary, and hadn't often an h.

Miss Grizel Hopkins, too – the cousin of an Earl, and Mrs Bedley the 'Mother' of the English Colony, both had been ignored. It was true Ann Bedley kept a circulating library and a tea-room combined and gave 'Information' to tourists as well (a thing she had done these forty years), but was that a sufficient reason why she should be totally taboo? *No*, in old Lord Clanlubber's time all had been made welcome, and there had been none of these heartburnings at all. Even the Irish coachman of the Archduchess was known to have been received – although it had been outside of course upon the lawn. Only gross carelessness, it was felt, on the part of those attachés could account for the extraordinary present neglect.

'I don't myself mind much,' Mrs Bedley said, who was seated over a glass of morning milk and 'a plate of fingers' in the *Circulating*

1 The Capital of Pisuerga.

end of the shop: 'going out at night upsets me. And the last time Dr Babcock was in he warned me not.'

'What is the Embassy there for but to be hospitable?' Mrs Barleymoon demanded from the summit of a ladder, from where she was choosing herself a book.

'You're shewing your petticoat, dear – excuse me telling you,' Mrs Bedley observed.

'When will you have something new, Mrs Bedley?'

'Soon, dear . . . soon.'

'It's always "soon",' Mrs Barleymoon complained.

'Are you looking for anything, Bessie, in particular?' a girl, with loose blue eyes that did not seem quite firm in her head, and a literary face enquired.

'No, only something,' Mrs Barleymoon replied, 'I've not had before and before and before.'

'By the way, Miss Hopkins,' Mrs Bedley said, 'I've to fine you for pouring tea over *My Stormy Past*.'

'It was coffee, Mrs Bedley – not tea.'

'Never mind, dear, what it was the charge for a stain is the same as you know,' Mrs Bedley remarked, turning to attend to Mrs Montgomery who, with his Naughtyness, Prince Olaf, had entered the Library.

'Is it in?' Mrs Montgomery mysteriously asked.

Mrs Bedley, assumed her glasses.

'*Mmnops*,' she replied, peering with an air of secretiveness in her private drawer where she would sometimes reserve or 'hold back' a volume for a subscriber who happened to be in her special good graces.

'I've often said,' Mrs Barleymoon from her ladder sarcastically let fall, 'that Mrs Bedley has her pets!'

'You are all my pets, my dear,' Mrs Bedley softly cooed.

'Have you read *Men – my Delight*, Bessie?' Miss Hopkins asked, 'by Cora Velasquez.'

'No!'

'It's not perhaps a very . . . It's about two dark, and three fair, men,' she added vaguely.

'Most women's novels seem to run off the rails before they reach the end, and I'm not very fond of them,' Mrs Barleymoon said.

'And anyway, dear, it's out,' Mrs Bedley asserted.

'*The Passing of Rose* I read the other day,' Mrs Montgomery said, 'and *so* enjoyed it.'

'Isn't that one of Ronald Firbank's books?'

'No, dear, I don't think it is. But I never remember an author's name and I don't think it matters!'

'I suppose I'm getting squeamish! But this Ronald Firbank I can't take to at all. *Valmouth!* Was there ever a novel more coarse. I assure you I hadn't gone very far when I had to put it down.'

'It's *out*,' Mrs Bedley suavely said, 'as well,' she added, 'as the rest of them.'

'I once met him,' Miss Hopkins said, dilating slightly the *retinae* of her eyes: 'He told me writing books was by no means easy!'

Mrs Barleymoon shrugged.

'Have you nothing more enthralling, Mrs Bedley,' she persuasively asked, 'tucked away?'

'Try *The Call of the Stage*, dear,' Mrs Bedley suggested.

'You forget, Mrs Bedley,' Mrs Barleymoon replied, regarding solemnly her *crêpe*.

'Or *Mary of the Manse*, dear.'

'I've read *Mary of the Manse* twice, Mrs Bedley – and I don't propose to read it again.'

'.........?'

'.........!'

Mrs Bedley became abstruse.

'It's dreadful how many poets take to drink,' she reflected.

A sentiment to which her subscribers unanimously assented.

'I'm taking *Men are Animals*, by the Hon Mrs Victor Smythe, and *What Every Soldier Ought to Know*, Mrs Bedley,' Miss Hopkins breathed.

'And I *The East is Whispering*,' Mrs Barleymoon in hopeless tones affirmed.

'Robert Hitchinson! He's a good author.'

'Do you think so? I feel his books are all written in hotels with the bed unmade at the back of the chair.'

'And I daresay you're right, my dear.'

'Well, Mrs Bedley, I must go – if I want to walk to my husband's grave,' Mrs Barleymoon declared.

'Poor Bessie Barleymoon,' Mrs Bedley sighed, after Mrs Barleymoon and Miss Hopkins had gone: 'I fear she frets!'

'We all have our trials, Mrs Bedley.'

'And some more than others.'

'Court life, Mrs Bedley, it's a funny thing.'

'It looks as though we may have an English Queen, Mrs Montgomery.'

'I don't believe it!'

'Most of the daily prints I see are devoting leaders to the little dog the Princess Elsie sent out the other day.'

'Odious, ill-mannered, horrid little beast . . .'

'It seems, dear, he ran from room to room looking for her until he came to the prince's door, where he just lay down and whined.'

'And what does that prove, Mrs Bedley?'

'I really don't know, Mrs Montgomery. But the press seemed to find it "significant",' Mrs Bedley replied as a Nun of the Flaming-Hood with a jolly face all gold with freckles entered the shop:

'Have you *Valmouth* by Ronald Firbank or *Inclinations* by the same author?' she asked.

'Neither I'm sorry – both are out!'

'Maladetta ✠ ✠ ✠ ✠! But I'll be passing soon again,' the Sister answered as she twinkingly withdrew.

'You'd not think now by the look of her that she had been at Girton!' Mrs Bedley remarked.

'Once a Girton girl always a Girton girl, Mrs Bedley.'

'It seems a curate drove her to it . . .'

'I'm scarcely astonished. Looking back I remember the average curate at home as something between a eunuch and a snigger.'

'Still, dear, I could never renounce my religion. As I said to the dear Chaplain only the other day (while he was having some tea), Oh, if only I were a man, I said! Wouldn't I like to *denounce* the disgraceful goings on every Sabbath down the street at the church of the Blue Jesus.'

'And I assure you it's positively *nothing*, Mrs Bedley, at the Jesus to what it is at the church of St Mary the Fair! I was at the wedding of one of the equerries lately, and never saw anything like it.'

'It's about time there was an English wedding, in *my* opinion, Mrs Montgomery!'

'There's not been one in the Colony indeed for some time.'

Mrs Bedley smiled undaunted.

'I trust I may be spared to dance before long at Dr and Mrs Babcock's!' she exclaimed.

'Kindly leave Cunnie out of it, Mrs Bedley,' Mrs Montgomery begged.

'So it's Cunnie already you call him!'

'Dr Cunliffe and I scarcely meet.'

'People talk of the immense sameness of marriage, Mrs Montgomery; but all the same, my dear, a widow's not much to be envied.'

'There are times, it's true, Mrs Bedley, when a woman feels she needs fostering; but it's a feeling she should try to fight against.'

'Ah my dear, I never could resist *a mon*!' Mrs Bedley exclaimed.

Mrs Montgomery sighed.

'Once,' she murmured meditatively, 'men (those procurers of delights) engaged me utterly . . . I was their *slave* . . . Now . . . One does not burn one's fingers twice, Mrs Bedley.'

Mrs Bedley grew introspective.

'My poor husband sometimes would be a little frightening, a little fierce . . . at night, my dear, especially. Yet how often now I miss him!'

'You're better off as you are, Mrs Bedley, believe me,' Mrs Montgomery declared, looking round for the little prince who was amusing himself on the library-steps.

'You must find him a handful to educate, my dear.'

'It will be a relief *indeed*, Mrs Bedley, when he goes to Eton!'

'I'm told so long as a boy is grounded . . .'

'His English accent is excellent, Mrs Bedley, and he shews quite a talent for languages,' Mrs Montgomery assured.

'I'm delighted, I'm sure, to hear it!'

'Well, Mrs Bedley, I mustn't stand dawdling: I've to 'ave my 'air shampooed and waved for the Embassy party tonight you know!' And taking the little prince by the hand, the Royal Governess withdrew.

## V

Among those attached to the Chedorlahomor expedition was a young – if thirty-five be young – eccentric Englishman from Wales, the Hon. 'Eddy' Monteith, a son of Lord Intriguer. Attached first to one thing and then another, without ever being attached to any, his life had been a gentle series of attachments all along. But this new attachment was surely something better than a temporary secretaryship to a minister, or 'aiding' an ungrateful general, or waiting in through draughts (so affecting to the constitution) in the ante-rooms of hard-worked royalty, in the purlieus of Pall Mall. Secured by the courtesy of his ex-chief, Sir Somebody Something, an old varsity friend of his father, the billet of 'surveyor and occasional help' to the Chedorlahomorian excavation party had been waywardly accepted by the Hon. 'Eddy' just as he had been upon the point of attaching himself, to the terror of his relatives and the amusement of his friends, to a monastery of the Jesuit Order, as a likely candidate for the cowl.

Indeed he had already gone so far as to sit to an artist for his portrait in the habit of a monk, gazing ardently at what looked to be the Escurial itself, but in reality was nothing other than an 'impression' from the kitchen garden of Intriguer Park. And now this sudden change, this call to the East instead. There had been no time, unfortunately, before setting out to sit again in the picturesque 'sombrero' of an explorer, but a ready camera had performed miracles, and the relatives of the Hon. 'Eddy' were relieved to behold his smiling countenance in the illustrated-weeklies, pick in hand, or with one foot resting on his spade while examining a broken jar, with just below the various editors' comments: *To Join the Expedition to*

*Chedorlahomor – the Hon. 'Eddy' Monteith, only son of Lord Intriguer*; or, *Off to Chedorlahomor!* or, *Bon Voyage . . . !*

Yes, the temptation of the expedition was not to be withstood, and for vows and renunciations there was always time! . . . And now leaning idly on his window ledge in a spare room of the Embassy, while his man unpacked, he felt, as he surveyed the distant dome of the Blue Jesus above the dwarf-palm trees before the house, half-way to the East already. He was suffering a little in his dignity from the contretemps of his reception, for having arrived at the Embassy among a jobbed troop of serfs engaged for the night, Lady Something had at first mistaken him for one: 'The cloakroom will be in the Smoking-room!' she had said, and in spite of her laughing excuses and ample apologies, he could not easily forget it. What was there in his appearance that could conceivably recall a cloak-room attendant –? *He* who had been assured he had the profile of a 'Rameses'! And going to a mirror he scanned, with less perhaps than his habitual contentment, the light, liver-tinted hair, grey narrow eyes, hollow cheeks, and pale mouth like a broken moon. He was looking just a little fatigued he fancied from his journey, and really, it was all his hostess deserved, if he didn't go down.

'I have a headache, Mario,' he told his man (a Neapolitan who had been attached to almost as many professions as his master). 'I shall not leave my room! Give me a kimono: I will take a bath.'

Undressing slowly, he felt as the garments dropped away, he was acting properly in refraining from attending the soirée, and only hoped the lesson would not be 'lost' on Lady Something, whom he feared must be incurably dense.

Lying amid the dissolving bath crystals while his man-servant deftly bathed him, he fell into a sort of coma, sweet as a religious trance. Beneath the rhythmic sponge, perfumed with *Kiki*, he was St Sebastian, and as the water became cloudier and the crystals evaporated amid the steam, he was Teresa . . . and he would have been, most likely, the Blessed Virgin herself, but that the bath grew gradually cold.

'You're looking a little pale, sir, about the gills!' the valet solicitously observed, as he gently dried him.

The Hon. 'Eddy' winced: 'I forbid you ever to employ the word gill, Mario,' he exclaimed. 'It is inharmonious, and in English it jars; whatever it may do in Italian.'

'Overtired, sir, what was I meant to say.'

'Basta!' his master replied, with all the brilliant glibness of the Berlitz-school.

Swathed in towels, it was delicious to relax his powder-blanched limbs upon a comfy couch, while Mario went for dinner: 'I don't care what it is! So long as it isn't –' (naming several dishes that he particularly abhorred, or might be 'better', perhaps, without) – 'And be sure, fool, not to come back without Champagne.'

He could not choose but pray that the Ambassadress had nothing whatever to do with the Embassy cellar, for from what he had seen of her already, he had only a slight opinion of her discernment.

Really he might have been excused had he taken her to be the cook instead of the social representative of the Court of St James, and he was unable to repress a caustic smile on recollecting her appearance that afternoon, with her hat awry, crammed with *Maréchal Niel* roses, hot, and decoiffed, flourishing a pair of garden-gauntlets as she issued her commands. What a contrast to his own Mamma – 'so different,' . . . and his thoughts returned to Intriguer – 'dear Intriguer, . . .' that if only to vex his father's ghost, he would one day turn into a Jesuit college! The Confessional should be fitted in the paternal study, and engravings of the Inquisition, or the sweet faces of Lippi and Fra Angelico, replace the Agrarian certificates and tiresome trophies of the chase; while the crack of the discipline in Lent would echo throughout the house! How 'useful' his friend Robbie Renard would have been; but alas poor Robbie. He had passed through life at a rapid canter, having died at nineteen . . .

Musingly he lit a cigarette.

Through the open window a bee droned in on the blue air of evening and closing his eyes he fell to considering whether the bee of one country would understand the remarks of that of another. The effect of the soil of a nation, had it consequences upon its Flora? Were plants influenced at their roots? People sometimes spoke (and especially ladies) of the language of flowers . . . the pollen therefore of an English rose would probably vary, not inconsiderably, from that of a French, and a bee born and bred at home (at *Intriguer* for instance) would be at a loss to understand (it clearly followed) the conversation of one born and bred, here, abroad. A bee's idiom varied then, as did man's! And he wondered, this being proved the case, where the best bees' accents were generally acquired . . .

Opening his eyes, he perceived his former school chum, Lionel Limpness – Lord Tiredstock's third (and perhaps most gifted) son, who was an honorary attaché at the Embassy, standing over him, his spare figure already arrayed in an evening suit.

'Sorry to hear you're off colour, Old Dear!' he exclaimed, sinking down upon the couch beside his friend.

'I'm only a little shaken, Lionel . . . : have a cigarette.'

'And so you're off to Chedorlahomor, Old Darling?' Lord Tiredstock's third son said.

'I suppose so . . .' the only son of Lord Intriguer replied.

'Well, I wish I was going too!'

'It would be charming, Lionel, of course to have you: but they might appoint you Vice-Consul at Sodom or something?'

'Why *Vice*? Besides . . . ! There's no consulate there yet,' Lord Tiredstock's third son said, examining the objects upon the portable altar, draped in prelatial purple of his friend.

'Turn over, Old Dear, while I chastise you!' he exclaimed, waving what looked to be a tortoiseshell lorgnon to which had been attached three threads of 'cerulean' floss silk.

'Put it down, Lionel, and don't be absurd.'

'Over we go. Come on.'

'Really, Lionel.'

'Penitence! To thy knees, Sir!'

And just as it seemed that the only son of Lord Intriguer was to be deprived of all his towels, the Ambassadress mercifully entered.

'*Poor* Mr Monteith!' she exclaimed in tones of concern bustling forward with a tablespoon and a bottle containing physic, '*so* unfortunate . . . Taken ill at the moment you arrive! But Life is like that!'

Clad in the flowing circumstance of an oyster satin ball dress, and all a-glitter like a Christmas tree (with jewels), her arrival perhaps saved her guest a 'whipping'.

'Had I known, Lady Something, I was going to be ill, I would have gone to the Ritz!' the Hon. 'Eddy' gasped.

'And you'd have been bitten all over!' Lady Something replied.

'Bitten all over?'

'The other evening we were dining at the Palace, and I heard the dear King say – but I oughtn't to talk and excite you —'

'By the way, Lady Something,' Lord Tiredstock's third son asked: 'what is the etiquette for the Queen of Dateland's eunuch?'

'It's all according; but you had better ask Sir Somebody, Mr Limpness,' Lady Something replied, glancing with interest at the portable altar.

'I've done so, and he declared he'd be jiggered!'

'I recollect in Pera when we occupied the Porte, they seemed (those of the old Grand Vizier – oh what a good-looking man he was –! such eyes –! and such a *way* with him –! *Despot!!*) only too thankful to crouch in corners.'

'Attention with that castor-oil . . . !'

'It's not castor-oil; it's a little decoction of my own, – aloes, gregory, a dash of liquorice. And the rest is buckthorn!'

'Euh!'

'It's not so bad, though it mayn't be very nice . . . Toss it off like a brave man, Mr Monteith (nip his nostrils, Mr Limpness), and while he takes it, I'll offer a silent prayer for him at that duck of an altar,' and as good as her word, the Ambassadress made towards it.

'You're altogether too kind,' the Hon. 'Eddy' murmured seeking refuge in a book – a volume of *Juvenilia* published for him by 'Blackwood of Oxford', and becoming absorbed in its contents: 'Ah Doris' – 'Lines to Doris' – 'Lines to Doris: written under the influence of wine, sun and fever' – 'Ode to Swinburne' – 'Sad Tamarisks' – 'Rejection' – 'Doigts Obscènes' – 'They Call me *Lily*!' – 'The Land of Titian! Land of Verdi! Oh Italy!' – 'I heard the Clock:

> I heard the clock strike seven,
> Seven strokes I heard it strike!
> His Lordship's gone to London
> And won't be back tonight.'

He had written it at Intriguer, after a poignant domestic disagreement, his Papa, – the 'his lordship' of the poem – had stayed away however considerably longer . . . And here was a sweet thing suggested by an old Nursery Rhyme, 'Loves, have you Heard':

> Loves, have you heard about the rabbits??
> They have such odd fantastic habits . . .
> Oh, Children . . . ! I daren't disclose to You
> The licentious things *some* rabbits do.

It had 'come to him' quite suddenly out ferreting one day with the footman . . .

But a loud crash as the portable altar collapsed beneath the weight of the Ambassadress aroused him unpleasantly from his thoughts.

'Horrid dangerous thing!' she exclaimed as Lord Tiredstock's third son assisted her to rise from her 'Silent' prayer: 'I had no idea it wasn't solid! But Life is like that . . .' she added somewhat wildly.

'Pity oh my God! Deliver me!' the Hon. 'Eddy' breathed, but the hour of *deliverance* it seemed was not just yet; for at that instant the Hon. Mrs Chilleywater, the 'literary' wife of the first attaché, thrust her head in at the door.

'How are you?' she asked. 'I thought perhaps I might find *Harold* . . .'

'He's with Sir Somebody.'

'Such mysteries!' Lady Something said.

'This betrothal of Princess Elsie's is simply wearing him out,' Mrs Chilleywater declared, sweeping the room with half-closed, expressionless eyes.

'It's a pity you can't pull the strings for us,' Lady Something ventured: 'I was saying so lately to Sir Somebody.'

'I wish I could, dear Lady Something: I wouldn't mind wagering I'd soon bring it off!'

'Have you fixed up Grace Gillstow yet, Mrs Chilleywater?' Lord Tiredstock's third son asked.

'She shall marry Baldwin: but not before she has been seduced first by Barnaby . . .'

'What are you talking about?' the Hon. 'Eddy' queried.

'Of Mrs Chilleywater's forthcoming book.'

'Why should Barnaby get Grace –? Why not Tex!'

But Mrs Chilleywater refused to enter into reasons.

'She is looking for cowslips,' she said, 'and oh I've such a wonderful description of a field of cowslips . . . They make quite a darling setting for a powerful scene of lust.'

'So Grace loses her virtue! . . . !' Lord Tiredstock's third son exclaimed.

'Even so she's far too good for Baldwin: after the underhand shabby way he behaved to Charlotte, Kate, and Millicent!'

'Life is like that, dear,' the Ambassadress blandly observed.

'It ought not to be, Lady Something!' Mrs Chilleywater looked vindictive.

*Née* Victoria Gellybore Frinton, and the sole heir of Lord Seafairer of Sevenelms, Kent, Mrs Harold Chilleywater, since her marriage 'for Love', had developed a disconcerting taste for fiction – a taste that was regarded at the Foreign Office with disapproving forbearance . . . So far her efforts (written under her maiden name in full with her husband's as well appended) had been confined to lurid studies of low life (of which she knew nothing at all), but the Hon. Harold Chilleywater had been gently warned, that if he was not to remain at Kairoulla until the close of his career, the style of his wife must really grow less *virile*.

'I agree with V.G.F.,' the Hon. Lionel Limpness murmured fondling meditatively his 'Charlie Chaplin' moustache – 'Life ought not to be.'

'It's a mistake to bother oneself over matters that can't be remedied.'

Mrs Chilleywater acquiesced: 'You're right indeed, Lady Something,' she said, 'but I'm so sensitive . . . I seem to *know* when I talk to a man, the colour of his braces . . . ! I say to myself: "Yours are violet . . ." "Yours are blue . . ." "His are red . . ."'

'I'll bet you anything, Mrs Chilleywater, you like, you won't guess what mine are,' the Hon. Lionel Limpness said.

'I should say, Mr Limpness, that they were *multihued* – like Jacob's,' Mrs Chilleywater replied, as she withdrew her head.

The Ambassadress prepared to follow:

'Come, Mr Limpness,' she exclaimed, 'we've exhausted the poor fellow quite enough – and besides, here comes his dinner.'

'Open the champagne, Mario,' his master commanded immediately they were alone.

'"Small" beer is all the butler would allow, sir.'

'Damn the b . . . butler!'

'What he calls a *demi-brune*, sir. In Naples we say *spumanti*!'

'Non è tanto amaro, sir; it's more sharp, as you'd say, than bitter . . .'

'. . . . . . ! ! ! ! ! !'

And language *unmonastic* far into the night reigned supreme.

Standing beneath the portraits of King Geo and Queen Glory, Lady Something, behind a large sheaf of mauve malmaisons, was growing stiff. Already, for the most part, the guests were welcomed, and it was only the Archduchess now, who as usual was late, that kept their Excellencies lingering at the head of the stairs. Her Majesty Queen Thleeanouhee of the Land of Dates had just arrived, but seemed loath to leave the stairs, while her hostess, whom she addressed affectionately as her *dear gazelle*, remained upon them – 'Let us go away by and by, my dear gazelle,' she exclaimed with a primitive smile, 'and remove our corsets and talk.'

'Unhappily Pisuerga is not the East, ma'am!' Lady Something replied.

'Never mind, my dear; we will introduce this innovation . . .'

But the arrival of the Archduchess Elizabeth spared the Ambassadress from what might too easily have become an 'incident'.

In the beautiful chandeliered apartments several young couples were pirouetting to the inevitable waltz from the *Blue Banana*, but most of the guests seemed to prefer exploring the conservatories and Winter Garden, or elbowing their way into a little room where a new portrait of Princess Elsie had been discreetly placed . . .

'One feels, of course, there *was* a sitting –; but still, it isn't like her!' those that had seen her said.

'The artist has attributed to her at least the pale spent eyes of her father!' the Duchess of Cavaljos remarked to her niece, who was standing quite silent against a rose-red curtain.

Mademoiselle de Nazianzi made no reply. Attaching not the faintest importance to the rumours afloat, still, she could not but feel, at times, a little heartshaken . . .

The duchess plied her fan.

'She will become florid in time like her mother!' she cheerfully predicted turning away just as the Archduchess approached herself to inspect the painting.

Swathed in furs, on account of a troublesome cough contracted paddling, she seemed nevertheless in charming spirits.

'Have you been to my new *Pipi*?' she asked.

'Not yet —'

'Oh but you must!'

'I'm told it's even finer than the one at the Railway Station. Ah, from musing too long on that Hellenic frieze, how often I've missed my train!' the Duchess of Cavaljos murmured, with a little fat deep laugh.

'I have a heavenly idea for another – Yellow tiles with Thistles . . .'

'Your Royal Highness never repeats herself!'

'Nothing will satisfy me this time,' the Archduchess declared, 'but files of state-documents in all the dear little boxes: In secret, secrets!' she added archly fixing her eyes on the assembly.

'It's positively pitiable,' the Duchess of Cavaljos commented, 'how the Countess of Tolga is losing her good looks: She has the air tonight of a tired businesswoman!'

'She looks at other women as though she would inhale them,' the Archduchess answered, throwing back her furs with a gesture of superb grace, in order to allow her robe to be admired by a lady who was scribbling busily away behind a door, with little nervous lifts of the head. For *noblesse oblige* the correspondent of the *Jaw-Waw*, the illustrious Eva Schnerb, was not to be denied.

'Among the many balls of a brilliant season,' the diarist, with her accustomed fluency wrote: 'none surpassed that which I witnessed at the English Embassy last night. I sat in a corner of the Winter Garden and literally gorged myself upon the display of dazzling uniforms and jewels. The Ambassadress Lady Something was looking really regal in dawn-white draperies, and holding a bouquet of the new mauve malmaisons (which are all the vogue just now), but no one, *I* thought, looked better than the *Archduchess*, etc. . . . Helping the hostess, I noticed Mrs Harold Chilleywater, in an "aesthetic" gown of flame-hued Kanitra silk edged with Armousky fur (to possess a dear woolly Armousk as a pet, is considered *chic* this season), while over her brain – an intellectual caprice, I wonder? – I saw a tinsel bow . . . She is a daughter of the fortieth Lord Seafairer of Sevenelms-Park (so famous for its treasures) and is very artistic and literary having written several novels of English life under her maiden name of Victoria Gellybore-Frinton: – She inherits considerable cleverness *also* from her Mother. Dancing indefatigably (as she always does!) Miss Ivy Something seemed to be thoroughly enjoying her Father's ball: I hear on *excellent authority* there is no foundation in the story of her engagement to a certain young Englishman, said to be bound ere long for the ruins of Sodom and Gomorrah. Among the late arrivals were the Duke and Duchess of Varna – *she* all in golden tissues: they came together with Madame Wetme, who is one of the new hostesses of the season you know, and they say has bought the Duke of Varna's palatial townhouse in Samaden Square —'

'There,' the Archduchess murmured, drawing her wraps about her with a sneeze: 'she has said quite enough now I think about my *toilette*!'

But the illustrious Eva was in unusual fettle, and only closed her notebook towards Dawn, when the nib of her pen caught fire.

## *VI*

And suddenly the Angel of Death passed by and the brilliant season waned. In the Archduchess' bedchamber, watching the antics of priests and doctors, he sat there unmoved. Propped high, by many bolsters, in a vast blue canopied bed, the Archduchess lay staring laconically at a diminutive model of a flight of steps, leading to what appeared to be intended, perhaps, as a hall of Attent, off which opened quite a lot of little doors, most of which bore the word: 'Engaged'. A doll, with a ruddy face, in charge, smiled indolently as she sat feigning knitting, suggesting vague 'fleshly thoughts', whenever he looked up, in the Archduchess' spiritual adviser.

And the mind of the sinking woman, as her thoughts wandered, appeared to be tinged with 'matter' too: 'I recollect the first time I heard the *Blue-Danube* played!' she broke out: 'it was at Schönbrunn – schönes Schönbrunn – My cousin Ludwig of Bavaria came – I wore – the Emperor said —'

'If your royal highness would swallow this!' Dr Cuncliffe Babcock started forward with a glass.

'Trinquons, trinquons et vive l'amour! Schneider sang that —'

'If your royal highness —'

'Ah my dear Vienna. Where's Teddywegs?'

At the Archduchess' little escritoire at the foot of the bed, her Dreaminess was making ready a few private telegrams, breaking without undue harshness the melancholy news: 'Poor Lizzie has ceased articulating,' she did not think she could improve on it, and indeed had written it several times in her most temperamental hand, when the Archduchess had started suddenly cackling about Vienna.

'*Ssssh*, Lizzie – I never can write when people talk!'

'I want Teddywegs.'

'The Countess Yvorra took him for a run round the courtyard.'

'I think I must undertake a convenience next for dogs . . . It is disgraceful they have not got one already, poor creatures,' the Archduchess crooned accepting the proffered glass.

'Yes, yes, dear,' the Queen exclaimed rising and crossing to the window.

The bitter odour of the oleander flowers outside oppressed the breathless air and filled the room as with a faint funereal music. So still a day. Tending the drooping sun-saturated flowers, a gardener with long ivory arms alone seemed animate.

'Pull up your skirt, Marquise! Pull it up . . . It's dragging, a little, in the water.'

'*Judica me, Deus*,' in imperious tones, the priest by the bedside besought: '*et discerne causam meum de gente non sancta. Parce, Domine! Parce populo tuo –! ne in aeternum irascaris nobis*.'

'A whale! A whale!'

'*Sustinuit anima mea in verbo ejus speravit anima mea in Domino*.'

'Elsie?' A look of wondrous happiness overspread the Archduchess' face – She was wading – wading again among the irises and rushes; wading, her hand in Princess Elsie's hand, through a glittering golden sea, towards the wide horizon.

The plangent cry of a peacock rose disquietingly from the garden.

'I'm nothing but nerves, doctor,' her Dreaminess lamented, fidgeting with the crucifix that dangled at her neck upon a chain. *Ultra* feminine, she disliked that another – even *in extremis* – should absorb *all* the limelight.

'A change of scene, ma'am, would be probably beneficial,' Dr Cuncliffe Babcock replied, eyeing askance the Countess of Tolga who unobtrusively entered:

'The couturiers attend your pleasure, ma'am,' in impassive undertones she said: 'to fit your mourning.'

'Oh tell them the Queen is too tired to try on now,' her Dreaminess answered repairing in agitation towards a glass.

'They would come here, ma'am,' the Countess said, pointing persuasively to the little anteroom of the Archduchess, where two nuns of the Flaming-Hood were industriously telling their beads.

'— I don't know why, but this glass refuses to flatter me!'

'*Benedicamus Domino! Ostende nobis Domine misericordiam tuam. Et salutare tuum da nobis!*'

'Well just a toque,' the Queen sadly assented.

'*Indulgentiam absolutionem et remissionem peccatorum nostrorum tribuat nobis omnipotens et misericors Dominus.*'

'Guess who is at the Ritz, ma'am, this week!' the Countess demurely murmured.

'Who is at the Ritz this week, I can't,' the Queen replied.

'*Nobody!*'

'Why how so?'

'The Ambassadress of England, it seems has alarmed the world away. I gather they mean to prosecute!'

The Archduchess sighed.

'I want mauve sweet-peas,' she listlessly said.

'Her spirit soars; her thoughts are in the *Champs-Elysées*,' the Countess exclaimed, withdrawing noiselessly to warn the milliners.

'Or in the garden,' the Queen reflected, returning to the window. And she was standing there, her eyes fixed half wistfully upon the long ivory arms of the kneeling gardener, when the Angel of Death (who had sat unmoved throughout the day) arose.

It was decided to fix a period of mourning of fourteen days for the late Archduchess.

## *VII*

Swans and sunlight. A little fishing boat with coral sails. A lake all grey and green. Beatitude intense. Consummate calm. It was nice to be at the Summer-Palace after all.

'The way the air will catch your cheek and make a rose of it,' the Countess of Tolga breathed. And as none of the company heeded her: 'How sweetly the air takes one's cheek,' she sighed again.

The post-prandial exercise of the members of the Court through the palace grounds was almost an institution.

The first half of the mourning prescribed, had as yet not run its course, but the tongues of the Queen's ladies had long since made an end of it.

'I hate dancing with a fat man,' Mademoiselle de Nazianzi was saying: 'for if you dance at all near him, his stomach hits you, while if you pull away, you catch either the scent of his breath or the hair of his beard.'

'But, you innocent baby, *all* big men haven't beards,' Countess Medusa Rappa remarked.

'Haven't they? Never mind. Everything's so beautiful,' the young girl inconsequently exclaimed: 'Look at that Thistle! and that Bee! O, you darling!'

'Ah, how one's face unbends in gardens!' the Countess of Tolga said, regarding the scene before her, with a far-away pensive glance.

Along the lake's shore, sheltered from the winds by a ring of wooded hills, shewed many a proud retreat, mirroring its marble terraces to the waveless waters of the lake.

Beneath a twin-peaked crag (known locally as the White Mountain whose slopes frequently would burst forth into patches of garlic that from the valley resembled snow) nestled the Villa Clement, rented each season by the Ambassador of the Court of St James, while half-screened by conifers and rhododendrons, and in the lake itself, was St Helena – the home and place of retirement of a 'fallen' minister of the Crown.

Countess Medusa Rappa cocked her sunshade; 'Whose boat is that,' she asked, 'with the azure oars?'

'It looks nothing but a pea-pod!' the Countess of Tolga declared.

'It belongs to a darling, with delicious lips and eyes like brown chestnuts,' Mademoiselle de Lambèse informed.

'Ah! . . . Ah! . . . Ah! . . . Ah! . . .' her colleagues crooned.

'A sailor?'

The Queen's maid nodded: 'There's a partner, though,' she added, 'a blue-eyed, gashed-cheeked angel . . .'

Mademoiselle de Nazianzi looked away.

'I love the lake with the white wandering ships,' she sentimentally stated, descrying in the distance the Prince.

It was usually towards this time, the hour of the siesta, that the lovers would meet and taste their happiness, but, today, it seemed ordained otherwise.

Before the heir apparent had determined whether to advance or retreat, his father and mother were upon him, attended by two dowagers newly lunched.

'The song of the pilgrim women, how it haunts me,' one of the dowagers was holding forth: 'I could never tire of that beautiful, beautiful music! Never tire of it. Ne-ver . . .'

'Ta, ta, ta, ta,' the Queen vociferated girlishly, slipping her arm affectionately through that of her son.

'How spent you look, my boy . . . Those eyes . . .'

His Weariness grimaced.

'They've just been rubbing in Elsie!' he said.

'Who?'

'"Vaseline" and "Nanny-goat"!'

'Well?'

'Nothing will shake me.'

'What are your objections?'

'She's so extraordinarily uninteresting!'

'Oh Yousef!' his mother faltered: '*Do you wish to break my heart?*'

'We had always thought you too lacking in initiative,' King William said (tucking a few long hairs back into his nose) 'to marry against our wishes.'

'They say she walks too wonderfully,' the Queen courageously pursued.

'What? Well?'

'Yes.'

'Thank God for it.'

'And can handle a horse as few others can!'

Prince Yousef closed his eyes.

He had not forgotten how as an undergraduate in England he had come upon the Princess once while out with the hounds. And it was only by a consummate effort that he was able to efface the sinister impression she had made – her lank hair falling beneath a man's felt-hat, her habit skirt torn to tatters, her full cheeks smeared in blood; the blood, so it seemed, of her 'first' fox.

A shudder seized him.

'No, nothing can possibly shake me,' he murmured again.

With a detached, cold face, the Queen paused to inhale a rose.

(Oh you gardens of Palaces . . . ! How often have you witnessed agitation and disappointment? You smooth, adorned paths . . . ! How often have you known the extremes of care . . . ?)

'It would be better to do away I think next year with that bed of cinerarias altogether,' the Queen of Pisuerga remarked, 'since persons won't go around it.'

Traversing the flower plat now, with the air of a black-beetle with a purpose, was the Countess Yvorra.

'We had supposed you higher-principled, Countess,' her sovereign admonished.

The Countess slightly flushed.

'I'm looking for groundsel for my birds, Sire,' she said – 'for my little dickies!'

'We understand your boudoir is a sort of menagerie,' His Majesty affirmed.

The Countess tittered.

'Animals love me,' she archly professed. 'Birds perch on my breast if only I wave . . . The other day a sweet red robin came and stayed for hours . . . !'

'The Court looks to you to set a high example,' the Queen declared, focusing quizzically a marble shape of Leda green with moss, for whose time-corroded plinth the late Archduchess' toy-terrier was just then shewing a certain contempt.

The Countess' long, slightly pulpy fingers strayed nervously towards the rosary at her thigh.

'With Your Majesty's consent,' she said, 'I propose a campaign to the Island.'

'What? And beard the Count?'

'The salvation of one so fallen, in my estimation should be worth hereafter (at the present rate of exchange, but the values vary) . . . a Plenary perpetual-indulgence: I therefore,' the Countess said, with an upward fleeting glance (and doubtless guileless of intention of irony), 'feel it my *duty* to do what I can.'

'I trust you will take a bodyguard when you go to St Helena?'

'And pray tell Count Cabinet from us,' the King looked implacable: 'we forbid him to serenade the Court this year! or to throw himself into the Lake again or to make himself a nuisance!'

'He was over early this morning, Willie,' the Queen retailed: 'I saw him from a window. Fishing, or feigning to! And with white kid gloves, and a red carnation.'

'Let us catch him stepping ashore!' the King displayed displeasure.

'And as usual the same mignon youth had the charge of the tiller.'

'I could tell a singular story of that young man,' the Countess said: 'for he was once a choir-boy at the Blue Jesus. But, perhaps, I would do better to spare your ears . . .'

'You would do better, a good deal, to spare my cinerarias,' her Dreaminess murmured, sauntering slowly on.

Sun so bright, trees so green, it was a perfect day. Through the glittering fronds of the palms shone the lake like a floor of silver glass strewn with white sails.

'It's odd,' the King observed, giving the dog Teddywegs a sly prod with his cane, 'how he follows Yousef.'

'He seems to know!' the Queen replied.

A remark that so annoyed the Prince that he curtly left the garden.

## VIII

But this melancholy period of *crêpe*, a time of idle secrets, and unbosomings, was to prove fatal to the happiness of Mademoiselle de Nazianzi. She now heard she was not the first in the Prince's life, and that most of the Queen's maids, indeed, had had identical experiences with her own. She furthermore learned, amid ripples of laughter, of her lover's relations with the Marquesa Pizzi-Parma and of his light dealings with the dancer April Flowers, a negress (to what depths??) at a time when he was enjoying the waxen favours of the wife of his Magnificence, the Master of the Horse.

Chilled to the point of numbness, the mortified girl had scarcely winced, and when on repairing to her room a little later, she had found his Weariness wandering in the corridor on the chance of a surreptitious kiss, she had bolted past him without look, or word, and sharply closed her door.

The Court had returned to colours when she opened it again, and such had been the trend of her meditations, that her initial steps were directed, with deliberate austerity, towards the basilica of the Palace.

Except for the Countess Yvorra, with an *écharpe de décence* drawn over her hair, there was no one in it.

'I thank Thee God for this *escape*,' she murmured falling to her knees before the silver branches of a cross: 'It is terrible; for I did so love him ........................................
.....................................................................
.....................................................................
....... and oh how could he ever with *a negress*? ...............
.....................................................................
....... Pho .........................................................

................................I fear this complete upset has considerably aged me ........................................
....... But to Thee I cling ..........................................
..................................................................
..................................................................
Preserve me at all times from the toils of the wicked, and forgive him, as *I* hope to forgive him soon.' Then kindling several candles with a lingering hand, she shaped her course towards the Kennels, called Teddywegs to her and started, with an aching heart, for a walk.

It was a day of heavy somnolence. Skirting the Rosery where gardeners with their slowly moving rakes were tending the sandy paths, she chose a neglected footway that descended towards the lake. Indifferent to the vivacity of Teddywegs, who would race on a little before her, then wait with leonine accouchments of head until she had almost reached him, when he would prick an ear and spring forward with a yap of exhortation, she proceeded leisurely, and with many a pause, wrapped in her own mournful thoughts.

Alack! Among the court circle there was no one to whom in her disillusion she could look for solace, and her spirit yearned for Sister Ursula, and the Convent of the Flaming-Hood.

Wending her way amid the tall trees, she felt she had never cared for Yousef as she had for Ursula . . . and broodingly, in order to ease her heart, she began comparing the two together as she walked along.

After all what had he ever said that was not either commonplace or foolish? Whereas Sister Ursula's talk was invariably pointed; and often indeed so delicately, that words seemed almost too crude a medium to convey her ethereal meanings, and she would move her evocative hands, and flash her aura, and it was no fault of hers if you hadn't a peep of the beyond. And the infinite tenderness of her least caress. Yousef's lips had seldom conveyed to hers the spell of Ursula's; and once indeed lately, when he had kissed her, there had been an unsavoury aroma of tobacco and *charcuterie*, which, to deal with, had required both tact and courage . . . Ah dear Hood! What harmony life had held within. Unscrupulous and deceiving men might lurk around its doors (they often did) coveting the chaste, but Old Jane, the porteress, would open to no man beyond the merest crack. And how right they were, the nuns in their mistrust of man! Sister Ursula one day had declared, in uplifted mood, that 'marriage was obscene'. Was it –? . . . ?? . . . Perhaps it might be –! How appalling if it was!

She had reached the lake.

Beneath a sky as white as platinum it lay, pearly, dove-like, scintillating capriciously where a heat-shrouded sun kindled its torpid waters into fleeting diamonds. A convulsive breeze strayed gratefully from the opposite shore, descending from the hills that rose up all veiled, and without detail, against the brilliant whiteness of the morning.

Sinking down upon the shingle by an upturned boat, she heaved a brief sigh, and drawing from her vanity-case the last epistles of the Prince, she began methodically to arrange them in their proper sequence.

(*1*) 'What is the matter with my Dearest Girl?'

(*2*) 'My own tender little Lita, I do not understand –'

(*3*) 'Darling, what's this –?'

(*4*) 'Beloved one, I swear –'

(*5*) 'Your cruel silence –'

If published in a dainty brochure form at about the time of his Coronation, they ought to realise no contemptible sum, and the proceeds might go to Charity, she reflected, thrusting them back again carefully into the bag.

Then, finding the shingle too hard through her thin gown to remain seated long, she got up, and ran a mournful race with Teddywegs along the shore.

Not far along the lake was the 'village', with the Hôtel d'Angleterre et du Lac, its stucco, belettered-walls professing: 'Garages, Afternoon Tea, Modern Comfort!' Flitting by this, and the unpretentious pier (where long blonde fishing-nets lay drying in the sun), it was a relief to reach the remote plage beyond.

Along the banks stretched vast brown carpets of corn and rye, broken by an occasional olive-garth, beneath whose sparse shade the heavy-eyed oxen blinked and whisked their tails, under the attacks of the water-gnats that were swarming around.

Musing on Negresses – and Can-Can dancers in particular – she strolled along a strand all littered with shells and little jewel-like stones.

The sun shone down more fiercely now, and soon, for freshness' sake, she was obliged to take to the fields.

Passing among the silver drooping olives, relieved here and there by a stone-pine, or slender cypress-tree eternally green, she sauntered on, often lured aside to pluck the radiant wild-flowers by the way. On the banks the pinkest cyclamens were in bloom, and cornflowers of the hue of paradise, and fine-stemmed poppies flecked with pink.

'Pho! A Negress . . .' she murmured, following the flight of some waterfowl towards the opposite shore.

The mists had fallen from the hills, revealing old woods wrapped in the blue doom of Summer.

Beyond those glowing heights, towards this hour, the nuns, each in her cool, shuttered, cell, would be immersed at noontide prayer.

'Ursula – for thee!' she sighed, proffering her bouquet in the direction of the town.

A loud splash . . . the sight of a pair of delicate legs (mocking the Law's requirements under the Modesty Act as relating to bathers) . . . Mademoiselle de Nazianzi turned and fled. She had recognised *the Prince*.[1]

1 The recollection of this was never quite forgotten.

# IX

And in this difficult time of spiritual distress, made more trying perhaps because of the blazing midsummer days, and long, pent feverish nights, Mademoiselle de Nazianzi turned in her tribulation towards religion.

The Ecclesiastical set at Court, composed of some six, or so, ex-Circes, under the command of the Countess Yvorra, were only too ready to welcome her, and invitations to meet Monsignor this, or 'Father' that, who constantly were being *coaxed* from their musty sacristies and wan-faced acolytes in the capital, in order that they might officiate at Masses, Confessions and Breakfast-parties *à la fourchette*, were lavished daily upon the bewildered girl.

Messages, and hasty informal lightly-pencilled notes, too, would frequently reach her; such as: 'I shall be pouring out cocoa after dinner in bed. Bring your biscuits and join me!' . . . or a rat-a-tat from a round-eyed page and: 'The Countess' comp'ts and she'd take it a Favour if you can make a "Station" with her in chapel later on,' or: 'The Marchioness will be birched tomorrow, and *not* today.'

O, the charm, the flavour of the religious world! Where match it for interest or variety!

An emotion approaching sympathy had arisen, perhaps a trifle incongruously, between the injured girl and the Countess Yvorra, and before long, to the amusement of the sceptical element of the Court, the Countess and her Confessor, Father Nostradamus, might often be observed in her society.

'I need a cage-companion, Father, for my little bird,' the Countess one evening said, as they were ambling, all the three of them before Office up and down the perfectly tended paths: 'ought it to be of the same species and sex, or does it matter? For as I said to myself just now (while listening to a thrush), *All* birds are His creatures.'

The priest discreetly coughed.

'Your question requires reflection,' he said: 'What is the bird?'

'A hen canary! – and with a voice, Father! Talk of soul!!'

'H—m . . . a thrush and a canary, I would not myself advise.'

Mademoiselle de Nazianzi tittered.

'Why not let it go?' she asked, turning her eyes towards the window-panes of the palace, that glanced like rows of beaten-gold in the evening sun.

'A hawk might peck it!' the Countess returned, looking up as if for one, into a sky as imaginative, and as dazzling as Shelley poetry.

'Even the Court,' Father Nostradamus ejaculated wryly, 'will peck at times.'

The Countess' shoulder-blades stiffened.

'After over thirty years,' she said, 'I find Court-life *pathetic* . . .'

'Pathetic?'

'Tragically pathetic . . .'

Mademoiselle de Nazianzi considered wistfully the wayward outline of the hills.

'I would like to escape from it all for a while,' she said, 'and travel.'

'I must hunt you out a pamphlet, by and by, dear child, on the "Dangers of Wanderlust".'

'The Great Wall of China and the Bay of Naples! It seems so frightful never to have seen them!'

'I have never seen the Great Wall, either,' the Countess said, 'and I don't suppose, my dear, I ever shall; though I once did spent a fortnight in Italy.'

'Tell me about it.'

The Countess became reminiscent.

'In Venice,' she said, 'the indecent movements of the Gondolieri quite affected my health, and, in consequence, I fell a prey to a sharp nervous fever. My temperature rose and it rose, ah, yes . . . until I became quite ill. At last I said to my maid (she was an English girl from *Wales*, and almost equally as sensitive as me): "Pack . . . Away!" And we left in haste for Florence. Ah, and Florence, too, I regret to say I found very far from what it ought to have been!!! I had a window giving on the Arno, and so I could *observe* . . . I used to see some curious sights! I would not care to scathe your ears, my Innocent, by an inventory of one half of the wantonness that went on; enough to say the tone of the place forced me to fly to Rome, where beneath the shadow of dear St Peter's I grew gradually less distressed.'

'Still, I should like, all the same, to travel!' Mademoiselle de Nazianzi exclaimed, with a sad little snatch of a smile.

'We will ask the opinion of Father Geordie Picpus, when he comes again.'

'It would be more fitting,' Father Nostradamus murmured (professional rivalry leaping to his eye), 'if Father Picpus kept himself free of the limelight a trifle more!'

'Often I fear our committees would be corvées without him . . .'

'Tchut.'

'He is very popular . . . too popular, perhaps . . .' the Countess admitted. 'I remember on one occasion in the Blue Jesus, witnessing the Duchess of Quaranta and Madame Ferdinand Fishbacher, fight like wild cats as to which should gain his ear – (any girl might envy Father Geordie his ear) – at Confession next. The odds seemed fairly equal, until the Duchess gave the Fishbacher-woman, such a violent push – (well down from behind, in the crick of the joints) – that she overturned The Confessional Box, with Father Picpus within: and when we scared ladies, standing by, had succeeded in dragging him out, he was too shaken, naturally as you can gather, to absolve anyone else *that* day.'

'He has been the object of so many unseemly incidents, that one can scarcely recall them all,' Father Nostradamus exclaimed, stooping to pick up a dropped pocket-handkerchief with 'remembrance' knots tied to three of the corners.

'Alas . . . Court life is not uplifting,' the Countess said again, contemplating her muff of *self-made* lace, with a half-vexed forehead. What that muff contained was a constant problem for conjecture;

but it was believed by more than one of the maids-in-waiting to harbour 'goody' books and martyrs' bones.

'By generous deeds and Brotherly love,' Father Nostradamus exclaimed, 'we should endeavour to rise above it!'

With the deftness of a virtuoso, the Countess seized, and crushed with her muff, a pale-winged passing gnat.

'Before Life,' she murmured, 'that saddest thing of all, was thrust upon us, I believe I was an angel . . .'

Father Nostradamus passed a musing hand across his brow.

'It may be,' he replied, 'and it very well may be,' he went on, 'that our ante-nativity was a little more brilliant, a little more *h—m* . . . ; and there is nothing unorthodox in thinking so.'

'O what did I do then to lose my wings?? What did I ever say to Them?! Father, Father. How did I annoy God? Why did He put me here?'

'My dear child, you ask me things I do not know; but it may be you were the instrument appointed above to lead back to Him our neighbour yonder,' Father Nostradamus answered, pointing with his breviary in the direction of St Helena.

'Never speak to me of that wretched old man.'

For despite the ablest tactics, the most diplomatic angling, Count Cabinet had refused to rally.

'We followed the sails of your skiff today,' Mademoiselle de Nazianzi sighed, 'until the hazes hid them!'

'I had a lilac passage.'

'You delivered the books?'

The Countess shrugged.

'I shall never forget this afternoon,' she said. 'He was sitting in the window over a decanter of wine when I floated down upon him; but no sooner did he see me, than he gave a sound, like a bleat of a goat, and disappeared: I was determined however to call! There is no bell to the villa, but two bronze door-knockers, well out of reach, are attached to the front-door. These with the ferrule of my parasol I tossed and I rattled, until an adolescent, with Bougainvillea at his ear, came and looked out with an insolent grin, and I recognised Peter Passer from the Blue Jesus grown quite fat.'

'Eh mon Dieu!' Father Nostradamus half-audibly sighed.

'Eh mon Dieu . . .' Mademoiselle de Nazianzi echoed, her gaze roving over the palace, whose long window-panes in the setting sun gleamed like sumptuous tissues.

'So that,' the Countess added, 'I hardly propose to venture again.'

'What a site for a Calvary!' Father Nostradamus replied, indicating with a detached and pensive air the cleft in the White Mountain's distant peaks.

'I adore the light the hills take on when the sun drops down,' Mademoiselle de Nazianzi declared.

'It must be close on *Salut* . . .'

It was beneath the dark colonnades by the Court Chapel door that they received the news from the lips of a pair of vivacious dowagers that the Prince was to leave the Summer-Palace on the morrow to attend 'the Manoeuvres', after which it was expected his Royal Highness would proceed '*to England*'.

# X

And meanwhile the representatives of the Court of St James were enjoying the revivifying country air and outdoor-life of the Villa Clement. It was almost exquisite how rapidly the casual mode of existence adopted during the summer villeggiatura by their Excellencies, drew themselves and their personnel together, until soon they were as united and as *sans gêne* as the proverbial family party. No mother, in the 'acclimatization' period, could have dosed her offspring more assiduously than did her Excellency the attachés in her charge; flavouring her little inventions frequently with rum or gin until they resembled cocktails. But it was Sir Somebody himself if anyone that required a tonic. Lady Something's pending litigation, involving as it did the Crown, was fretting the Ambassador more than he cared to admit, and the Hon. Mrs Chilleywater, ever alert, told 'Harold' that the injudicious chatter of the Ambassadress (who even now notwithstanding her writ, would say to every other visitor that came to the villa: 'Have you heard about the Ritz?? The other night we were dining at the Palace, and I heard the King,' *etc.*) was wearing their old Chief out.

And so through the agreeable vacation life there twitched the grim vein of tension.

One day disturbed by her daughter's persistent trilling of the last coster song *When I sees 'im I topple giddy*, Lady Something gathered up her morning letters and stepped out upon the lawn.

Oh so formal, oh so slender towered the Cypress-trees against the rose-farded hills and diamantine waters of the lake. The first hint of Autumn was in the air; and over the gravel paths, and in the basins of the fountains, a few shed leaves lay hectically strewn already.

Besides an under-stamped missive, with a foreign postmark, from her Majesty the Queen of the Land of Dates beginning 'My dear Gazel,' there was a line from the eloquent, and moderately-victorious, young barrister, engaged in the approaching suit with the Ritz: He had spared himself no pains he assured his client in preparing the defence, which was he said to be *the respectability of Claridge's*.

'Why bring in Claridge's? . . . ?' the Ambassadress murmured, prodding with the tip of her shoe a decaying tortoiseshell leaf; 'but anyway,' she reflected, 'I'm glad the proceedings fall in winter, as I always look well in furs.'

And mentally she was wrapped in leopard skins and gazing round the crowded court saluting with a bunch of violets an acquaintance here and there, as her eyes fell on Mrs Chilleywater seated in the act of composition beneath a cedar-tree.

Mrs Chilleywater extended a painful smile of welcome which revealed her pointed teeth and pale-hued gums, repressing, simultaneously, an almost irresistible inclination to murder.

'What! . . . Another writ?' she suavely asked.

'No, dear; but these legal men *will* write . . .'

'I love your defender. He has an air of d'Alembert's sympathetic soul.'

'He proposes pleading Claridge's.'

'Claridge's?'

'Its respectability.'

'Are hotels ever respectable, – I ask you? Though, possibly, the horridest are.'

'Aren't they all horrid!'

'*Natürlich*; but do you know those cheap hotels where the guests are treated like naughty children?'

'No. I must confess I don't,' the Ambassadress laughed.

'Ah, there you are . . .'

Lady Something considered a moment a distant gardener employed in tying Chrysanthemum blooms to little sticks.

'I'm bothered about a cook,' she said.

'And I, about a maid! I dismissed Ffoliott this morning – well I simply *had* to – for a figure salient.'

'So awkward out here to replace anyone; I'm sure I don't know . . .' the Ambassadress replied, her eyes hovering tragically over the pantaloons strained to *splitting* point, of the stooping gardener.

'It's a pretty prospect . . .'

'Life is a compound!' Lady Something defined it at last.

Mrs Chilleywater turned, surprised. 'Not even Socrates,' she declared, 'said anything truer than that.'

'A compound!' Lady Something twittered again.

'I should like to put that into the lips of Delitsiosa.'

'Who's Delitsiosa?' the Ambassadress asked as a smothered laugh broke out beside her.

Mrs Chilleywater looked up.

'I'd forgotten you were there. Strange thing among the cedar-boughs,' she said.

The Hon. Lionel Limpness tossed a slippered foot flexibly from his hammock.

'You may well ask "who's Delitsiosa"!' he exclaimed.

'She is my new heroine,' Mrs Chilleywater replied, after a few quick little clutches at her hair.

'I trust you won't treat her, dear, quite so shamefully as your last.'

The Authoress tittered.

'Delitsiosa is the wife of Marsden Didcote,' she said, 'the manager of a pawnshop in the district of Maida Vale, and in the novel he seduces an innocent seamstress, Iris Drummond, who comes in one day to redeem her petticoat (and really I don't know how I did succeed in drawing the portrait of a little fool!) . . . and when Delitsiosa, her suspicions aroused, can no longer doubt or ignore her husband's intimacy with Iris, already engaged to a lusty young farmer in Kent – (some boy) – she decides to yield herself to the entreaties of her brother-in-law Percy, a junior partner in the firm, which brings about the great tussle between the two brothers on the edge of the Kentish cliffs. Iris and Delitsiosa – Iris is anticipating a babelet soon – are watching them from a cornfield, where they're boiling a kettle for afternoon tea; and oh, I've such a darling description of a cornfield. I make you *feel* England!'

'No really, my dear,' Lady Something exclaimed.

'Harold pretends it would be wonderful, arranged as an Opera . . . with duos and things and a *Liebestod* for Delitzi towards the close.'

'No, no,' Mr Limpness protested: 'What would become of our modern fiction at all if Victoria Gellybore Frinton gave herself up to the stage?'

'That's quite true, strange thing among the cedar-boughs,' Mrs Chilleywater returned fingering the floating strings of the bandelette at her brow: 'It's lamentable; yet who is there doing anything at present for English Letters . . . ? Who among us today,' she went on peering up at him, 'is carrying on the tradition of Fielding? Who really cares? I know *I* do what I can . . . and there's Madam Adrian Bloater, of course. But I can think of no one else; – we two.'

Mr Limpness rocked, critically.

'I can't bear Bloater's books,' he demurred.

'To be frank, neither can I. I'm very fond of Lilian Bloater, I adore her *weltbürgerliche* nature, but I feel like you about her books; I *cannot* read them. If only she would forget Adrian; but she will thrust him headlong into all her work. Have *I* ever drawn Harold? No. (Although many of the public seem to think so!) And please heaven, however *great* my provocation at times may be, I never shall!'

'And there I think you're right,' the Ambassadress answered, frowning a little as the refrain that her daughter was singing caught her ear.

> 'And when I sees 'im
> My heart goes BOOM! . . .
> And I topple over;
> I topple over, over, over,
> All for Love!'

'I dreamt last night my child was on the Halls.'

'There's no doubt, she'd dearly like to be.'

'Her Father would never hear of it!'

'And when she sees me
O, when she sees me –
(*The voice slightly false was Harold's*)
My heart goes BOOM! . . .
And she topples over;
She topples over, over, over,
All for Love!'

'There; they've routed Sir Somebody . . .'

'And when anything vexes him,' Lady Something murmured, appraising the Ambassador's approaching form with a glassy eye, 'he always, you know, blames me!'

Shorn of the sombre, betailed attire, so indispensable for the town-duties of a functionary, Sir Somebody, while rusticating, usually wore a white-twill jacket, and black multi-pleated pantaloons; while for headgear, he would favour a Mexican sugar-loaf, or green-draped pugaree: 'He looks half-Irish,' Lady Something would sometimes say.

'Infernal Bedlam,' he broke out: 'the house is sheer pandemonium.'

'I found it so too, dear,' Lady Something agreed; 'and so,' she added, removing a fallen tree-bug tranquilly from her hair, 'I've been digesting my letters out here upon the lawn.'

'And no doubt,' Sir Somebody murmured, fixing the placid person of his wife, with a keen psychological glance: 'you succeed, my dear, in digesting them?'

'Why shouldn't I.'

'. . .' the Ambassador displayed discretion.

'We're asked to a Lion hunt in the Land of Dates; quite an *entreating* invitation from the dear Queen –; really most pressing and affectionate, but Princess Elsie's nuptial negotiations and this pending Procès with the Ritz, may tie us here for some time.'

'Ah Rosa.'

'Why these constant moans? . . . ? A clairvoyant once told me I'd "the bump of Litigation" – a *cause célèbre* unmistakably defined; so it's as well, on the whole, to have it over.'

'And quite probably; had your statement been correct —'

The Ambassadress gently glowed.

'I'm told it's simply swarming!' she impenitently said.

'Oh Rosa, Rosa . . .'

'And if you doubt it at all, here is an account direct from the Ritz itself,' her Excellency replied, singling out a letter from among the rest: 'It is from dear old General Sir Trotter-Stormer. He says: "I am the only guest here. I must say, however, the attendance is beyond all praise, more *soigné* and better than I've ever known it to be, but after what you told me, dear friend, I feel *distinctly uncomfortable* when the hour for bye-bye comes!"'

'Pish; what evidence, pray, is that?'

'I regard it as of the very first importance! Sir Trotter admits – a distinguished soldier admits, his uneasiness; and who knows, he is so brave about concealing his woes – his two wives left him! – what he may not have patiently and stoically endured?'

'Less I am sure, my dear, than I of late in listening sometimes to you.'

'I will write I think and press him for a more detailed report . . .'

The Ambassador turned away.

'She should no more be trusted with ink than a child with firearms!' he declared, addressing himself with studious indirectness to a garden-snail.

Lady Something blinked.

'Life is a compound,' she murmured again.

'Particularly for women!' the Authoress agreed.

'Ah, well,' the Ambassadress majestically rose: 'I must be off and issue household orders; although I derive hardly my usual amount of enjoyment at present, I regret to say, from my morning consultations with the cook . . .'

# *XI*

It had been once the whim, and was now the felicitous habit of the Countess of Tolga to present Count Cabinet annually with a bouquet of flowers. It was as if Venus-Anadyomene herself, standing[1] on a shell and wafted by all the piquant whispers of the town and court, would intrude upon the flattered exile (with her well-wired orchids, and malicious, soulless, laughter), to awaken delicate, pagan images, of a trecento, Tuscan Greece.

But upon this occasion desirous of introducing some new features, the Countess decided on presenting the fallen senator with a pannier of well-grown, early pears, a small 'heath', and the Erotic Poems bound in half calf with tasteful tooling of a Schoolboy Poet, cherishable chiefly, perhaps, for the vignette frontispiece of the author. Moreover, acting on an impulse she was never able afterwards to explain, she had invited Mademoiselle Olga Blumenghast to accompany her.

Never had summer shown a day more propitiously clement, than the afternoon in mid-Autumn they prepared to set out.

Fond of a compliment, when not too frankly racy,[2] and knowing how susceptible the exile was to clothes, the Countess had arrayed herself in a winter gown of kingfisher-tinted silk turning to turquoise, and stencilled in purple at the arms and neck with a crisp Greek-key design; while a voluminous violet veil, depending behind her to a point, half-concealed a tricorne turquoise toque from which arose a shaded lilac aigrette branching several ways.

1 *Vide* Botticelli.

2 In Pisuerga compliments are apt to rival in this respect those of the ardent South.

'I shall probably die with heat, and of course it's most unsuitable; but poor old man, he likes to recall the Capital!' the Countess panted, as, nursing heath, poems and pears, she followed Mademoiselle Olga Blumenghast blindly towards the shore.

Oars, and swaying drying nets, a skyline lost in sun, a few moored craft beneath the little rickety wooden pier awaiting choice: – 'The boatmen, today, darling, seem all so ugly; let's take a sailing-boat and go alone!'

'I suppose there's no danger, darling?' the Countess replied, and scarcely had she time to make any slight objection, than the owner of a steady wide-bottomed boat – the *Calypso* – was helping them to embark.

The Island of St Helena, situated towards the lake's bourne, lay distant some two miles or more, and within a short way of the open sea.

With sails distended to a languid breeze the shore eventually was left behind; and the demoiselle cranes, in mid-lake, were able to observe there were two court dames among them.

'Although he's dark, Vi,' Mademoiselle Olga Blumenghast presently exclaimed, dropping her cheek to a frail hand upon the tiller, 'although he's dark, it's odd how he gives one the impression somehow of perfect fairness!'

'Who's that, darling?' the Countess murmured, appraising with fine eyes, faintly weary, the orchid-like style of beauty of her friend.

'Ann-Jules, of course.'

'I begin to wish, do you know, I'd brought Pomegranates, and worn something else!'

'What are those big burley-worleys?'

'Pears . . .'

'Give me one.'

'Catch, then.'

'Not that I could bear to be married; especially like *you*, Vi!'

'A marriage like ours, dear, was so utterly unworthwhile . . .'

'I'm not sure, dear, that I comprehend altogether?'

'Seagulls' wings as they fan one's face . . .'

'It's vile and wrong to shoot them: but oh! How I wish your happiness depended, even ever so little, on me.'

The Countess averted her eyes.

Waterfowl, like sadness passing, hovered, and soared overhead, casting their dark, fleeting shadows to the white, drowned clouds, in the receptive waters of the lake.

'I begin to wish I'd brought grapes,' she breathed.

'Heavy stodgy pears. So do I.'

'Or a few special peaches,' the Countess murmured, taking up the volume of verse beside her, with a little, mirthless, half-hysterical laugh.

*To a Faithless Friend.*
*To V.O.I. and S.C.P.*
*For Stephen.*
*When the Dormitory Lamp burns Low.*

Her gaze travelled over the Index.

'Read something, dear,' Mademoiselle Blumenghast begged, toying with the red-shaded flower in her burnished curls.

'Gladly; but oh, Olga!' the Countess crooned.

'What!'

'Where's the wind?'

It had gone.

'We must row.'

There was nothing for it.

To gain the long, white breakwater, with the immemorial willow-tree at its end, that was the most salient feature of the island's approach, required, nevertheless, resolution.

'It's so far, dear,' the Countess kept on saying. 'I had no idea how far it was! Had you any conception at all it was so far?'

'Let us await the wind, then. It's bound to rally.'

But no air swelled the sun-bleached sails, or disturbed the pearly patine of the paralysed waters.

'I shall never get this peace, I only realize it *exists* . . .' the Countess murmured with dream-glazed eyes.

'It's astonishing . . . the stillness,' Mademoiselle Blumenghast murmured, with a faint tremor, peering round towards the shore.

On the banks young censia-trees raised their boughs like strong white whips towards the mountains, upon whose loftier heights lay, here and there, a little stray patch of snow.

'Come hither, ye winds, come hither!' she softly called.

'Oh, Olga! Do we really want it?' the Countess in agitation asked, discarding her hat and veil with a long, sighing breath.

'I don't know, dear; no; not, not much.'

'Nor I, – at all.'

'Let us be patient then.'

'It's all so beautiful it makes one want to cry.'

'Yes; it makes one want to cry,' Mademoiselle Blumenghast murmured, with a laugh that in brilliance vied with the October sun.

'Olga!'

'So,' as the *Calypso* lurched: 'lend me your hanky, dearest.'

'*Olga* –? –? Thou fragile, and exquisite thing!'

. . . . . . . . . . .

Meanwhile Count Cabinet was seated with rod-and-line at an open window idly ogling a swan. Owing to the reluctance of tradespeople to call for orders, the banished statesman was often obliged to supplement the larder himself. But hardly had he been angling ten minutes today, when lo! a distinguished mauvish fish with vivid scarlet spots. Pondering on the mysteries of the deep, and of the subtle variety there is in Nature, the veteran ex-minister lit a cigar. Among the more orthodox types that stocked the lake, such as carp, cod, tench, eels, sprats, shrimps, etc., this exceptional fish must have known its trials and persecutions, its hours of superior difficulty . . . and the Count, with a stoic smile recalled his own. Musings on the advantages and disadvantages of personality, of 'party' viewpoints, and of morals in general, the Count was soon too self-absorbed to observe the approach of his 'useful' secretary and amanuensis, Peter Passer.

More valet perhaps than secretary, and more errand-boy than either, the former chorister of the Blue Jesus had followed the fallen statesman into exile at a moment when the Authorities of Pisuerga were making minute enquiries for sundry missing articles[1] from the *Trésor* of the Cathedral, and since the strain of constant choir-practice is apt to be injurious for a youngster suffering from a delicate chest, the adolescent had been willing enough to accept, for a time, at least, a situation in the country.

'O, sir,' he exclaimed, and almost in his excitement forgetting altogether the insidious, lisping tones he preferred as a rule to employ: 'O, sir, here comes that old piece of rubbish again with a fresh pack of tracts!'

'Collect yourself, Peter, pray do: what, lose our heads for a visit?' the Count said getting up and going to a glass.

'I've noticed, sir, it's impossible to live on an island long without feeling its effects; you *can't* escape being insular!'

'Or insolent.'

'Insular, sir!'

'No matter much, but if it's the Countess Yvorra, you might shew her round the garden this time, perhaps, for a change,' the Count replied, adjusting a demure-looking fly, of indeterminate sex, to his line.

And brooding on life and baits, and what *A* will come for while *B* won't, the Count's thoughts grew almost humorous as the afternoon wore on.

Evening was approaching, when weary of the airs of a common carp, he drew in, at length, his tackle.

Like a shawl of turquoise silk the lake seemed to vie, in serenity and radiance, with the bluest day in June, and it was no surprise, on descending presently for a restricted ramble – (the island, in all, amounted to scarcely one acre) – to descry the invaluable Peter enjoying a pleasant swim.

When not boating or reading or feeding his swans, to watch Peter's fancy-diving off the terrace end, was perhaps the favourite pastime of the veteran *viveur*: to behold the lad trip along the riven

1 The missing articles were:
5 chasubles
A relic-casket in lapis and diamonds, containing the Tongue of St Thelma
4¾ yards of black lace, said to have 'belonged' to the Madonna

breakwater, as naked as a statue, shoot out his arms and spring, the *Flying-head-leap* or the *Backsadilla*, was a beautiful sight, looking up now and again – but more often *now* – from a volume of old Greek verse; while to hear him warbling in the water with his clear alto voice – of Kyries and Anthems he knew no end – would often stir the old man to the point of tears. Frequently the swans themselves would paddle up to listen, expressing by the charmed or rapturous motions of their necks (recalling to the exile the ecstasies of certain musical, or 'artistic' dames at Concert-halls, or the Opera House, long ago) their mute appreciation, their touched delight . . .

'Old goody Two-shoes never came, sir,' Peter archly lisped, admiring his adventurous shadow upon the breakwater wall.

'How is that?'

'Becalmed, sir,' Peter answered, culling languidly a small, nodding rose, that was clinging to the wall:

> 'O becalmed is my soul
> I rejoice in the Lord!'

At one extremity of the garden stood the Observatory, and after duly appraising various of Peter's neatest feats, the Count strolled away towards it. But before he could reach the Observatory, he had first to pass his swans.

They lived, with an ancient water-wheel, beneath a cupola of sun-glazed tiles, sheltered, partially, from the lake by a hedge of towering red geraniums, and the Count seldom wearied of watching these strangely gorgeous creatures as they sailed out and in through the sanguine-hued flowers. A few, with their heads sunk back beneath their wings, had retired for the night already; nevertheless, the Count paused to shake a finger at one somnolent bird, in disfavour for pecking Peter: 'Jealous, doubtless of the lad's grace,' he mused, fumbling with the key of the Observatory door.

The unrivalled instrument that the Observatory contained, whose intricate lenses were capable of drawing even the remote Summer-Palace to within an appreciable range, was, like most instruments of merit, sensitive to the manner of its manipulation; and fearing lest the inexpert tampering of a homesick housekeeper (her native village was visible in clear weather, with the aid of a glass) should break or injure the delicate lenses, the Count kept the Observatory usually under key.

But the inclination to focus the mundane, and embittered features of the fanatic Countess, as she lectured her boatmen for forgetting their oars, or, being considerably superstitious, to count the moles on their united faces as an esoteric clue to the Autumn Lottery, waned a little before the mystery of the descending night.

Beneath a changing tide of deepening shadow, the lifeless valleys were mirroring to the lake the sombreness of dusk. Across the blue forlornness of the water, a swan, here and there, appeared quite violet, while coiffed in swift clinging, golden clouds, the loftiest hills alone retained the sun.

A faint nocturnal breeze, arising simultaneously with the Angelus-bell, seemed likely to relieve, at the moon's advent, the trials to her patience of the Countess Yvorra: 'who must be cursing,' the Count reflected, turning the telescope about with a sigh, to suit her sail.

Ah poignant moments when the heart stops still! Not since the hour of his exile had the Count's been so arrested.

From the garden Peter's voice rose questingly; but the Count was too wonderstruck, far, to heed it.

Caught in the scarlet radiance of the after-glow, the becalmed boat, for one brief and most memorable second, was his to gaze on.

In certain lands with what diplomacy falls the night, and how discreetly is the daylight gone: Those dimmer-and-dimmer, darker-and-lighter twilights of the North, so disconcerting in their playfulness, were unknown altogether in Pisuerga. There, Night pursued Day, as though she meant it. No lingering, or arctic sentiment! No concertinaishness . . . Hard on the sun's heels, pressed Night. And the wherefore of her haste; Sun-attraction? Impatience to inherit? An answer to such riddles as these may doubtless be found by turning to the scientists' theories on Time and Relativity.

Effaced in the blue air of evening became everything, and with the darkness returned the wind.

'Sir, sir? . . . Ho, Hi, hiiiiiiiiiii!!' Peter's voice came again.

But transfixed, and loath just then for company, the Count made no reply.

A green-lanterned barge passed slowly, coming from the sea, and on the mountainside a village light winked wanly here and there.

'Oh, why was I not *sooner*?' he murmured distractedly aloud.

. . . . . . . . . . . .

'Oh Olga!'

'Oh Vi!'

'. . . I hope you've enough money for the boat, dear? . . . ?'

'. . . !!?'

'Tell me, Olga: Is my hat all sideways?'

'. . . . . . . . . . . .'

The long windows of the Summer-Palace were staring white to the moon, as the Countess of Tolga, her aigrettes casting *heroic* shadows and hugging still her heath, re-entered the Court's precincts on the arm of her friend.

## XII

One evening, as Mrs Montgomery was reading *Vanity Fair* for the fifteenth time, there came a tap at the door. It was not the first interruption since opening the cherished green-bound book, and Mrs Montgomery seemed disinclined to stir. With the Court about to return to winter quarters, and the Summer-Palace upside down, the royal governess was still able to command her habitual British phlegm. It had been decided, moreover, that she should remain behind in the forsaken palace with the little prince, the better to 'prepare' him for his forthcoming Eton exam.

Still, with disputes as to the precedence of trunks and dress-baskets, simmering in the corridors without, it was easier to enjoy the Barley-sugar stick in one's mouth, than the Novel in one's hand.

'Thank God I'm not touchy!' Mrs Montgomery reflected, rolling her eyes lazily about the little white wainscoted room.

It was as if something of her native land had crept in through the doorway with her, so successfully had she inculcated its tendencies, or spiritual Ideals, upon everything around.

A solitary teapot, on a bracket, above the door, two *Jubilee* plates, some peacock's feathers, an image of a little Fisher-boy in bathing-drawers and a broken hand; – 'a work of delicate beauty!' A mezzotint: *The Coiffing of Maria* – these were some of the treasures which the room contained.

'A blessing to be sure when the Court has gone!' she reflected half-rising to drop a curtsy to Prince Olaf who had entered.

'Word from your country,' sententiously he broke out: 'My brother's betrothed! So need I go on with my preparation?'

'Put your tie straight! And just look at your socks all tumbling down. Such great jambons of knees! . . . What will become of you, I ask myself, when you're a lower boy at Eton.'

'How can I be a lower boy when I'm a Prince?'

'Probably, the Rev. Ruggles-White, when you enter his House, will be able to explain.'

'I won't be a lower boy! I will *not*!'

'Cs, Cs.'

'Damn the democracy.'

'Fie, sir.'

'Down with it.'

'For shame.'

'Revenge.'

'That will do: and now, let me hear your lessons: I should like,' Mrs Montgomery murmured, her eyes set in detachment upon the floor; 'the present-indicative tense of the Verb *To be*! Adding the words, Political h-Hostess; – more for the sake of the pronunciation than for anything else!'

And after considerable persuasion, prompting, and 'bribing', with various sorts of sweets:

> 'I am a Political Hostess,
> Thou art a Political Hostess,
> He is a Political Hostess,
> We are Political Hostesses,
> Ye are Political Hostesses,
> They are Political Hostesses.'

'Very good, dear, and only one mistake. *He* is a Political h-Hostess: Can you correct yourself? The error is so slight . . .'

But alas the Prince was in no mood for study; and Mrs Montgomery very soon afterwards was obliged to let him go.

Moving a little anxiously about the room, her meditations turned upon the future.

With the advent of Elsie a new régime would be established: increasing Britishers would wish to visit Pisuerga; and it seemed a propitious moment to abandon teaching, and to inaugurate in Kairoulla an English hotel.

'I have no more rooms. I am quite full up!' she smiled, addressing the silver andirons in the grate.

And what a deliverance to have done with instructing unruly children, she reflected going towards the glass mail-box attached to her vestibule door. Sometimes about this hour there would be a letter in it, but this evening there was only a picture postcard of a field mouse in a bonnet, from her old friend Mrs Bedley.

'We have *Valmouth* at last,' she read, 'and was it you, my dear, who asked for *The Beard Throughout the Ages*? It is in much demand, but I am keeping it back anticipating a *reply*. Several of the plates are missing I see, among them, those of the late King Edward, and of Assur Bani Pal; I only mention it, that you may know I shan't blame you! We are having wonderful weather, and I am keeping pretty well, although poor Mrs Barleymoon, I fear, will not see through another winter. Trusting you are benefiting by the beautiful country air: your obedient servant to command, ANN BEDLEY.

'P.S. – *Man, and All About Him*, is rebinding. Ready I expect soon.'

'Ah! Cunnie, Cunnie . . . ?' Mrs Montgomery murmured, laying the card down near a photograph of the Court-physician with a sigh: 'Ah! Arthur Amos Cuncliffe Babcock . . . ?' she invoked his name dulcetly in full: and as though in telepathic response, there came a tap at the door, and the doctor himself looked in.

He had been attending, it seemed, the young wife of the Comptroller of the Household at the extremity of the corridor; a creature, who, after two brief weeks of marriage, imagined herself to be in an interesting state: '*I believe baby's coming!*' she would cry out every few hours.

'Do I intrude?' he demanded, in his forceful, virile voice, that ladies knew and liked: 'pray say so if I do.'

'Does he intrude!' Mrs Montgomery flashed an arch glance towards the cornice.

'Well, and how are you keeping?' the doctor asked, dropping on to a rep causeuse that stood before the fire.

'I'm only semi-well, doctor, thanks!'

'Why, what's the trouble?'

'You know my organism is not a very strong one, Dr Cuncliffe . . .'

Mrs Montgomery replied, drawing up a chair, and settling a cushion with a sign of resignation at her back.

'Imagination!'

'If only it were!'

'Imagination!' he repeated, fixing a steady eye on the short train of her black brocaded robe that all but brushed his feet.

'If that's your explanation for continuous broken sleep . . .' she gently snapped.

'Try mescal.'

'I'm trying Dr Fritz Millar's treatment' the lady stated, desiring to deal a slight *scratch* to his masculine *amour propre*.

'Millar's an Ass.'

'I don't agree at all!' she incisively returned, smiling covertly at his touch of pique.

'What is it?'

'Oh it's horrid. You first of all lie down; and then you drink cold water in the sun.'

'Cold what? I never *heard* of such a thing: It's enough to kill you.'

Mrs Montgomery took a deep-drawn breath of languor.

'And would you care, doctor, so *very* much if it did?' she asked, as a page made his appearance with an ice-bucket and champagne.

'To toast our young Princess!'

'Oh, oh, Dr Cuncliffe? What a wicked man you are.' And for a solemn moment their thoughts went out in unison to the sea-girt land of their birth – Barker's, Selfridge's, Brighton-pier, the Zoological gardens on a Sunday afternoon.

'Here's to the good old country!' the doctor quaffed.

'The Bride, and,' Mrs Montgomery raised her glass, 'the Old Folks at h-home.'

'The Old Folks at home!' he vaguely echoed.

'Bollinger, you naughty man,' the lady murmured, amiably seating herself on the causeuse at his side.

'You'll find it dull here all alone after the Court has gone,' he observed, smiling down, a little despotically, on to her bright, abundant hair.

Mrs Montgomery sipped her wine.

'When the wind goes whistling up and down under the colonnades: oh, then!' she shivered.

'You'll wish for a fine, bold Pisuergian husband; shan't you?' he answered, his foot drawing closer to hers.

'Often of an evening, I feel I need fostering,' she owned, glancing up yearningly into his face.

'Fostering, eh?' he chuckled, refilling with exuberance her glass.

'Why is it that wine always makes me feel *so good*?'

'Probably, because it fills you with affection for your neighbour!'

'It's true; I feel I could be very affectionate: I'm what they call an "amoureuse" I suppose, and there it is . . .'

There fell a busy silence between them.

'It's almost too warm for a fire,' she murmured, repairing towards the window; 'but I like to hear the crackle!'

'Company, eh?' he returned, following her (a trifle unsteadily) across the room.

'The night is so clear the moon looks to be almost transparent,' she languorously observed, with a long tugging sigh.

'And so it does,' he absently agreed.

'I adore the Pigeons in my wee court towards night, when they sink down like living sapphires upon the stones,' she sentimentally said, sighing languorously again.

'Ours,' he assured her; 'since the surgery looks on to it, too . . .'

'Did you ever see anything so ducky-wucky, so completely twee!' she inconsequently chirruped.

'Allow me to fill this empty glass.'

'I want to go out on all that gold floating water!' she murmured listlessly, pointing towards the lake.

'Alone?'

'Drive me towards the sweet seaside,' she begged, taking appealingly his hand.

'Aggie?'

'Arthur – Arthur, for God's sake!' she shrilled, as with something between a snarl and a roar, he impulsively whipped out the light.

'H-Help! Oh Arth —'

Thus did they celebrate the 'Royal engagement'.

# XIII

Behind the heavy moucharabi in the little dark shop of Haboubet of Egypt all was song, *fête* and preparation. Additional work had brought additional hands, and be-tarbouched boys in burnooses, and baskets of blossoms, lay strewn all over the floor.

'Sweet is the musk-rose of the Land of Punt!
Sweet are the dates from Khorassân . . .
But bring *me* (O wandering Djinns) the English rose, the
English apple!
O sweet is the land of the Princess Elsie,
Sweet indeed is England —'

Bachir's voice soared, in improvisation, to a long-drawn, strident, wail.

'Pass me the scissors, O Bachir ben Ahmed, for the love of Allah,' a young man with large lucent eyes, and an untroubled face, like a flower, exclaimed, extending a slender, keef-stained hand.

'Sidi took them,' the superintendent of the Duchess of Varna replied, turning towards an olive-skinned Armenian youth, who, seated on an empty hamper, was reading to a small, rapt group, the *Kairoulla Intelligence* aloud.

'"Attended by Lady Canon-of-Noon and by Lady Bertha Chamberlayne (she is a daughter of Lord Frollo's[1]) the Princess was seen to alight from her saloon, in a *chic* toque of primrose paille, stabbed

1 Although the account of Princess Elsie's arrival in Kairoulla is signed 'Green Jersey', it seems not unlikely that 'Eva Schnerb' herself was the reporter of this eventful occasion.

with the quill of a nasturtium-coloured bird, and, darting forward, like the Bird of Paradise that she *is*, embraced her future Parents-in-law with considerable affection . . .'"'

'Scissors, for the love of Allah!'

"'And soon I heard the roll of drums! And saw the bobbing plumes in the jangling browbands of the horses: it was a moment I shall never forget. She passed . . . and as our Future Sovereign turned smiling to bow her acknowledgments to the crowd, I saw a happy tear . . . !'"

'Ah Allah.'

'Pass me two purple pinks.'

"'Visibly gratified at the cordial ovation to her Virgin Daughter was Queen Glory, a striking and impressive figure, all a-glitter in a splendid dark dress of nacre and nigger tissue, her many Orders of Merit almost bearing her down.'"

'Thy scissors, O Sidi, for the love of Muhammad?'

"'It seemed as if Kairoulla had gone wild with joy. Led by the first Life-Guards and a corps of ladies of great fashion disguised as peasants, the cortège proceeded amid the whole-hearted plaudits of the people towards Constitutional Square, where, with the sweetest of smiles and thanks the princess received an exquisite sheaf of Deflas (they are the hybrids of slipper-orchids crossed with maidens-rue, and are all the mode at present), tendered her by little Paula Exelmans, the Lord Mayor's tiny daughter. Driving on, amid showers of confetti, the procession passed up the Chaussée, which presented a scene of rare animation; boys, and even quite elderly dames swarming up the trees, to obtain a better view of their new Princess. But it was not until Lilianthal Street and the Cathedral Square were reached, that the climax reached its height! Here, a short standstill was called, and after an appropriate address from the Archbishop of Pisuerga, the stirring strains of the National Anthem, superbly rendered by Madame Marguerite Astorra of the State Theatre (she is in perfect voice this season), arose on the air. At that moment a black cat and its kitties rushed across the road, and I saw the Princess smile.'"

'Thy scissors, O Sidi, in the Name of the Prophet!'

"'A touching incident,'" Sidi with equanimity pursued, "'was just before the English Tea Rooms, where the English Colony had mustered together in force . . .'"

But alack for those interested. Owing to the clamour about him much of the recital was lost: "'Cheers and tears . . . Life's benison . . . Honiton lace . . . If I live to be *forty*, it was a moment I shall never forget . . . Panic . . . congestion . . . Police.'"

But it was scarcely needful to peruse the paper, when on the boulevards outside, the festivities were everywhere in full swing. The arrival of the princess for her wedding had brought to Kairoulla unprecedented crowds from all parts of the kingdom, as much eager to see the princess, as to catch a glimpse of the fine pack of beagles, that it was said had been brought over with her, and which had taken an half eerie hold of the public mind. Gilderoy, Beausire, Audrey, many of the dogs' names were known pleasantly to the crowd already; and anecdotes of Audrey, picture-postcards of Audrey, were sold as rapidly almost as those even of the princess. Indeed mothers among the people had begun to threaten their disobedient offspring with Audrey, whose silky, thickset frame was supported, it appears, daily on troublesome little boys and tiresome little girls . . .

'Erri, erri, get on with thy bouquet, oh Lazari Demitraki!' Bachir exclaimed in plaintive tones, addressing a blonde boy with a skin of amber, who was 'charming' an earwig with a reed of grass.

'She dance the *Boussadilla* just like in the street of Halfaouine in Gardaïa my town any Ouled Nail!' he rapturously gurgled.

'Get on with thy work, oh Lazari Demitraki,' Bachir besought him, 'and leave the earwigs alone for the clients to find.'

'What with the heat, the smell of the flowers, the noise of you boys, and with filthy earwigs Boussadillaing all over one, I feel I could I could *swoon*,' the voice, cracked yet cloying, was Peter Passer's.

He had come to Kairoulla for the 'celebrations', and also, perhaps, aspiring to advance his fortunes, in ways known best to himself. With Bachir, his connection dated from long ago, when as a Cathedral choir-boy it had been his habit to pin a shoulder, or bosom-blossom to his surplice, destroying it with coquettish, ring-laden fingers in the course of an anthem, and scattering the petals from the choir-loft leaf by leaf, on to the grey heads of the monsignori below.

'Itchiata wa?' Bachir grumbled, playing his eyes distractedly around the shop. And it might have been better for the numerous orders there were to attend to had he called fewer of his acquaintance to assist him. Sunk in torpor, a cigarette smouldering at his ear, a Levantine Greek known as 'Effendi darling' was listening to a dark-cheeked Tunisian engaged at the Count of Tolga's private Hammam Baths – a young man, who, as he spoke, would make mazy gestures of the hands as though his master's ribs, or those of some illustrious guest, lay under him. But by no means all of those assembled in the little shop, bore the seal of Islam. An American who had grown too splendid for the copper 'Ganymede' or Soda-fountain of a Café bar and had taken to teaching the hectic dance-steps of his native land in the night-halls where Bachir sold, was achieving wonders with some wires and Eucharist lilies, while discussing with a shy-mannered youth the many difficulties that beset the foreigner in Kairoulla.

'Young chaps that come out here, don't know what they're coming to,' he sapiently remarked, using his incomparable teeth in place of scissors. 'Gosh! Talk of advancement,' he growled.

'There's few can mix as I can, yet I don't never get no rise!' the shy youth exclaimed, producing a card that was engraved: *Harry Cummings, Salad-Dresser to the King*: 'I expect I've arrived,' he murmured, turning to hide a modest blush towards a pale young man who looked on life through heavy horn glasses.

'Salad dressing? I'd sooner it was hair! You do get tips there anyway,' the Yankee reasoned.

'I wish *I* were – arrived,' the young man with the glasses, by name Guy Thin, declared. He had come out but recently from England to establish a 'British Grocery', and was the owner of what is sometimes called an expensive voice, his sedulously clear articulation missing out no syllable or letter of anything he might happen to be saying, as though he were tasting each word, like the Pure tea, or the Pure marmalade, or any other of the so very Pure goods he proposed so exclusively to sell.

'If Allah wish it then you arrive,' Lazari Demitraki assured him with a dazzling smile, catching his hand in order to construe the lines.

'Finish thy bouquet, O Lazari Demitraki,' Bachir faintly moaned.

'It is finished – arranged: it with Abou!' he announced, pointing to an aged negro with haunted sin-sick eyes who appeared to be making strange grimaces at the wall. A straw hat of splendid dimensions was on his head, flaunting bravely the insignia of the Firm.

But the old man seemed resolved to run no more errands:

'Nsa, nsa,' he mumbled: 'Me walk enough for one day! Me no go out any more. Old Abou too tired to take another single step! As soon would me cross the street again dis night as the Sahara! . . .'

And it was only after the promise of a small gift of Opium that he consented to leave a débutante's bouquet at the Théâtre Diana.[1]

'In future,' Bachir rose remarking, 'I only employ the women; I keep only girls,' he repeated, for the benefit of 'Effendi darling' who appeared to be attaining Nirvâna.

'And next I suppose you keep a Harem?' 'Effendi darling' somnolently returned.

Most of the city shops had closed their shutters for the day, when Bachir shouldering a pannier bright with blooms, stepped with his companions forth into the street.

Along the Boulevards thousands were pressing towards the Regina Gardens to view the Fireworks, all agog to witness the pack of beagles wrought in brilliant lights due to course a stag across the sky, and which would change, if newspaper reports might be believed, at the critical moment, into '"something of the nature of a surprise".'

Pausing before a plate-glass window that adjoined the shop to adjust the flowing folds of his gandourah, and to hoist his flower tray to his small scornful head, Bachir allowed his auxiliaries to drift, mostly two by two, away among the crowd. Only the royal salad-dresser, Harry Cummings, expressed a demure inclination (when the pushing young grocer caressed his arm), to 'be alone'; but Guy Thin, who had private designs upon him, was loath to hear

1 The Théâtre Diana; a Music Hall dedicated to Spanish Zarzuelas and Operettes. It enjoyed a somewhat doubtful reputation.

of it! He wished to persuade him to buy a bottle of Vinegar from his Store, when he would print on his paper-bags *As supplied to his Majesty the King*.

'Grant us, O Allah, each good Fortunes,' Bachir beseeched, looking up through his eyelashes towards the moon, that drooped like a silver amulet in the firmament above: in the blue nocturnal air he looked like a purple poppy. 'A toute à l'heure mes amis!' he murmured as he moved away.

And in the little closed shop behind the heavy moucharabi, now that they all had gone, the exhalations of the *flowers* arose; pungent, concerted odours, expressive of natural antipathies and feuds, suave alliances, suffering, pride, and joy . . . Only the shining moon through the moucharabi, illumining here a lily, there a leaf, may have guessed what they were saying:

'My wires are hurting me: my wires are hurting me.'

'I have no water. I cannot reach the water.'

'They have pushed me head down into the bottom of the bowl.'

'I'm glad I'm in a Basket! No one will hurl *me* from a window to be bruised under foot by the callous crowd.'

'It's uncomfy, isn't it, without one's roots?'

'You Weed you! You, you, you . . . *buttercup*! How dare you to *an Orchid*!'

'I shouldn't object to sharing the same water with him, dear . . . Ordinary as he is! If *only* he wouldn't smell . . .'

'She's nothing but a piece of common grass and so I tell her!'

When upon the tense pent atmosphere surged a breath of cooler air, and through the street-door slipped the Duchess of Varna.

Overturning a jar of great heavy-headed Gladioli with a crash, she sailed, with a purposeful step, towards the till.

Garbed in black and sleepy citrons, she seemed, indeed, to be equipped for a long, long Voyage, and was clutching, in her arms, a pet Poodle dog, and a levant-covered case, in which, doubtless, reposed her jewels.

Since her rupture with Madame Wetme (both the King and Queen had refused to receive her), the money *ennuis* of the Duchess had become increasingly acute. Tormented by tradespeople, dunned and bullied by creditors, menaced, mortified, insulted – an offer to 'star' in the *rôle* of *A Society Thief* for the cinematograph had particularly shocked her – the inevitable hour to quit the Court so long foreseen had come. And now with her departure definitely determined upon, the Duchess experienced an insouciance of heart unknown to her assuredly for many a year. Replenishing her reticule with quite a welcome sheaf of the elegant little banknotes of Pisuerga, one thing only remained to do, and taking pen and paper, she addressed to the Editor of the *Intelligence* the supreme announcement: – '*The Duchess of Varna has left for Dateland.*'

Eight light words! But enough to set *tout* Kairoulla in a rustle.

'I only so regret I didn't go sooner,' she murmured to herself aloud, breaking herself a rose to match her gown from an arrangement in the window.

Many of the flowers had been newly christened, 'Elsie', 'Audrey', 'London-Madonnas' (black Arums these), while the Roses from the 'Land of Punt' had been renamed 'Mrs Lloyd George' – and priced accordingly. A basket of Odontoglossums eked out with Gypsophila seemed to anticipate the end, when supplies from Punt must necessarily cease. However, bright boys, like Bachir, seldom lacked patrons, and the duchess recalled glimpsing him one evening from her private sitting-room at the Ritz Hotel, seated on a garden bench in the Regina Gardens beside the Prime Minister himself; both, to all seeming, on the most cordial terms, and to have reached a perfect understanding as regards the Eastern Question. Ah, the Eastern Question! It was said that, in the Land of Dates, one might study it well. In Djezira, the chief town, beneath the great golden sun, people, they said, might grow wise. In the simoon that scatters the silver sand, in the words of the nomads, in the fairy mornings beneath the palms, society with its foolish *cliché* . . . the duchess smiled.

'But for that poisonous woman, I should have gone last year,' she told herself, interrupted in her cogitations by the appearance of her maid.

'The train your Grace we shall miss it . . .'

'Nonsense!' the duchess answered following, leaving the flowers alone again to their subtle exhalations.

'I'm glad *I'm* in a Basket!'
'I have no water. I cannot reach the water.'
'Life's bound to be uncertain when you haven't got your roots!'

# XIV

On a long-chair with tired, closed eyes lay the Queen. Although spared from henceforth the anxiety of her son's morganatic marriage, yet, now that his destiny was sealed, she could not help feeling perhaps he might have done better. The bride's lineage was nothing to boast of – over her great-great-grandparents, indeed, in the year 17– it were gentler to draw a veil – while, for the rest, disingenuous, undistinguished, more at home in the stables than in a drawing-room, the Queen much feared that she and her future daughter-in-law would scarcely get on.

Yes, the little Princess was none too engaging, she reflected, and her poor sacrificed child if not actually trapped . . .

The silken swish of a fan, breaking the silence, induced the Queen to look up.

In waiting at present was the Countess Olivia d'Omptyda, a person of both excellent principles and birth, if lacking, somewhat, in social boldness. Whenever she entered the royal presence she would begin visibly to tremble, which considerably flattered the Queen. Her Father, Count 'Freddie' d'Omptyda, an infantile and charming old man, appointed in a moment of unusual vagary Pisuergan Ambassador to the Court of St James, had lately married a child wife scarcely turned thirteen, whose frivolity, and numerous pranks on the high dames of London, were already the scandal of the *Corps Diplomatique*.

'Sssh! Noise is the last vulgarity,' the Queen commented, raising a cushion embroidered with raging lions and white uncanny unicorns higher behind her head.

Unstrung from the numerous *fêtes*, she had retired to a distant boudoir to relax, and, having partly disrobed, was feeling remotely

Venus of Miloey with her arms half-hidden in a plain white cape.

The Countess d'Omptyda furled her fan.

'In this Age of push and shriek . . .' she said and sighed.

'It seems that neither King Geo, nor Queen Glory, *ever* lie down of a day!' her Dreaminess declared.

'Since his last appointment, neither does Papa.'

'The affair of your step-mother and Lady Diana Duff Semour,' the Queen remarked, 'appears to be assuming the proportions of an Incident!'

The Countess dismally smiled. The subject of her step-mother, mistaken, frequently for her grand-daughter, was a painful one: 'I hear she's like a colt broke loose!' she murmured, dropping her eyes fearfully to her costume.

She was wearing an apron of Parma-violets, and the Order of the Holy Ghost.

'It's a little a pity she can't be more sensible,' the Queen returned, fingering listlessly some papers at her side. Among them was the *Archaeological Society*'s initial report relating to the recent finds among the Ruins of Sodom and Gomorrah. From Chedorlahomor came the good news that an *amphora* had been found, from which it seemed that men, in those days, rode sideways, and women straddle-legs, with their heads to the horses' tails, while a dainty cup, ravished from a rock-tomb in the Vale of Akko, ornamented with naked boys and goblets of flowers, encouraged a yet more extensive research.

'You may advance, Countess, with the Archaeōlogists' report,' the Queen commanded. 'Omitting (skipping, I say) the death of the son of Lord Intriguer.'[1]

'It was in the Vale of Akko, about two miles from Sââda,' the Countess tremblingly began, 'that we laid bare a superb tear-bottle, a unique specimen in *grisaille*, severely adorned with a matron's head. From the inscription, there can be no doubt whatever that we have here an authentic portrait of Lot's disobedient, though

1 The Hon. 'Eddy' Monteith had succumbed: the shock received by meeting a jackal while composing a sonnet had been too much for him. His tomb is in the Vale of Akko, beside the River Dis. Alas, for the *triste* obscurity of his end!

unfortunate wife. Ample and statuesque (as the salten image she was afterwards to become), the shawl-draped, masklike features are by no means beautiful. It is a face that you may often see today, in downtown "Dancings", or in the bars of the dockyards, or wharfs, of our own modern cities, Tilbury, 'Frisco, Vera Cruz – a sodden, gin-soaked face, that helps to vindicate, if not, perhaps, excuse, the conduct of Lot . . . With this highly interesting example of the Potters' Art, was found a novel object, of an unknown nature, likely to arouse, in scientific circles, considerable controversy . . .'

And just as the lectrice was growing hesitant, and embarrassed, the Countess of Tolga, who had the *entrée*, unobtrusively entered the room.

She was looking particularly well in one of the new standing-out skirts ruched with rosebuds, and was showing more of her stockings than she usually did.

'You bring the sun with you!' the Queen graciously exclaimed.

'Indeed,' the Countess answered, 'I ought to apologise for the interruption, but the *poor little thing* is leaving now.'

'What? has the Abbess come?'

'She has sent Sister Irene of the Incarnation, instead . . .'

'I had forgotten it was today.'

With an innate aversion for all farewells, yet the Queen was accustomed to perform a score of irksome acts daily that she cordially disliked, and when, shortly afterwards, Mademoiselle de Nazianzi accompanied by a Sister from the Flaming-Hood were announced, they found her quite prepared.

Touched, and reassured at the ex-maid's appearance, the Queen judged, at last, it was safe to unbend. Already very remote and unworldly in her novice's dress, she had ceased, indeed, to be a being there was need any more to either circumvent, humour, or suppress; and now that the threatened danger was gone, her Majesty glanced, half-lachrymosely, about among her personal belongings for some slight token of 'esteem' or *souvenir*. Skimming from cabinet to cabinet, in a sort of hectic dance, she began to fear, as she passed her bibelots in review, that beyond a Chinese Buddha that she believed to be ill-omened, and which for a nun seemed hardly suitable, she could spare nothing about her after all, and in some dilemma, she raised her eyes, as though for a crucifix, towards the wall. Above the long-chair a sombre study of a strangled negress in a ditch by Gauguin conjured up today with poignant force a vivid vision of the Tropics.

'The poor Duchess!' she involuntarily sighed, going off into a train of speculation of her own.

Too tongue-tied, or, perhaps, too discreet, to inform the Queen that anything she might select would immediately be confiscated by the Abbess, Sister Irene, while professing her rosary, appraised her surroundings with furtive eyes, crossing herself frequently with a speed, and facility due to practice whenever her glance chanced to alight on some nude shape in stone. Keen, meagre, and perhaps slightly malicious, hers was a curiously pinched face – like a cold violet.

'The Abbess is still in retreat; but sends her duty,' she ventured as the Queen approached a guéridon near which she was standing.

'Indeed? How I envy her,' the Queen wistfully said, selecting, as suited to the requirements of the occasion, a little volume of a mystic trend, the *Cries of Love* of Father Surin,[1] bound in grey velvet, which she pressed upon the reluctant novice, with a brief, but cordial, kiss of farewell.

'She looked quite pretty!' she exclaimed, sinking to the long-chair as soon as the nun had gone.

'So like the Cimabue in the long corridor . . .' the Countess of Tolga murmured chillily. It was her present policy that her adored ally, Olga Blumenghast, should benefit by Mademoiselle de Nazianzi's retirement from Court, by becoming nearer to the Queen, when they would work all the wires between them.

'I'd have willingly followed her,' the Queen weariedly declared, 'at any rate, until after the wedding.'

'It seems that I and Lord Derbyfield are to share the same closed carriage in the wake of the bridal coach,' the Countess of Tolga said, considering with a supercilious air her rose *suède* slipper on the dark carpet.

1 Author of *In the Dusk of the Dawn*.

'He's like some great Bull. What do you suppose he talks about?'

The Countess d'Omptyda repressed a giggle.

'They tell me Don Juan was nothing – *nothing* to him . . . He cannot see, he cannot be, oh every hour. It seems he can't help it, and that he simply *has* to!'

'Fortunately Lady Lavinia Lee-Strange will be in the landau as well!'

The Queen laid her cheek to her hands.

'I all but died, dear Violet,' she crooned, 'listening to an account of her Ancestor, who fell fighting Scotland, at the battle of Pinkie Cleugh.'

'These well-bred, but detestably insular women, how they bore one.'

'They are not to be appraised by any ordinary standards. Crossing the state saloon while coming here what should I see, ma'am, but Lady Canon of Noon on her hands and knees (all fours!) peeping below the loose-covers of the chairs in order to examine the Gobelins-tapestries beneath . . .'

'Oh —'

'"Absolutely authentic" I said! as I passed on, leaving her looking like a pickpocket caught in the act.'

'I suppose she was told to make a quiet survey . . .'

'Like their beagles and deer-hounds, that their Landseer so loved to paint, I fear the British character is, at bottom, *nothing* if not rapacious!'

'It's said, I believe, to behold the Englishman at his *best*, one should watch him play at tip-and-run.'

'You mean of course at cricket?'

The Queen looked doubtful: She had retained of a cricket-match at Lord's a memory of hatless giants waving wooden sticks.

'I only wish it could have been a long engagement,' she abstrusely murmured, fastening her attention on the fountains whitely spurting in the gardens below.

Valets in cotton-jackets and light blue aprons bearing baskets of crockery and *argenterie*, were making ready beneath the tall Tuba trees, a supper *buffet* for the evening's Ball.

'Flap your wings, little bird
O flap your wings —'

A lad's fresh voice, sweet as a robin's, came piping up.

'These wretched workpeople —! There's not a peaceful corner,' the Queen complained as her husband's shape appeared at the door. He was followed by his first secretary – a simple commoner, yet, with the air, and manner, peculiar to the husband of a Countess.

'Yes, Willie? I've a hundred headaches. What is it?'

'Both King Geo and Queen Glory, are wondering where you are.'

'Oh, really, Willie?'

'And dear Elsie's asking after you too.'

'Very likely,' the Queen returned with quiet complaisance, 'but unfortunately, I have neither her energy, or,' she murmured with a slightly sardonic laugh, 'her appetite!'

The Countess of Tolga tittered.

'She called for fried-eggs and butcher's-meat, this morning, about the quarter before eight,' she averred.

'An excellent augury for our dynasty,' the King declared, reposing the eyes of an adoring grandparent upon an alabaster head of a boy attributed to Donatello.

'She's terribly foreign, Willie . . . ! Imagine ham and eggs . . .' the Queen dropped her face to her hand.

'So long as the Royal-House —' The King broke off, turning gallantly to raise the Countess d'Omptyda, who had sunk to the floor with a gesture of exquisite allegiance.

'Sir . . . Sir!' she faltered in confusion, seeking with fervent lips her Sovereign's hand.

'What is she doing, Willie?'

'Begging for Strawberry-leaves!' the Countess of Tolga brilliantly commented.

'Apropos of Honours . . . it appears King Geo has signified his intention of raising his present representative in Pisuerga to the peerage.'

'After her recent *Cause*, Lady Something should be not a little consoled.'

'She was at the début of the new diva, little Miss Hellvellyn (the foreign invasion has indeed begun!), at the Opera-House last night, so radiant . . .'

'When she cranes forward out of her own box to smile at someone into the next, I can't explain . . . but one feels she ought to hatch,' the Queen murmured, repairing capriciously from one couch to another.

'We neglect our guests, my dear,' the King expostulatingly exclaimed, bending over his consort anxiously from behind.

'Tell me, Willie,' she cooed, caressing the medals upon his breast, and drawing him gently down: 'tell me? Didst thou enjoy thy cigar, dear, with King Geo?'

'I can recall in my time, Child, a suaver flavour . . .'

'Thy little chat, though, dearest, was well enough?'

'I would not call him crafty, but I should say he was a man of considerable subtlety . . .' the King evasively replied.

'One does not need, my dearest nectarine, a prodigy of intelligence however to take him in!'

'Before the proposed Loan, love, can be brought about, he may wish to question thee as to thy political opinions.'

The Queen gave a little light laugh.

'No one knows what my political opinions are; I don't myself!'

'And I'm quite confident of it: But, indeed, my dear, we neglect our functions.'

'I only wish it could have been a *long* engagement, Willie . . .'

## *XV*

In the cloister eaves, the birds were just awakening, and all the spider scales, in the gargoyled gables, glanced fresh with dew. Above the Pietà, on the porter's gate, slow-speeding clouds, like knots of pink roses, came blowing across the sky, sailing away in titanic bouquets towards the clear horizon. All virginal in the early sunrise what enchantment the world possessed! The rhythmic sway-sway of the trees, the exhalations of the flowers, the ethereal candour of this early hour, – these raised the heart up to their Creator.

Kneeling at the casement of a postulant's cell, Laura de Nazianzi recalled that scene, and just thus had she often planned must dawn her bridal day!

Beyond the cruciform flower-beds, and the cloister wall, soared the Blue Jesus, the storied windows of its lofty galleries aglow with light.

'Most gracious Jesus. Help me to forget. For my heart aches. Uphold me now.'

But to forget today, was well-nigh she knew impossible . . .

Once it seemed she caught the sound of splendid music from the direction of the Park, but it was too early for music yet. Away in the palace, the Princess Elsie must be already astir . . . in her peignoir, perhaps? The bridal-garment unfolded upon the bed: But no; it was said the bed indeed was where usually her Royal-Highness' dogs . . .

With a long and very involuntary sigh, she began to sweep, and put in some order, her room.

How forlorn her cornette looked upon her *prie-Dieu*! And, oh, how stern, and 'old'!

Would an impulse to bend it slightly but only so, *so* slightly, to an angle to suit her face, be attended, later, by remorse?

'Confiteor Deo omnipotenti, beatae Mariae semper vergini, beato Michaeli Archangelo (et *tibi* Pater), quia peccavi nimis cogitatione, verbo et opere,' she entreated, reposing her chin in meditation, upon the handle of her broom.

The bluish shadow of a cypress-tree, on the empty wall, fascinated her as few pictures had.

'Grant my soul Eyes,' she prayed, cheerfully completing her task.

In the corridor, being a general holiday, all was yet quite still. A sound, as of gentle snoring, came indeed from behind more than one closed door, and the new *pensionnaire* was preparing to beat a retreat, when she perceived, in the cloister, the dumpish form of Old Jane.

Seated in the sun by the convent well, the Porteress was sharing a scrap of breakfast with the birds.

'You're soonish for Mass, love,' she broke out, her large archaic features surcharged with smiles.

'It's such a perfect morning, I felt I must come down.'

'I've seen many a more promising sunrise before now, my dear, turn to storm and blast! An orange sky overhead, brings back to me the morning that I was received; ah, I shall never forget, as I was taking my Vows, a flash of forked lightning, and a clap of Thunder (Glory be to God!) followed by a water-spout (Mercy save us!) bursting all over my Frinch lace veil . . .'

'What is your book, Old Jane?'

'Something light, love, as it's a holiday.'

'*Pascal* . . .'

'Though it's mostly a *Fête* day I've extra to do!' the Porteress averred, dropping her eyes to the great, glistening spits, upon the Cloister flags. It was her boast she could distinguish Monsignor Potts' round splash from Father Geordie Picpus' more dapper fine one, and again the Abbess' from Mother Martinez de la Rosa's – although these indeed shared a certain opaque sameness.

'Of course it's a day for private visits.'

'Since the affair of Sister Dorothea and Brother Bernard Soult, private visits are no longer allowed,' the Porteress returned, reproving modestly, with the cord of her discipline, a pert little lizard, that seemed to be proposing to penetrate between the nude toes of her sandalled foot.

But on such a radiant morning it was preposterous to hint at 'Rules'.

Beneath the clement sun a thousand cicadas were insouciantly chirping, while birds, skimming about without thoughts of money, floated lightly from tree to tree.

'Jesus – Mary – Joseph!' the Porteress purred, as a Nun, with her face all muffled up in wool, crossed the Cloister, glancing neither to right nor left, and sharply slammed a door: for, already, the Convent was beginning to give signs of animation. Deep in a book of Our Lady's Hours, a biretta'd priest was slowly rounding a garden path, while repairing from a *Grotto-sepulchre*, to which was attached a handsome indulgence, Mother Martinez de la Rosa appeared, all heavily leaning on her stick.

Simultaneously the matins bell rang out, calling all to prayer.

The Convent Chapel founded by the tender enthusiasm of a wealthy widow, the Countess d'Acunha, to perpetuate her earthly comradeship with the beautiful Andalusian, the Doña Dolores Baatz, was still but thinly peopled some few minutes later, although the warning bell had stopped.

Peering around, Laura was disappointed not to remark Sister Ursula in her habitual place, between the veiled fresco of the 'Circumcision' and the stoup of holy-water by the door.

Beyond an offer to 'exchange whippings' there had been a certain coolness in the greeting with her friend, that had both surprised and pained her.

'When those we rely on wound and betray us, to whom should we turn but Thee?' she breathed, addressing a crucifix, in ivory, contrived by love, that was a miracle of wonder.

Finished Mass, there was a general rush for the Refectory!

Preceded by Sister Clothilde, and followed, helter-skelter, by an exuberant bevy of nuns, even Mother Martinez, who being short-sighted would go feeling the ground with her cane, was propelled to the measure of a hop-and-skip.

Passing beneath an archway, labelled 'Silence' (the injunction today being undoubtedly ignored), the company was welcomed by the mingled odours of tea, *consommé*, and fruit. It was a custom of the Convent for one of the Sisters during meal-time to read aloud from some standard work of fideism, and these edifying recitations, interspersed by such whispered questions as: 'Tea, or *Consommé*?' 'A Banana, or a Pomegranate?' gave to those at all foolishly, or hysterically inclined, a painful desire to giggle. Mounting the pulpit-lectern, a nun with an aristocratic, though gourmand little face, was about to resume the arid life of the Byzantine monk, Basilius Saturninus, when Mother Martinez de la Rosa took it upon herself, in a few patriotic words, to relax all rules for that day.

'We understand in the world now,' a little faded woman murmured to Laura upon her right: 'that the latest craze among ladies is to gild their tongues; but I should be afraid,' she added diffidently, dipping her banana into her tea, 'of poison, myself!'

Unhappy at her friend's absence from the Refectory, Laura, however, was in no mood to entertain the nuns with stories of the present pagan tendencies of society.

Through the bare, blindless windows, framing a sky so bluely luminous, came the swelling clamour of the assembling crowds, tinging the languid air as with some sultry fever. From the *Chaussée*, music of an extraordinary intention – heated music, crude music, played with passionate élan to perfect time, conjured up, with vivid, heartrending prosaicness, the seething Boulevards beyond the high old creeper-covered walls.

'I forget now, Mother, which of the Queens it is that will wear a velvet train of a beautiful orchid shade. But one of them will!' Sister Irene of the Incarnation was holding forth.

'I must confess,' Mother Martinez remarked, who was peeling herself a peach, with an air of far attention: 'I must confess, I should have liked to have cast my eye upon the *lingerie* . . .'

'I would have rather seen the ballwraps, Mother, or the shoes, and evening slippers!'

'Yes, or the fabulous jewels . . .'

'Of course Sister Laura saw the *trousseau*?'

But Laura made feint not to hear.

Discipline relaxed, a number of nuns had collected provisions and were picnicking in the window, where Sister Innez (an ex-Repertoire actress) was giving some spirited renderings from her chief successful parts – *Jane de Simerose*, *Frou-Frou*, *Sappho*, *Cigarette* . . .

'My darling child! I always sleep all day and only revive when there's a *Man*,' she was saying with an impudent look, sending the scandalised Sisters into delighted convulsions.

Unable to endure it any longer, Laura crept away.

A desire for air and solitude, led her towards the Recreation ground. After the hot refectory, sauntering in the silken shade of the old astounding cedars, was delightful quite. In the deserted alleys, the golden blossoms of the censia-trees, unable to resist the sun, littered in perfumed piles the ground, overcoming her before long with a sensation akin to *vertige*. Anxious to find her friend, Laura turned towards her cell.

She found Sister Ursula leaning on her window-ledge, all crouched up – like a Duchess on 'a First Night'.

'My dear, my dear, the *crowds*!'

'Ursula?'

'Yes, what is it?'

'Perhaps I'll go, since I'm in the way.'

'Touchy Goose,' Sister Ursula murmured wheeling round with a glance of complex sweetness.

'Ah, Ursula,' Laura sighed, smiling reproachfully at her friend.

She had long almond eyes, one longer and larger than the other, that gave to her narrow, etiolated face, an exalted, mystic air. Her hair, wholly concealed by her full coif, would be inclined to rich copper or chestnut: Indeed, below the pinched and sensitive nostrils, a moustache (so slight as to be scarcely discernible) proved this beyond all controversy to be so. But perhaps the quality and beauty of her hands were her chief distinction.

'Do you believe it would cause an earthquake, if we climbed out, dear little one, upon the leads?' she asked.

'I had forgotten you overlooked the street by leaning out,' Laura answered, sinking fatigued to a little cane armchair.

'Listen, Laura . . . !'

'This cheering racks my heart . . .'

'Ah, Astaroth! There went a very "swell" carriage.'

'Perhaps I'll come back later: It's less noisy in my cell.'

'Now you're here, I shall ask you, I think, to whip me.'

'Oh, no . . .'

'Bad dear Little-One. Dear meek soul,' Sister Ursula softly laughed.

'This maddening cheering,' Laura breathed, rolling tormented eyes about her.

A crucifix, a text: *I would lay Pansies at Jesus' Feet*, two fresh eggs in a blue paper bag, some ends of string, a breviary, and a birch, were the chamber's individual, if meagre, contents.

'You used *not* to have that text, Ursula,' Laura observed, her attention arrested by the preparation of a Cinematograph Company on the parapet of the Cathedral.

The Church had much need indeed of Reformation! The Times were incredibly low: A new crusade . . . she ruminated, revolted at the sight of an old man holding dizzily to a stone-winged angel, with a wine-flask at his lips.

'Come dear, won't you assist me now to mortify my senses?' Sister Ursula cajoled.

'No, really, no –! –! –!'

'Quite lightly: For I was scourged, by Sister Agnes, but yesterday, with a heavy bunch of keys, head downwards, hanging from a bar.'

'Oh . . .'

'This morning she sent me those pullets' eggs. I perfectly was touched by her delicate sweet sympathy.'

Laura gasped.

'It must have hurt you?'

'I assure you I felt nothing – my spirit had travelled so far,' Sister Ursula replied, turning to throw an interested glance at the street.

It was close now upon the critical hour, and the plaudits of the crowd were becoming more and more uproarious, as 'favourites' in Public life, and 'celebrities' of all sorts, began to arrive in brisk succession at the allotted door of the Cathedral.

'I could almost envy the fleas in the Cardinal's vestments,' Sister Ursula declared, overcome by the venal desire to see.

Gazing at the friend upon whom she had counted in some disillusion, Laura quietly left her.

The impulse to witness something of the spectacle outside was, nevertheless, infectious, and recollecting that from the grotto-sepulchre in the garden it was not impossible to attain the convent wall, she determined, moved by some wayward instinct, to do so. Frequently, as a child, had she scaled it, to survey the doings of the city streets beyond – the streets, named by the nuns often 'Sinward-ho'. Crossing the cloisters, and through old gates crowned by vast fruit-baskets in stone, she followed, feverishly, the ivy-masked bricks of the sheltering wall, and was relieved to reach the grotto without encountering anyone. Surrounded by heavy boskage, it marked a spot where, once, long ago, one of the Sisters, it was said, had received the mystic stigmata . . . With a feline effort (her feet supported by the Grotto boulders), it needed but a bound to attain an incomparable post of vantage.

Beneath a blaze of bunting, the street seemed paved with heads. 'Madonna,' she breathed, as an official on a white horse, its mane stained black, began authoritatively backing his steed into the patient faces of the mob, startling an infant in arms below, to a frantic fit of squalls.

'Just so shall we stand on the Day of Judgment,' she reflected, blinking at the glare.

Street boys vending programmes, 'Lucky' horseshoes, Saturnalian emblems – (these for gentlemen only), offering post-cards of 'Geo and Glory', etc., wedged their way however where it might have been deemed indeed impossible for anyone to pass.

And *he*, she wondered, her eyes following the wheeling pigeons, alarmed by the recurrent salutes of the signal guns, he must be there already: Under the dome! Restive a little beneath the busy scrutiny, his tongue like the point of a blade . . .

A burst of cheering seemed to announce the Queen. But no, it was only a lady, with a parasol sewn with diamonds, that was exciting the rah-rahs of the crowd. Followed by mingled cries of 'Shame!' 'Waste!' and sighs of envy, Madame Wetme was enjoying a belated triumph. And now a brief lull, as a brake containing various delegates and 'representatives of English Culture', rolled by at a stately trot – Lady Alexander, E. V. Lucas, Robert Hichens, Clutton Brock, etc., – the ensemble the very apotheosis of worn-out *cliché*.

'There's someone there wot's got enough heron plumes on her head!' a young girl in the crowd remarked.

And nobody contradicted her.

Then troops and outriders, and at last the Queen.

She was looking charming in a Corinthian chlamyde, in a carriage lined in deep delphinium blue, behind six restive blue roan horses.

Finally, the bride and her father, bowing this way and that . . .

Cheers.

'Huzzas' –

A hushed suspense.

Below the wall the voice of a beggar arose, persistent, haunting: 'For the Love of God . . . In the Name of Pity . . . of Pity.'

'Of Pity,' she echoed, addressing a frail, wind-sown harebell, blue as the sky: And leaning upon the shattered glass ends, that crowned the wall, she fell to considering the future – Obedience, Solitude – death.

The troubling *valse* theme from *Dante in Paris* interrupted her meditations.

How often had they valsed it together, he and she . . . sometimes as a two-step . . . ! What souvenirs . . . Yousef, Yousef . . . Above the Cathedral, the crumbling clouds, had eclipsed the sun. In the intense meridian glare the thronged street seemed even as though half-hypnotised; occasionally only the angle of a parasol would change, or some bored soldier's legs would give a little. When brusquely, from the belfry, burst a triumphant clash of bells.

Laura caught her breath.

Already?

A shaking of countless handkerchiefs in wild ovation: From roof-tops, and balconies, the air was thick with falling flowers – the bridal pair!

But only for the bridegroom had she eyes.

Oblivious of what she did, she began to beat her hands, until they streamed with blood, against the broken glass ends upon the wall: 'Yousef, Yousef, Yousef . . .

*July 1921, May 1922*
*Versailles, Montreux, Florence*

# *Sorrow in Sunlight*

# *I*

Looking gloriously bored, Miss Miami Mouth gaped up into the boughs of a giant silk-cotton-tree. In the lethargic noontide nothing stirred: all was so still, indeed, that the sound of someone snoring was clearly audible among the cane-fields far away.

'After dose yams an' pods an' de white falernum, I dats way sleepy too,' she murmured, fixing heavy, somnolent, eyes upon the prospect that lay before her.

Through the sun-tinged greenery shone the sea, like a floor of silver glass strewn with white sails.

Somewhere out there, fishing, must be her boy, Bamboo!

And, inconsequently, her thoughts wandered from the numerous shark-casualties of late to the mundane proclivities of her mother; for to quit the little village of Mediavilla for the capital was that dame's fixed obsession.

Leave Mediavilla, leave Bamboo! The young negress fetched a sigh.

In what, she reflected, way would the family gain by *entering Society*, and how did one enter it, at all? There would be a gathering, doubtless, of the elect (probably armed), since the best Society is exclusive, and difficult to enter. And then? Did one burrow? Or charge? She had sometimes heard it said that people 'pushed' . . . and closing her eyes, Miss Miami Mouth sought to picture her parents, assisted by her small sister, Edna, and her brother, Charlie, forcing their way, perspiring, but triumphant, into the highest social circles of the city of Cuna-Cuna.

Across the dark savannah country the city lay, one of the chief alluring cities of the world: The Celestial city of Cuna-Cuna, Cuna, city of Mimosa, Cuna, city of Arches, Queen of the Tropics, Paradise – almost invariably travellers referred to it like that.

Oh, everything must be fantastic there, where even the very pickneys put on clothes! And Miss Miami Mouth glanced fondly down at her own plump little person, nude, but for a girdle of creepers that she would gather freshly twice a day.

'It would be a shame, sh'o, to cover it,' she murmured drowsily, caressing her body; and moved to a sudden spasm of laughter, she tittered: 'No! really. De ideah!'

## II

'Silver bean-stalks, silver bean-stalks, oh hé, oh hé,' down the long village street from door to door, the cry repeatedly came, until the vendor's voice was lost on the evening air.

In a rocking chair, before the threshold of a palm-thatched cabin, a matron with broad, bland features, and a big untidy figure, surveyed the scene with a nonchalant eye.

Beneath some tall trees, bearing flowers like flaming bells, a few staid villagers sat enjoying the rosy dusk, while, strolling towards the sea, two young men passed by with fingers intermingled.

With a slight shrug, the lady plied her fan.

As the Mother of a pair of oncoming girls, the number of ineligible young men, or confirmed *bachelors* around the neighbourhood was a constant source of irritation . . .

'Sh'o, dis remoteness bore an' weary me to death,' she exclaimed, addressing someone through the window behind; and receiving no audible answer, she presently rose, and went within.

It was the hour when, fortified by a siesta, Mrs Ahmadou Mouth was wont to approach her husband on general household affairs, and to discuss, in particular, the question of their removal to the town; for, with the celebration of their Pearl-wedding, close at hand, the opportunity to make the announcement of a change of residence to their guests, ought not, she believed, to be missed.

'We leave Mediavilla for de education ob my daughters,' she would say; or, perhaps: 'We go to Cuna-Cuna for de finishing ob *mes filles*!'

But, unfortunately, the reluctance of Mr Mouth to forsake his Home seemed to increase from day to day.

She found him asleep, bolt upright, his head gently nodding, beneath a straw-hat beautifully browned.

'Say, nigger, lub,' she murmured, brushing her hand featheringly along his knee, 'say, nigger, lub, I gotta go!'

It was the tender prelude to the storm.

Evasive (and but half-awake), he warned her. 'Let me alone; Ah'm thinkin'.'

'Prancing Nigger, now come on!'

'Ah'm thinkin'.'

'Tell me what for dis procrastination?' Exasperated, she gripped his arm.

But for all reply, Mr Mouth drew a volume of revival hymns towards him, and turned on his wife his back.

'You ought to shame o' you-self, sh'o,' she caustically commented, crossing to the window.

The wafted odours of the cotton-trees without, oppressed the air. In the deepening twilight, the rising moonmist, already obscured the street.

'Dis place not healthy. Dat damp! Should my daughters go off into a decline . . .' she apprehensively murmured, as her husband started softly to sing.

> 'For ebber wid de Lord!
> Amen; so let it be;
> Life from de dead is in dat word,
> 'Tis immortality.'

'If it's de meeting-house dats de obstruction, dair are odders, too, in Cuna-Cuna,' she observed.

'How often hab I bid you nebba to mention dat modern Sodom in de hearing ob my presence!'

'De Debil frequent de village, fo' dat matter, besides de town.'

'Sh'o nuff.'

'But yestiddy, dat po' silly negress Ottalie was seduced again in a Mango track –; an' dats de third time!'

'Heah in de body pent,
Absent from Him I roam,
Yet nightly pitch my movin' tent
A day's march nearer home.'

'Prancing Nigger, from dis indifference to your fambly, be careful lest you do arouse de vials ob de Lord's wrath!'

'Yet nightly pitch –' he was beginning again, in a more subdued key, but the tones of his wife arrested him.

'Prancing Nigger, lemme say sumptin' more!' Mrs Mouth took a long sighing breath: 'In dis dark jungle my lil jewel Edna, I feah, will wilt away . . .'

'Wh'a gib you cause to speak like dat?'

'I was tellin' my fortune lately wid de cards,' she reticently made reply, insinuating, by her half-turned eyes, that more disclosures of an ominous nature concerning others besides her daughter had been revealed to her as well.

'Lordey Lord; what is it den you want?'

'I want a Villa with a watercloset –' flinging wiles to the winds, it was a cry from the heart.

'De Lord hab pity on dese vanities an' innovations!'

'In town, you must rememba, often de houses are far away from de parks; – de city, in dat respect, not like heah.'

'Say nothin' more! De widow ob my po' brudder Willie, across de glen, she warn me I ought nebba to listen to you.'

'Who care for a common woman, dat only read de *Negro World*, an' nebba see anyt'ing else!' she swelled.

Mr Mouth turned conciliatingly.

'Tomorrow me arrange for de victuals for our ebenin' at Home!'

'Good, bery fine,' she murmured, acknowledging through the window the cordial 'good-night' of a few late labourers, returning from the fields, each with a bundle of sugar-cane poised upon the head.

'As soon as marnin' dawn me take dis bizniz in hand.'

'Only pramas, nigger darlin',' she cajoled, 'dat durin' de course of de reception you make a lil speech to inform de neighbours ob our gwine away bery soon, for de sake of de education ob our girls.'

'Ah cyan pramas nothin'.'

'I could do wid a change too, honey, after my last miscarriage.'

'Change come wid our dissolution,' he assured her, 'quite soon enuff!'

'Bah,' she murmured, rubbing her cheek to his: 'we set out on our journey sh'o in de season ob Novemba.'

To which with asperity he replied: '*Not for two Revolutions!*' and rising brusquely, strode solemnly from the room.

'Hey-ho-day,' she yawned, starting a wheezy gramophone, and sinking down upon his empty chair; and she was lost in ball-room fancies (whirling in the arms of some blonde young foreigner), when she caught sight of her daughter's reflection in the glass.

Having broken, or discarded her girdle of leaves, Miss Miami Mouth, attracted by the gramophone, appeared to be teaching a hectic two-step to the cat.

'Fie, fie, my lass. Why you be so *Indian*?' her mother exclaimed, bestowing, with the full force of a carpet-slipper, a well-aimed spank from behind.

'*Aïe, aïe!*'

'Sh'o: you nohow select!'

'*Aïe* . . .'

'De low exhibition!'

'I had to take off my apron, 'cos it seemed to draw de bees,' Miami tearfully explained, catching up the cat in her arms.

'Ob course, if you choose to wear roses . . .'

'It was but ivy!'

'De berries ob de ivy, entice de same,' Mrs Mouth replied, nodding graciously, from the window, to Papy Paul, the next-door neighbour, who appeared to be taking a lonely stroll with a lanthorn and a pineapple.

'I dats way wondering why Bamboo, no pass, dis ebenin', too; as a rule, it is seldom he stop so late out upon de sea,' the young girl ventured.

'After I shall introduce you to de world (de advantage ob a good marriage; when I t'ink ob mine!), you will be ashamed, sh'o, to recall dis infatuation.'

'De young men ob Cuna-Cuna (tell me, Mammee), are dey den so nice?'

'Ah, Chile! If I was your age again . . .'

'Sh'o, dair's nothin' so much in dat.'

'As a young girl of eight (Tee-hee!), I was distracting to all the gentlemen,' Mrs Mouth asserted, confiding a smile to a small, long-billed bird, in a cage, of the variety known as Bequia-Sweet.

'How I wish I'd been born, like you, in August-Town, across de Isthmus!'

'It gib me dis taste fo' S'ciety, Chile.'

'In S'ciety, don' dey dress wid clothes on ebery day?'

'Sh'o; surtainly.'

'An' don't dey nebba tickle?'

'In August-Town, de aristocracy conceal de best part ob deir bodies; not like heah!'

'An' tell me, Mammee . . . ? De first lover you eber had . . . was he half as handsome as Bamboo?'

'De first dude, Chile, I eber had, was a lil, lil buoy, . . . wid no hair (whatsoeber at all), bal' like a calabash!' Mrs Mouth replied, as her daughter Edna entered with the lamp.

'Frtt!' the wild thing tittered, setting it down with a bang: with her cincture of leaves and flowers, she had the éclat of a butterfly.

'Better fetch de shade,' Mrs Mouth exclaimed, staring squeamishly at Miami's shadow on the wall.

'Already it grow dark; no one about now at dis hour ob night at all.'

'Except thieves an' ghouls,' Mrs Mouth replied, her glance straying towards the window.

But only the little blue-winged Bats were passing beneath a fairyland of stars.

'When I do dis, or dis, my shadow appear as formed as Mimi's!'

'Sh'o, Edna, she dat provocative today.'

'Be off at once, Chile, an' lay de table for de ebenin' meal; an' be careful not to knock de shine off de new tin-teacups,' Mrs Mouth commanded, taking up an Estate-Agent's catalogue, and seating herself comfortably beneath the lamp.

'"City of Cuna-Cuna,"' she read, '"*in the Heart of a Brainy District* (within easy reach of University, shops, etc.). A charming, Freehold Villa. Main drainage. Extensive views. Electric light. Every convenience."'

'Dat sound just de sort ob lil shack for me.'

## *III*

The strange sadness of evening, the *détresse* of the Evening Sky! Cry, cry, white Rain Birds out of the West, cry . . . !

'An' so, Miami, you no come back no more?'

'No, no come back.'

Flaunting her boredom by the edge of the sea one close of day, she had chanced to fall in with Bamboo, who, stretched at length upon the beach, was engaged in mending a broken net.

'An' I dats way glad,' she half-resentfully pouted, jealous a little of his toil.

But, presuming deafness, the young man laboured on, since, to support an aged mother, and to attain one's desires, perforce necessitates work; and his fondest wish, by dint of saving, was to wear on his wedding-day a pink starched, cotton shirt – a starched, pink cotton shirt, stiff as a boat's-sail when the North winds caught it! But a pink shirt would mean trousers . . . and trousers would lead to shoes . . . 'Extravagant nigger, don't you dare!' he would exclaim, in dizzy panic, from time to time, aloud.

'Forgib me, honey,' he begged, 'but me obliged to finish, while de daylight last.'

'Sh'o,' she sulked, following the amazing strategy of the sunset-clouds.

'Miami angel, you look so sweet: I dat amorous ob you, Mimi!'

A light laugh tripped over her lips:

'Say, buoy, how you getting on?' she queried, sinking down on her knees beside him.

'I dat amorous ob you!'

'Oh, ki,' she tittered, with a swift mocking glance at his crimson loincloth. She had often longed to snatch it away.

'Say you lub me, just a lil, too, deah?'

'Sh'o,' she answered softly, sliding over on to her stomach, and laying her cheek to the flats of her hands.

Boats with crimson spouts, to wit, steamers, dotted the skyline far away, and barques, with sails like the wings of butterflies, borne by an idle breeze, were bringing more than one ineligible young mariner back to the prose of shore.

'Ob wha' you t'inking?'

'Nothin',' she sighed, contemplating laconically a little transparent shell of violet pearl, full of sea-water and grains of sand, that the wind ruffled as it blew.

'Not ob *any* sort ob lil t'ing?' he caressingly insisted, breaking an open dark flower from her belt of wild Pansy.

'I should be gwine home,' she breathed, recollecting the undoing of the negress Ottalie.

'Oh, I dat amorous ob you, Mimi.'

'If you want to finish dat net, while de daylight last.'

For oceanward, in a glowing ball, the sun had dropped already.

'Sho', nigger, I only wish to be kind,' she murmured, getting up and sauntering a few paces along the strand.

Lured, perhaps, by the nocturnal phosphorescence from its lair, a water-scorpion, disquieted at her approach, turned and vanished amid the sheltering cover of the rocks. 'Isht, isht,' she squealed, wading after it into the surf; but to find it, look as she would, was impossible. Dark, curious and anxious, in the fast failing light, the sea disquieted her too, and it was consoling to hear close behind her the solicitous voice of Bamboo.

'Us had best soon be movin', befo' de murk ob night.'

The few thatched cabins, that comprised the village of Mediavilla, lay not half a mile from the shore. Situated between the savannah and the sea, on the southern side of the island known as Tacarigua (the 'burning Tacarigua' of the Poets), its inhabitants were obliged, from lack of communication with the larger island centres, to rely to a considerable extent for a livelihood among themselves. Local

Market days, held, alternatively, at Valley Village, or Broken Hill (the nearest approach to industrial towns in the district around Mediavilla), were the chief source of rural trade, when such merchandise as fish, coral, beads, bananas and loincloths, would exchange hands amid much animation, social gossip and pleasant fun.

'Wh'a you say to dis?' she queried as they turned inland through the cane-fields, holding up a fetish known as a 'luck-ball', attached to her throat by a chain.

'Who gib it you?' he shortly demanded, with a quick suspicious glance.

'Mammee, she bring it from Valley Village, an' she bring another for my lil sister, too.'

'Folks say she attend de Market only to meet de Obi man, who cast a spell so dat your Dada move to Cuna-Cuna.'

'Dat so!'

'Your Mammee no seek ebber de influence ob Obeah?'

'Not dat I know ob!' she replied; nevertheless, she could not but recall her mother's peculiar behaviour of late, especially upon Market days, when, instead of conversing with her friends, she would take herself off, with a mysterious air, saying she was going to the Baptist Chapel.

'Mammee, she hab no faith in de Witch-Doctor, at all,' she murmured, halting to lend an ear to the liquid note of a Pea-dove among the canes.

'I no care; me follow after wherebber you go,' he said, stealing an arm about her.

'True?' she breathed, looking up languidly towards the white mounting moon.

'I dat amorous ob you, Mimi.'

## *IV*

It was the Feast night. In the grey spleen of evening through the dusty lanes towards Mediavilla, county-society flocked.

Peering round a cow-shed door, Primrose and Phoebe, procured as waitresses for the occasion, felt their valour ooze as they surveyed the arriving guests, and dropping prostrate amid the straw, declared, in each others arms, that never, never would they find the courage to appear.

In the road, before a tall tamarind-tree, a well-spread supper board exhaled a pungent odour of fried cascadura fish, exciting the plaintive ravings of the wan pariah dogs, and the cries of a few little stark naked children engaged as guardians to keep them away. Defying an ancient and inelegant custom, by which the hosts welcomed their guests by the side of the road, Mrs Mouth had elected to remain within the precincts of the house, where, according to tradition, the bridal trophies – cowrie-shells, feathers, and a bouquet of faded orange blossom – were being displayed.

'It seem no more dan yestidday,' she was holding forth gaily over a goblet of Sangaree wine, 'it seems no more dan yestidday dat I put on me maiden wreath ob arange blastams to walk wid me nigger to church.'

Clad in rich-hued creepers, she was both looking and feeling her best.

'Sh'o,' a woman with blonde-dyed hair and Buddery eyes exclaimed, 'it seem no more dan just like yestidday; dat not so, Papy Paul?' she queried, turning to an old man in a raspberry-pink kerchief, who displayed (as he sat) more of his person than he seemed to be aware of.

But Papy Paul was confiding a receipt for pickling yuccas to Mamma Luna, the mother of Bamboo, and made as if not to hear.

Offering a light, lilac wine, sweet and heady, Miami circled, here and there. She had a cincture of white rose-oleanders, and a bandeau of blue convolvuli. She held a fan.

'Or do you care for anyt'ing else?' she was enquiring, automatically, of Mr Musket (the Father of three very common girls), as a melodious tinkle of strings announced the advent of the minstrels from Broken Hill.

Following the exodus roadward, it was agreeable to reach the outer air.

Under the high trees by the yard-door gate, the array of vehicles and browsing quadrupeds was almost as numerous as upon a Market day. Coming and going between the little Café, of the 'Forty Parrots' (with its Bar, spelled *Biar* in twinkling lights), the quiet village road was agog, with bustling folk, as perhaps never before. All iris in the dusk, a few loosely-loin-clothed young men, had commenced dancing aloofly among themselves, bringing down some light (if bitter) banter from the belles.

Pirouetting with these, Miami recognized the twinkling feet of her brother Charlie, a lad who preferred roaming the wide savannah country after butterflies with his net, to the ever-increasing etiquette of his home.

'Sh'o, S'ciety no longer what it wa',' the mother of two spare lean girls, like young giraffes, was lamenting, when a clamorous gong summoned the assembly to the festal board.

In the glow of blazing palm logs, stoked by capering pickneys, the company, with some considerable jostling, became seated by degrees.

'Fo' what we gwine to recebe, de Lord make us to be truly t'ankful,' Mr Mouth's low voice was lost amid the din. Bending to the decree of Providence, and trusting in God for the welfare of his house, he was resigned to follow the call of duty, by allowing his offspring such educational advantages and worldly polish that only a city can give.

'An' so I heah you gwine to leab us!' the lady at his elbow exclaimed, helping herself to a claw of a crab.

'Fo' de sake ob de chillen's schoolin',' Mr Mouth made reply, blinking at the brisk lightning play through the foliage of the trees.

'Dey tell me de amount of licence dat go on ober dah,' she murmured, indicating with her claw the chequered horizon, 'but de whole world needs revising, as de Missionary truly say!'

'Indeed, an' dat's de trute.'

'It made me cry,' a plump little woman declared, 'when de Minister speak so serious on de scandal ob close dancing . . .'

'Fo' one t'ing lead sh'o to de nex'!' Mr Mouth abstrusely assented, turning his attention upon an old negress answering to the name of Mamma May, who was retailing how she had obtained the sunshade, beneath which, since noon, she had walked all the way to the party.

'Ah could not afford a parasol, so Ah just cut miself a lil green bush, an' held it up ober my head,' she was crooning in gleeful triumph.

'It's a wonder, indeed, no one gib you a lif'!' several voices observed, but the discussion was drowned by an esoteric song of remote, tribal times, from the lips of Papy Paul.

> '*I am King Elephant-bag,*
> *Ob de rose-pink Mountains!*
> *Tatou, tatouay, tatou . . .*'

provoking a giggle from Miss Stella Spooner, the marvellous daughter of an elderly father, and in which she was joined by the youngest Miss Mouth.

Incontestably a budding Princess, the playful mite was enjoying, with airy nonchalance, her initial experience of Society.

'Ob course she is very *jeune*,' Mrs Mouth murmured archly, behind her hand, into the ear of Mr Musket.

'It's de Lord's will,' he cautiously replied, rolling a mystified eye towards his wife (a sable negress out of Africa), continually vaunting her foreign extraction: 'I'm Irish,' she would say: 'I'm Irish, deah . . .'

'Sh'o she de born image ob her elder sister!'

'De world all say she to marry de son ob ole Mamma Luna, dat keep de lil shop.'

'Suz! Wha' nex'? Mrs Mouth returned, breaking off to focus Papy Paul, apparently, already, far from sober: 'I hav' saw God, an' I hav' spoke wid de President, too!' he was announcing impressively to Mamma Luna, a little old woman in whose veins ran the blood of many races.

'Dair's no trute at all in *dat* report,' Mrs Mouth quietly added, signalling directions to a sturdy, round-bottomed little lad, who had undertaken to fill the gap caused by Primrose and Phoebe.

Bearing a pannier piled with fruit, he had not got far before the minstrels called forth several couples to their feet.

The latest jazz, bewildering, glittering, exuberant as the soil, a jazz, throbbing, pulsating, with a zim, zim, zim, a jazz all abandon and verve that had drifted over the glowing savannah and the waving cane-fields from Cuna-Cuna by the Violet Sea, invited, irresistibly, to motion every boy and girl.

'Prancing Nigger, hab a dance?' his wife, transported, shrilled: but Mr Mouth was predicting a Banana slump to Mrs Walker, the local midwife, and paid no heed.

Torso-to-torso, the youngsters twirled, while even a pair of majestic matrons, Mrs Friendship and Mrs Mother, went whirling away (together) into the brave summer dusk. Accepting the invitation of Bamboo, Miami rose, but before dancing long complained of the heat.

'Sh'o, it cooler in de Plantation,' he suggested, pointing along the road.

'Oh, I too much afraid!'

'What for you afraid?'

But Miami only laughed, and tossed her hand as if she were scattering dewdrops.

Following the roving fireflies, and the adventurous flittermice, they strolled along in silence. By the roadside, two young men, friends, walking with fingers intermingled, saluted them softly. An admirable evening for a promenade! Indescribably sweet, the floating field-scents enticed them witchingly on.

'Shi!' she exclaimed as a bird skimmed swiftly past with a chattering cry.

'It noddin', deah, but a lil wee owl!'

'An' it to make my heart go so,' she murmured, with a sidelong smiling glance.

He had a new crimson loincloth, and a blood pink carnation at his ear.

'What for you afraid?' he tenderly pressed.

'It much cooler heah, doh it still very hot,' she inconsequently answered, pausing to listen to the fretting of the hammer tree-frogs in the dusk.

'Dey hold a concert honey lub, all for us.'

Rig a jig jig, rig a jig jig . . .

'Just hark to de noise!' she murmured, starting a little at the silver lightning behind the palms.

'Just hark,' he repeated, troubled.

Rig a jig jig, rig a jig jig . . .

# *V*

Little jingley trot-trot-trot, over the Savannah, hey –!

Joggling along towards Cuna-Cuna the creaking caravan shaped its course. Seated in a hooded chariot, berced by mule-bells, and nibbling a shoot of ripe cane, Mrs Mouth appeared to have attained the heights of bliss. Disregarding, or insensitive to her husband's incessant groans, (wedged in between a case of pineapples, and a box marked 'lingerie'), she abandoned herself voluptuously to her thoughts. It was droll to contemplate meeting an old acquaintance, Nini Snagg, who had gone to reside in Cuna-Cuna long ago: 'Fancy seein' you!' she would say, and how they both would laugh.

Replying tersely to the innumerable 'what would you do ifs' of her sister, supposing attacks from masked-bandits or ferocious wild-animals, Miami moped.

All her whole heart yearned back behind her, and never had she loved Bamboo so much as now.

'– if a big, shaggy buffalo, wid two, sharp, horns, dat long, were to rush right at you?' Edna was plaguing her, when a sudden jolt of the van set up a loud cackling from a dozen scared cocks and hens.

'Drat dose fowl; as if dair were none in Cuna-Cuna!' Mrs Mouth addressed her husband.

'Not birds ob dat brood,' he retorted, plaintively starting to sing.

> 'I t'ink when I read dat sweet story ob old,
> When Jesus was here among men,
> How He called lil chillens as lambs to His fold,
> I should hab like to hab been wid dem den!

I wish dat His hands had been placed ahn my head,
Dat His arms had been thrown aroun' me,
An' dat I might hab seen His kind look when He said,
Let de lil ones come unto me!'

'Mind de dress-basket don't drop down, deah, an' spoil our clo',' Mrs Mouth exclaimed, indicating a cowskin trunk that seemed to be in peril of falling; for, from motives of economy and ease, it had been decided that not before Cuna-Cuna should rear her queenly towers above them would they change their floral garlands for the more artificial fabrics of the town, and, when Edna, vastly to her importance, should go into a pair of frilled 'invisibles' and a petticoat for the first amazing time; nor, indeed, would Mr Mouth himself take 'to de pants', until his wife and daughters should have assumed their skirts. But this, from the languid pace at which their vehicle proceeded, was unlikely to be just yet. In the torrid tropic noontime, haste, however, was quite out of the question. Bordered by hills, long, yellow and low, the wooded savannah rolled away beneath a blaze of trembling heat.

'I don't t'ink much ob dis part of de country,' Mrs Mouth commented. 'All dese common palms . . . de cedar wood-tree, dat my tree. Dat is de timber I prefer.'

'An' some,' Edna pertly smiled, 'dey like best de bamboo . . .'

A remark that was rewarded by a blow on the ear.

'Now she set up a hullabaloo like de time de scorpion bit her botty,' Mrs Mouth lamented, and, indeed, the uproar made, alarmed from the boskage a cloud of winsome soldier-birds and inquisitive parroquets.

'Oh my God,' Mr Mouth exclaimed. 'What for you make all dat dere noise?' But his daughter paid no attention, and soon sobbed herself to sleep.

Advancing through tracks of acacia-scrub, or groves of nutmeg-trees, they jolted along in the gay, exalting sunlight. Flowers brighter than love, wafting the odour of spices, strewed in profusion the long guinea-grass on either side of the way.

'All dose sweet aprons, if it weren't fo' de flies!' Mrs Mouth murmured, regarding some heavy, ambered, Trumpet flowers, with a covetous eye.

'I trust Charlie get bit by no snake!'

'Prancing Nigger! It a lil too late now to t'ink ob dat.'

Since to avoid overcrowding the family party, Charlie was to follow with his butterfly net, and arrive as he could. And never were butterflies (seen in nigger-boys' dreams) as brilliant, or frolicsome, as were those of mid-savannah. Azure Soledads, and radiant Conquistadors with frail flamboyant wings, wove about the labouring mules perpetual fresh rosettes.

'De Lord protect de lad,' Mr Mouth remarked, relapsing into silence.

Onward through the cloudless noontide, beneath the ardent sun, the caravan drowsily crawled. As the afternoon advanced, Mrs Mouth produced a pack of well-thumbed cards, and cutting, casually, twice, began interrogating Destiny with these. Reposing as best she might, Miami gave herself up to her reflections. The familiar aspect of the wayside palms, the tattered pennons of the bananas, the big silk-cottons (known, to children, as 'Mammee-trees'), all brought to her mind Bamboo.

'Dair's somet'in' dat look like a death dah, dat's troublin' me,' Mrs Mouth remarked, moodily fingering a greasy ace.

'De Almighty forgib dese foolish games!' Mr Mouth protestingly said.

'An' from de lie ob de cards . . . it seem as ef de corpse were ob de masculine species.'

'Wha' gib you de notion ob dat?'

'Sh'o, a sheep puts his wool on his favourite places,' Mrs Mouth returned, reshuffling slowly her pack.

Awakened by her Father's psalms, Edna's 'What would you do's' had commenced with volubility anew, growing more eerie with the gathering night.

'. . . if a Wood-Spirit wid two heads an' six arms, were to take hold ob you, Mimi, from behind?'

'I no do nothin' at all,' Miami answered briefly.

'Talk not so much ob de jumbies, Chile, as de chickens go to roost!' Mrs Mouth admonished.

'Or, if de debil himself should?' Edna insisted, allowing Snowball, the cat, to climb on to her knee.

'Nothin', sh'o,' Miami murmured, regarding dreamily the sun's sinking disk, that was illuminating all the Western sky with incarnadine and flamingo-rose. Ominous in the falling dusk, the savannah rolled away, its radiant hues effaced beneath a rapid tide of deepening shadow.

'Start de gramophone gwine girls, an' gib us somet'in' bright!' Mrs Mouth exclaimed, depressed by the forlorn note the Twa-oo-Twa-oo bird, that mingled its lament with a thousand night cries from the grass.

'When de saucy female sing: "My Ice Cream Girl", fo' sh'o she scare de elves.'

And as though by force of magic, the nasal soprano of an invisible songstress rattled forth with tinkling gusto a music-hall air with a sparkling refrain.

> 'And the boys shout Girlie, hi!
> Bring me soda, soda, soda,
> [Aside, spoken] (Stop your fooling there and let me alone!)
> For I'm an Ice Cream Soda Girl.'

'It put me in mind ob de last sugar-factory explosion! It was de same day dat Snowball crack de Tezzrazine record. Drat de cat.'

'O, Lordey Lord! Wha' for you make dat din?' Mr Mouth complained, knotting a cotton handkerchief over his head.

'I hope you not gwine to be billeous, honey, afore we get to Lucia?'

'Lemme alone. Ah'm thinkin' . . .'

Pressing on by the light of a large clear moon, the hamlet of Lucia, the halting-place proposed for the night, lay still far ahead.

Stars, like many Indian pinks, flecked with pale brightness the sky above; towards the horizon shone the Southern Cross, while the Pole Star, through the palm-fronds, came and went.

> '*And the men cry Girlie, hi!*
> *Bring me –*'

'Silence, dah! Ah'm thinkin' . . .'

## *VI*

Cuna, full of charming roses, full of violet shadows, full of music, full of Love, Cuna . . . !

Leaning from a balcony of the Grand Savannah hotel, their instincts all aroused, Miami and Edna gazed out across the Alameda, a place all foliage, lamplight, and flowers. It was the hour when Society, in slowly-parading carriages, would congregate to take the air beneath the pale mimosas that adorned the favourite promenade. All but recumbent, as though agreeably fatigued by their recent emotions (what wild follies were not committed in shuttered-villas during the throbbing hours of noon?), the Cunans, in their elegant equipages, made for anyone, fresh from the provinces, an interesting and absorbing sight. The liquid-eyed loveliness of the women, and the handsomeness of the men, with their black moustaches and their treacherous smiles – these, indeed, were things to gaze on.

'Oh ki!' Miami laughed delightedly, indicating a foppish, pretty youth, holding in a restive little horse dancing away with him.

Rubbing herself repeatedly, as yet embarrassed by the novelty of her clothes, Edna could only gasp.

'. . . ,' she jabbered, pointing at some flaunting belles in great evening hats and falling hair.

'All dat fine,' Miami murmured, staring in wonderment around.

Dominating the city soared the Opera House, uplifting a big, naked man, all gilt, who was being bitten, or mauled, so it seemed, by a pack of wild animals carved of stone, while near by were the University, and the Cathedral with its low white dome crowned by moss-green tiles.

Making towards it, encouraged by the Vesper bell, some young girls, in muslin masks, followed by a retinue of bustling nuns, were running the gauntlet of the profligates that clustered on the curb.

'Oh, Jesus honey!' Edna cooed, scratching herself in an ecstasy of delight.

'Fo' shame, Chile, to act so unladylike; if any gen'leman look up he t'ink you make a wicked sign,' Mrs Mouth cautioned, stepping out upon the balcony from the sitting-room behind.

Inhaling a bottle of sal volatile, to dispel *de megrims*, she was looking dignified in a *décolleté* of smoke-blue tulle.

'Nebba do *dat* in S'ciety,' she added, placing a protecting arm around each of her girls.

Seduced, not less than they, by the animation of the town, the fatigue of the journey seemed amply rewarded. It was amusing to watch the crowd before the Ciné Lara, across the way, where many were flocking attracted by the hectic posters of *A Wife's Revenge*.

'I keep t'inking I see Nini Snagg,' Mrs Mouth observed, regarding a negress in emerald-tinted silk, seated on a public-bench beneath the glittering greenery.

'Cunan folk dat fine,' Edna twittered, turning about at her Father's voice:

> 'W'en de day ob toil is done,
> W'en de race ob life is run,
> Heaven send thy weary one
> Rest for evermore!'

'Prancing Nigger! Is it worth while to wear dose grimaces?'

'Sh'o, dis no good place to be.'

'Why, what dair wrong wid it?'

'Ah set out to look fo' de Meetin'-House, but no sooner am Ah in de street, dan a female wid her har droopin' loose down ober her back, an' into her eyes, she tell me to Come along.'

'Some of dose bold women, dey ought to be shot through dair bottoms!' Mrs Mouth indignantly said.

'But I nebba answer nothin'.'

'May our daughters respect dair virtue same as you!' Mrs Mouth returned, focusing wistfully the vast flowery parterre of the Café McDhu'l.

Little city of cocktails, Cuna! The surpassing excellence of thy Barmen, who shall sing?

'See how dey spell "Biar", Mammee,' Miami tittered: 'Dey forget de *i*!'

'Sh'o, Chile, an' so dey do . . .'

'Honey Jesus!' Edna broadly grinned: 'Imagine de ignorance ob dat.'

## *VII*

Now, beyond the Alameda, in the modish faubourg of Farananka, there lived a lady of both influence and wealth – the widow of the Inventor of Sunflower Piquant. Arbitress absolute of Cunan society, and owner, moreover, of a considerable portion of the town, the *veto* of Madame Ruiz, had caused the suicide indeed of more than one social climber. Unhappy, nostalgic, disdainful, selfish, ever about to abandon Cuna-Cuna to return to it no more, yet never budging, adoring her fairy villa far too well, Madame Ruiz while craving for the International-world, consoled herself by watching from afar European Society going speedily to the dogs. Art loving, and considerably musical (many a dizzy venture at the Opera-house had owed its audition to her), she had, despite the self-centredness of her nature, done not a little to render more brilliant the charming city it amused her with such vehemence to abuse.

One softly gloomy morning, preceding Madame Ruiz's first *cotillon* of the Season, the lodge-keeper of the Villa Alba, a negress, like some great, violet bug, was surprised, while tending the brightly-hanging Grape-Fruit in the drive, by an imperative knocking on the gate. At such a matutinal hour only trashy errand-boys shouldering baskets might be expected to call, and giving the summons no heed, the mulatress continued her work.

The Villa Alba, half-buried in spreading awnings, and surrounded by many noble trees, stood but a short distance off the main road, its pleasaunces enclosed by flower-enshrouded walls, all a-zig-zag, like the folds of a screen. Beloved of lizards, and velvet-backed humming-birds, the shaded gardens led on one side to the sea.

'To make such a noise at dis hour,' the negress murmured,

going grumblingly at length to the gate, disclosing, upon opening, a gentleman in middle-life, with a toothbrush moustache and a sapphire ring.

'De mist'ess still in bed, sah.'

'In bed?'

'She out bery late, sah, but you find Miss Edwards up.'

And with a nod of thanks, the visitor directed his footsteps discreetly towards the house.

Although not, precisely, *in* her bed when the caller, shortly afterwards, was announced, Madame Ruiz was nevertheless as yet in deshabille.

'Tiresome man, what does he want to see me about?' she exclaimed, gathering around her a brocaded-wrap formed of a priestly cope.

'He referred to a lease, ma'am,' the maid replied.

'A lease!' Madame Ruiz raised eyes dark with spleen.

The visit of her agent, or man of affairs, was apt to ruffle her composure for the day: 'Tell him to leave it, and go,' she commanded, selecting a nectarine from a basket of iced-fruits beside her.

Removing reflectively the sensitive skin, her mind evoked, in ironic review, the chief salient events of society, scheduled to take place on the face of the map in the course of the day.

The marriage of the Count de Nozhel, in Touraine, to Mrs Exelmans of Cincinnati, the divorce of poor Lady Luckcock in London (it seemed quite certain that one of the five co-respondents was the little carrot-haired Lord Dubelly again), the last 'pomps', at Vienna, of Princess de Seeyohl *née* Mitchening-Meyong (Peace to her soul! She had led her life) . . . The christening in Madrid of the girl-twins of the Queen of Spain . . .

'At her time, I really *don't* understand it,' Madame Ruiz murmured to herself aloud, glancing, as though for an explanation, about the room.

Through the flowing folds of the mosquito curtains of the bed, that swept a cool, flagged-floor, spread with skins, showed the oratory, with its waxen flowers, and pendant flickering lights, that burned, night and day, before a Leonardo saint with a treacherous smile. Beyond the little recess came a lacquer commode, bearing a masterly marble group, depicting a pair of amorous hermaphrodites amusing themselves, while above, against the spacious wainscoting of the wall, a painting of a man, elegantly corseted, with a Violet in his moustache, *Study of a Parisian*, was suspended, and which, with its pendant *Portrait of a Lady*, signed Van Dongen, were the chief outstanding objects that the room contained.

'One would have thought that at forty she would have given up having babies,' Madame Ruiz mused, choosing a glossy cherry from the basket at her side.

Through the open window a sound of distant music caught her ear.

'Ah! If only he were less weak,' she sighed, her thoughts turning towards the player, who seemed to be enamoured of the opening movement (rapturously repeated) of *L'Après midi d'un Faune*.

The venatorial habits of Vittorio Ruiz had been from his earliest years the source of his mother's constant chagrin and despair. At the age of five he had assaulted his Nurse, and, steadily onward, his passions had grown and grown . . .

'It's the fault of the wicked climate,' Madame Ruiz reflected, as her companion, Miss Edwards, came in with the post.

'Thanks, Eurydice,' she murmured, smilingly exchanging a butterfly kiss.

'It's going to be oh so hot, today!'

'Is it, dear?'

'Intense,' Miss Edwards predicted, fluttering a gay-daubed paper fan.

Sprite-like, with a little strained ghost-face beneath a silver shock of hair, it seemed as if her long blue eyes had absorbed the Cunan sea.

'Do you remember the giant with the beard?' she asked, 'at the Presidency fête?'

'Do I?'

'And we wondered who he could be!'

'Well?'

'He's the painter of Women's Backs, my dear!'

'The painter of women's *what*?'

'An artist.'

'Oh.'

'I wanted to know if you'd advise me to sit.'

'Your back is charming, dear, *c'est un dos d'élite*.'

'I doubt, though, it's classic,' Miss Edwards murmured, pirouetting slowly before the glass.

But Madame Ruiz was perusing her correspondence, and seemed to be absorbed.

'They're to be married, in Munich, on the fifth,' she chirruped.

'Who?'

'Elsie and Baron Sitmar.'

'Ah, Ta-ra, dear! In those far worlds . . .' Miss Edwards impatiently exclaimed, opening wide a window and leaning out.

Beneath the flame-trees, with their spreading tops, one mass of crimson flower, coolly, white-garbed gardeners, with naked feet and big bell-shaped hats of straw, were sweeping slowly, as in some rhythmic dance, the flamboyant blossoms that had fallen to the ground.

'Wasn't little Madame Haase, dear, born Kattie von Guggenheim?'

'I really don't know,' Miss Edwards returned, flapping away a fly with her fan.

'This villainous climate! My memory's going . . .'

'I wish I cared for Cuna less, that's all!' Miss Edwards said, her glance following a humming-bird, poised in air, above the sparkling turquoise of a fountain.

'Captain Moonlight . . . duty . . . (tedious word) . . . can't come!'

'Oh?'

'Such a dull post,' Madame Ruiz murmured, pausing to listen to the persuasive tenor-voice of her son.

> 'Little mauve nigger boy,
> I t'ink you break my heart!'

'My poor Vitti! Bless him.'

'He was out last night with some Chinese she.'

'I understood him to be going to *Pelléas and Mélisande*.'

'He came to the Opera-house, but only for a minute.'

'Dios!'

'And, oh, dearest,' Miss Edwards dropped her cheek to her hand.

'Was Hatso as ever delicious?' Madame Ruiz asked, changing the topic as her woman returned, following by a pomeranian of parts, 'Snob'; a dog beautiful as a child.

'We had Gebhardt instead.'

'In Mélisande she's so huge,' Madame Ruiz commented, eyeing severely the legal-looking packet which her maid had brought her.

'Business, Camilla; *how* I pity you!'

Madame Ruiz sighed.

'It seems,' she said, 'that for the next nine-and-ninety years, I have let a Villa to a Mr and Mrs Ahmadou Mouth.'

# VIII

Floor of copper, floor of gold . . . Beyond the custom-house door, ajar, the street at sunrise seemed aflame.

'Have you nothing, young man, to declare?'

'. . . Butterflies!'

'Exempt of duty. Pass.'

Floor of silver, floor of pearl . . .

Trailing a muslin net, and laughing for happiness, Charlie Mouth marched into the town.

Oh, Cuna-Cuna! Little city of Lies and Peril! How many careless young nigger boys have gone thus to seal their Doom?

Although the Sun-god was scarcely risen, already the radiant street teemed with life.

Veiled dames, flirting fans, bent on church or market, were issuing everywhere from their doors, and the air was vibrant with the sweet voice of bells.

To rejoin his parents promptly at their hotel was a promise he was tempted to forget.

Along streets all fresh and blue in the shade of falling awnings, it was fine, indeed, to loiter. Beneath the portico of a church, a running fountain drew his steps aside. Too shy to strip and squat in the basin, he was glad to bathe freely his head, feet and chest: then stirred by curiosity to throw a glance at the building, he lifted the long yellow nets that veiled the door.

It was the fashionable church of La Favavoa, and the extemporary address of the Archbishop of Cuna was in full, and impassioned, swing.

'Imagine the world, my friends, had Christ been born a girl!' he was saying in tones of tender dismay as Charlie entered.

Subsiding bashfully to a bench, Charlie gazed around.

So many sparkling fans. One, a delicate light mauve one: 'Shucks! If only you wa' butterflies!' he breathed, contemplating with avidity the nonchalant throng; then perceiving a richer specimen splashed with silver of the same amative tint: 'Oh you lil beauty!' And, clutching his itching net to his heart, he regretfully withdrew.

Sauntering leisurely through the cool, Mimosa-shaded streets, he approached, as he guessed, the Presidency. A score of shoeblacks, lolled at cards, or gossip, before its gilded pales. Amazed at their audacity (for the President had threatened more than once to 'wring the Public's neck'), Charlie hastened by. Public gardens, brilliant with sarracenias, lay just beyond the palace, where a music-pavilion, surrounded by palms and rocking-chairs, appeared a favourite, and much-frequented, resort; from here he observed the Cunan bay strewn with sloops and white-sailed yachts, asleep upon the tide. Strolling on, he found himself in the busy vicinity of the Market. Although larger, and more varied, it resembled, in other respects, the village one at home.

'Say, honey, say' – crouching in the dust before a little pyre of mangoes, a lean-armed woman besought him to buy.

Pursued by a confusion of voices, he threaded his way deftly down an alley dressed with booths. Pomegranates, some open with their crimson seeds displayed, banana-combs, and big, veined water-melons, lay heaped on every side.

'I could do wid a slice ob watteh-million,' he reflected: 'but to lick an ice-cream dat tempt me more!' Nor would the noble fruit of the baobab, the paw-paw, or the pine, turn him from his fancy.

But no ice-cream stand met his eye, and presently he resigned himself to sit down upon his heels, in the shade of a potter's stall, and consider the passing crowd.

Missionaries with freckled hands and hairy, care-worn faces, followed by pale girls wielding tambourines of the Army of the Soul, foppish nigger bucks in panamas and palm-beach suits so cocky, Chinamen with osier baskets their nostalgic eyes aswoon, heavily straw-hatted nuns trailing their dust-coloured rags, and suddenly, oh could it be, but there was no mistaking that golden waddle: 'Mamma!'

Mamma, Mammee, Mrs Ahmadou Mouth. All in white, with snow-white shoes and hose so fine, he hardly dare.

'Mammee, Mammee, oh, Mammee . . .'

'Sonny mine! My lil boy!'

'Mammee.'

'Just to say!'

And, oh, honies! Close behind, behold Miami, and Edna too: The Miss Lips, the fair Lips, the smiling Lips. How spry each looked. The elder (grown a trifle thinner), sweet *à ravir* in tomato-red, while her sister, plump as a corn-fattened partridge, and very perceptibly powdered, seemed like the flower of the prairie sugar-cane when it breaks into bloom.

'We've been to a Music-hall, an' a pahty, an' Snowball has dropped black kittens.' Forestalling Miami, Edna rapped it out.

'Oh shucks!'

'An' since we go into S'ciety, we keep a boy in buttons!'

Mrs Mouth turned about.

'Where is dat ijit coon?'

'He stay behind to bargain for de pee-wee birds, Mammee, fo' to make de taht.'

'De swindling tortoise.'

'An' dair are no vacancies at de University: not fo' any ob us!' Edna further retailed, going off into a spasm of giggles.

She was swinging a wicker basket, from which there dangled the silver forked tail of a fish.

'Fo' goodness' sake gib dat sea-porcupine to Ibum, Chile,' Mrs Mouth commanded, as a perspiring niggerling in livery presented himself.

'Ibum, his arms are full already.'

'Just come along all to de Villa now! It dat mignon an' all so nice. An' after de collation,' Mrs Mouth (shocked on the servant's account at her son's nude neck), raised her voice: 'we go to de habadasher in Palmbranch Avenue, an' I buy you an Eton colleh!'

# IX

'Prancing Nigger, I t'ink it bery strange, dat Madame Ruiz, she nebba call.'

'Sh'o.'

'In August-Town, S'ciety less stuck-up dan heah!'

Ensconced in rocking-chairs, in the shade of the ample porch of the Villa Vista Hermosa, Mr and Mrs Mouth had been holding a desultory *tête-à-tête*.

It was a Sabbath evening, and a sound of reedy pipes and bafalons, from a neighbouring café, filled with a feverish sadness the brilliantly lamp-lit street.

'De airs ob de nabehs, dat dair affair, what matter mo', am de chillen's schoolin'.'

'Prancing Nigger, I hope your Son an' Daughters will yet take dair Degrees, an' if not from de University, den from Home. From heah.'

'Hey-ho-day, an' dat would be a miracle!' Mr Mouth mirthlessly laughed.

'Dose chillens hab learnt quite a lot already.'

''Bout de shaps an' cynemas!'

Mrs Mouth disdained a reply.

She had taken the girls to the gallery at the Opera one night to hear *Louise*, but they had come out, by tacit agreement, in the middle of it: the plainness of Louise's blouse, and the lack of tunes . . . added to which, the suffocation of the gallery . . . And – once bit twice shy – they had not gone back again.

'All your fambly need, Prancing Nigger, is social opportunity! But what is de good ob de Babtist parson?'

Mr Mouth sketched a gesture.

'Sh'o, Edna, she some young yet . . . But Miami dat *distinguée*; an', doh I her mother, b'lieb me dat is one ob de choicest girls I see; an 'dat's de trute.'

'It queer,' Mr Mouth abstrusely murmured, 'how many skeeter-bugs dair are 'bout dis ebenin'!'

'De begonias in de window-boxes most lik'ly draw dem. But as I was saying, Prancing Nigger, I t'ink it bery strange dat Madame Ruiz nebba call.'

'P'raps, she out ob town.'

'Accordin' to de paper, she bin habing her back painted, but what dat fo' I dunno.'

'Ah shouldn't wonder ef she hab some trouble ob a dorsal kind; same as me gramma mumma long agone.'

'Dair'd be no harm in sendin' one ob de chillens to enquire. Wha' you t'ink, sah?' Mrs Mouth demanded, plucking from off the porch a pale hanging flower with a languorous scent.

Mr Mouth glanced apprehensively skyward.

The mutters of thunder and intermittent lightning of the finest nights.

'It's a misfortnit we eber left Mediavilla,' he exclaimed uneasily, as a falling star, known as a thief star, sped swiftly down the sky.

'Prancing Nigger,' Mrs Mouth rose, remarking, 'befo' you start to grummle, I leab you alone to your Jereymiads!'

'A misfortnit sho' nuff,' he mused, and regret for the savannah country, and the tall palm-trees of his village, oppressed his heart. Moreover, his means (derived from the cultivation of the *Musa paradisica*, or Banana) seemed likely to prove ere long inadequate to support the whims of his wife, who after a lifetime of contented nudity, appeared to be now almost insatiable for dress.

A discordant noise from above interrupted the trend of his thoughts.

'Sh'o, she plays wid it like a toy,' he sighed, as the sound occurred again.

'Prancing Nigger, de water-supply cut off!'

'It's de Lord's will.'

'Dair's not a drop, my lub, in de privy.'

''Cos it always in use!'

'I b'lieb dat lil half-caste Ibum, 'cos I threaten to gib him notice, do somet'in' out ob malice to de chain.'

'Whom de Lord loveth, He chasteneth!' Mr Mouth observed, 'an' dose bery words (ef you look) you will find in de twelfth chapter, an' de sixth berse ob de Book ob Hebrews.'

'Prancing Nigger, you datways selfish! Always t'inkin 'ob your soul, instead ob your obligations towards de fambly.'

'Why, wha' mo' can I do dan I've done?'

Mrs Mouth faintly shrugged.

'I had hoped,' she said, 'dat Nini would hab bin ob use to de girls, but dat seem now impossible!' For Mrs Snagg had been traced to a house of ill-fame, where, it appeared, she was an exponent of the Hodeidah – a lascive Cunan dance.

'Understand dat any sort ob intimacy 'tween de Villa an' de *Closerie des Lilas* Ah must flatly forbid.'

'Prancing Nigger, as ef I should take your innocent chillens to call on po' Nini; not dat everyt'ing about her at de *Closerie* is not elegant an' nice. Sh'o, some ob de inmates ob dat establishment possess mo' diamonds dan dair betters do outside! You'd be surprised ef you could see what two ob de girls dair, Dinah an' Lew . . .'

'Enuf!'

'It isn't always Virtue, Prancing Nigger, dat come off best!' And Mrs Mouth might have offered further observations on the matter of ethics, had not her husband left her.

# X

Past the Presidency and the public park, the Theatres Maxine Bush, Eden-Garden, and Apollo, along the Avenida, and the Jazz Halls by the wharf, past little suburban shops, and old, deserted churchyards where bloom geraniums, through streets of squalid houses, and onward skirting pleasure lawns and orchards, bibbitty-bobbitty, beneath the sovereign brightness of the sky, the Farananka tram crawled along.

Surveying the landscape listlessly through the sticks of her fan, Miss Edna Mouth grew slightly bored – alas, poor child; couldst thou have guessed the blazing brightness of thy Star, thou wouldst doubtless have been more alert!

'Sh'o, it dat far an' tejus,' she observed to the conductor, lifting upon him the sharp-soft eyes of a parroquet.

She was looking bewitching in a frock of silverish *mousseleine* and a violet tallyho cap, and dangled upon her knees an intoxicating sheaf of blossoms, known as Marvel of Peru.

'Hab patience, lil Missey, an' we soon be dah.'

. . . . . . . . . . .

'He tells me, dear child, he tells me,' Madame Ruiz was rounding a garden path, upon the arm of her son, 'he tells me, Vitti, that the systole and diastole of my heart's muscles are slightly inflamed; and that I ought, darling, to be *very* careful . . .'

Followed by a handsome borzoi, and the pomeranian Snob, the pair were taking their usual post-prandial exercise beneath the trees.

'Let me come, Mother, dear,' he murmured without interrupting, 'over the other side of you; I always like to be on the right side of my profile!'

'And, really, since the affair of Madame de Bazvalon, my health has hardly been what it was.'

'That foolish little woman,' he uncomfortably laughed.

'He tells me my nerves need rest,' she declared, looking pathetically up at him.

He had the nose of an actress, and ink-black hair streaked with gold, his eyes seemed to be covered with the freshest of fresh dark pollen, while nothing could exceed the vivid pallor of his cheeks, or the bright sanguine of his mouth.

'You go out so much, Mother.'

'Not so much!'

'So very much.'

'And he forbids me my opera-box for the rest of the week! So last night I sat at home, dear child, reading the Life of Lazarillo de Tormes.'

'I don't give a damn,' he said, 'for any of your doctors.'

'So vexing, though; and apparently Lady Bird has been at death's door, and poor Peggy Povey too. It seems she got wet on the way to the Races; and really I was *sorry* for her when I saw her in the paddock; for the oats and the corn, and the wheat and the tares, and the barley and the rye, and all the rest of the reeds and grasses in her pretty Lancret hat, looked like nothing so much as manure.'

'I adore to folly her schoolboy's moustache!'

'My dear, Age is the one disaster,' Madame Ruiz remarked, raising the rosy dome of her sunshade a degree higher above her head.

They were pacing a walk radiant with trees and flowers as some magician's garden, that commanded a sweeping prospect of long, livid sands, against a white green sea.

'There would seem to be several new yachts, darling,' Madame Ruiz observed.

'The Duke of Wellclose with his duchess (on their wedding-tour) arrived with the tide.'

'Poor man; I'm told that he only drove to the church after thirty brandies!'

'And the *Sea-Thistle*, with Lady Violet Valesbridge, and, *oh*, such a crowd.'

'She used to be known as "The Cat of Curzon Street", but I hear she is still quite incredibly pretty,' Madame Ruiz murmured, turning to admire a somnolent peacock, with moping fan, poised upon the curved still arm of a marble maenad.

'How sweet something smells.'

'It's the China lilies.'

'I believe it's my handkerchief . . .' he said.

'Vain wicked boy; ah, if you would but decide, and marry some nice, intelligent girl.'

'I'm too young yet.'

'You're *twenty-six*!'

'And past the age of folly-o,' he made airy answer, drawing from his breast-pocket a flat, jewel-encrusted case, and lighting a cigarette.

'Think of the many men, darling, of twenty-six . . .' Madame Ruiz broke off, focusing the fruit-bearing summit of a slender areca palm.

'Foll-foll-folly-o!' he laughed.

'I think I'm going in.'

'Oh, why?'

'Because,' Madame Ruiz repressed a yawn, 'because, dear, I feel armchairish.'

With a kiss of the finger tips (decidedly distinguished hands had Vittorio Ruiz), he turned away.

Joying frankly in excess, the fiery noontide hour had a special charm for him.

It was the hour, to be sure, of 'the Faun'!

'Aho, Ahi, Aha!' he carolled, descending half-trippingly a few white winding stairs, that brought him upon a fountain. Palms, with their floating fronds, radiating light, stood all around.

It was here 'the creative mood' would sometimes take him, for he possessed no small measure of talent of his own.

His *Three Hodeidahs*, and *Five Phallic Dances for Pianoforte and Orchestra*, otherwise known as 'Suite in Green', had taken the whole concert world by storm, and, now, growing more audacious, he was engaged upon an opera to be known, by and by, as *Sumaïa*.

'Ah Atthis, it was Sappho who told me –' tentatively he sought an air.

A touch of banter there.

'*Ah Atthis* –' One must make the girl feel that her little secret is out . . . ; quiz her; but let her know, and pretty plain, that the Poetess had been talking . . .

'Ah Atthis –'

But somehow or other the lyric mood today was obdurate, and not to be persuaded.

'I blame the oysters! After oysters –' he murmured, turning about to ascertain what was exciting the dogs.

She was coming up the drive with her face to the sun, her body shielded behind a spreading bouquet of circumstance.

'It's all right; they'll not hurt you.'

'Sh'o, I not afraid!'

'Tell me who it is you wish to see.'

'Mammee send me wid dese flowehs . . .'

'Oh! But how scrumptious.'

'It strange how dey call de bees; honey-bees, sweat-bees, bumble-bees an' all!' she murmured, shaking the blossoms into the air.

'That's only natural,' he returned, his hand falling lightly to her arm.

'Madame Ruiz is in?'

'She is: but she is resting; and something tells me,' he suavely added, indicating a grassy bank, 'you might care to repose yourself too.'

And indeed after such a long and rambling course, she was glad to accept.

'De groung's as soft as a cushom,' she purred, sinking with nonchalance to the grass.

'You'd find it,' he said, 'even softer, if you'll try it nearer me.'

'Dis a mighty pretty place!'

'And you –' but he checked his tongue.

'Fo' a villa so grand, dair must be mo' dan one privy?'

'Some six, or seven!'

'Ours is broke.'

'You should get it mended.'

'De aggervatiness'!' she wriggled.

'Tell me about them.'

And so, not without digressions, she unfolded her life.

'Then you, Charlie, and Mimi are here, dear, to study?'

'As soon as de University is able to receibe us; but dair's a waiting list already dat long.'

'And what do you do with all your spare time?'

'Goin' round de shops takes up some ob it. An' den ob course, dair's de Cinés. Oh, I love de Lara. We went last night to see *Souls in Hell.*'

'I've not been!'

'Oh it was choice.'

'Was it? Why?'

'De scene ob dat story,' she told him, 'happen foreign; 'way crost de big watteh, on de odder side ob de world . . . an' de principal gal, she merried to a man who neglect her (ebery ebenin' he go to pahtys an' biars), while all de time his wife she sit at home wid her lil pickney at her breas'. But dair anodder gemplum (a friend ob de fambly) an' he afiah to woe her; but she only shake de head, slowly, from side to side, an' send dat man away. Den de hubsom lose his fortune, an', oh, she dat 'stracted, she dat crazed . . . at last, she take to gamblin,' but dat only make t'ings worse. Den de friend ob de fambly come back, an' offer to pay all de expenses ef only she unbend: so she cry, an' she cry, 'cos it grieb her to leab her pickney to de neglect ob de serbants (dair was three ob dem, an old buckler, a boy, an' a cook), but, in de end, she do, an' frtt! away she go in de fambly carriage. An' den, bimeby, you see dem in de bedroom doin' a bit ob funning.'

'What?'

'Oh ki; it put me in de gigglemints . . .'

'Exquisite kid.'

'Sh'o, de coffee-concerts an' de pictchures, I don't nebba tiah ob dem.'

'Bad baby.'

'I turned thirteen.'

'You are?'

'By de Law ob de Island, I a spinster ob age!'

'I might have guessed it was the Bar! These Law-students,' he murmured, addressing the birds.

'Sh'o, it's de trute,' she pouted, with a languishing glance through the sticks of her fan.

'I don't doubt it,' he answered, taking lightly her hand.

'Mercy,' she marvelled: 'is dat a watch dah, on your arm?'

'Dark, bright baby!'

'Oh, an' de lil "V.R." all in precious stones so blue.' Her frail fingers caressed his wrist.

'Exquisite kid.' She was in his arms.

'Vitti, Vitti! –' It was the voice of Eurydice Edwards. Her face was strained and quivering. She seemed about to faint.

# XI

Ever so lovely are the young men of Cuna-Cuna – Juarez, Jotifa, Enid – (these, from many, to distinguish but a few) – but none so delicate, charming, and squeamish, as Charlie Mouth.

'Attractive little Rose . . .' 'What a devil of a dream . . .' the avid belles would exclaim when he walked abroad, while impassioned widows would whisper 'Peach!'

One evening, towards sundown, just as the city lifts its awnings, and the deserted streets start seething with delight, he left his home to enjoy the grateful air. It had been a day of singular oppressiveness, and not expecting overmuch of the vesperal breezes, he had borrowed his mother's small Pompadour fan.

Ah, little did that nigger boy know as he strolled along what novel emotions that promenade held in store!

Disrelishing the dust of the Avenida, he directed his steps towards the Park.

He had formed already an acquaintanceship with several young men, members, it seemed, of the University, and these he would sometimes join, about this hour, beneath the Calabash-trees in the Marcella Gardens.

There was Abe, a lad of fifteen, whose father ran a Jazz Hall on the harbour-beach, and Ramon, who was destined to enter the Church, and the intriguing Esmé, whose dream was the Stage, and who was supposed to be 'in touch' with Miss Maxine Bush, and there was Pedro, Pedro ardent and obese, who seemed to imagine that to be a dress-designer to foreign Princesses would yield his several talents a thrice-blessed harvest.

Brooding on these and other matters, Charlie found himself in Liberty Square.

Here, the Cunan Poet, Samba Marcella's effigy arose – that 'sable singer of Revolt'.

Aloft, on a pedestal, soared the Poet, laurel-crowned, thick-lipped, woolly, a large weeping Genius, with a bold taste for draperies, hovering just beneath; her one eye closed, the other open, giving her an air of winking confidentially at the passer-by: 'Up Cunans, up! To arms, to arms!' he quoted, lingering to watch the playful swallows wheeling among the tubs of rose-oleanders that stood around.

And a thirst, less for bloodshed, than for a sherbet, seized him.

It was a square noted for the frequency of its bars, and many of their names, in flickering lights, shewed palely forth already.

Cuna! City of Moonstones; how faerie art thou in the blue blur of dusk!

Costa Rica. Chile Bar. To the Island of June . . .

Red roses, against tall mirrors, reflecting the falling night.

Seated before a cloudy cocktail, a girl with gold cheeks like the flesh of peaches, addressed him softly from behind: 'Listen, lion!'

But he merely smiled on himself in the polished mirrors, displaying moist-gleaming teeth and coral gums.

An aroma of aromatic cloves . . . a mystic murmur of ice . . .

A little dazed after a Ron Bacardi, he moved away: 'Shine, sah?' the inveigling squeak of a shoeblack followed him.

Sauntering by the dusty benches by the pavement-side, where white-robed negresses sat communing in twos and threes, he attained the Avenue Messalina with its spreading palms, whose fronds hung nerveless in the windless air.

Tinkling mandolines from restaurant gardens, light laughter, and shifting lights.

Passing before the Café de Cuna, and a people's 'Dancing', he roamed leisurely along. Incipient Cyprians, led by vigilant, blanched-faced queens, youths of a certain life, known as bwam-wam bwam-wams, gaunt pariah dogs with questing eyes, all equally were on the prowl. Beneath the Pharaonic pilasters of the Theatre Maxine Bush, a street crowd had formed before a notice described 'Important', which informed the Public that, owing to a 'temporary hoarseness', the rôle of Miss Maxine Bush would be taken, on that occasion, by Miss Pauline Collier.

The Marcella Gardens lay towards the end of the Avenue, in the animated vicinity of the Opera. Pursuing the glittering thoroughfare, it was interesting to observe the pleasure announcements of the various theatres, picked out in signs of fire: *Aïda: The Jewels of the Madonna: Clara Novotny and Lily Lima's Season.*

Vending bags of roasted peanuts, or sapadillos and avocado pears, insistent small boys were importuning the throng.

'Go away; I can't be bodder,' Charlie was saying, when he seemed to slip; it was as though the pavement were a carpet snatched from under him, and looking round, he was surprised to see, in a Confectioner's window, a couple of marble-topped tables start merrily waltzing together.

Driven onward by those behind, he began stumblingly to run towards the Park. It was the general goal. Footing it a little ahead, two loose women and a gay young man (pursued by a waiter with a napkin and a bill), together with the horrified, half-crazed crowd; all, helter-skelter, were intent upon the Park.

Above the Calabash-trees, bronze, demoniac, the moon gleamed sourly from a starless sky, and although not a breath of air was stirring, the crests of the loftiest palms were set arustling by the vibration at their roots.

'Oh, will nobody *stop* it?' a terror-struck lady implored.

Feeling quite white and clasping a fetish, Charlie sank all panting to the ground.

Safe from falling chimney-pots and signboards (that, for 'Pure Vaseline', for instance, had all but caught him), he had much to be thankful for.

'Sh'o nuff, dat was a close shave,' he gasped, gazing dazed about him.

Clustered back to back near by upon the grass, three stolid matrons, matrons of hoary England, evidently not without previous earthquake experience, were ignoring resolutely the repeated shocks:

'I always follow the Fashions, dear, at a distance!' one was saying: 'this little gingham gown I'm wearing, I had made for me after a design I found in a newspaper at my hotel.'

'It must have been a pretty old one, dear – I mean the paper, of course.'

'New things are only those you know that have been forgotten.'

'Mary . . . there's a sharp pin, sweet, at the back of your . . . *Oh!*'

Venturing upon his legs, Charlie turned away.

By the Park palings a few 'Salvationists' were holding forth, while in the sweep before the bandstand, the artists from the Opera in their costumes of *Aïda*, were causing almost a greater panic, among the ignorant, than the earthquake was itself. A crowd, promiscuous rather than representative, composed variously of chauffeurs (making a wretched pretence, poor chaps, of seeking out their masters), Cyprians, patricians (these in opera cloaks and sparkling diamonds), tourists, for whom the Hodeidah girls would *not* dance that night, and bwam-wam bwam-wams, whose equivocal behaviour, indeed, was perhaps more shocking even than the shocks, set the pent Park ahum. Yet, notwithstanding the upheavals of Nature, certain persons there were bravely making new plans.

'How I wish I could, dear! But I shall be having a houseful of women over Sunday – that's to say.'

'Then come the week after.'

'Thanks, then, I *will*.'

Hoping to meet with Abe, Charlie took a pathway, flanked with rows of tangled roses, whose leaves shook down at every step.

And it occurred to him with alarming force that perhaps he was an orphan.

Papee, Mammee, Mimi and lil Edna – the villa drawing-room on the floor . . .

His heart stopped still.

'An' dey in de spirit world – in heaven hereafter!' He glanced with awe at the moon's dark disk.

'All in dair cotton shrouds . . .'

What if he should die and go to the Bad Place below?

'I mizzable sinneh, Lord. You heah, Sah? You heah me say dat?

Oh, Jesus, Jesus, Jesus,' and weeping, he threw himself down among a bed of flowers.

When he raised his face it was towards a sky all primrose and silver pink. Sunk deep in his dew-laved bower, it was sweet to behold the light. Above him great spikes of blossom were stirring in the idle wind, while birds were chaunting voluntaries among the palms. And in thanksgiving, too, arose the matins bells. From Our Lady of the Pillar, from the church of La Favavoa in the West, from Saint Sebastian, from Our Lady of the Sea, from Our Lady of Mount Carmel, from Santa Theresa, from Saint Francis of the Poor.

# XII

But although by the grace of Providence the city of Cuna-Cuna had been spared, other parts of the island had sustained irremediable loss. In the Province of Casuby, beyond the May Day Mountains, many a fair Banana, or Sugar estate, had been pitifully wrecked, yet what caused perhaps the widest regret among the Cunan public was the destruction of the famous convent of Sasabonsam. One of the beauties of the island, one of the gems of tropic architecture, celebrated, made immortal (in *The Picnic*), by the Poet Marcella, had disappeared. A Relief Fund for those afflicted had at once been started, and as if this were not enough, the doors of the Villa Alba were about to be thrown open for 'An Evening of Song and Gala', in the causes of charity.

'Prancing Nigger, dis an event to take exvantage ob; dis not a lil t'ing love to be sneezed at at all,' Mrs Mouth eagerly said upon hearing the news, and she had gone about ever since, reciting the names of the list of Patronesses, including that of the Cunan Archbishop.

It was the auspicious evening.

In their commodious, jointly-shared bedroom, the Miss Lips, the fair Lips, the smiling Lips were maiding one another in what they both considered to be the 'Parisian way'; a way, it appeared, that involved much nudging, arch laughter, and, even, some prodding.

'In love? Up to my ankles! Oh, yes,' Edna blithely chuckled.

'Up to your topnot!' her sister returned, making as if to pull it.

But with the butt end of the curling-tongs, Edna waved her away.

Since her visit to the Villa Alba 'me, an' Misteh Ruiz' was all her talk, and to be his reigning mistress the summit of her dreams.

'Come on man wid dose tongs; 'cos I want 'em myself,' Miami murmured, pinning a knot of the sweet Night Jasmyn deftly above her ear.

Its aroma evoked Bamboo.

Oh, why had he not joined her? Why did he delay? Had he forgotten their delight among the trees, the giant silk-cotton-trees, with the hammer tree-frogs chanting in the dark: Rig-a-jig-jig, rig-a-jig-jig?

'Which you like de best man, dis lil necklash or de odder?' Edna asked, essaying a strand of orchid tinted beads about her throat.

'I'd wear dem both,' her sister advised.

'I t'ink, on de whole, I wear de odder; de one he gib me de time he take exvantage ob my innocence.'

'Since dose imitation pearls, honey, – he gib you anyt'ing else?'

'No; but he dat generous! He say he mean to make me a lil pickney gal darter: An', oh, won't dat be a day,' Edna fluted, breaking off at the sound of her mother's voice in the corridor.

'. . . and tell de cabman to take de fly-bonnets off de horses,' she was instructing Ibum as she entered the room.

She had a gown of the new mignonette satin, with 'episcopal' sleeves lined with red.

'Come, girls, de cab is waiting; but perhaps you no savey dat.'

They didn't; and, for some time, dire was the confusion.

In the Peacock drawing-room of the Villa Alba, the stirring ballet music from *Isfahan* filled the vast room with its thrilling madness. Upon a raised estrade, a corps of dancing boys, from Sankor, had glided amid a murmur of applause.

The combination of charity and amusement had brought together a crowded and cosmopolitan assembly, and early though it was, it was evident already that with many more new advents there would be a shortage of chairs. From their yachts had come several distinguished birds of passage, exhaling an atmosphere of Paris and Park Lane.

Wielding a heavy bouquet of black feathers, Madame Ruiz, robed in a gown of malmaison cloth-of-silver, watched the dancers from an alcove by the door.

Their swaying torsos, and weaving gliding feet, fettered with chains of orchids and hung with bells, held a fascination for her.

'My dear, they beat the Hodeidahs! I'm sure I never saw anything like it,' the Duchess of Wellclose remarked admiringly: 'That little one Fred,' she murmured, turning towards the Duke.

A piece of praise, a staid, small body in a demure lace cap chanced to hear.

This was 'the incomparable' Miss McAdam, the veteran ballet mistress of the Opera-house, and inventrix of the dance. Born in the frigid High Street of Aberdeen, 'Alice', as she was universally known among enthusiastic patrons of the ballet, had come originally to the tropics as companion to a widowed clergyman in Orders, when, as she would relate (in her picturesque, native brogue), at the sight of *Nature* her soul had awoke. Self-expression had come with a rush; and, now that she was ballet mistress of the Cunan opera, some of the daring *ensembles* of the Scottish spinster would embarrass even the good Cunans themselves.

'I've warned the lads,' she whispered to Madame Ruiz: 'to cut their final figure, on account of the Archbishop. But young boys are so excitable, and I expect they'll forget!'

Gazing on their perfect backs, Madame Ruiz could not but mourn the fate of the Painter, who, like Dalou, had specialized almost exclusively on this aspect of the human form; for, alas, that admirable Artist had been claimed by the Quake; and although his portrait of Madame Ruiz remained unfinished . . . there was still a mole . . . nevertheless, in gratitude, and as a mark of respect, she had sent her Rolls car to the Mass in honour of his obsequies, with the *crêpe* off an old black dinner-dress tied across the lamps.

'I see they're going to,' Miss McAdam murmured, craning a little to focus the Archbishop, then descanting to two ladies with deep purple fans.

'Ah, well! It's what they do in *Isfahan*,' Madame Ruiz commented, turning to greet her neighbour Lady Bird.

'Am I late for Gebhardt?' she asked, as if Life itself hinged upon the reply.

A quietly silly woman, Madame Ruiz was often obliged to lament the absence of intellect at her door: accounting for it as the consequence of a weakness for negroes, combined with a hopeless passion for the Regius Professor of Greek at Oxford.

But the strident cries of the dancers, and the increasing volume of the music, discouraged all talk, though ladies with collection-boxes (biding their time) were beginning furtively to select their next quarry.

Countess Katty Taosay, *née* Soderini, a little woman and sure of the giants, could feel in her psychic veins which men were most likely to empty their pockets: English Consul . . . pale and interesting, he would not refuse to stoop and fumble, nor Follinsbe 'Peter', the slender husband of a fashionable wife, or Charlie Campfire, a young boy like an injured camel, heir to vast banana estates, the darling, and six foot high if an inch.

'Why do big men like little women?' she wondered, waving a fan powdered with blue *paillettes*: and she was still casting about for a reason, when the hectic music stopped.

And now the room echoed briefly with applause, while admiration was divided between the superexcellence of the dancers, and the living beauty of the rugs which their feet had trod – rare rugs from Bokhara-i-Shareef, and Kairouan-city-of-Prayer, lent by the mistress of the house.

Entering on the last hand-clap, Mr and Mrs Mouth, followed by their daughters, felt, each, in their several ways, they might expect to enjoy themselves.

'Prancing Nigger, what a *furore*!' Mrs Mouth exclaimed. 'You b'lieb, I hope, now, dat our tickets was worth de money.'

Plucking at the swallow-tails of an evening 'West-End', Mr Mouth was disinclined to reopen a threadbare topic.

'It queah how few neegah dair be,' he observed, scanning the brilliant audience, many of whom, taking advantage of an interval, were flocking towards a buffet in an adjoining conservatory.

'Prancing Nigger, I feel I could do wid a glass ob champagne.'

Passing across a corridor, it would have been interesting to have explored the spacious vistas that loomed beyond: 'Dat must be one ob de priveys,' Edna murmured, pointing to a distant door.

'Seben, Chile, did you say?'

'If not more!'

'She seem fond ob flowehs,' Mr Mouth commented, pausing to notice the various plants that lined the way: from the roof swung showery azure flowers that commingled with the theatrically-hued cañas, set out in crude, bold, colour-schemes below, that looked best at night. But in their malignant splendour, the orchids were the thing. Mrs Abanathy, Ronald Firbank (a dingy lilac blossom of rarity untold), Prince Palairet, a heavy blue-spotted flower, and rosy Olive Moonlight, were those that claimed the greatest respect from a few discerning connoisseurs.

'Prancing Nigger, you got a chalk mark on your 'West-End'. Come heah, sah, an' let me brush it.'

Hopeful of glimpsing Vittorio, Miami and Edna sauntered on. With arms loosely entwined about each other's hips, they made, in their complete insouciance, a conspicuous couple.

'I'd give sumpin' to see de bedrooms, man, 'cos dair are chapels, an' barf-rooms, besides odder conveniences off dem,' Edna related, returning a virulent glance from Miss Eurydice Edwards, with a contemptuous, pitying smile.

Traversing a throng, sampling sorbets, and ices, the sisters strolled out upon the lawn.

The big silver stars, how clear they shone – infinitudes, infinitudes.

'Adieu, hydrangeas, adieu, blue, burning South!'

The concert, it seemed, had begun.

'Come chillens, come!'

In the vast drawing-room, the first novelty of the evening – an aria from *Sumaïa* – had stilled all chatter. Deep-sweet, poignant, the singer's voice was conjuring Sumaïa's farewell to the Greek isle of Mitylene, bidding farewell to its gracious women, and to the trees of white, or turquoise, in the gardens of Lesbos.

'Adieu, hydrangeas – '

Hardly a suitable moment, perhaps, to dispute a chair! But neither the Duchess of Wellclose or Mrs Mouth were creatures easily abashed.

'I pay, an' I mean to hab it.'

'You can't; it's taken!' the duchess returned, nodding meaningly towards the buffet, where the duke could be seen swizzling whisky at the back of the bar.

'Sh'o! Dese white women seem to t'ink dey can hab ebberyt'ing.'

'Taken,' the duchess repeated, who disliked what she called the *parfum d'Afrique* of the 'sooties', and as though to intimidate Mrs Mouth, she gave her a look that would have made many a Peeress in London quail.

Nevertheless in the stir that followed the song, chairs were forthcoming.

'From de complexion dat female hab, she look as doh she bin boiling bananas!' Mrs Mouth commented comfortably, loud enough for the duchess to hear.

'Such a large congregation should su'tinly assist de fund!' Mr Mouth resourcefully said, envisaging with interest the audience; it was not every day that one could feast the gaze on the noble baldness of the Archbishop, or on the subtle *silhouette* of Miss Maxine Bush, swathed like an idol in an Egyptian tissue woven with magical eyes.

'De woman in de window dah,' Mrs Mouth remarked, indicating a dowager who had the hard, but resigned look of the Mother of six daughters, in immediate succession. 'Hab a look, Prancing Nigger, ob your favourite statesman.'

'De immortal Wilberforce!'

'I s'poge it's de whiskers,' Mrs Mouth replied, ruffling gently her 'Borgia' sleeves for the benefit of the Archbishop. Rumour had it he was fond of negresses, and that the black private secretary he employed was his own natural son, while some suspected indeed a less natural connexion.

But Madame Hatso (of Blue Brazil, the Argentine; those nights in Venezuela and Buenos Ayres, 'bis' and 'bravas'! How the public had roared) was curtseying right and left, and glancing round to address her daughters, Mrs Mouth perceived with vexation that Edna had vanished.

In the garden he caught her to him:

'Flower of the Sugar cane!'

'Misteh Ruiz . . .'

'Exquisite kid.'

'I saw you thu de window-glass all de time, an' dair was I! laughing so silent-ly . . .'

'My little honey.'

'. . . no; 'cos ob de nabehs,' she fluted, drawing him beneath the great flamboyants that stood like temples of darkness all around.

'Sweetheart.'

'I 'clar to grashis!' she delightedly crooned as he gathered her up in his arms.

'My little Edna . . . ? . . . ? . . . ?'

'Where you goin' wid me to?'

'There,' and he nodded towards the white sea sand.

A yawning butler, an insolent footman, a snoring coachman, a drooping horse . . .

The last conveyance had driven away, and only a party of 'b—d—y niggers', supposed to be waiting for their daughter, was keeping the domestics from their beds.

Ernest, the bepowdered footman, believed them to be thieves, and could have sworn he saw a tablespoon in the old coon's pocket.

Hardly able to restrain his tears, Mr Mouth sat gazing vacuously at the floor.

'What' can keep de chile? . . . Oh Lord . . . I hope dair noddin' wrong.'

'On such a lovely ebenin' what is time!' Mrs Mouth exclaimed, taking up an attitude of night-enchantment by the open door.

A remark that caused Butler, and subordinate, to cough.

'It not often I see de cosmos look so special!'

'Ef she not heah soon, we better go widout her,' Miami murmured, who was examining the visitors' cards on the hall table undismayed by the eye of Ernest.

'It's odd she should so procrastinate; but la jeunesse, c'est le temps où l'on s'amuse,' Mrs Mouth blandly declared, seating herself tranquilly by her husband's side.

'Dair noddin', I hope, de matteh . . .'

'Eh, suz, my deah! Eh, suz.' Reassuringly, she tapped his arm.

'Sir Victor Virtue, Lady Bird, Princess Altamisal,' Miami tossed their cards.

'Sh'o it was a charming ebenin'! Doh I was sorry for de duchess, wid de duke, an' he all nasty drunk wid spirits.'

'I s'poge she use to it.'

'It was a perfect skangle! Howebber, on de whole, it was quite an enjoyable pahty – doh dat music ob Wagner, it gib me de retches.'

'It bore me, too,' Miami confessed, as a couple of underfootmen made their appearance, and joining their fidgeting colleagues by the door, waited for the last guests to depart, in a mocking, whispering group.

'Ef she not here bery soon,' Miami murmured, vexed by the servants' impertinent smiles.

'Sh'o, she be here directly,' Mrs Mouth returned, appraising through her fan-sticks the footmen's calves.

'It daybreak already!' Miami yawned, moved to elfish mirth by the over-emphasis, of rouge on her mother's round cheeks.

But under the domestics' mocking stare, their talk at length was chilled to silence.

From the garden come the plaintive wheepling of a bird (intermingled with the coachman's spasmodic snores), while above the awning of the door, the stars were wanly paling.

'Prancing Nigger, sah, heah de day. Dair no good waitin' any more.'

It was on their return from the Villa Alba, that they found a letter signed 'Mamma Luna', announcing the death of Bamboo.

## *XIII*

He had gone out, it seemed, upon the sea to avoid the earthquake (leaving his mother at home to take care of the shop), but the boat had overturned, and the evil sharks . . .

In a room darkened against the sun, Miami, distracted, wept. Crunched by the maw of a great blue shark: 'Oh honey.'

Face downward with one limp arm dangling to the floor, she bemoaned her loss: such love-blank, and aching void! Like some desolate, empty cave, filled with clouds, so her heart.

'An' to t'ink dat I eber teased you!' she moaned, reproaching herself for the heedless past; and as day passed over day, still she wept.

One mid-afternoon, it was some two weeks later, she was reclining lifelessly across the bed, gazing at the sunblots on the floor. There had been a mild disturbance of a seismic nature that morning, and indeed slight though unmistakable shocks had been sensed repeatedly of late.

'Intercession' services, fully choral – the latest craze of society – filled the churches at present, sadly at the expense of other places of amusement; many of which had been obliged to close down. A religious revival was in the air, and in the Parks and streets elegant dames would stop one another in their passing carriages, and pour out the stories of their iniquitous lives.

Disturbed by the tolling of a neighbouring bell, Miami reluctantly rose.

'Lord! What a din; it gib a po' soul de grabe-yahd creeps,' she murmured, lifting the jalousie of a sun-shutter and peering idly out.

Standing in the street was a Chinese Laundrymaid, chatting with two Chinamen with osier baskets, while a gaunt pariah dog was rummaging among some egg-shells and banana-skins in the dust before the gate.

'Dat lil fool-fool Ibum, he throw ebbery-t'ing out ob de window, an' nebba t'ink ob de stink,' she commented, as an odour of decay was wafted in on a gust of the hot trade wind. The trade winds! How pleasantly they used to blow in the village of Mediavilla. The blue trade wind, the gold trade wind caressing the bending canes . . . City life, what had it done for any of them, after all? Edna nothing else than a harlot (since she had left them there was no other word), and Charlie fast going to pieces, having joined the Promenade of a notorious Bar with its bright particular galaxy of boys.

'Sh'o, ebberyt'ing happier back dah,' she mused, following the slow gait across the street of some barefooted nuns; soon they would be returning, with many converts and pilgrims, to Sasabonsam, beyond the May Day Mountains, where remained a miraculous image of Our Lady of the Sorrows still intact. How if she joined them, too? A desire to express her grief, and thereby ease it, possessed her. In the old times there had been many ways: tribal dances, and wild austerities . . .

She was still musing, self-absorbed, when her mother, much later, came in from the street.

There had been a great Intercessional, it seemed, at the Cathedral, with hired singers, from the Opera-house and society women as thick as thieves, '*gnats*', she had meant to say (Tee-hee!), about a corpse. Arturo Arrivabene . . . a voice like a bull . . . and she had caught a glimpse of Edna driving on the Avenue Amanda, looking almost Spanish in a bandeau beneath a beautiful grey tilt hat.

But Miami's abstraction discouraged confidences.

'Why you so triste, Chile? Dair no good, at all, in frettin'.'

'Sh'o nuff.'

'Dat death was on de cards, my deah, an' dair is no mistakin' de fac'; an' as de shark is a rapid feeder it all ober sooner dan wid de crocodile, which is some consolation for dose dat remain to mourn.'

'Sh'o, it bring not an attom to me!'

''Cos de process ob de crocodile bein' sloweh dan dat ob de shark –'

'Ah, say no more,' Miami moaned, throwing herself in a storm of grief across the bed. And as all efforts to appease made matters only worse, Mrs Mouth prudently left her.

'Prancing Nigger, she seem dat sollumcholly an' depressed,' Mrs Mouth remarked at dinner, helping herself to some guava-jelly, that had partly dissolved through lack of ice.

'Since de disgrace ob Edna dat scarcely s'prisin',' Mr Mouth made answer, easing a little the napkin at his neck.

'She is her own woman, me deah sah, an' *I* cannot prevent it!'

In the convival ground-floor dining-room of an imprecise style, it was hard, at times, to endure such second-rate company, as that of a querulous husband.

Yes, marriage had its dull side, and its drawbacks; still, where would society be (and where morality!) without the married women?

Mrs Mouth fetched a sigh.

Just at her husband's back, above the ebony sideboard, hung a Biblical engraving after Rembrandt, *Woman Taken in Adultery*, the conception of which seemed to her exaggerated and overdone, knowing full well, from previous experience, that there need not, really, be so much fuss . . . Indeed, there need not be any: but to be *Taken* like that! A couple of idiots.

'W'en I look at our chillen's chairs, an' all ob dem empty, in my opinion, we both betteh deaded,' Mr Mouth brokenly said.

'I dare say dair are dose dat may t'ink so,' Mrs Mouth returned, refilling her glass; 'but, Prancing Nigger, I am not like dat; no, sah!'

'Where's Charlie?'

'I s'poge he choose to dine at de lil Cantonese restaurant on de quay,' she murmured, setting down her glass with a slight grimace: how *ordinaire* this cheap red wine! Doubtless Edna was lapping the wines of paradise! Respectability had its trials . . .

'Dis jelly mo' like lemon squash,' Mr Mouth commented.

''Cos dat lil liard Ibum, he again forget de ice! Howebber, I hope soon to get rid ob him: for de insolence ob his bombax is more dan

I can stand,' Mrs Mouth declared, lifting her voice on account of a piano-organ in the street just outside.

'I s'poge today Chuesd'y? It was a-Chuesd'y – God forgib dat po' frail chile.'

'Prancing Nigger, I allow Edna some young yet for dat position; I allow dat to be de matteh ob de case but, me good sah! Bery likely she marry him later.'

'Pah.'

'An', why not?'

'Chooh, nebba!'

'Prancing Nigger, you seem to forget dat your elder daughter was a babe ob four, w'en I put on me nuptial arange blastams to go to de Church.'

'Sh'o, I wonder you care to talk ob it!'

'An', today, honey, as I sat in de Cathedral, lis'nin' to de Archbishop, I seemed to see Edna, an' she all in *dentelles* so *chic*, comin' up de aisle, followed by twelve maids, all ob good blood, holdin' flowehs an' wid hats kimpoged ob feddehs – worn raddeh to de side, an' I heah a stranger say: "Excuse me, sah, but who dis fine marriage?" an' a voice make reply: "Why, dat Mr Ruiz de milliona'r-'r-'r'," an' as he speak, one ob dese Italians from de Opera-house, commence to sing, "De voice dat brieved o'er Eden", an' Edna she blow a kiss at me an' laugh dat arch.'

'Nebba!'

'Prancing Nigger, "wait an' see"!' Mrs Mouth waved prophetically her fan.

'No, nebba,' he repeated, his head sunk low in chagrin.

'How you know, sah?' she queried, rising to throw a crust of loaf to the organ man outside.

The wind with the night had risen, and a cloud of blown dust was circling before the gate.

'See de raindrops, deah; here come at last de big rain.'

'. . .'

'Prancing Nigger!'

'Ah'm thinkin'.'

# XIV

Improvising at the piano, Piltzenhoffer, kiddy-grand, he was contented, happy. The creative fertility, bursting from a radiant heart, more than ordinary, surprised him: 'My most quickening affair, since – ' he groped, smiling a little at several particular wraiths, more, or less, bizarre, that, in their time, had especially disturbed him. 'Yes; probably!' he murmured, enigmatically, striking an intricate, virile chord.

'Forgib me, dearest! I was wid de manicu' of de fingeh-nails.'

'Divine one.'

She stood before him.

Hovering there between self-importance and madcapery, she was exquisite quite.

'All temperament . . . !' he murmured, capturing her deftly between his knees.

She was wearing a toilette of white *crêpe de chine*, and a large favour of bright purple Costa-Rica roses.

'Soon as de sun drop, dey set out, deah: so de manicu' say.'

'What shall we do till then?'

'. . . or, de pistols!' she fluted, encircling an arm about his neck.

'Destructive kitten,' he murmured, kissing, one by one, her red, polished nails.

'Honey! Come on.'

He frowned.

It seemed a treason almost to his last mistress, an exotic English girl, perpetually shivering, even in the sun, this revolver practice on the empty Quinine-bottles she had left behind. Poor Meraude. It was touching what faith she had had in a dose of quinine! Unquestionably she had been faithful to *that*. And, dull enough, too, it had made her. With her albums of photographs, nearly all of midshipmen, how insufferably had she bored him: – 'This one, darling, tell me, isn't he – I, really – he makes me – and this one, darling! An Athenian viking, with hair like mimosa, and what ravishing hands! – oh my God! – I declare – he makes me –' Poor Meraude; she had been extravagant as well.

'Come on, an' break some bokkles!'

'There's not a cartridge left,' he told her, setting her on his knee.

> 'Ha-ha! Oh, hi-hi!
> Not a light;
> Not a bite!
> What a Saturday Night!'

she trilled, taking off a comedian from the Eden Garden.

Like all other negresses she possessed a natural bent for mimicry, and a voice of that lisping quality that would find complete expression in songs such as: Have you see my sweet garden ob Flowehs? Sst! Come closter, Listen heah, Lead me to the Altar, Dearest, and His Little Pink, proud, Spitting-lips are Mine.

'What is that you're wearing?'

'A souvenir ob today; I buy it fo' Luck,' she rippled, displaying a black briar cross pinned to her breast.

'I hope it's blessed?'

'De nun dat sold it, didn't say: Sh'o, its dreadful to t'ink ob po' Mimi, an' she soon a pilgrim all in blistehs an' rags,' she commented, as a page boy with bejasmined ears appeared at the door.

'Me excuse . . .'

'How dare you come in, lil saucebox, widdout knockin'?'

'Excuse, missey, but . . .'

'What ?'

Ibum hung his head.

'I only thoughted, it bein' Crucifix day, I would like to follow in de procession thu de town.'

'Bery well: but be back in time fo' dinner.'

'T'ank you, missey.'

'An' mind fo' once you are!'

'Yes, missey,' the niggerling acquiesced, bestowing a slow smile on Snob and Snowball, who had accompanied him into the room. Easy of habit, as tropical animals are apt to be, it was apparent that the aristocratic pomeranian was paying sentimental court to the skittish mouser, who, since her *περιπέτεια* of black kittens looked ready for anything.

'Sh'o, but she hab a way wid her!' Ibum remarked, impressed.

'Lil monster, take dem both, an' den get out ob my sight,' his mistress directed him.

Fingering a battered volume, that bore the book-plate of Meraude, Vittorio appeared absorbed.

'Honey.'

'Well?'

'Noddin'.'

In the silence of the room a restless bluebottle, attracted by the wicked leer of a chandelier, tied up incredibly in a bright green net, blended its hum with the awakening murmur of the streets.

'Po' Mimi. I hope she look up as she go by.'

'Yes, by Jove.'

'Doh after de rude t'ings she say to me –' she broke off, blinking a little at the sunlight through the thrilling shutters.

'If I remember, beloved, you were both equally candid,' he remarked, wandering out upon the balcony.

It was on the palm-grown Messalina, an avenue that comprised a solid portion of the Ruiz estate, that he had installed her, in a many-storied building, let out in offices and flats.

Little gold, blue, lazy and romantic Cuna, what chastened mood broods over thy life today?

'Have you your crucifix? Won't you buy a cross?' persuasive, feminine voices rose up from the pavement below. Active again with the waning sun, 'workers', with replenished wares, were emerging forth from their respective depots nursing small lugubrious baskets.

'Have you bought your cross?' The demand, when softly cooed, by some solicitous patrician, almost compelled an answer; and most of the social world of Cuna appeared to be vending crosses, or

'Pilgrims' medals' in imitation 'bronze', this afternoon upon the kerb. At the corner of Valdez Street, across the way, Countess Katty Taosay (*née* Soderini), austere in black with Parma violets, was presiding over a depot festooned with nothing but rosaries, that 'professed' themselves, as they hung, to the suave trade wind.

> 'Not a light:
> Not a bite!
> What a —'

Edna softly hummed, shading her eyes with a big feather fan.

It was an evening of cloudless radiance; sweet and mellow as is frequent at the close of summer.

'Oh, ki, honey! It so cleah, I can see de lil iluns ob yalleh sand, far away b'yond de Point.'

'Dearest!' he inattentively murmured, recognizing on the Avenue the elegant cobweb wheels of his mother's Bolivian buggy.

Accompanied by Eurydice Edwards, she was driving her favourite mules.

'An' de shipwreck off de coral reef, oh, ki!'

'Let me find you the long-glass, dear,' he said, glad for an instant to step inside.

Leaning with one foot thrust nimbly out through the balcony-rails towards the street, she gazed absorbed.

Delegates of agricultural guilds bearing banners, making for the Cathedral square (the pilgrims' starting-point), were advancing along the avenue amidst applause: fruit-growers, rubber-growers, sugar-growers, opium-growers all doubtless wishful of placating Nature that redoubtable Goddess, by showing a little honour to the Church. 'Oh Lord, *not* as Sodom,' she murmured, deciphering a text attached to the windscreen of a luxurious automobile.

'Divine one, here they are.'

'T'anks, honey, I see best widdout,' she replied, following the Bacchic progress of two girls in soldiers' forage-caps, who were exciting the gaiety of the throng.

'Be careful, kid; don't lean too far . . .'

'Oh, ki, if dey don't exchange kisses!'

But the appearance of the Cunan Constabulary, handsome youngsters, looking the apotheosis themselves of earthly lawlessness, in their feathered sun-hats and bouncing kilts, created a diversion.

'De way dey stare up; I goin' to put on a tiara!'

'Wait, do, till supper,' he entreated, manipulating the long-glass to suit his eye.

Driving or on foot, were the usual faces.

Seated on a doorstep, Miss Maxine Bush, the famous actress, appeared to be rehearsing a smart society rôle, as she flapped the air with a sheet of street-foul paper, while, rattling a money-box, her tame monkey, 'Jutland-ho', came as prompt for a coin as any demned Duchess.

'Ha-ha, Oh, hi-hi!' Edna's blasted catches: 'Bless her,' he exclaimed, relevelling the glass. Perfect. Good lenses these; one could even read a physician's doorplate across the way: 'Hours 2–4, Agony guaranteed' – obviously, a dentist, and the window-card too, above, 'Miss –? Miss –? Miss –? – *Speciality*: Men past thirty.'

Four years to wait. Patience.

Ooof! There went 'Alice' and one of her boys. Bad days for the ballet! People afraid of the Opera-house . . . that chandelier . . . and the pictures on the roof . . . And wasn't that little Lady Bird? Running at all the trousers: '*have* you your crucifix! . . . ? ?'

'Honey . . .'

She had set a crown of moonstones on her head, and had moonstone bracelets on her arms.

'My queen.'

'I hope Mimi look up at me!'

'Vain one.'

Over the glistering city the shadows were falling, staining the white-walled houses here and there as with some purple pigment.

'Accordin' to de lates' 'ticklers, de Procession follow de Paseo only as far as de fountain.'

'Oh . . .'

'Where it turn up thu Carmen Street, into de Avenue Messalina.'

Upon the metallic sheen of the evening sky she sketched the itinerary lightly with her fan.

And smiling down on her uplifted face, he asked himself whimsically how long he would love her. She had not the brains poor child, of course, to keep a man for ever. Heigho. Life indeed was often hard . . .

'Honey, here dey come!'

A growing murmur of distant voices, jointly singing, filled liturgically the air, together as the warning salute, fired at sundown, from the fort heights, above the town, reverberated sadly.

'Oh, la, la,' she laughed, following the wheeling flight of some birds that rose startled from the palms.

'The Angelus . . .'

'Hark, honey: what is dat dey singin'?'

*A thousand ages in Thy sight*
*Are like an evening gone,*
*Short as the watch that ends the night*
*Before the rising sun.*

Led by an old negress leaning on her hickory staff, the procession came.

Banners, banners, banners.

'I hope Mimi wave!'

Floating banners against the dusk . . .

'Oh, honey! See dat lil pilgrim-boy?'

*Time like an ever-rolling stream,*
*Bears all its sons away;*
*They fly forgotten, as a dream*
*Dies at the opening day.*

'Mimi, Mimi!' She had flung the roses from her dress: 'Look up, my deah, look up.'

But her cry escaped unheard.

*They fly forgotten, as a dream*
*Dies —*

The echoing voices of those behind lingered a little.

'Edna.'

She was crying.

'It noddin'; noddin', at all! But it plain she refuse to forgib me!'

'Never.'

'Perspirin', an' her skirt draggin', sh'o, she looked a fright.'

He smiled: for indeed already the world was perceptibly moulding her . . .

'Enuff to scare ebbery crow off de savannah!'

'And wouldn't the Farmers bless her.'

'Oh, honey!' Her glance embraced the long, lamp-lit avenue with suppressed delight.

'Well.'

'Dair's a new dancer at de Apollo tonight. Suppose we go?'

*Havana – Bordighera*

# *Concerning the Eccentricities of Cardinal Pirelli*

# I

Huddled up in a cope of gold wrought silk he peered around. Society had rallied in force. A christening – and not a child's.

Rarely had he witnessed, before the font, so many brilliant people. Were it an heir to the DunEden acres (instead of what it *was*) the ceremony could have hardly drawn together a more distinguished throng.

Monsignor Silex moved a finger from forehead to chin, and from ear to ear. The Duquesa DunEden's escapades, if continued, would certainly cost the Cardinal his hat.

> 'And ease my heart by splashing fountains.'

From the choir loft a boy's young voice was evoking Heaven.

'His hat!' Monsignor Silex exclaimed aloud, blinking a little at the immemorial font of black Macael marble that had provoked the screams of pale numberless babies.

Here Saints and Kings had been baptized, and royal Infantas, and sweet Poets, whose high names thrilled the heart.

Monsignor Silex crossed his breast. He must gather force to look about him. Frame a close report. The Pontiff, in far-off Italy, would expect precision.

Beneath the state baldequin, or Grand Xaymaca, his Eminence sat enthroned ogled by the wives of a dozen grandees. The Altamissals, the Villarasas (their grandeeships' approving glances, indeed, almost eclipsed their wives'), and Catherine, Countess of Constantine, the most talked-of beauty in the Realm, looking like some wild limb of Astaroth in a little crushed 'toreador' hat round as an athlete's coif with hanging silken balls, while beside her, a stout, dumpish dame, of enormous persuasion, was joggling, solicitously, an object that was of the liveliest interest to all.

Head archly bent, her fine arms divined through darkling laces, the Duquesa stood, clasping closely a week-old police-dog in the ripple of her gown.

'Mother's pet!' she cooed, as the imperious creature passed his tongue across the splendid uncertainty of her chin.

Monsignor Silex's large, livid face grew grim.

What, – disquieting doubt, – if it were her Grace's offspring after all? Praise heaven, he was ignorant enough regarding the schemes of nature, but in an old lutrin once he had read of a young woman engendering a missel-thrush through the channel of her nose. It had created a good deal of scandal to be sure at the time: the Holy Inquisition, indeed, had condemned the impudent baggage, in consequence, to the stake.

'That was the style to treat them,' he murmured, appraising the assembly with no kindly eye. The presence of Madame San Seymour surprised him; one habitually so set apart and devout! And Madame La Urench, too, gurgling away freely to the four-legged Father: 'No, my naughty Blessing; no, not now! . . . By and by, a *bone*.'

Words which brought the warm saliva to the expectant parent's mouth.

Tail awag, sex apparent (to the affected slight confusion of the Infanta Eulalia-Irene), he crouched, his eyes fixed wistfully upon the nozzle of his son.

Ah, happy delirium of first parenthood! Adoring pride! Since Times primaeval by what masonry does it knot together those that have succeeded in establishing, here, on earth, the vital bonds of a family's claim? Even the modest sacristan, at attention by the font, felt himself to be superior in parts to a certain unproductive chieftain of a princely House, who had lately undergone a course of asses' milk in the surrounding mountains – all in vain!

But, supported by the Prior of the Cartuja, the Cardinal had arisen for the act of Immersion.

Of unusual elegance, and with the remains, moreover, of perfect looks, he was as wooed and run after by the ladies as any *matador*.

'And thus being cleansed and purified, I do call thee "Crack"!' he addressed the Duquesa's captive burden.

Tail sheathed with legs 'in master's drawers', ears cocked, tongue pendent . . .

'Mother's mascot!'

'Oh, take care, dear; he's removing all your rouge!'

'*What?*'

'He's spoilt, I fear, your roses': the Countess of Constantine tittered.

The duquesa's grasp relaxed. To be seen by all the world at this disadvantage.

'Both?' she asked distressed, disregarding the culprit, who sprang from her breast with a sharp, sportive bark.

What rapture, what freedom.

'Misericordia!' Monsignor Silex exclaimed, staring aghast at a leg poised, inconsequently, against the mural-tablet of the widowed duchess of Charona – a woman, who, in her lifetime, had given over thirty million pezos to the poor!

Ave Maria purissima! What challenging snarls and measured mystery marked the elaborate recognition of father and son, and would no one then forbid their incestuous frolics?

In agitation Monsignor Silex sought fortitude from the storied windows overhead, aglow in the ambered light as some radiant missal.

It was Saint Eufraxia's Eve, she of Egypt, a frail unit numbered above among the train of the Eleven Thousand Virgins: an immaturish schoolgirl of a saint, unskilled, inexperienced in handling a prayer, lacking the vim and native astuteness of the incomparable Theresa.

Yes, divine interference, 'twixt father and son, was hardly to be looked for, and Eufraxia (she, of Egypt) had failed too often before . . .

Monsignor Silex started slightly, as from the estrade beneath the dome, a choir-boy let fall a little white spit.

Dear child, as though *that* would part them!

'Things must be allowed to take their "natural" course,' he concluded, following the esoteric antics of the reunited pair.

Out into the open, over the Lapis Lazuli of the floor, they flashed, with stifled yelps like things possessed.

'He'll tear my husband's drawers!' the duquesa lamented.

'The duque's legs. Poor Decima.' The Infanta fell quietly to her knees.

'Fortify . . . asses . . .' the royal lips moved.

'Brave darling,' she murmured gently rising.

But the duquesa had withdrawn it seemed to repair her ravaged roses, and from the obscurity of an adjacent confessional-box, was calling to order Crack.

'Come, Crack!'

And to the Mauro-Hispanic rafters the echo rose.

'Crack, Crack, Crack, Crack . . .'

## *II*

From the Calle de la Pasión, beneath the blue-tiled mirador of the garden wall, came the soft brooding sound of a seguidilla. It was a twilight planned for wooing, unbending, consent; many, before now, had come to grief on an evening such. 'It was the moon.'

Pacing a cloistered walk, laden with the odour of sun-tired flowers, the Cardinal could not but feel the insidious influences astir. The bells of the institutions of the *Encarnacion* and the Immaculate Conception, joined in confirming Angelus, had put on tones half-bridal, enough to create vague longings, or sudden tears, among the young patrician boarders.

'Their parents' daughters – convent-bred,' the Cardinal sighed.

At the Immaculate Conception, dubbed by the Queen, in irony, once 'The school for harlots' the little Infanta Maria-Paz must be lusting for her Mamma and the Court, and the lilac carnage of the ring, while chafing also in the same loose captivity would be the roguish *niñas* of the pleasure-loving duchess of Sarmento, girls whose Hellenic ethics had given the good Abbess more than one attack of fullness.

Morality. Poise! For without temperance and equilibrium — The Cardinal halted.

But in the shifting underlight about him the flushed camellias and the sweet Night-jasmines suggested none; neither did the shape of a garden-Eros pointing radiantly the dusk.

'For unless we have balance –' the Cardinal murmured, distraught, admiring against the elusive nuances of the afterglow the cupid's voluptuous hams.

It was against these, once, in a tempestuous mood, that his mistress had smashed her fan-sticks.

'Would that all liaisons would break as easily!' his Eminence framed the prayer: and musing on the appalling constancy of a certain type, he sauntered leisurely on. Yes, enveloping women like Luna Sainz, with their lachrymose tactless, 'mys', how shake them off? 'My' Saviour, 'my' lover, 'my' parasol – and, even, 'my' virtue . . .

'Poor dearie.'

The Cardinal smiled.

Yet once in a way, perhaps, he was not averse to being favoured by a glimpse of her: 'A little visit on a night like this' – Don Alvaro Narciso Hernando Pirelli, Cardinal-Archbishop of Clemenza, smiled again.

In the gloom there, among the high thickets of bay and flowering-myrtle . . . For, after all, bless her, one could not well deny she possessed the chief essentials: 'such, poor soul, as they are!' he reflected, turning about at the sound as of the neigh of a horse.

'Monseigneur . . .'

Bearing a biretta and a silver shawl, Madame Poco, the venerable Superintendent-of-the-palace, looking, in the blue moonlight, like some whiskered skull, emerged, after inconceivable peepings, from among the leafy limbo of the trees.

'Ah, Don Alvaro, sir! Come here.'

'Pest?' His Eminence evinced a touch of asperity.

'Ah, Don, Don, . . .' and skimming forward with the grace of a Torero, lassoing a bull, she slipped the scintillating fabric about the prelate's neck.

'Such nights breed fever, Don Alvaro, and there is mischief in the air.'

'Mischief?'

'In certain quarters of the city you would take it almost for some sortilege.'

'What next.'

'At the *Encarnación*, there's nothing, of late, but seedyness. Sister Engracia with a chickenpox, and Mother Claridad with the itch, while at the College of Noble Damosels in the Calle Santa Fé, I hear a daughter of Don José Illescas, in a fit of caprice, has set a match to her coronet.'

'A match to her what?'

'And how explain, Don Alvaro of my heart, these constant shots in the Cortes? Ah *sangre mio* in what Times we live!'

Ambling a few steps pensively side by side, they moved through the brilliant moonlight. It was the hour when the awakening fireflies are first seen like atoms of rosy flame floating from flower to flower.

'Singular times, sure enough,' the Cardinal answered, pausing to enjoy the transparent beauty of the white dripping water of a flowing fountain.

'And ease my heart by splashing – tum-tiddly-um-tum,' he hummed: 'I trust the choir-boys, Dame, are all in health?'

'Ah, Don Alvaro, no, sir!'

'Eh?'

'No, sir,' Madame Poco murmured, taking up a thousand golden poses.

'Why, how's that?'

'But few now seem keen on Leapfrog, or Bossage, and when a boy shows no wish for a game of Leap, sir, or Bossage —'

'Exactly,' his Eminence nodded.

'I'm told it's some time, young cubs, since they've played pranks on Tourists! Though only this afternoon little Ramón Ragatta came over queazy while demonstrating before foreigners the Dance of the Arc, which should teach him in future not to be so profane: and as to the acolytes, Don Alvaro, at least half of them are absent, confined to their cots, in the wards of the pistache Fathers!'

'Tomorrow, all well, I'll take them some melons.'

'Ah, Don, Don!!'

'And, perhaps, a cucumber,' the Cardinal added, turning valedictionally away.

The tones of the seguidilla had deepened and from the remote recesses of the garden arose a bedlam of nightingales and frogs.

It was certainly incredible how he felt immured.

Yet to forsake the Palace for the Plaza he was obliged to stoop to creep.

With the Pirelli pride, with resourceful intimacy he communed with his heart: deception is a humiliation; but humiliation is a Virtue – a Cardinal, like myself, and one of the delicate violets of our Lady's crown . . . Incontestably, too, – he had a flash of inconsequent insight, many a prod to a discourse, many a sapient thrust, delivered ex-cathedra, amid the broken sobs of either sex, had been inspired, before now, by what prurient persons might term, perhaps, a 'frolic'. But away with all scruples! Once in the street in mufti, how foolish they became.

The dear street. The adorable Avenidas. The quickening stimulus of the crowd: Truly it was exhilarating to mingle freely with the throng!

Disguised as a caballero from the provinces or as a matron (disliking to forgo altogether the militant bravura of a skirt), it became possible to combine philosophy, equally, with pleasure.

The promenade at the Trinidades seldom failed to be diverting, especially when the brown Bettita or the Ortiz danced! *Olé*, he swayed his shawl. The Argentina with Blanca Sanchez was amusing too; her ear-tickling little song 'Madrid is on the Manzanares', trailing the "ares' indefinitely, was sure, in due course, to reach the Cloisters.

Deliberating critically on the numerous actresses of his diocese, he traversed lightly a path all enclosed by pots of bergamot.

And how entrancing to perch on a bar-stool, over a glass of old golden sherry!

'Ah Jesus-Maria,' he addressed the dancing lightning in the sky.

Purring to himself, and frequently pausing, he made his way, by ecstatic degrees, towards the mirador on the garden wall.

Although a mortification, it was imperative to bear in mind the consequences of cutting a too dashing figure. Beware display. Vanity once had proved all but fatal: 'I remember it was the night I wore ringlets, and was called "my queen".'

And with a fleeting smile, Don Alvaro Pirelli recalled the persistent officer who had had the effrontery to attempt to molest him: 'Stalked me the whole length of the Avenue Isadora!' It had been a lesson. 'Better to be on the drab side,' he reflected, turning the key of the garden tower.

Dating from the period of the Reformation of the Nunneries, it commanded the privacy of many a drowsy patio.

'I see the Infanta has begun her Tuesdays!' he serenely noted sweeping the panorama with a glance.

It was a delightful prospect.

Like some great guitar the city lay engirdled ethereally by the snowy Sierras.

'Foolish featherhead,' he murmured, his glance falling upon a sunshade of sapphire chiffon, left by Luna: '"my" parasol!' he twirled the crystal hilt.

'Everything she forgets, bless her,' he breathed, lifting his gaze towards the Magnolia blossom cups that overtopped the tower, stained by the eternal treachery of the night to the azure of the Saint Virgin. Suspended in the miracle of the moonlight their elfin globes were at their zenith.

'Madrid is on the Manzan-ares,' he intoned.

But 'Clemenza', of course, is in white Andalucia.

## *III*

After the tobacco-factory and the railway-station, quite the liveliest spot in all the city was the cathedral-sacristia. In the interim of an Office it would be besieged by the laity, often to the point of scrimmage: aristocrats and mendicants, relatives of acolytes – each had some truck or other in the long lofty room. Here the secretary of the chapter, a burly little man, a sound judge of women and bulls, might be consulted gratis, preferably, before the supreme heat of the day. Seated beneath a sombre study of the Magdalen waylaying our lord (a work of wistful interest ascribed to Valdés Leal), he was, with tactful courtesy, at the disposal of anyone soliciting information as to 'vacant dates', or 'hours available', for some impromptu function. Indulgences, novenas, terms for special masses – with flowers and music? Or, just plain; the expense, it varied! Bookings for baptisms, it was certainly advisable to book well ahead; some mothers booked before the birth –; Ah-hah, the little Juans and Juanas; the angelic babies! And arrangements for a Corpse's lying-in-state: 'Leave it to me.' These, and such things, were in his province.

But the secretarial bureau was but merely a speck in the vast shuttered room. As a rule, it was by the old pagan sacrophaguses, outside the vestry-door, 'waiting for Father', that *aficionados* of the cult liked best to forgather.

It was the morning of the Feast of San Antolín of Panticosa, a morning so sweet, and blue and luminous, and many were waiting.

'It's queer the time a man takes to slip on a frilly!' the laundress of the Basilica, Doña Consolación, observed, through her fansticks, to Tomás the beadle.

'Got up as you get them . . .'

'It's true, indeed, I've a knack with a rochet!'

'Temperament will out, Doña Consolación; it cannot be hid.'

The laundress beamed.

'Mine's the French.'

'It's God's will *whatever* it is.'

'It's the French,' she lisped, considering the silver rings on her honey-brown hands. Of distinguished presence, with dark matted curls at either ear, she was the apotheosis of flesh triumphant.

But the entry from the vestry of a file of monsignori imposed a transient silence – a silence which was broken only by the murmur of passing mule bells along the street.

Tingaling, tingaling: evocative of grain and harvest the sylvan sound of mule bells came and went.

Doña Consolación flapped her fan.

There was to be question directly of a Maiden Mass.

With his family all about him, the celebrant, a youth of the People, looking childishly happy in his first broidered cope, had bent, more than once, his good-natured head, to allow some small brothers and sisters to inspect his tonsure.

'Like a little, little star!'

'No. Like a *perra gorda*.'

'No, like a little star,' they fluted, while an irrepressible grandmother, moved to tears and laughter, insisted on planting a kiss on the old 'Christian' symbol: 'He'll be a Pope some day, if he's spared!' she sobbed transported.

'Not he, the big burly bull,' Mother García of the Company of Jesus addressed Doña Consolación with a mellifluent chuckle.

Holding a bouquet of sunflowers and a basket of eggs she had just looked in from Market.

'Who knows, my dear?' Doña Consolación returned, fixing her gaze upon an Epitaph on a vault beneath her feet: '"He was a boy and she dazzled him." Heigh-ho! Heysey-ho . . . ! Yes, as I was saying.'

'Pho: I'd like to see him in a Papal tiara.'

'It's mostly luck. I well recall his Eminence when he was nothing but a trumpery curate,' Doña Consolación declared, turning to admire the jewelled studs in the ears of the President of the College of Noble Damosels.

'Faugh!' Mother García spat.

'It's all luck.'

'There's luck and luck,' the beadle put in. Once he had confined by accident a lady in the souterrains of the cathedral, and only many days later had her bones and a diary, a diary documenting the most delicate phases of solitude and loneliness, *a woman's contribution to Science*, come to light; a piece of carelessness that had gone against the old man in his preferment.

'Some careers are less fortunate than others,' Mother García exclaimed, appraising the sleek silhouette of Monsignor Silex, then precipitantly issuing from the Muniment-Room.

It was known he was not averse to a little stimulant in the bright middle of the morning.

'He has the evil Eye, dear, he has the evil Eye,' Doña Consolación murmured, averting her head. Above her hung a sombre Ribera, in a frame of elaborate, blackened gilding.

'Ah, well, I do not fear it,' the Companion of Jesus answered, making way for a dark, heavy belle in a handkerchief and shawl.

'Has any one seen Jositto, my little José?'

Mother García waved with her bouquet towards an adjacent portal, surmounted, with cool sobriety, by a long, lavender marble cross: 'I expect he's through there.'

'In the cathedral?'

'How pretty you look, dear, and what a very gay shawl!'

'Pure silk.'

'I don't *doubt* it!'

Few women, however, are indifferent to the seduction of a Maiden mass, and all in a second there was scarcely one to be found in the whole sacristia.

The secretary at his bureau looked about him: without the presence of *las mujares* the atmosphere seemed to weigh a little, still, being a Holiday of Obligation, a fair sprinkling of boys, youthful chapter hands whom he would sometimes designate as the 'lesser delights', relieved the place of its austerity.

Through the heraldic windows, swathed in straw-mats to shut out the heat, the sun-rays entered, tattooing with piquant freckles the pampered faces of the choir.

A request for a permit to view the fabled Orangery in the cloisters, interrupted his siestose fancies.

Like luxurious cygnets in their cloudy lawn, a score of young singing-boys were awaiting their cue: Low-masses, cheapness, and economy, how they despised them, and how they would laugh at 'Old Ends' who snuffed out the candles.

'Why should the Church charge *higher* for a short *Magnificat* than for a long *Miserere*?'

The question had just been put by the owner of a dawning moustache and a snub, though expressive nose.

'Because happiness makes people generous, stupid, and often as not they'll squander, boom, but unhappiness makes them calculate. People grudge spending much on a snivel – even if it lasts an hour.'

'It's the choir that suffers.'

'This profiteering . . . The Chapter . . .' there was a confusion of voices.

'Order!' A slim lad, of an ambered paleness, raised a protesting hand: Indulged, and made much-of by the hierarchy, he was Felix Ganay, known as Chief-dancing-choir-boy to the cathedral of Clemenza.

'Aren't they awful?' he addressed a child with a very finished small head. Fingering a score of music he had been taking lead in a mass of Palestrina, and had the vaguely distraught air of a kitten that had seen visions.

'After that, I've not a dry stitch on me,' he murmured, with a glance towards the secretary, who was making lost grimaces at the Magdalen's portrait.

A lively controversy (becoming increasingly more shrill) was dividing the acolytes and choir.

'Tiny and Tibi! Enough.' The intervention came from the full-voiced Cristóbal, a youngster of fifteen, with soft, peach-textured cheeks, and a tongue never far away. Considered an opportunist, he was one of the privileged six dancing-boys of the cathedral.

'Order!' Felix enjoined anew. Finely sensitive as to his prerogatives, the interference of his colleague was apt to vex him. He would be trying to clip an altar pose next. Indeed, it was a matter of scandal already, how he was attempting to attract attention, in influential places, by the unnecessary undulation of his loins, and by affecting strong scents and attars, such as Egyptian Tahetant, or Long flirt through the violet Hours. Himself, Felix, he was faithful to Royal Florida, or even to plain *eau-de-Cologne*, and to those slow Mozarabic movements which alone are seemly to the Church.

'You may mind your business, young Cristóbal,' Felix murmured, turning towards a big, serious, melancholy boy, who was describing a cigarette-case he had received as fee for singing 'Say it with Edelweiss' at a society wedding.

'Say it with what?' the cry came from an oncoming-looking child, with caressing liquid eyes, and a little tongue the colour of raspberry-cream – *so bright.* Friend of all sweets and dainties, he held San Antolín's day chiefly notable for the Saint's sweet biscuits, made of sugar and white-of-egg.

'And you, too, Chicklet. Mind your business, can't you?' Felix exclaimed, appraising in some dismay a big, bland woman, then descending upon the secretary at his desk, with a slow, but determined, waddle.

Amalia Bermudez, the fashionable Actress-manageress of the Teatro Victoria Eugenia, was becoming a source of terror to the chapter of Clemenza. Every morning, with fatal persistence, she would aboard the half-hypnotised secretary with the request that the Church should make 'a little christian' of her blue-chow, for unless it could be done it seemed the poor thing wasn't *chic.* To be *chic* and among the foremost vanward, this apart from the Theatre meant all to her in life, and since the unorthodox affair of 'the DunEdens', she had been quite upset by the chapter's evasive refusals.

'If a police-dog, then why not a chow?' she would ask: 'Why not my little Whisky? Little devil. Ah, believe me, Father, she has need of it; For she's supposed to have had a snake by my old dog Conqueror! . . . And yet you won't receive her? Oh, it's heartless. Men are cruel . . .'

'There she is! Amalia – the Bermudez': the whisper spread, arresting the story of the black Bishop of Bechuanaland, just begun by the roguish Ramón.

And in the passing silence the treble voice of Tiny was left talking all alone.

'. . . frightened me like Father did, when he kissed me in the dark like a lion': – a remark that was greeted by an explosion of coughs.

But this morning the clear, light laugh of the comedienne rang out merrily: 'No, no, *hombre*,' she exclaimed (tapping the secretary upon the cheek, archly with her fan), 'now don't, don't stare at me, and intimidate me like that! I desire only to offer "a Mass of Intention", fully choral, *that the Church may change her mind*.'

And when the cannon that told of Noon was fired from the white fortress by the river far away, she was still considering programmes of music by Rossini and Cimarosa, and the colour of the chasubles which the clergy should wear.

# IV

At the season when the Oleanders are in their full perfection, at the season when the oleanders are in their choicest bloom, it was the Pontiff's innovation to install his American type-writing apparatus in the long Loggie of the Apostolic Palace that had been in disuse since the demise of Innocent XVI. Out-of-doorish, as Neapolitans usually are, Pope Tertius II was no exception to the rule, preferring blue skies to golden ceilings – a taste for which indeed many were inclined to blame him. A compromise between the state-saloons and the modest suite occupied by his Holiness from choice, these open Loggie, adorned with the radiant frescoes of Luca Signorelli, would be frequently the scene of some particular Audience, granted after the exacting press of official routine.

Late one afternoon the Pontiff after an eventful and arduous day was walking thoughtfully here alone. Participating no longer in the joys of the world, it was, however, charming to catch, from time to time, the distant sound of Rome – the fitful clamour of trams and cabs, and the plash of the great twin-fountains in the court of Saint Damascus.

Wrapped in grave absorption, with level gaze, the lips slightly pinched, Pope Tertius II paced to and fro, occasionally raising a well-formed (though hairy) hand, as though to dismiss his thoughts with a benediction. The nomination of two Vacant Hats, the marriage annulment of an ex-hereditary Grand Duchess, and the 'scandals of Clemenza', were equally claiming his attention and ruffling his serenity.

He had the head of an elderly lady's-maid, and an expression concealed by layers of tactful caution.

'Why can't they all behave?' he asked himself, plaintively, descrying Lucrezia, his prized white squirrel, sidling shyly towards him.

She was the gift of the Archbishop of Trebizond who had found her in the region of the Coelian hill.

'Slyboots, slyboots,' Pope Tertius exclaimed, as she skipped from reach. It was incredible with what playful zest she would spring from statue to statue; and it would have amused the Vicar of Christ to watch her slip and slide, had it not suggested many a profound moral metaphor applicable to the Church: 'Gently, gently,' he enjoined; for once, in her struggles, she had robbed *a fig-leaf* off a 'Moses'.

'Yes, why can't they all behave?' he murmured, gazing up into the far pale-blueness.

He stood a brief moment transfixed, as if in prayer, oblivious of two whispering chamberlains.

It was the turn-in-waiting of Baron Oschatz, a man of engaging exquisite manners, and of Count Cuenca, an individual who seemed to be in perpetual consternation.

Depositing a few of the most recent camera portraits of the Pontiff requiring autograph in a spot where he could not fail but see them, they formally withdrew.

It had been a day distinguished by innumerable Audiences, several not uninteresting to recall . . .

Certainly the increasing numbers of English were decidedly promising, and bore out the sibylline predictions of their late great and sagacious ruler – that of Queen Victoria.

'The dear *santissima* woman,' the Pontiff sighed, for he entertained a sincere, if brackish, enthusiasm for the lady who for so many years had corresponded with the Holy See under the signature of *the Countess of Lostwaters*.

'Anglicans . . . ? Heliolaters and sun-worshippers,' she had written in her most masterful hand, 'and your Holiness may believe us,' she had added, 'when we say especially our beloved Scotch.'

'I shouldn't wonder enormously if it were true,' the Pope exclaimed, catching through a half-shut door a glimpse of violet stockings.

Such a display of old, out-at-heel hose could but belong to Cardinal Robin.

There had been a meeting of the board for Extraordinary Ecclesiastical Affairs, and when shortly afterwards the Cardinal was admitted, he bore still about him some remote trace of faction.

He had the air of a cuttle-fish, and an inquiring voice. Inclined to gesture, how many miles must his hands have moved in the course of the sermons that he had preached!

Saluting the sovereign Pontiff with a deep obeisance, the Cardinal came directly to the point.

'These schisms in Spain . . .'

'They are ever before me,' his Holiness confessed.

'With priests like Pirelli, the Church is in peril!' the Cardinal declared, with a short, abysmal laugh.

'Does he suppose we are in the Times of Bâal and Moloch?' the Pope asked, pressing a harassed hand to his head. A Neapolitan of Naples (oh, Bay of Napoli. See Vesuvius, *and die*), he had curly hair that seemed to grow visibly; every few hours his tonsure would threaten to disappear.

The Cardinal sent up his brows a little.

'If I may tender the advice of the secret Consistory,' he said, 'your Holiness should Listen in.'

'To what end?'

'A snarl, a growl, a bark, a yelp, coming from the font, would be quite enough to condemn . . .'

'Per Bacco. I should take it for a baby.'

'. . . condemn,' the Cardinal pursued, 'this Pirelli for a *maleficus pastor*. In which case, the earlier, the better, the unfrocking . . .'

The Pontiff sighed.

The excellent Cardinal was as fatiguing as a mission from Salt Lake City.

'Evidently,' he murmured, detecting traces of rats among the papyrus plants in the long walk below.

'They come up from the Tiber!' he exclaimed, piloting the Cardinal dexterously towards a flight of footworn steps leading to the Court of Bramante.

'It's a bore there being no lift!' he commented (the remark was Vatican cliché), dismissing the Cardinal with a benediction.

'A painful interview,' the Holy Father reflected, regarding the Western sky. An evening rose and radiant altogether . . .

Turning sadly, he perceived Count Cuenca.

A nephew of the Dean of the Sacred College, it was rumoured that he was addicted, in his 'home' above Frascati, to the last excesses of the pre-Adamite Sultans.

'A dozen blessings, for a dozen Hymens – but only eleven were sent,' he was babbling distractedly to himself. He had been unstrung all day, 'just a mass of foolish nerves,' owing to a woman, an American, it seemed, coming for her Audience in a *hat* edged with white and yellow water-lilies. She had been repulsed successfully by the Papal Guard, but it had left an unpleasant impression.

'How's that?' the Vicar of Christ exclaimed: he enjoyed to tease his Chamberlains – especially Count Cuenca.

The Count turned pale.

'———,' he replied inaudibly rolling eyes at Lucrezia.

Baron Oschatz had 'deserted' him; and what is one Chamberlain, alas, without another?

'The photographs of your Holiness are beside the bust of Bernini!' he stammered out, beating a diplomatic retreat.

Pope Tertius II addressed his squirrel.

'Little slyboots,' he said, 'I often laugh when I'm alone.'

## V

Before the white façade of the DunEden Palace, commanding the long, palm-shaded Paseo del Violón, an array of carriages and limousines was waiting, while passing, in brisk succession, beneath the portico, like a swarm of brilliant butterflies, each instant was bringing more. Dating from the period of Don Pedro *el cruel*, the palace had been once the residence of the famous Princesse des Ursins, who had left behind something of her conviviality and glamour. But it is unlikely that the soirées of the exuberant and fanciful Princesse eclipsed those of the no less exuberant Duquesa DunEden. It was to be an evening (flavoured with rich heroics) in honour of the convalescence of several great ladies, from an attack of 'Boheara', the new, and fashionable epidemic, diagnosed by the medical faculty, as 'hyperaesthesia with complications'; a welcoming back to the world in fact of several despotic dowagers, not one perhaps of whom had she departed this life would have been really much missed or mourned! And thus, in deference to the intimate nature of the occasion, it was felt by the solicitous hostess, that a Tertulia (that mutual exchange of familiar, or intellectual ideas) would make less demand, on arms and legs, than would a ball: just the mind and lips . . . a skilful rounding-off here, developing there, chiselling, and putting-out feelers; an evening dedicated to the furtherance of intrigue, scandal, love, beneath the eager eyes of a few young girls, still at school, to whom a quiet party was permitted now and then.

Fingering a knotted-scapular beneath a windy arch, Mother Saint-Mary-of-the-Angels was asking God His will. Should she wait for Gloria and Clyte (they might be some time) or return to the convent and come back again at twelve? 'The dear girls are with their mother,' she informed her Maker, inclining respectfully before the Princess Aurora of the Asturias, who had just arrived attended by two bearded gentlemen with tummies.

Hopeful of glimpsing perhaps a colleague, Mother Saint-Mary moved a few steps impulsively in their wake. It was known that Monseigneur the Cardinal-Archbishop himself was expected, and not infrequently one ecclesiastic will beget another.

The crimson saloon, with its scattered groups of chairs, was waxing cheery.

Being the day it was, and the social round never but slightly varying, most of the guests had flocked earlier in the evening to the self-same place (*i.e.*), the Circus, or *Arena Amanda*, where it was subscription night, and where, at present, there was an irresistibly comic clown.

'One has only to think of him to —' the wife of the Minister of Public Instruction exclaimed, going off into a fit of wheezy laughter.

'What power, what genius, what —!' the young wife of the Inspector of Rivers and Forests was at a loss. Wedded to one of the handsomest, though dullest of men, Marvilla de Las Espinafres' perfervid and exalted nature kept her little circle in constant awe, and she would be often jealous of the Forests (chiefly scrub) which her husband, in his official capacity, was called upon to survey. 'Don't lie to me. I know it! You've been to the woods.' And after his inspection of the aromatic groves of Lograno, Phaedra in full fury tearing her pillow with her teeth was nothing to Marvilla. 'Why, dear? Because you've been *among the Myrtles*,' was the explanation she chose to give for severing conjugal relations.

'Vittorio forbids the circus, on account of germs,' the wife of the president of the National Society of Public Morals murmured momentously.

'Really with this ghastly Boheara, I shall not be grieved when the time comes to set out for dear Santander!' a woman with dog-rose cheeks, and puffed, wrinkled eyes, exclaimed, focusing languishingly the Cardinal.

'He is delicious in handsomeness tonight!'

'A shade battered. But a lover's none the worse in my opinion for acquiring technique,' the Duchess of Sarmento declared.

'A lover; what? His Eminence . . . ??'

The duchess tittered.

'Why not? I expect he has a little woman to whom he takes off his clothes,' she murmured, turning to admire the wondrous *Madonna of the Mule-mill* attributed to Murillo.

On a wall-sofa just beneath crowned with flowers and aigrettes sat Conca, Marchioness of Macarnudo.

'*Que tal?*'

'My joie de vivre is finished; still, it's amazing how I go on!' the Marchioness answered, making a corner for the duchess. She had known her 'dearest Luiza' since the summer the sun melted the church bells and their rakish, pleasure-loving, affectionate hearts had dissolved together. But this had not been yesterday; no; for the Marchioness was a *grandmother* now.

'Conca, Conca: one sees you're in love.'

'He's from *Avila*, dear – the footman.'

'What!'

'Nothing *classic* – but, *oh*!'

'Fresh and blond? I've seen him.'

'Such sep . . .'

'Santiago be praised!'

The Marchioness of Macarnudo plied her fan.

'Our hands first met at table . . . yes, dear; but what I always say is, one spark explodes the mine!' And with a sigh she glanced rhapsodically at her fingers, powdered and manicured and encrusted with rings: 'Our hands met first at table,' she repeated.

'And . . . and the rest?' the duchess gasped.

'I sometimes wish though I resembled my sister more, who cares only for amorous, "delicate" men – the Claudes, so to speak. But there it is! And, anyway, dear,' the Marchioness dropped her voice, 'he keeps me from thinking (ah perhaps more than I should) of my little grandson. Imagine, Luiza . . . Fifteen, white and vivid rose, and ink-black hair . . .' And the Marchioness cast a long, pencilled eye towards the world-famous Pietà above her head.

'Queen of Heaven, defend a weak woman from *that*!' she besought.

Surprised, and considerably edified, by the sight of the dowager in prayer, Mother Saint-Mary-of-the-Angels was emboldened to advance: The lovely, self-willed donkey (or was it a mule?) that Our Lady was prodding, one could almost stroke it, hear it bray . . .

Mother Saint-Mary-of-the-Angels could have almost laughed.

But the recollection of the presence of royalty steadied her.

Behind pink lowered portières it had retired, escorted by the mistress of the house. She wore a gown of ivory-black with heavy golden roses and a few of her large diamonds of ceremony.

'I love your Englishy-Moorishy cosy comfort, Decima, and, I love —' the Princess Aurora had started to rave.

'An hyperaesthesia injection? . . . a beaten egg?' her hostess solicitously asked.

'*Per caritad!*' the Princess fluted, stooping to examine a voluptuous small *terre cuite*, depicting a pair of hermaphrodites amusing themselves.

She was looking like the ghost in the Ballet of Ghislaine, after an unusually sharp touch of Boheara; eight-and-forty hours in bed, and scandal declared not alone.

'A Cognac? . . . a crème de Chile? . . .'

'Nothing, nothing,' the Princess negligently answered, sweeping her long, primrose trailing skirts, across the floor.

It was the boudoir of the Winterhalters and Isabeys, once the bright glory of the Radziwollowna collection, and which, after several decades of disesteem, were returning to fashion and favour.

'And I love —' she broke off, nearly stumbling over an old blind spaniel, that resided in a basket behind the 'supposed original' of the *Lesbia of Lysippus*.

'Clapsey, Clapsey!' her mistress admonished. The gift of a dear, and once intimate friend, the dog seemed inclined to outlive itself and become a nuisance.

Alas, poor, fawning Clapsey! Fond, toothless bitch. Return to your broken doze, and dream again of leafy days in leafy Parks, and comfy drives and escapades long ago. What sights you saw when you could see; fountains, and kneeling kings, and grim beggars at

Church doors (those at San Eusebio were the worst). And sheltered spas by glittering seas: Santander! And dark adulteries and dim woods at night.

'And I love your Winterhalters!'

Beneath one of these, like a red geranium, was Cardinal Pirelli.

'Oh, your Eminence, the utter forlornness of Society! . . . Besides, (oh, my God!) to be the *one* Intellectual of a Town . . .' a wizened little woman, mistaken, not infrequently, for 'Bob Foy', the jockey, was exclaiming plaintively.

'I suppose?' Monseigneur nodded. He was looking rather Richelieu, draped in ermines and some old lace of a beautiful fineness.

'It's pathetic how entertaining is done now. Each year meaner. There was a time when the DunEdens gave balls, and one could count, as a rule, on supper. Tonight, there's nothing but a miserable Buffet, with flies trimming themselves on the food; and the champagne that I tasted, well, I can assure your Eminence it was more like foul flower-water than Mumm.'

'Disgraceful,' the Cardinal murmured, surrendering with suave dignity his hand to the lips of a pale youth all mouchoir and waist.

These kisses of young men, ravished from greedy Royalty, had a delicate savour.

The One Intellectual smiled obliquely.

'Your Eminence I notice has several devout salve-stains already,' she murmured, defending her face with her fan.

'Believe me, not all these imprints were left by men!'

The One Intellectual glanced away.

'The poor Princess, I ask you, has one the right to look *so* dying!'

'Probably not,' the Cardinal answered, following her ethereal transit.

It was the turn of the tide, and soon admittance to the boudoir had ceased causing 'heartburnings'.

Nevertheless, some few late sirens were only arriving.

Conspicuous among these was Catherine (the ideal-questing, God-groping and insouciant), Countess of Constantine, the aristocratic heroine of the capital, looking half-charmed to be naked and alive. Possessing but indifferent powers of conversation – at Tertulias and dinners she seldom shone – it was yet she who had coined that felicitous phrase: *Some men's eyes are sweet to rest in.*

Limping a little (she had sprained her foot, alas, while turning backward somersaults to a negro band in the Black Ballroom of the Infanta Eulalia-Irene), her reappearance on her misadventure was a triumph.

'Poor Kitty: It's a shame to ask her, if it's not a ball!' the Inspector of Rivers and Forests exclaimed, fondling the silvery branches of his moustache.

But, at least, a Muse, if not musicians, was at hand.

Clasping a large bouquet of American Beauty-roses, the Poetess Diana Beira Baixa was being besieged by admirers, to 'give them something; just something! *Anything* of her own.' Wedded, and proclaiming (*in vers libres*) her lawful love, it was whispered she had written a paean to her husband's '. . .' beginning: *Thou glorious wonder!* which was altogether too conjugal and intimate for recitation in society.

'They say I utter the cry of sex throughout the Ages,' she murmured, resting her free hand idly on a table of gold and lilac lacquer beside her.

The Duchess-Dowager of Vizeu spread prudishly her fan.

'Since me maid set me muskito net afire, I'm just a bunch, me dear, of hysterics,' she declared.

But requests for 'something; just something!' were becoming insistent, and indeed the Muse seemed about to comply, when, overtaken by the first alarming symptoms of 'Boheara', she fell with a longdrawn sigh to the floor.

## VI

Repairing the vast armholes of a chasuble, Madame Poco, the venerable Superintendent-of-the-palace, considered, as she worked, the social status of a Spy. It was not without a fleeting qualm that she had crossed the borderland that divides mere curiosity from professional vigilance, but having succumbed to the profitable proposals of certain monsignori, she had grown as keen on her quarry as a tigress on the track.

'It's a wearing life you're leading me, Don Alvaro; but I'll have you,' she murmured, singling out a thread.

For indeed the Higher-curiosity is inexorably exacting, encroaching, all too often, on the hours of slumber and rest.

'It's not the door-listening,' she decided, 'so much as the garden, and when he goes awenching Calle Nabuchodonosor.'

She was seated by an open window, commanding the patio and the gate.

'*Vamos, vamos!*' Madame Poco sighed, her thoughts straying to the pontifical supremacy of Tertius II, for already she was the Pope's Poco, his devoted Phoebe, his own true girl: 'I'm true blue, dear. True blue.'

Forgetful of her needle, she peered interestedly on her image in a mirror on the neighbouring wall. It was a sensation of pleasant novelty to feel between her skull and her mantilla the notes of the first instalment of her bribe.

'Earned, every *perra gorda*, earned!' she exclaimed, rising and pirouetting in elation before the glass.

Since becoming the courted favourite of the chapter, she had taken to strutting-and-languishing in private before her mirror, improvising occult dance-steps, semi-sacred in character, modelled on those of Felix Ganay at white Easter, all in the flowery Spring. Ceremonial poses such as may be observed in storied-windows and olden *pietàs* in churches (Dalilaesque, or Shulamitish, as the case might be) were her especial delight, and from these had been evolved an eerie 'Dance of Indictment'.

Finger rigid, she would advance ominously with slow, Salomé-like liftings of the knees upon a phantom Cardinal: 'And thus I accuse thee!' or, 'I denounce thee, Don Alvaro, for,' etc.

'*Dalila!* You old sly gooseberry,' she chuckled, gloating on herself in the greenish spotted-depth of a tall, time-corroded glass.

Punch and late hours had left their mark.

'All this Porto and stuff to keep awake make a woman liverish,' she commented, examining critically her tongue.

It was a Sunday evening of *corrida*, towards the Feast of Corpus, and through the wide open window came the near sound of bells.

Madame Poco crossed and recrossed her breast.

They were ringing 'Paula', a bell which, tradition said, had fused into its metal one of the thirty pieces of silver received by the Iscariot for the betrayal of Christ.

'They seem to have asked small fees in those days,' she reflected, continuing her work.

It was her resolution to divide her reward on masses for herself and the repose and 'release' (from Purgatory) of her husband's soul, while anything over should be laid-out on finery for a favourite niece, the little Leonora, away in the far Americas.

Madame Poco plied pensively her needle.

She was growing increasingly conscious of the physical demands made by the Higher-curiosity upon a constitution already considerably far-through, and the need of an auxiliary caused her to regret her niece. More than once, indeed, she had been near the point of asking Charlotte Chiemsee, the maid of the Duchess of Vizeu, to assist her. It was Charlotte who had set the duchess's bed-veils on fire while attempting to nip a romance.

But alone and unaided it was astonishing the evidence Madame

Poco had gained, and she smiled, as she sewed, at the recollection of her latest capture – the handkerchief of Luna Sainz.

'These hennaed heifers that come to confess! . . .' she scoffed sceptically: For Madame Poco had some experience of men – those brown humbugs (so delicious in tenderness) – in her time: 'Poor soul! He had the prettiest teeth . . .' she murmured, visualising forlornly her husband's face. He had been coachman for many years to the sainted Countess of Triana, and he would tell the story of the pious countess and the vermin she had turned to flowers of flame while foraging one day among some sacks before a secondhand-clothes shop. It was she, too, who, on another occasion, had changed a handful of marsh-slush into fine slabs of chocolate, each slab engraved with the insignia of a Countess and the sign of the Cross.

'Still, she didn't change *him*, though!' Madame Poco reflected dryly, lifting the lid to her work-box.

Concealed among its contents was a copy of the gay and curious *Memoirs of Mlle Emma Crunch*, so famous as 'Cora Pearl' –; a confiscated bedside-book once belonging to the Cardinal-Archbishop.

'Ps, ps!' she purred, feeling amorously for her scissors beneath the sumptuous oddments of old church velvet and brocade that she loved to ruffle and ruck.

'Ps.'

She had been freshening a little the chasuble worn last by his Eminence at the baptism of the blue-eyed police-pup of the Duquesa DunEden, and which bore still the primrose trace of an innocent insult.

'A disgraceful business altogether,' Madame Poco sighed.

Not everyone knew the dog was christened in *white menthe* . . .

'Sticky stuff,' she brooded: 'and a liqueur I never cared for! It takes a lot to beat Aniseed brandy; when it's old. Manzanilla runs it close; but it's odd how a glass or two turns me muzzy.'

She remained a moment lost in idle reverie before the brilliant embroideries in her basket. Bits of choice beflowered brocade, multi-tinted, inimitably faded silks of the epoca of Theresa de Ahumada, exquisite tatters, telling of the Basilica's noble past, it gladdened the eyes to gaze on. What garden of Granada could show a pink to match that rose, or what sky show a blue as tenderly serene as that azure of the Saint Virgin?

'*Vamos*,' she exclaimed rising: 'it's time I took a toddle to know what he's about.'

She had last seen the Cardinal coming from the orange orchard with a dancing-boy and Father Fadrique, who had a mark on his cheek left by a woman's fan.

Her mind still dwelling on *men* (those divine humbugs), Madame Poco stepped outside.

Traversing a white-walled corridor, with the chasuble on her arm, her silhouette, illumined by the splendour of the evening sun, all but caused her to start.

It was in a wing built in the troublous reign of Alfonso the Androgyne that the vestments were kept. Whisking by a decayed and ancient painting, representing 'Beelzebub' at Home, she passed slowly through a little closet supposed to be frequented by the ghosts of evil persons long since dead. Just off it was the vestry, gay with blue azulejos-tiles of an admirable lustre.

They were sounding Matteo now, a little bell with a passionate voice.

'The pet!' Madame Poco paused to listen. She had her 'favourites' among the bells, and Matteo was one of them. Passiaflora, too: – but Anna, a light slithery bell, 'like a housemaid in hysterics', offended her ear by lack of tone; Sebastián, a complaining, excitable bell, was scarcely better –; 'a fretful lover'! She preferred old 'Wanda' the Death-bell, a trifle monotonous, and fanatical perhaps, but 'interesting', and opening up vistas to varied thought and speculation.

Lifting a rosary from a linen-chest, Madame Poco laid the chasuble within. It was towards this season she would usually renew the bags of bergamot among the Primate's robes.

'This espionage sets a woman all behindhand,' she commented to Tobit, the vestry cat.

Black as the Evil One, perched upon a Confessional's ledge, cleansing its belly, the sleek thing sat.

It was the 'ledge of Forgotten fans', where privileged Penitents would bring their tales of vanity, infidelity and uncharitableness to the Cardinal once a week.

'Directing half-a-dozen duchesses must be frequently a strain!' Madame Poco deliberated, picking up a discarded mitre and trying it absently on.

With a plume at the side or a cluster of balls, it would make quite a striking toque, she decided, casting a fluttered glance on the male effigy of a pale-faced member of the Quesada family, hewn in marble by the door.

'*Caramba!* I thought it was the Cardinal; it gave me quite a turn,' she murmured, pursuing lightly her way.

Being a Sunday evening of *corrida*, it was probable the Cardinal had mounted to his aerie, to enjoy the glimpse of Beauty returning from the fight.

Oh, mandolines of the South, warm throats, and winged songs, winging . . .

Following a darkened corridor with lofty windows closely barred, Madame Poco gained an ambulatory, terminated by a fresco of Our Lady, ascending to heaven in a fury of paint.

'These damp flags'll be the death of me,' she complained, talking with herself, turning towards the garden.

Already the blue pushing shadows were beguiling from the shelter of the cloister eaves the rueful owls. A few flittermice, too, were revolving around the long apricot chimneys of the Palace, that, towards sunset, looked like the enchanted castle of some sleeping Princess.

'Bits of pests,' she crooned, taking a neglected alley of old bay-tree laurels, presided over by a plashing fountain comprised of a Cupid sneezing. Wary of mole-hills and treacherous roots, she roamed along, preceded by the floating whiteness of a Persian peacock, mistrustful of the intentions of a Goat-sucker owl. Rounding a sequestered garden seat, beneath an aged cypress, the bark all scented knots, Madame Poco halted.

Kneeling before an altar raised to the cult of Our Lady of Dew, Cardinal Pirelli was plunged in prayer.

'Salve. Salve Regina . . .' Above the tree-tops, a bird was singing.

## *VII*

The College of Noble Damosels in the Calle Santa Fé was in a whirl. It was 'Foundation' day, an event annually celebrated with considerable fanfaronade and social éclat. Founded during the internecine wars of the Middle Age, the College, according to early records, had suffered rapine on the first day of term. Hardly it seemed had the last scholar's box been carried upstairs, than a troop of military had made its appearance at the Pension gate demanding, with 'male peremptoriness', a billet. 'I, alone,' the Abbess ingeniously states, in relating the poignant affair in her unpublished diary: 'I alone did all I was able to keep them from them, for which they (the scholars) called me "greedy".' Adding, not without a touch of modern socialism in disdain for titles, that she had preferred 'the staff-officers to the Field-Marshal,' while as to ensigns, in her estimation, why, 'one was worth the lot'.

Polishing urbanely her delicate nails, the actual President, a staid, pale woman with a peacock nose, recalled the chequered past. She hoped his Eminence when he addressed the girls, on handing them their prizes, would refer to the occasion with all the tactfulness required.

'When I think of the horrid jokes the old Marqués of Illescas made last year,' she murmured, bestowing a harrowed smile on a passing pupil.

She was ensconced in a ponderous fauteuil of figured velvet (intended for the plump posterior of Royalty), beneath the incomparable 'azulejos' ceiling of the Concert-room, awaiting the return of Madame Always Alemtejo, the English governess, from the printers, in the Plaza de Jesús, with the little silver-printed programmes (so like the paste-board cards of brides!), and which, as usual, were late.

'Another year we'll type them,' she determined, awed by the ardent tones of a young girl rehearsing an aria from the new opera, *Leda* – 'Gaze not on Swans'.

'Ah, gaze not so on Swan-zzz! . . .'

'Crisper, child. Distinction. Don't exaggerate,' the President enjoined, raising a hand to the diamonds on her heavy, lead-white cheeks.

Née an Arroyolo, and allied by marriage with the noble house of Salvaterra, the head mistress in private life was the Dowager-Marchioness of Pennisflores.

'*Nosotros*, you know, are not candidates for the stage! Bear in mind your moral,' she begged, with a lingering glance at her robe of grey georgette.

The word 'moral', never long from the President's lips, seemed, with her, to take on an intimate tinge, a sensitiveness of its own. She would invest the word at times with an organic significance, a mysterious dignity, that resembled an avowal made usually only in solemn confidence to a doctor or a priest.

The severity of my moral. The prestige of my moral. The perfection of my moral. She has no dignity of moral. I fear a person of no positive moral. Nothing to injure the freshness of her moral. A difficulty of moral. The etiquette of my moral. The majesty of my moral, etc., etc. – as uttered by the President, became, psychologically, interesting *data*.

'Beware of a facile moral!' she added, for the benefit of the singer's accompanist, a young nun with a face like some strange white rock, who was inclined to give herself married airs, since she had been debauched, one otiose noon, by a demon.

'Ah, Madame Always.' The President swam to meet her.

British born, hailing from fairy Lisbon, Madame Always Alemtejo seemed resigned to live and die in a land of hitches.

'The delay is owing to the Printers' strike,' she announced. 'The Plaza's thronged: the Cigar factory girls, and all the rag-tag and bobtail, from the Alcazaba to the Puerta del Mar, are going out in sympathy, and —'

'The tarts?'

'The t's from Chamont are on the way.'

It was the President's custom to lay all vexations before Nostra Señora de los Remedios, the college's divine Protectress, with whose gracious image she was on the closest footing.

Consulting her now as to the concert-programmes, the President recalled that no remedy yet had been found for Señorita Violeta de las Cubas, who had thrown her engagement ring into a place of less dignity than convenience, and refused to draw it out.

'Sapphires, my favourite stones,' the President reflected, wondering if she should ask 'la Inglesa' to recover it with the asparagus-tongs.

But already a few *novios*, eager to behold their *novias* again, were in the Patio beneath the 'Heiresses' Wing', exciting the connoisseurship of a bevy of early freshness.

'You can tell *that* by his eyebrows!' a girl of thirteen and just beginning as a woman, remarked.

'*Que barbaridad.*'

'Last summer at Santander I and Maria-Manuela bathed with him, and one morning there was a tremendous sea, with *terrific* waves, and we noticed unmistakably.'

'I can't explain; but I adore all that mauvishness about him!'

'I prefer Manolito to Gonzalito, though neither thrill me like the Toreador Tancos.'

Assisted by Fräulein Pappenheim and Muley, the president's negress maid, they were putting the final touches to their vestal frocks.

'Men are my raging disgust,' a florid girl of stupendous beauty declared, saturating with a flacon of *Parfum cruel* her prematurely formed silhouette.

'Nsa, nsa, señorita,' Muley mumbled. 'Some know better dan dat!'

'To hell with them!'

'*Adios*, Carlo. *Adios*, Juan. Join you down dah in one minute.' The negress chuckled jauntily.

'Muley, Muley.' Fräulein chided.

'What wonder next I 'bout to hear?'

Delighting in the tender ferocities of Aphrodite, she was ever ready to unite the *novio* to the *novia.* For window-vigils (where all is hand play), few could contrive more ingeniously than she those fans of fresh decapitated flowers, tuberose punctuated with inebriating jasmine, so beloved in the East by the dark children of the sun. Beyond Cádiz the blue, the Beautiful, in palm-girt Marrakech, across the sea, she had learnt other arts besides . . .

'Since seeing Peter Prettylips on the screen the Spanish type means nothing to me,' Señorita Soledad, a daughter of the first Marqués of Belluga, the greatest orange-king in the Peninsula, remarked.

'How low. She is not noble.'

'I *am* noble.'

'Oh no; you're not.'

'Cease wrangling,' Fräulein exclaimed, 'and enough of that,' she added sharply, addressing a *novio*less little girl looking altogether bewitching of naughtiness as she tried her ablest to seduce by her crude manoeuvres the fiancé of a friend. Endowed with the lively temperament of her grandmother, Conca, Marchioness of Macarnudo, the impressionable, highly amative nature of the little Obdulia gave her governesses some grounds for alarm. At the Post Office one day she had watched a young man lick a stamp. His rosy tongue had vanquished her. In fact, at present, she and a class-chum, Milagros, were 'collecting petals' together – and much to the bewilderment of those about them, they might be heard on occasion to exclaim, at Mass, or in the street: 'Quick, did you see it?' 'No.' 'Santissima! *I* did!'

'Shrimp. As if Gerardo would look at her!' his *novia* scoffed: 'But let me tell you, young woman,' she turned upon the shrinking Obdulia, 'that social ostracism, and even, in certain cases' (she slapped and pinched her), '*assassination* attends those that thieve or tamper with another's lover! And Fräulein will correct me if I exaggerate.'

Fräulein Pappenheim was a little woman already drifting towards the sad far shores of forty, with no experience of the pains of Aphrodite caused by men; only at times she would complain of stomach aches in the head.

'Dat is so,' Muley struck in sententiously for her: 'Dair was once a young lady ob Fez —'

But from the Patio the college chaplain, Father Damien Forment, known as 'Shiney-nose' was beckoning to the heiresses to join their relatives in the reception-hall below.

Since that sanguinary period of Christianity, synchronising with the foundation of the institution of learning in the Calle Santa Fé, what changes in skirts and trousers the world has seen. Alone unchanging are women's ambitions and men's desires.

'Dear child . . . She accepts him . . . but a little à contre-coeur,' the president was saying to the Marchioness of las Cubas, an impoverished society belle, who went often without bread, in order to buy lip-sticks and rouge.

'With Violeta off my hands . . . Ah, President, if only Cecilio could be suitably *casado*.'

'In my little garden I sometimes work a brother. The heiresses' windows are all opening to the flowers and trees . . . The boy should be in Polo kit. A uniform interests girls,' the President murmured, turning with an urbane smile to welcome the Duquesa DunEden.

She had a frock of black kasha, signed Paul Orna, with a cluster of brown-and-pink orchids, like sheep's-kidneys, and a huge feather hat.

'I'm here for my God-girl, Gloria,' she murmured, glancing mildly round.

Incongruous that this robust, rich woman should have brought to the light of heaven no heir, while the unfortunate Marchioness needy, and frail of physique, a wraith, did not know what to do with them!

The President dropped a sigh.

She was prepared to take a dog of the daughterless Duquesa. A bitch, of course . . . But let it be Police, or Poodle! It would lodge with the girls. A cubicle to itself in the heiresses' wing; and since there would be no extra class-charge for dancing or drawing, no course *in belle arti*, some reduction of fees might be arranged . . . 'We would turn her out a creature of breeding . . . An eloquent tail-wave, a disciplined moral, and with a reverence moreover for house-mats and carpets.' The President decided to draw up the particulars of the prospectus by and by.

'Your Goddaughter is quite one of our most promising

exhibitioners,' she exclaimed, indicating with her fan some water-colour studies exposed upon the walls.

'She comes of a mother with a mania for painting,' the Duquesa declared, raising a lorgnon, critically, before the portrait of a Lesbian, with dying, fabulous eyes.

'Really?'

'A positive passion,' the Duquesa answered, with a swift, discerning glance at an evasive 'nude', showing the posterior poudrederizé of a Saint.

'I had no idea,' the President purred, drawing attention to a silvery streetscape.

'It's the Rambla from the back of Our Lady of the Pillar! It was rare fun doing it, on account of the *pirapos* of the passers-by,' the artist, joining them, explained.

'Dear child, I predict for her a great deal of admiration very soon,' the President murmured, with a look of reproach at a youthful pupil as she plied her boy-Father with embarrassing questions: 'Who are the chief society women in the moon? What are their names? Have they got motor-cars there? Is there an Opera-House? Are there bulls?'

When the leering aspect of a lady in a costume of blonde Guadalmedina lace and a hat wreathed with clipped black cocks' feathers arrested her.

Illusion-proof, with a long and undismayed service in Love's House (sorry brutes, all the same, though, these men, with their selfishness, fickleness and lies!), the Marchioness of Macarnudo with her mysterious 'legend' (unscrupulous minxes, all the same, though, these women, with their pettiness, vanity and . . . !), was too temperamentally intriguing a type, to be ignored.

'Isn't that little Marie Dorothy with the rosebuds stuck all over her?' she asked her granddaughter who was teasing her brother on his moustache.

'To improve the growth, the massage of a *novia*'s hand,' she fluted, provoking the marchioness to an involuntary nervous gesture. Exasperated by resistance, struggling against an impossible infatuation, her Spanish ladyship was becoming increasingly subject to passing starts. Indeed only in excitement and dissipation could her unsatisfied longings find relief. Sometimes she would run out in her car to where the men bathe at Ponte Delgado, and one morning, after a ball, she had been seen standing on the main road to Cádiz in a cabuchon tiara, watching the antics of some nude muleteers: *Black as young Indians* – she had described them later.

'My sweet butterfly! What next?' she exclaimed, ogling Obdulia, whose elusive resemblance to her brother was really curiously disturbing.

Averting a filmy eye, she recognised Marvilla de las Espinafres, airing anti-patriotic views on Birth control, her arms about an adopted daughter: 'Certainly not; most decidedly *no*! I should scream!' she was saying as from the Concert-room the overture began thinning the crowd.

'It's nothing else than a National disaster,' the marchioness declared to her grandson, 'how many women nowadays seem to shirk their duty!'

'Well the de las Cubas hasn't anyway,' he demurred.

'Poor thing. They say she jobs her mules,' the marchioness murmured, exchanging a nod with the passing President.

Something, manifestly, had occurred to disturb the equilibrium of her moral.

'Such a disappointment, *Nostra Señora*!' she exclaimed. 'Monseigneur, it seems, has thrown me over.'

'Indeed; how awkward!'

'I fear though even more so for his chapter.'

'He is not ill?'

'*Cardinal Pirelli has fled the capital!*'

# VIII

Standing amid gardens made for suffering and delight, is the disestablished, and, *sic transit*, slowly decaying monastery of the Desierto. Lovely as Paradise, oppressive perhaps as Eden, it had been since the days of the mystic Luigi of Granada a site well suited to meditation and retreat. Here, in the stilly cypress-court, beneath the snowy sierras of Santa Maria la Blanca, Theresa of Ávila, worn and ill, though sublime in laughter, exquisite in beatitude, had composed a part of the *Way of Perfection*, and, here, in these same realms of peace, dominating the distant city of Clemenza and the fertile plains of Andalucia, Cardinal Pirelli, one blue midday towards the close of summer, was idly considering his Defence: '*Apologia*, no; merely a defence,' he mused: 'Merely,' he flicked the ash-tip of a cigar: 'a defence! I defend myself, that's all! . . .'

A sigh escaped him.

Divided by tranquil vineyards and orange-gardens from the malice and vindictiveness of men it was difficult to experience emotions other than of forgiveness and love.

'Come, dears, and kiss me,' he murmured, closing consentingly his eyes.

It was the forgetful hour of noon, when Hesperus from his heavens confers on his pet Peninsula the boon of sleep.

'A nice nap he's having, poor old gentleman,' Madame Poco surveyed her master.

Ill-at-ease and lonely in the austere dismantled house, she would keep an eye on him at present almost as much for company as for gain.

As handsome and as elegant as ever, his physiognomy in repose revealed a thousand strange fine lines, suggestive subtleties, intermingled with less ambiguous signs, denoting stress and care.

'He's growing almost huntedish,' she observed, casting a brief glance at the literature beside him – The Trial of Don Fernando de la Cerde, Bishop of Barcelona, defrocked for putting young men to improper uses; a treatise on The Value of Smiles; an old volume of Songs, by Sà de Miranda; The Lives of Five Negro Saints, from which escaped a bookmark of a dancer in a manton.

'Everything but his Breviary,' she commented, perceiving a soutaned form through the old flowered ironwork of the courtyard gateway.

Regretting her better gown of hooped water-silk, set aside while in retreat (for economy's sake), Madame Poco fled to put it on, leaving the visitor to announce himself.

The padre of Our Lady of the Valley, the poor padre of Our Lady, would the Primate know? Oh, every bird, every rose, could have told him that: the padre of Our Lady bringing a blue trout for his Eminence's supper from the limpid waters of Lake Orense.

Respecting the Primate's rest Father Felicitas, for so, also, was he named, sat down discreetly to await his awakening.

It was a rare sweetness to have the Cardinal to himself thus intimately. Mostly, in the city, he would be closely surrounded. Not that Father Felicitas went very much to town; no; he disliked the confusion of the streets, and even the glories of the blessed basilicas made him scarcely amends for the quiet shelter of his hills.

The blessed basilicas, you could see them well from here. The giralda of Saint Xarifa, and the twin august towers of the cathedral, and the azulejos dome of Saint Eusebio, that was once a pagan mosque; while in Santissima Marias, Maria del Carmen, Maria del Rosario, Maria de la Soledad, Maria del Dolores, Maria de las Nieves, few cities in all the wide world could show as many.

'To be sure, to be sure,' he exclaimed absently, lifting his eyes to a cloudlet leisurely pointing above the lofty spur of the Pico del Mediodia. 'To be sure,' he added, seeking to descry the flower-like bellcot of Our Lady of the Valley just beneath.

But before he had discovered it, half concealed by trees, he was reminded by the sound of a longdrawn, love-sick wail, issuing out of the very entrails of the singer, of the lad left in charge of his rod by the gate.

'On the Bridge to Alcantara.'

With its protracted cadences and doleful, vain-yearning reaches, the voice, submerged in all the anguish of a Malagueña, troubled, nostalgically, the stillness.

God's will be done. It was enough to awaken the Primate. Not everyone relished a Malagueña, a dirgeful form of melody introduced, tradition said, and made popular in the land, long, long ago, beneath the occupation of the Moors.

Father Felicitas could almost feel the sin of envy as he thought of the flawless choir and noble triumphal organ of the cathedral yonder.

Possessed of no other instrument, Our Lady of the Valley depended at present on a humble guitar. Not that the blessed guitar, with its capacity for emotion, is unworthy to please God's listening ear, but Pepe, the lad appointed to play it, would fall all too easily into those Jotas, Tangos, and Cuban Habaneras, learnt in wayside fondas and fairs. Some day, Father Felicitas did not doubt, Our Lady would have an organ, an organ with pipes. He had prayed for it so often; oh, so often; and once, quite in the late of twilight while coming through the church, he had seen her it seemed standing just where it should be. It had been as though a blinding whiteness.

'A blinding whiteness,' he murmured, trembling a little at the recollection of the radiant vision.

Across the tranquil court a rose-red butterfly pursued a blue. 'I believe the world is all love, only no one understands,' he meditated, contemplating the resplendent harvest plains steeped in the warm sweet sunlight.

'My infinite contrition!' The Cardinal spoke.

A rare occurrence in these days was a visitor, and now with authority ebbing, or in the balance at least, it was singular how he felt a new interest in the concerns of the diocese. The birth-rate and the death-rate, and the super-rate, which it was to be feared that the *Cortes* —

Sailing down the courtyard in her watered-silken gown, Madame

Poco approached with Xeres and Manzanilla, fresh from the shuttered snowery or nieveria.

'And I've just buried a bottle of champagne, in case your Eminence should want it,' she announced as she inviolably withdrew.

'As devoted a soul as ever there was, and loyal to all my interests,' the Primate exclaimed, touched.

'God be praised!'

'An excellent creature,' the Cardinal added, focusing on the grey high road beyond the gate two youths on assback, seated close.

'Andalucians, though of another parish.'

'I should like much to visit my diocese again; it's some while since I did,' the Cardinal observed, filling the Padre's glass.

'You'd find up at Sodré a good many changes.'

'Have they still the same little maid at the Posada de la Melodia?'

'Carmencita?'

'A dainty thing.'

'She went Therewards about the month of Mary.'

'America? It's where they all go.'

'She made a ravishing corpse.'

'Ahi.'

And Doña Beatriz too had died; either in March or May. It was she who would bake the old Greek Sun-bread, and although her heirs had sought high and low, no one could find the receipt.

The Cardinal expressed satisfaction.

'Bestemmia,' he breathed, 'and I trust they never may; for on the Feast of the Circumcision she invariably caused to be laid before the high-altar of the cathedral a peculiarly shaped loaf to the confusion of all who saw it.'

And the Alcalde of Ayamonte, Don Deniz, had died on the eve of the bachelor's party he usually gave, when he took off his winter beard.

'Ahi; this death . . .'

Ah, yes, and since the delicacies ordered by the corpse could not well be countermanded, they had been divided among Christ's poor.

Left to himself once more Cardinal Pirelli returned reluctantly to his Defence.

Half the diocese it seemed had gone 'Therewards', while the rest were at Biarritz or Santander . . .

'A nice cheery time this is!' he murmured, oppressed by the silent cypress-court. Among the blue, pointing shadows, a few frail Oleanders in their blood-rose ruby invoked warm brief life and earth's desires.

'A nice cheery time,' he repeated, rising and going within.

The forsaken splendour of the vast closed cloisters seemed almost to augur the waning of a cult. Likewise the decline of Apollo, Diana, Isis, with the gradual downfall of their Temples, had been heralded, in past times, by the dispersal of their priests. It looked as though Mother Church, like Venus, or Diana, was making way in due turn for the beliefs that should follow: 'and we shall begin again with intolerance, martyrdom and converts,' the Cardinal ruminated, pausing before an ancient fresco depicting the eleven thousand virgins, or as many as there was room for.

Playing a lonely ball game against them was the disrespectful Chicklet.

'Young vandal,' the Cardinal chided, caressing the little acolyte's lustrous locks.

'Monseigneur? . . .'

'There: Run along; and say a fragrant prayer for me, Child.'

Flinging back a shutter drawn fast against the sun, the boundless prospect from the balcony of his cell recalled the royal Escorial. The white scattered terraces of villas set in dark deeps of trees, tall palms, and parasol-pines so shady, and almost indistinguishable the white outline of the sea, made insensibly for company.

Changing into a creation of dull scarlet crêpe, a cobweb dubbed 'summer-exile', Cardinal Pirelli felt decidedly less oppressed: 'Madrid is on the Manzanares,' he vociferated, catching sight of the diligence from Sodré. Frequently it would bring Frasquisto, the postman – a big tawny boy overgiven to passing the day in the woods with his gun and his guitar.

'The mail bag is most irregular,' he complained, fastening a few dark red, almost black, roses, to his cincture. It was Cardinal Pirelli's fancy while in retreat to assume his triple-Abraham, or mitre, and with staff in hand to roam abroad as in the militant Springtide of the Church.

'When kings were cardinals,' he murmured quietly as he left the room.

It was around the Moorish water-garden towards shut of day he liked most to wander, seeking like some Adept to interpret in the still, deep pools, the mirrored music of the sky.

All, was it vanity; these pointing stars and spectral leaning towers, this mitre, this jewelled ring, these trembling hands, these sweet reflected colours, white of daffodil and golden rose. All, was it vanity?

Circling the tortuous paths like some hectic wingless bird, he was called to the refectory by the tintinnabulation of a bell.

In the deep gloominous room despoiled of all splendour but for a dozen old Zurbarans flapping in their frames, a board, set out with manifest care, was prepared for the evening meal.

Serving both at Mass and table, it was the impish Chicklet who, with a zealous napkin-flick (modelled on the *mozos* of the little café-cum-restaurant 'As in Ancient Andalucia' patronised by rising toreadors and *aficionados* of the Ring), showed the Primate to his chair.

Having promised José the chef a handsome indulgence, absolved him from bigamy, and raised his wages, Cardinal Pirelli, in gastronomy nothing if not fastidious, had succeeded in inducing him to brave the ghostly basements of the monastery on the mount.

Perhaps of the many charges brought against the Primate by his traducers, that of making the sign of the cross with his left foot at meals was the most utterly unfounded – looking for a foot-cushion would have been nearer the truth.

Addressing the table briefly in the harmonious Latin tongue, his Eminence sat down with an impenetrable sigh.

With vine-sprays clinging languorously to the candle-stands, rising from a bed of nespoles, tulips, and a species of wild orchid known as Devil's-balls, the Chicklet, to judge from his floral caprices, possessed a little brain of some ambition, not incapable of excess.

'I thought you were tired of jasmine, sir, and th'orange bloom's getting on,' he chirruped, coming forward with a cup of cold, clear consommé, containing hearts, coronets, and most of the alphabet in vermicelli.

'I'm tired, true, child; but not of jasmine,' the Primate returned, following a little contretemps of a marqués' crown, sinking amid a frolicsome bevy of *O*s.

'I hope it's right, sir?'

'Particularly excellent, child – tell José so.'

'Will I bring the trout, sir?'

'Go, boy,' the Cardinal bade him, opening a volume by the menu-stand formed of a satyr, sentimentalising over a wood-nymph's breasts.

While in retreat it was his fancy, while supping, to pursue some standard work of devotion, such as Orthodoxy so often encourages or allows: it was with just such a golden fairy-tale as this that he had once won a convert: Poor woman. What had become of her? Her enthusiasm, had it lasted? She had been very ardent. Perfervid! 'Instruction' would quite wear it out of them. Saint Xarifa's at fall of day; . . . an Autumn affair! Chrysanthemums; big bronze frizzlies. A Mrs Mandarin Dove. American. Ninety million sterling. Social pride and religious humility, how can I reconcile? The women in Chicago. My God!!! My little stepdaughter . . . Her Father, fortunately . . . Yes, your Eminence, he's dead. And, oh, I'm *glad*. Is it naughty? And then her photograph à la Mary of Magdala, her hair unbound, décolletée, with a dozen long strands of pearls. 'Ever penitently yours, Stella Mandarin Dove.'

'I'd rather have had the blonde Ambassadress to the Court of St James,' he reflected, toying with the fine table-glass of an old rich glamour. A fluted bell cup sadly chipped provoked a criticism and a citation from Cassiodorus on the 'rude' ways of boys.

Revolving around an austere piece of furniture, that resembled a Coffin-upon-six-legs, the Chicklet appeared absorbed.

'I hear it's the Hebrew in heaven, sir. Spanish is seldom spoken,' he exclaimed seraphically.

'Tut, dear child. Who says so?' the Primate wondered, his eyes wandering in melancholy towards the whitest of moons illumining elusively the room – illumining a long, sexless face with large, mauve, heroic lips in a falling frame, and an 'apachey', blue-cheeked, Christ, the Cardinal noticed.

'Who, sir? Why, a gentleman I was guide to once!'

The Cardinal chuckled comprehensively.

'I should surmise, dear child, there was little to show.'

'What, not the crypt, sir? Or the tomb of the beautiful Princess Eboli, the beloved of Philip II, sir?'

'Jewel boy. Yum-yum,' the Cardinal raised his glass.

'And the bells, sir? Last night, I'll tell you, sir. I thought I heard old "Wanda" on the wind.'

'Old Wanda, boy.'

'She rings for deaths, sir.'

'Nonsense, child; your little ears could never hear as far,' the Cardinal answered, deliberating if a lad of such alertness and perception might be entrusted to give him a henna shampoo: it was easy enough to remove the towels before it got too red. The difficulty was to apply the henna; evenly everywhere; fair play all round; no favouring the right side more than the left, but golden Justice for each grey hair. Impartiality: proportion! 'Fatal, otherwise,' the Primate reasoned.

'Are you ready for your Quail, sir?'

'Quail, quail? Bring on the *dulces*, boy,' his Eminence murmured, regarding absently through the window the flickering arc-lights of Clemenza far away. Dear beckoning lamps, dear calling lamps; lamps of theatres, cinemas, cabarets, bars and dancings; lamps of railway-termini, and excessively lit hotels, *olé* to you, enchantress lights!

'And, after all, dears, if I did,' the Cardinal breathed, tracing a caricature of his Holiness upon the table-cloth lightly with a dessert-fork. ('Which I certainly deny' . . .), he brooded, disregarding the dissolving Orange ice *à la* Marchioness of Macarnudo.

'Had you anything in the Lottery, sir?'

'Mind your business, boy, and remove this ball-room nastiness,' the Primate snapped.

It was while lingering, after dinner, over some choice vintage, that he oftenest would develop the outline of his Defence. To escape the irate horns of the Pontiff's bull (Die, dull beast) he proposed pressing the 'Pauline Privilege', unassailable, and confirmed *A.D. 1590* by Pope Sixtus V, home to the battered beauty of the Renaissance hilt: 'With the elegance and science,' he murmured, 'of a *matador*.'

'I have the honour to wish you, sir, a good, and pleasant night.'

'Thanks, boy.'

'And if you should want me, sir' . . . the youthful acolyte possessed the power to convey the unuttered.

'If?? . . . And say a fragrant prayer for me, child,' the Cardinal enjoined.

Resting an elbow among the nespoles and tulips (dawn-pink and scarlet, awakening sensitively in the candle-glow), he refilled reflectively his glass.

'God's providence is over all,' he told himself, considering dreamfully a cornucopia heaped with fruit. Being just then the gracious Autumn, a sweet golden-plum called 'Don Jaime of Castile' was in great perfection. It had been for the Southern orchards a singularly fertile year. Never were seen such gaily rouged peaches, such sleek, violet cherries, such immensest white grapes. Nestling delectably amid its long, deeply lobed leaves, a pomegranate (fruit of joy) attracted the Cardinal's hand.

Its seeds, round and firm as castanets, evoked the Ortiz. 'Ah, Jesus-Maria. The evening she waved her breasts at me!' he sighed, attempting to locate the distant lights of the Teatro Trinidades. Interpreting God's world, with her roguish limbs and voice, how witching the Child had been but lately in *The Cistus of Venus*. Her valse-refrain 'Green Fairy Absinthe' (with a full chorus in tights), had been certainly, theatrically (if, perhaps, not socially), the hit of the season.

'The oleanders come between us,' he deliberated, oppressed by the amative complaint of some sweet-throated, summer night-bird.

'It's queer, dears, how I'm lonely!' he exclaimed, addressing the ancient Zurbarans flapping austerely in their frames.

The Archbishop of Archidona, for all his air of pomposity, looked not unsympathetic, neither, indeed, did a little lady with a nimbus, casting melting glances through the spokes of a mystic wheel.

'It's queer –; you'd be surprised!' he murmured, rising and setting an oval moon-backed chair beside his own.

As usual the fanciful watch-dogs in the hills had begun their disquieting barking.

'The evenings are suicide,' he ruminated, idly replenishing his glass.

Sometimes, after the fifth, or sixth, bumper, the great Theresa herself would flit in from the garden. Long had her radiant spirit 'walked' the Desierto, seeking, it was supposed, a lost sheet of the manuscript of her *Way of Perfection*. It may have been following on the seventh, or, even, the eighth bumper, that the Primate remarked he was not alone.

She was standing by the window in the fluttered moonshine, holding a knot of whitish heliotropes.

'Mother?'

Saint John of the Cross could scarcely have pronounced the name with more wistful ecstasy.

Worn and ill, though sublime in laughter, exquisite in tenderness she came towards him.

'. . . Child?'

'Teach me, oh, teach me, dear Mother, the Way of Perfection.'

# IX

Verifying private dates, revising here and there the cathedral list of charges, Don Moscosco, the secretary of the chapter, seated before his usual bureau, was at the disposal of the public. A ministerial crisis had brought scattered Fashion home to town with a rush, and the pressure of work was enormous. 'Business' indeed had seldom been livelier, and chapels for Masses of special intention were being booked in advance as eagerly as opera-boxes for a Première, or seaside-villas in the season.

'If the boys are brisk we might work in Joseph,' he mused, consulting with closely buttoned lips his Tarifa and plan; 'although I'd rather not risk a clash.'

Unknown to double-let like his compères on occasion outside, the swarthy little man was a master organiser, never forgetting that the chapter's welfare and prestige were inseparable from his own. Before allotting a chapel for a mass of Intent, it was his rule to analyse and classify the 'purity' of the intention (adding five per cent where it seemed not altogether to be chaste, or where the purpose was 'obscure').

'I see no inconvenience,' he murmured, gauging delicately the motif of a couple of great ladies of the bluest blood in Spain who were commissioning masses for the safety of a favourite toreador in an approaching *corrida*.

'Five hundred flambeaux, at least, between them,' the secretary, negligently spat.

It was the twenty-first day of September (which is the Feast of Saint Firmín), and the sacristia, thronged with mantons and monsignori, resembled some vast shifting parterre of garden-flowers.

Having a little altercation together, Mother Mary of the Holy Face and Mother García of the Company of Jesus, alone, seemed stable. In honour of Saint Firmín the door of Pardon (closed half the year) had just been thrown open, bringing from the basilica an odour of burning incense and the strains of a nuptial march.

How many of the bridal guests knew of the coffin installed in the next chapel but one? the little man wondered, rising gallantly to receive a client.

She wore no hat but a loose veil of gold and purple enveloped her hair and face.

'I fear for him!'

'There, there. What is it?'

'I fear for him' – a man and the stars, nights of sweet love, oleander flowers were in her voice.

By her immense hooped earrings, as large as armlets, he knew her for the Adonira, the mistress of the toreador Tancos.

'Come to me after the Friday miserere,' the official objected: 'let me entreat an appointment.'

'No. Now.'

'Well.'

'I want a Mass.'

'The intention being . . . ?' the secretary sent up his brows a little.

'His safety.'

'Whose?'

'My lover's.'

'But, señorita, it's all done! It's all *done*, dear lady,' the words were on Don Moscosco's lips. Still, being the pink of chivalry with *las mujares* and a man of business, he murmured: 'With what quantity of lights?'

'Two. Just for him and me.'

'Tell me how you would prefer them,' he exclaimed, glancing whimsically towards the canvas of the Magdalen waylaying our Lord.

'How I would —' she stammered, opening and closing the fansticks in her painted, love-tired hands.

'You would like them long and, I dare say, gross?'

'The best,' she breathed, almost fainting as though from some fleeting delicious vision in the air.

'Leave it to me,' Don Moscosco said, and dropping expressively his voice he added: 'Come, señorita; won't you make a date with me?'

'A date with you?'

'Ah-hah, the little Juans and Juanas; the charming cherubs!' the secretary archly laughed.

Returning however no answer she moved distractedly away.

'Two tapers! *Two*. As many only as the animal's horns. It's amazing how some women stint,' he reflected, faintly nettled.

The marriage ceremony was over. From the summit of the giralda, volley on volley, the vibrant bells proclaimed the consummation.

'It was all so quick; I hope it's valid?' Madame la Horra, the mother of the 'Bride', looked in to say. With a rose mole here and a strawberry mole there, men (those adorable monsters) accounted her entirely attractive.

'As *though* we should hurry, as *though* we should clip!'

'Eh?'

'As though we were San Eusebio, or the Pilar!'

'Forgive me, I came only to – I, . . . I, . . . I, . . . I think I cried. The first Spring flowers looked so beautiful.'

A mother's love, and contrition, perhaps, for her own shortcomings, the secretary brooded: 'I shall knock her off five per cent.'

Lost in bland speculation Don Moscosco considered the assembly collected outside the curtained *camarín* of the Virgin, where the gowns of the Image were dusted and changed.

For Firmín she usually wore an osprey or two and perfumed ball-gloves of Córdoba, and carried a spread fan of gold Guadalmedina lace. Among devotees of the sacristia it was a perpetual wonder to observe how her costumes altered her. Sometimes she would appear quite small, dainty and French, at others she would recall the sumptuous women of the Argentine and the New World, and *aficionados* would lament their fairy isle of Cuba in the far-off Caribbean Sea.

Traversing imperiously the throng, Don Moscosco beheld the Duquesa DunEden.

Despite the optimism of the gazettes it looked as though the Government must indeed be tottering, since the Duquesa too was up from her Country quinta.

'I have a request to make,' she began, sinking gratefully to a chair.

'And charmed, in advance, to grant it.'

'I suppose you will have forgotten my old spaniel Clapsey?'

'Ah, no more dogs!'

'She is passing-out, poor darling; and if the Church could spare her some trifling favour —'

'Impossible.'

'She is the first toy tail for my little cemetery!'

'Quite impossible.'

'Poor pet,' the Duquesa exclaimed undaunted: 'she has shared in her time my most intimate secrets: she stands for early memories; what rambles we'd go together, she and I, at Santander long ago! I remember Santander, Don Moscosco (imagine), when there was not even a hotel! A little fishing-village, so quiet, so quiet; ah, it was nicer, far, and more exclusive then . . .'

'I dare say.'

'You know my old, blind and devoted friend was a gift from the king; and this morning I said to her: "Clapsey! Clapsey!" I said: "where's Carlos? Car-los . . . ?" And I'll take my oath she rallied.'

Don Moscosco unbent a shade: 'A token, is she, of royalty?'

'He also gave me "Flirt"!'

'Perhaps a brief mass . . .'

'Poor dearest: you'll keep it quiet and black?'

'We say all but the Black.'

'Oh?'

'One must draw the line somewhere!' Don Moscosco declared, his eye roving towards a sacristan piloting a party of travel-stained tourists, anxious to inspect the casket containing a feather from the Archangel Gabriel's wing.

'I know your creative taste! I rely on you,' the Duquesa rose remarking.

Nevertheless, beneath the routine of the sacristia, the air was surcharged with tension. Rival groups, pro- or anti-Pirellian, formed almost irreconcilable camps, and partisanship ran high. Not a few among the cathedral staff had remained true to his Eminence, and Mother Sunlight, a charwoman, (who sometimes performed odd jobs at the Palace) had taught her infant in arms to cry: 'Long live Spain and Cardinal Pirelli!'

Enough, according to some extreme anti-Pirellians, to be detrimental to her milk.

'I'm told the Pope has sent for him at last,' the laundress of the Basilica, Doña Consolación, remarked to Sister June of the Way Dolorous.

'Indeed, indeed; it scarcely does to think!'

'Does anyone call to mind a bit of a girl (from Bilbao she was) that came once to stop as his niece?'

'Inclined to a moustache! Perfectly.'

'Phoebe Poco protests she wasn't.'

'Ah, well; a little *Don Juanism* is good,' the laundress said, and sighed.

'She declares . . .'

'She tells the truest lies, dear, of anyone I know!'

'Be that as it may it's certain he's getting increasingly eccentric. But Sunday last, entertaining his solicitor, it seems he ordered coffee after the merienda to be served in two chamber-pots.'

'Shameful – and he in his sunset years!' Mother Mary of the Holy Face commented, coming up with Tomás the beadle.

'It wouldn't surprise me,' he declared, drowsily shaking a heavy bouquet of keys, 'if the thread of his life was about to break.'

'*Hombre* . . .' The laundress expressed alarm.

'Often now, towards Angelus, as I climb the tower, I hear the bell Herod talking with old Wanda in the loft. Eeeeeeee! Eeeeeeee! Horrible things they keep saying. Horrible things they keep saying.'

'Nonsense,' Doña Consolación exclaimed, bestowing a smile on Monsignor Cuxa. Old, and did-did-doddery, how frail he seemed beside Father Fadrique, the splendid swagger of whose chasuble every woman must admire.

'Sent for to Rome; ah, sangre mio, I wish someone would send for me,' a girl with a rose in the hair beautifully placed sighed romantically.

'Be satisfied with Spain, my dear, and remember that no other country can compare with it!' Doña Generosa, an Aunt of one of the cathedral dancing-boys (who drew a small pension as the widow of the late Leader of applause at the Opera-house) remonstrated.

'I've never travelled,' Doña Consolación blandly confessed: 'but I dare say, dear, you can't judge of Egypt by *Aïda*.'

'Oh, can't I, though,' Doña Generosa sniffed, as the Father of an acolyte raised his voice.

'Spain!' he exclaimed exalted, throwing a lover's kiss to the air: 'Spain! The most glorious country in God's universe, His admitted masterpiece, His gem, His —' He broke off, his eloquence dashed by the sad music of Monsignor Cuxa's haemorrhage.

An office in the Chapel of the Crucifix was about to begin, recalling to their duties the scattered employees of the staff.

Hovering by the collection-box for the Souls in Hades, the Moorish maid from the College of Noble Damosels, bound on an errand of trust as ancient as the world, was growing weary of watching the people come and go.

'I must have missed him beneath the trees of the Market Place,' she ruminated, straightening on her head a turban wreathed in blossoms.

It was the matter of a message from Obdulia and Milagros to the radiant youth whose lips they were so idyllically (if perhaps somewhat licentiously) sharing.

'Fo' sh'o dis goin' to put dose heiresses in a quandry,' she deliberated, oppressed by her surroundings.

Eastern in origin like the Mezquita of Córdoba, it was impossible to forget that the great basilica of Clemenza was a Mosque profaned.

Designed for the cult of Islam, it made her African's warm heart bleed to behold it now. Would it were reconverted to its virginal state, and the cry of the muezzin be heard again summoning men to Muhammad's house! Yes, the restitution of the cathedral to Allah was Muley's cherished dream, and it consoled her, on certain days when she was homesick, to stand before the desecrated mihrab in worship, her face turned towards Africa, and palm-girt Marrakech across the sea.

'I almost inclined to slip across to de Café Goya,' she breathed, moving aside for a shuffling acolyte, bearing a crucifix on a salver.

Led by the pious sisters of the noble order of the Flaming Hood, the Virgin was returning to her niche.

She was arrayed as though bound for the Bull-ring, in a robe of peacock silk, and a mantilla of black lace.

'*Santissima! . . .*'

'*Elegantissima!*' Devotees dropped adoring to the floor.

Alone, the African remained erect.

'Muhammad mine, how long?' she sighed, turning entreating eyes to the cabbalistic letters and Saracenic tracings of the azulejos arabesques.

# X

Midnight had ceased chiming from the Belfry tower, and the last seguidilla had died away. Looking fresh as a rose, and incredibly juvenile in his pyjamas of silver-grey and scarlet (the racing colours of Vittoria, Duchess of Vizeu), the Cardinal seemed disinclined for bed.

Surveying in detachment the preparatives for his journey (set out beneath an El Greco Christ, with outspread, delicate hands), he was in the mood to dawdle.

'These for the Frontier. Those for the train,' he exclaimed aloud, addressing a phantom porter.

Among the personalia was a Passport, the likeness of identity showing him in a mitre, cute to tears, though, essentially, orthodox; a flask of Napoleon Brandy, to be 'declared' if not consumed before leaving the Peninsula; and a novel, *Self-Essence*, on the Index, or about to be.

'A coin, child, and put them for me on the rack,' he enjoined the wraith, regarding through the window the large and radiant stars.

The rhythmic murmur of a weeping fountain filled momentously the night.

Its lament evoked the Chicklet's sobs.

'Did I so wrong my God to punish him? Was I too hasty?' the Primate asked, repairing towards an ivory crucifix by Cano, 'yet, Thou knowest, I adore the boy!'

He paused a moment astonished by the revelation of his heart.

'It must have been love that made me do it,' he smiled, considering the incident in his mind. Assuredly the rebuff was unpremeditated, springing directly from the boy's behaviour, spoiling what might have been a ceremony of something more than ordinary poignance.

It had come about so.

There had been held previously during the evening, after the Basilica's scheduled closing hour, a service of 'Departure', fastidiously private, in the presence only of the little Ostensoir-swinger 'Chicklet', who, missing all the responses, had rushed about the cathedral after mice; for which the Cardinal, his sensitiveness hurt by the lad's disdain and frivolity, had afterwards confined him alone with them in the dark.

'Had it been Miguelito or Joaquín, I should not have cared a straw for their interest in the mice! But somehow this one —' the Cardinal sighed.

Adjusting in capricious abstraction his cincture, he turned towards the window.

It was a night like most.

Uranus, Venus, Saturn showed overhead their wonted lights, while in the sun-weary cloisters, brightly blue-drenched by the moon, the oleanders in all their wonder – (how swiftly fleeting is terrestrial life) – were over, and the bougainvilleas reigned instead.

'It must have been that,' he murmured, smiling up at the cathedral towers.

Poor little Don Wilful. The chapter-mice, were they something so amusing to pursue? 'I've a mind, do you know, to join you, boy; I declare I feel quite rompish!' he told himself, gathering up, with a jocund pounce, a heavy mantle of violet cloth-of-gold.

'Tu-whit, tu-whoo.'

Two ominous owls answered one another across the troubled garden.

'I declare I feel —' his hand sought vaguely his heart: it went pit-a-pat for almost nothing now! 'The strain of the diocese,' he breathed, consulting a pier-glass of the period of Queen Isabella 'the Ironical'.

'The Court may favour Paul Orna, but in my opinion no one can rival Joey Paquin's "line"; I should like to see him "tailor" our Madonna; one of the worst and most expensively dressed little saints in the world,' his Eminence commented, folding toga-wise the obedient tissues about his slender form.

An aspect so correctly classic evoked the golden Rome of the Imperial Caesars rather than the so tedious Popes.

Repeating a sonorous line from Macrobius, the Cardinal measured himself a liqueur-glass of brandy.

Poor little Don Bright-eyes, alone in the obscurity. It was said a black dervish 'walked' the Coro – one of the old habitués of the Mosque.

'Jewel boy. Yum-yum,' he murmured, setting a mitre like a wondrous mustard-pot upon his head. *Omnia vanitas*; it was intended for Saint Peter's.

'Tu-whit, tu-whoo!'

Grasping a Bishop's stave, remotely shepherdessy, his Eminence opened softly the door.

Olé, the Styx!

Lit by Uranus, Venus, and Saturn only, the consummate tapestries on the stairs recording the Annunciation, Conception, Nativity, Presentation, Visitation, Purification and Ascension of the Virgin made welcome milestones.

'. . . Visitation, Purification,' the Primate paused on the penultimate step.

On a turn of the stair by the 'Conception', a sensitive panel, chiefly white, he had the impression of a wavering shadow, as of someone following close behind.

Continuing, preoccupied, his descent, he gained a postern door. A few deal cases, stoutly corded for departure, were heaped about it: 'His Holiness, I venture to predict, will appreciate the excellence of our home-grown oranges, not to be surpassed by those of any land,' the Primate purred, sailing forth into the garden.

Oh, the lovely night. Oh, the lovely night. He stood, leaning on his wand, lost in contemplation of the miracle of it.

'Kek, kex, kex.'

In the old lead aqua-butt, by the Chapter-house, the gossiping bull-frogs were discussing their great horned and hoofed relations . . .

'There was never yet one that didn't bellow!'

'Kek, kek, kek.'

'*Los toros*, forsooth!'

'A blessed climate . . .' The Primate pursued his way.

It was in the face of a little door like the door of a tomb in the cathedral's bare façade (troubled only by the fanciful shadows of the trees) that he presently slipped his key.

Olé, the Styx!

He could distinguish nothing clearly at first beyond the pale forked fugitive lightning through the triple titanic windows of the chancel.

'Sunny-locks, Don Sunny-locks?' the Cardinal cooed, advancing diffidently, as though mistrustful of meeting some Charwoman's pail. *Life* had prepared him for these surprises.

Traversing on his crozier a spectral aisle, he emerged upon the nave.

Flanked by the chapels of the Crucifix, of the Virgin, of the Eldest Son of God, and of divers others, it was here as bright as day.

Presumably Don April-showers was too self-abashed to answer, perhaps too much afraid . . . 'If I recollect, the last time I preached was on the theme of Flagellation,' the Primate mused, considering where it caught the moon the face of a fakir in ecstasy carved amid the corbels.

'A sermon I propose to publish,' he resolved, peering into the chapel of Santa Lucia. It was prepared, it seemed, in anticipation of a wedding, for stately palms and branches of waxen peach-bloom stood all about: 'Making circulation perilous,' the Primate mused, arrested by the determined sound of a tenacious mouse gnawing at a taper-box.

'An admirable example in perseverance!' he mentally told himself, blinking at the flickering mauve flowers of light in the sanctuary lamps.

Philosophising, he penetrated the engrailed silver doors connecting the chapel of the Magdalen.

The chapel was but seldom without a coffin, and it was not without one now.

Since the obsequies of the brilliant Princess Eboli, it had enjoyed an unbroken vogue.

Besides the triumphal monument of the beloved of Philip II, the happy (though, perhaps, not the happiest) achievement of Jacinto Bisquert, there were also mural tablets to the Duchesses of Pampeluna (*née* Mattosinhos), Polonio (*née* Charona), and Sarmento (*née* Tizzi-Azza), while the urn and ashes of the Marchioness of Orcasitas (*née* Ivy Harris) were to be found here too, far from the race and turmoil of her native New York.

'Misericordia! Are you there, boy?' the Cardinal asked, eyeing abstractedly the twin-hooded caryatides that bore the fragile casket white as frozen snow containing the remains of the all-amiable princess.

Folded in dainty sleep below, he perceived the lad.

Witching as Eros, in his loose-flowing alb, it seemed profane to wake him!

'. . . And lead us not into temptation,' the Primate murmured, stooping to gaze on him.

Age of bloom and fleeting folly: Don Apple-cheeks!

Hovering in benison he had almost a mind to adopt the boy, enter him for Salamanca or, remoter, Oxford, and perhaps (by some bombshell codicil) even make him his heir.

'How would you like my Velasquez, boy? . . .' his Eminence's hand framed an airy caress. 'Eh, child? Or my Cano Crucifix? . . . I know of more than one bottle-nosed dowager who thinks she'll get it! . . . You know my Venetian-glass, Don Endymion, is among the choicest in Spain . . .'

There was a spell of singing silence, while the dove-grey mystic lightning waxed and waned.

Aroused as much by it as the Primate's hand, the boy started up with a scream of terror.

'Ouch, sir!'

'Olé, boy?'

The panic appeared to be mutual.

'Oufarella! . . .' With the bound of a young faun the lad was enskied amid the urns and friezes.

The heart in painful riot, the Primate dropped to a chair.

Ouching, Oléing and Oufarellaing it, would they never have

done? Paternostering Phoebe Poco (shadowing her master) believed they never would. 'Old ogre: why can't he be brisk about it and let a woman back to bed?' she wondered.

Thus will egotism, upon occasion, eclipse morality outright.

'And always be obedient, dear child,' the Cardinal was saying; 'it is one of the five things in Life that matter most.'

'Which are the others, sir?'

'What others, boy?'

'Why, the other four!'

'Never mind now. Come here.'

'Oh, Tral-a-la, sir.' Laughing like some wild spirit, the lad leapt (Don Venturesome, Don Venturesome, his Eminence trembled) from the ledge of A Virtuous Wife and Mother (Sarmento, *née* Tizzi-Azza) to the urn of Ivy, the American marchioness.

'You'd not do that if you were fond of me, boy!' The Cardinal's cheek had paled.

'But I *am* fond of you, sir! Very. Caring without caring: don't you know?'

'So you do care something, child?'

'I care a lot! . . .'

Astride the urn of Ivy – poised in air – the Chicklet pellucidly laughed.

'Tell me so again,' the Cardinal begged, as some convent-bell near by commenced sounding for office before aurora.

For behind the big windows the stars were fading.

'It's today they draw the Lottery, sir.'

'Ah; well, I had nothing in it . . .'

'00050 – that's me!'

The Cardinal fetched a breath.

'Whose is it, boy?' he pointed towards the bier.

'A Poet, sir.'

'A Poet?'

'The name though he had escapes me . . .'

'No matter then.'

'Where would his soul be now, sir?'

'Never mind, boy; come here.'

'In the next world I should like to meet the Cid, and Christopher Columbus!'

'Break your neck, lad, and so you will.'

'Pablo Pedraza too . . .'

'Who's that, boy?'

'He was once the flower of the ring, sir; superior even to Tancos; you may recollect he was tossed and ruptured at Ronda; the press at the time was full of it.'

'Our press, dear youth, our press!!! . . .' the Primate was about to lament, but an apologetic sneeze from a chapel somewhere in the neighbourhood of the Eldest Son of God arrested him.

It seemed almost to confirm the legend of old, Mosque-sick 'Suliman', said to stalk the temple aisles.

The Cardinal twirled challengingly his stave – *Bible* v. *Koran*; a family case; cousins; Eastern, equally, each; hardy, old perennials, no less equivocal and extravagant often, than the ever-adorable *Arabian Nights*! 'If only Oriental literature *sprawled* less, was more concise! It should concentrate its roses,' he told himself, glancing out, inquiringly, into the nave.

Profoundly soft and effaced it was a place full of strange suggestion. Intersecting avenues of pillared arches, upbearing waving banners, seemed to beckon towards the Infinite.

'Will you be obliged to change, sir; or shall you go straight through?'

'Straight through, boy.'

'I suppose, as you cross the border, they'll want to know what you have to declare.'

'I have nothing, child, but myself.'

'If 00050 is fortunate, sir, I hope to travel, too – India, Persia, Peru!! . . . Ah, it's El Dorado, then.'

'El Dorado, boy?' The Cardinal risked an incautious gesture.

'Oh, Tral-a-la, sir.' Quick as Cupid the lad eluded him on the evasive wings of a laugh; an unsparing little laugh, sharp and mocking, that aroused the Primate like the thong of a lash.

Of a long warrior line, he had always regarded disobedience (in others) as an inexcusable offence. What would have happened before the ramparts of Zaragoza, Valladolid, León, Burgos, had the men commanded by Ipolito Pirelli in the Peninsula War refused to obey! To be set at defiance by a youngster, a mere cock-robin, kindled elementary ancestral instincts in the Primate's veins.

'Don't provoke me, child, again.'

From pillared ambush Don Prudent saw well, however, to effect a bargain.

'You'd do the handsome by me, sir; you'd not be mean?'

'Eh? . . .'

'The Fathers only give us texts; you'd be surprised, your Greatness, at the stinginess of some!'

'. . . ?'

'You'd run to something better, sir; you'd give me something more substantial?'

'I'll give you my slipper, child, if you don't come here!' his Eminence warned him.

'Oufarella . . .'

Sarabandish and semi-mythic was the dance that ensued. Leading by a dozen derisive steps Don Light-of-limb took the nave. In the dusk of the dawn it seemed to await the quickening blush of day like a white-veiled negress.

'Olé, your Purpleship!'

Men (eternal hunters, novelty seekers, insatiable beings), men in their natural lives, pursue the concrete no less than the ideal – qualities not inseldom found combined in fairy childhood.

'Olé.'

Oblivious of sliding mantle the Primate swooped.

Up and down, in and out, round and round 'the Virgin', over the worn tombed paving, through Saint Joseph, beneath the cobweb banners from Barocco to purest Moorish, by early Philip, back to Turân-Shâh: 'Don't exasperate me, boy' – along the raised tribunes of the choristers and the echoing coro – the great fane (after all) was nothing but a cage; God's cage; the cage of God! . . .

Through the chancel windows the day was newly breaking as the Oleanders will in Spring.

Dispossessed of everything but his fabulous mitre, the Primate was nude and elementary now as Adam himself.

'As you can perfectly see, I have nothing but myself to declare,' he addressed some phantom image in the air.

With advancing day Don Skylark *alias* Bright-eyes *alias* Don Temptation it seemed had contrived an exit, for the cathedral was become a place of tranquillity and stillness.

'Only myself,' he had dropped before a painting of old Dominic Theotocópuli, the Greek, showing the splendour of Christ's martyrdom.

Peering expectantly from the silken parted curtains of a confessional, paternostering Phoebe Poco caught her breath.

Confused not a little at the sight before her, her equilibrium was only maintained by the recollection of her status: 'I'm an honest widow; so I know what men are, bless them!' And stirred to romantic memories she added: 'Poor soul, he had the prettiest teeth . . .'

Fired by fundamental curiosity, the dame, by degrees, was emboldened to advance. All over, was it with him, then? It looked as though his Eminence was far beyond Rome already.

'May God show His pity on you, Don Alvaro of my heart.'

She remained a short while lost in mingled conjecture. It was certain no morning bell would wake him.

'So': she stopped to coil her brierwood chaplet about him in order that he might be less uncovered. 'It's wonderful what us bits of women do with a string of beads, but they don't go far with a gentleman.'

Now that the ache of life, with its fevers, passions, doubts, its routine, vulgarity, and boredom was over, his serene, unclouded face was a marvelment to behold. Very great distinction and sweetness was visible there, together with much nobility, and love, all magnified, and commingled.

'*Adios*, Don Alvaro of my heart,' she sighed, turning away towards the little garden door ajar.

Through the triple windows of the chancel the sky was clear and blue – a blue like the blue of lupins. Above him stirred the wind-blown banners in the Nave.